STEELE's FINAL ADVENTURE.

Fillmore

THE PRESIDENT'S HAIL MARY

A NOVEL

John P. Morse

IDLEKNOT PRESS

This is a work of fiction taking place in the near future. Names, characters, places and incidents are the product of the author's imagination or are used fictionally. Any resemblance to actual events, locales or persons, living or dead is entirely coincidental.

Copyright © 2024 by John P. Morse

www.johnpmorse.com
Idleknot Press
Morse, John P.

The President's Hail Mary

ISBN 978-0-9976450-5-7 (paperback)

ISBN 978-0-9976450-6-4 (eBook)

Cover Design/Artwork by Eric Van Gronigen

Formatting Design by Madeline Silva

ALSO BY JOHN P. MORSE

Half Staff 2018

Chokepoint

To Carole,

An incredible wife, a bright North Star, and my best friend

I Corinthians 13

PART I

PART I

PRELUDE

Newport, Rhode Island

January 2023

Dan Steele's life fell apart on November 11, 2017, the day that his wife and twin boys drowned at the bottom of the Chesapeake Bay at the hands of a terrorist. Meantime, he'd been engaged in fighting America's unannounced wars from the shadows against people who in one way or another represented a threat to the United States, either by themselves or as part of a larger group. The ranks of those people were growing at an alarming rate. The number of those selected to keep them at bay was shrinking, because of elusive transparency, because of a divided government and because it was increasingly clear that the battle was being lost. He had just begun to think about the future six years later.

Winter came early. The gray sky, filled with scudding clouds, and the dry wind brisked across Narragansett Bay unchecked, lashing his face with the briny smell of the sea and sucking a visible plume of wet air from his lungs. Dan Steele crunched over the newly frozen ground, heaved up here and there. Ice crystals in the soil sparkled as he arrived at the plain plot where his wife and twin sons were buried together five years ago. Jill's headstone was flanked by two smaller stones cut with "Alex" and "Andrew" in bold letters. The boys were just over three years old. Removing his gloves, Dan traced the letters on the middle stone:

Jill Murphy Steele

October 16, 1990 - November 11, 2017

Teacher, Daughter, Wife, Mother

Forever in Our Hearts

The wind froze the tears streaming from Steele's face as he stood there. He would never hear her voice again nor those of the boys with their early words. On this very day five short years ago, he'd promised her father that he would do everything he could to bring the man responsible for their short lives to account. Her father grabbed Steele's arms in a powerful grip and ordered him to find those responsible and teach them the "eye for an eye covenant." The man responsible was still breathing God's air.

Steele rubbed his red eyes with his coat-sleeve. Looking back, what had he done to avenge their deaths? Sure, he'd served his country but now, those missions seemed like meaningless excuses. "How did I lose focus?" he wondered aloud. He'd grown too distant from his commitment, blurred by time and the nation's dirty work assigned to men on no one's roster and with no place on any organization chart. Steele gave up his identity to fight those battles. Weary of allowing those fights to take all his time, he pounded the unyielding granite top of Jill's resting place, sobbing, falling to his knees and gathering the three people he truly loved in his life together in his arms.

The cold from the stones gave him no solace. His mind began a slide show. The first image was of a laughing Jill playing with the boys trying to squirm away from her grasp. In the next image, the three faces, eyes closed, when the family car was finally winched out of the salt water and the scavengers had been brushed away from the flesh they'd been feeding on for days. A tall, balding man next came into view. Haughty. Smiling. The man behind his family's death. The big shot who gave the orders, paid the bills and stood back to observe the results of his sick work. Steele shivered away the images and opened his eyes.

Finally, he rose slowly to his feet and whispered in a crackling voice.

"I love you, Jill. I love you Alex and Andrew. Forgive me for saving myself."

Steele turned his back to the cold salt air and crunched his way across the small cemetery back to the car. He would return with Jill's parents the following day. The temperature had dropped, but all he felt was a rekindled fire burning deep inside.

CHAPTER 1

Washington, DC
Six months later

Dan Steele glanced at his watch as he rounded the corner on M street in the Southeast sector of the District of Columbia. He'd left the Department of Transportation building to his home to pick up his duffle bag and passport. Another eight hours and he would be flying east for a long-awaited week with Sydney Garrison in Italy. *And where would that lead to, he wondered?*

There was an unusual sight in front of the Headquarters building that had assembled during his short absence: a small troupe of circus performers entertaining the lunchtime crowd. A boom box carried music straight from the midway. People were streaming out of the Transportation building or pressed up against its tall glass office windows, still inside to avoid the hot, humid air which had choked the city for the last week. Quite a crowd had formed, and, with the traffic blocked, some commuters on M street had abandoned their vehicles to join the fun.

DC certainly needed some lightening up, and this impromptu gathering filled the bill. People were mesmerized by the spectacle. There was a clown in a garish yellow and pink outfit riding a unicycle and juggling three bowling pins, a man with a handlebar mustache wearing black tights and lace-up boots swallowing a burning sword, and a one-man trapeze act with the acrobat suspended on a ladder-like set of poles twenty feet above the pavement by a strong man glistening in sweat as his companion performed death-defying somersaults above the asphalt. There was even a man dressed in a wide-striped red and white suit selling "Peanuts, Popcorn, Prackerjacks," obviously proud of his inventive alliteration.

Steele shook his head, suddenly turned and pushed his way through the crowd. He'd fallen for it too. He'd let his guard down. The circus act might be a clever diversion, and he had an uneasy feeling about what might be happening at the other end of the building which housed the small suite of offices carved into a bedrock bunker sixty feet under the street. His lightheartedness abandoned him quickly and the uneasiness took over as he approached his usual entrance. With his breathing quickening, he felt mildly panicked when he walked into the building, carrying a leather-trimmed green duffel bag packed for his trip. He felt an unfamiliar foreboding as he flashed his badge to a guard he didn't recognize and continued to a single elevator separated from the bank of elevators whisking people up and down the modern glass and chrome building. His foreboding turned to alarm when he saw the elevator door standing open. There was a dark shaft with cables leading down. How did the car end up at Pisces' level? Now on high alert, crouching as he looked back toward the guard station, he heard a sharp crack and felt a bullet whiz over his head at the same time. He dove behind a thin fabric-covered room divider and a second bullet hit the floor and ricocheted into his duffel bag. Coming off his knees into a low crouch, Steele guessed which side of the opaque divider the gunman would take. Right-handed. Steele didn't hesitate. Even though a wrong guess would be rewarded by a shot in the back.

Steele spotted the gun barrel first, a familiar matte black military-styled Eastern Bloc 9mm, peeking past the plane of the gray divider. He exploded from his stance as the man's forearm came into view. Hitting the uniform chest high, the gun spit fire as the two went down to the tiled floor. For a moment, Steele controlled the arm holding the gun before the man twisted it from Steele's grasp. Steele slammed his head under the man's chin, snapping his head back, causing him to drop the gun, which skittered along the tile against the opposite wall. An elbow smashed Steele's face as the guard tried to free himself to retrieve the gun, but Steele had a grip on his torso like a Burmese python. The guard drew a knife from the waistband of his trousers and flicked open the blade, trying to penetrate Steele's back. All he got was cloth and a few superficial cuts.

A quick kick from a steel-tipped boot forced Steele to his feet to face his attacker. Holding the knife in front of him, the guard began edging toward the gun and holding Steele at bay with the thin stiletto. There was nothing at hand to even the fight, so Steele once again resorted to brute force and charged the guard like an NFL linebacker with a straight shot at the opposing quarterback. He dove low under the extended knife and upended the attacker by putting air under his legs and moving them together, so they'd come down at an awkward angle. While initially successful, the tactic backfired as the guard got closer to the gun, and Steele came up with the knife. Both fighters were again upright. Not wanting to face a handgun, Steele threw the knife just as the guard's outstretched fingers grasped the gun. Finding its mark, the guard's muscled neck fountained blood as he pitched forward and took a breath from a mouth contorted with shock. Steele quickly retrieved the handgun and tapped its butt sharply against the man's left temple to keep him from re-joining the fight.

Steele headed into the open elevator shaft while checking the weapon. A series of cables standing away from the concrete attached to the top of the car and a set of rails anchored into the concrete shaft. No fixed ladder. The rails were greasy. Using his leather belt like a lineman's harness, Steele descended into the shaft relying on the metal standoffs supporting the rails every ten feet. The belt wore through halfway down, and Steele used his shirt and hands to slide down the cables. The access hatch opened easily, and the interior of the car was empty with its door open. He looked through the hatch before dropping down to the car's floor. The intruders were likely still in the Pisces suite.

Orient, he commanded himself. Grasping the gun with a two-handed grip from one side of the elevator, he saw that the landing between the elevator and the bedrock was clear. Beyond, the vault door stood open. Steele moved across the narrow concrete floor.

He thought about closing the vault door but reasoned that his colleagues might be in danger — because under the biometric reader lay a hand chopped off at the wrist, palm side up. Steele kept his eyes looking beyond the door into the hallway, dropping to one knee to get a closer look at the hand. He recognized the ragged pinkish scar from the base of index finger across the palm to the soft tissue under the fourth finger. His colleague, Paul Blanchard, the intelligence community liaison to Pisces, sliced it on a razor-sharp piece of shale when falling down a ravine the previous year during a hike on the Appalachian Trail in New Hampshire. Thirty stitches to close. Still on active duty, Paul was at the end of a two-year assignment to Pisces and was preparing to rotate to the Office of Naval Intelligence in Suitland, Maryland. Where was the rest of Paul? Steele knew he was back on the Trail for a winter hike in the Great Smoky Mountains in Tennessee. Was he still alive? What the hell is going on down here? Steele asked himself.

A repeating automated message from the Secure Sites Monitoring System blared from the office intercom as he edged forward. He had a gun and heard nothing other than the speakers, dismissing the idea that any intruders might still be in the facility. Pretty slick, he mused. Bring the circus to town and distract hundreds of people while breaking into Pisces. Very clever.

As he entered the vault, a familiar coppery, metallic smell greeted him. Steele knew the odor of blood all too well. Going to the first office, he found his boss, Admiral Wright, sitting upright in his chair with coagulating rivulets of dark red running from a head wound and two chest wounds, ending in a puddle on his thighs and filling the space between them and the chair's seat. Steele stepped behind the desk and felt his neck for a pulse. Thready and weak, but still there. How could this have happened? Steele had only been out of the office for thirty minutes.

Steele knew he had to clear the remainder of the facility. Sandy Matthews was headed to a conference in Florida. His office was empty. Steele checked the other offices in the compact facility. The deadly tally: two badly wounded, one dead. Paul Blanchard's hand used to gain access using the biometric reader. Cass Thomas had shot one of the intruders during his entry. Steele pressed a button on Wright's office phone.

"Department of Transportation, how may I help you?"

Steele shouted, "We have an emergency near the West entrance. Call for security and two ambulances now."

Steele hugged the almost dead weight from the chair and maneuvered Wright to the floor and ripped away his blood-soaked shirt. Grabbing a first aid kit from the hallway, Steele tore it open and extracted a handful of gauze pads and compression tape. One of the chest wounds was sucking air. He raced to the kitchenette and brought a roll of plastic wrap back to the office, smoothing a sheet against the frothy hole and then applied a compression bandage on top of it. He used an AMBU bag to force some fresh air into Wright's lungs, which strengthened his pulse. With Wright as stable as any man with two bullet holes in his chest and one in his forehead could be, Steele rushed to aid Cass Thomas, his savior on two previous occasions, bleeding from several wounds and shaking in shock.

Cass's eyes fluttered. She was communicating "I'm not ready to go."

Ambulances arrived and maneuvered past the security pylons onto the broad sidewalk. The first responders arrived in minutes, found Admiral Wright and relieved Steele of his first aid duties with Cass. Steele found an EMT preparing the admiral for transport.

"What's your prognosis?" asked Steele.

"He'll be back. While I was bagging him, I examined the head wound. It looked bad, but the slug hit his forehead at an angle and furrowed under his skin, following the curve of his skull. It is resting on top of his head, so I don't expect he suffered any internal damage there. The body shots punctured his left lung for sure, but I don't see any obvious signs of other organ damage. Seems like a tough guy. Did you apply the chest dressing? You must have done that before."

"A couple of times. Thanks."

Steele's phone vibrated in his pocket. It was Rear Admiral Hank Owens, military aide to the National Security Advisor.

"Dan Steele," he answered.

"The FBI forensics team is inbound from Quantico. Is the scene secure? Are you OK?"

"It's getting there. Yes, I'm OK."

After setting a land speed record from Quantico, a motorcade of three black Suburbans screeched to a halt with flashing lights and ear-piercing sirens. Two investigators button-holed Steele into the lobby-level conference room and began questioning him as the first person on the scene. The FBI's calm efficiency stopped Steele's hands from shaking with the adrenalin surge.

The team bagged the body of the phony guard and the real guard who had been stabbed and stuffed into a cleaning closet. They also zipped up the suit found outside Cass's office. Steele surrendered his bloody, grease-stained shirt to one of the investigators and retrieved a fresh one from his duffel bag, noticing it sported a vent hole from the bullet that passed through it and lodged in a paperback thriller. The bullet had penetrated 280 pages of the 420-page book. Steele felt relieved that he packed the novel rather than a collection of short stories. The Quantico team left the scene at 7:30 p.m. just as Steele's overseas flight started boarding at Dulles.

Feeling like he just finished Hell Week, Steele stumbled home, hoping that the glands which had been pumping adrenalin into his system for the last eight hours would finally take a break. After a quick shower, Steele changed into shorts and a tee shirt and lay down on the couch, sending Sydney a short text explaining that his trip was again cancelled. For a variety of reasons, the trip to Italy had been postponed a half dozen times starting with his first scheduled trip in January 2022, after he was medically cleared to travel. Since getting banged up on a mission to Yemen, he had worked hard to regain his SEAL-level of fitness, even though he had been riding a desk for the past seven months.

He fell asleep.

Steele's cell phone danced off the coffee table and fell on the floor. Still groggy, he picked it up and answered, "Dan Steele."

"Good morning," said a voice Steele didn't recognize. "This is Dr. Barrett, one of the medical examiners from Quantico. I wanted to give someone a rundown on what we found on the bodies brought in yesterday afternoon. Are you here on the base?"

"No doctor, I'm in Southeast DC." Steele looked at the digital clock on the TV — 3:45 a.m.

"I think you may want to come down and see things for yourself. I cannot get into any details over the phone. Or you could wait for the report that should be transcribed sometime later today."

"I'll be there within the hour," Steele said. He got up from the couch, feeling the effects of yesterday's excitement like a bad hangover. Without having eaten anything in the last twenty hours, he felt weak. A dozen chin-ups got his blood flowing and he grabbed a protein bar on his way out the door. Traffic was light, as he drove south though a gentle rain. He opened the door to the morgue just before 5:00 a.m.

Donning a mask and single-use plastic gown, Steele followed as the M.E. pushed open the airtight double doors taking a breath of the peculiar smell of death, exposed blood and bodily fluids mixed with the pungent fragrance of anti-bacterial soap. Not a good morning smell.

The first body lay draped on an oversized stainless-steel table with a drain hole in one corner. Dr. Barrett pulled back the drape, and Steele saw the man he found near Cass Thomas' office. His dark pinstriped suit was gone. To Steele, the narrow face, sunken cheeks and swarthy features placed him from somewhere in Eastern Europe or the Middle East.

"Shot three times," said the M.E. pointing at the clean entrance wounds. "What killed him was this shot to his face which removed a large chunk of his skull on its way out."

As the M.E. continued to the next table, Steele mused — Cass Thomas was a great shot.

"Here, you have a man who lived a very hard life before this knife severed everything on the way to his spinal cord. I never thought a butterfly knife could do all that damage."

"It's his knife. A lucky throw. He was reaching for a gun when I threw it."

"It certainly did the job. Over the years, this guy had every bone in his frame broken as the result of fighting, torture, or accidentally falling down hundreds of staircases. He's got old knife wounds, burns made by external tools, bullet holes, and a face beaten often by fists or clubs. I've never seen another specimen like this one."

Steele grimaced at the sight.

"By the way, are these two men on the same team?" the M.E. asked.

"Yes, they both came to kill our group. I don't know if there were others. We'll have to wait to see if the security cameras caught anything. Why do you ask?"

"What's unusual is that both men have the same tattoo."

The doctor rolled over the forearm of the battered man to reveal a tattoo that sent chills up Steele's spine. A crude two-headed black eagle had been inked on his arm four inches above the wrist. It looked like a prison tat, but the same image was centered in a field of blood red on the national flag of Albania. A flood of bad memories coursed through Steele's body, and his hands began to tremble, just the beginning of an autonomic response.

"I didn't see one on the first guy. Where is it?" whispered Steele.

The doctor rolled the swarthy man over on his side. The same image, done professionally, covered the man's back with the eagles' heads positioned over his shoulder blades, giving the birds the ability to move their heads.

Steele shuddered, "I'm familiar with the images. The same group responsible for killing my wife and two sons ordered this attack.

Two of my close friends and the real guard over there on the next table were collateral damage. I might have been the target."

CHAPTER 2

Gaeta, Italy
July 2023

Sydney Garrison woke from an anxious sleep just as her alarm clock was about to sound. Excited about the day ahead, she checked her cell phone, hoping Dan Steele was on his way and would soon be landing in Rome. But there was the text:

> *Sydney,*
>
> *Can't fly due to real crisis.*
>
> *Talk soon.*
>
> *Dan*

Falling back on her bed, disappointed and irked at the latest cancellation, Commander Sydney Garrison cursed her bad luck and began to parse the text message: Dan's not on the flight to Rome but is OK; Real crisis is something important requiring him to remain in DC: work related. Talk soon. He's under a lot of pressure and can't talk now. It's the middle of the night in the States. Maybe classified. Cryptic. Feeling better, this delay might prove to be lengthy. It was time to take another course. She was determined to run this long-distance relationship to reality. Dan Steele was becoming a dream instead of a reality.

First, to get the blood flowing, she completed a quick set of warm-up floor exercises and began her morning yoga routine before building herself a large mug of coffee with frothed milk and getting to work. *Newport* would begin a maintenance period the following week. Grabbing a lined tablet and calendar, she began to strategize how to get back to the east coast for ten days. She had done some thinking about a contingency plan and had already decided that if Dan was not able to come to Italy as planned, she would fly to him.

There were always good reasons to travel to Washington: visiting her sponsor for Submarine Warfare in the Pentagon, checking in with the Naval Sea Systems Command in the Navy Yard regarding technical sonar and periscope issues, and perhaps briefing the Chief of Naval Operations on his own program of overseas rotation. In a few hours, she had a working plan and a checklist of telephone calls and messages to organize the trip. Also included would be a visit to her parents living in Mystic, Connecticut. COVID had stymied their plans to fly to Italy.

She would set the plan in motion, build some momentum and then call her mother. She immediately silenced any contrary "what ifs" which invaded her thinking and pressed on. Sydney Garrison had not gotten to her position as the first woman commanding an attack submarine by being a passive observer watching life go by. Forehandedness had long been a hallmark among professional naval officers. The more she looked at her trip's outline, the more it made sense.

She picked up her landline, dialed the Pentagon and asked the DOD operator in Washington to patch her through to Dan's cell phone. The connection was as clear as if she was making a call to a restaurant around the corner.

"Good morning, Dan, it's Sydney. Can you talk?"

Steele tried to mentally shift gears away from the situation in Pisces. He had just left Quantico and was trying to sort out the meaning of the last twenty hours.

"Good morning, I'm glad you called."

"Me too. How are you doing?"

"Tired. Yesterday turned out to be a long day. I can't get into details, but my world has been turned upside down."

I got that sense from your text. Anyway, I wanted to tell you I'm planning to travel to DC next week for some meetings and wondered how clobbered your schedule might be on the weekend? I'm planning to fly on Thursday and will arrive early afternoon."

"Sounds great. I'm excited."

"So, am I," Sydney purred, "do you think your crisis will be resolved by then?"

"No. I expect it will take some more time. There's nothing else on the horizon so we should be able to carve out some time for ourselves. Where are you staying?" Steele bit his tongue after asking the question.

An awkward pause ensued. Sydney didn't miss a beat.

"I plan to make reservations at the Army-Navy Club near Dupont Circle if I can get a room. Otherwise, somewhere in Crystal City."

"Anything I can do from this end?" said Dan.

Sydney laughed, "No, just keep as much white space in your calendar as possible."

"I will," said Steele.

"And I'll look at the flight options."

"Great. I'm looking forward to it."

Even though it was a week away, Steele felt a little nervous about Sydney's visit. Should he have invited her to stay with him? Was he ready for that? Had he been able to make the trip to Italy, he assumed that he'd stay with her in Gaeta. Did she expect him to invite her to his house in DC? Why didn't he? His self-talk led to idle speculation about a woman he felt he knew. But really, how well did he know her? Was there something there more than the basic animal attraction that took place aboard *Newport*? Steele shut down that part of the conversation. It was repetitive, and it triggered round after round of internal questions. He would let it play out by itself.

Steele was facing some other realities that needed his full attention.

CHAPTER 3

The Walter Reed National Military Medical Center

Bethesda, Maryland
July 2023

Steele continued his long day with a trip to the former Naval National Medical Center where both Admiral Wright and Cass Thomas were recovering.

"Morning, admiral," said Steele.

"Good morning, Dan. Have you come to break me out of this place?" His gruff question confirmed he was on the mend.

"No," said Steele, "I'm here to see how you are recovering and if there's anything else I should be doing. Your shoes have plenty of room."

The admiral smiled and then laughed, wrinkling the bandage covering his scalp. "I know I'm not ready to leave here, but I sure would prefer to be at home recovering. Carole stayed here most of the night and just left, but it will take her longer to drive home than we are allowed to visit. The warden runs a tight ship here."

"How is she taking it?"

"Pretty well, considering she's got her good friends here in northern Virginia. Our retirement lasted less than a year, and she found living by ourselves on a bit of the ocean too calming. She still needs more action in her life. That's why we moved back to Virginia. But she prefers that it be different than the action which brought me here. I'm sure we'll talk about changing courses again a lot more now. How's Cass doing?"

"Her condition is improving, and she's been upgraded to stable. I managed to see her earlier for five minutes. She's alert and able to communicate, but still weak. She is missing the sparkle in her eyes, and I thought she was going to fall asleep while we were talking. Three body shots. Breathing on her own. She has another bowel resection scheduled today."

Wright continued, "Any news on Paul?"

"No. His last planned position on the Appalachian Trail was in Tennessee, so that's where we are concentrating our search. I'm worried. I think those butchers would have killed him to avoid having their break-in plans ruined," said Steele.

"Why now? It makes no sense to me that Spence would take the risk of coming for you after all these years. I think we need a better fix on what he's up to. Last I knew, the government was still keeping tabs on him but that was maybe a year ago. Something's changed."

"Yes, I agree. I'm taking the usual precautions. I wonder if he'll try again."

"I'd count on it. He's probably not happy this attempt was bungled. Watch your six, Dan."

After visiting both patients, Steele found himself fighting heavy traffic on Wisconsin Avenue heading back to the district. It seemed like the rush hour inside the beltway took up the entire morning. He was mentally preparing for the day ahead. A loud ring on the car phone jolted him out of his reverie. The caller ID showed an 865-area code labeled Private Caller.

"Morning, Dan. Can you talk?"

"Paul, what a relief! Where are you?"

"I'm in Gatlinburg, Tennessee at the Smokies Urgent Care. I got my hand chopped off at the wrist and was thrown over a ledge by a group I met on the trail. They left me for dead. Now I'm fighting a bad infection the doctors are treating with big antibiotic guns. I've got a broken leg and separated shoulder. Other than that, everything is peachy keen. I'm having a ball, and the hospital cuisine is four-star Michelin. I'm hope all is quiet there in the center of the universe."

"Not really. A group from Albania used your hand to gain access to our facility a couple of days ago. I just left Bethesda where the admiral and Cass are recovering from gunshot wounds. The prognosis is for a full recovery, but it will take some time. The bastards killed your buddy Nate. I'm sorry, Paul."

"I can't believe they killed Nate. He was a great guy. I'm having a hard time processing all this news. I didn't mean to dump on you at the beginning, Dan. How are you handling the load," asked Blanchard.

"OK, I guess. It's been non-stop since the attack. I was out of the building running an errand when they got in. I think they were after me again."

"Got it. Just so you know, I expect to be discharged in the next two to three days and plan to head your way. I've suddenly lost interest in continuing this hike."

"Do you need any help? Really. I'm certain Owens can commandeer an airplane to fly you back."

"Thanks for offering a helping hand — a bad joke — but I guess I'll have to get used to them. Sure, if you can send a plane to Gatlinburg or somewhere else, that would be great."

"I'll work it when I get back to the office. I'm relieved to hear from you, Paul. I look forward to catching up once we can meet face to face. We've got a lot of moving parts in the air."

"Thanks. I'll press the white coats here for a specific discharge day."

"OK. Take care of yourself. I can't believe what's happening. I'm just glad you are still alive."

"Thanks, Dan. I'll see you later this week."

CHAPTER 4

Tirana, Albania
July 2023

In Tirana, Spence busied himself with a standard routine. Three separate piles of reading lay on his desk. The first were intelligence reports that he often saw before the intended recipient. There were Head of State summaries that provided details on sensitive operations around the globe, delved into the behavior of key leaders, their personal lives and provided projections of any military movements from satellites. A quick status report on the situation in Syria. The overhead sensors had taken the place of operatives in the field. Second, newspapers from the major capitals. Spence had not mastered Chinese, but the translation service did a very thorough job of reporting what the Central Committee allowed. Spence recognized this was considered an old school habit, but he enjoyed thumbing through the world news rather than tuning in to the eight large screen monitors on his office wall. He found there were many silly advertisements and too many stories of contrived heroism, tragedy, and loss on cable television. The final straw: dogs on surfboards. The last stack dived into the current business details of Double Eagle Industries. He churned through messages sent from world-wide offices.

Known as a shipping and security firm, Double Eagle Industries had been dealt an economic blow by the US government almost five years ago when he'd planned to kill the US president and several world leaders who'd gathered in Boston for the United States' Independence Day celebration The plan had been perfect. Had he succeeded, the US would have been forced to respond to the terrorist attack and go on a new offensive in the Middle East. Maybe they would have constructed sufficient evidence to finally go after Iran.

But the plan was foiled, largely because of the efforts of a single very tenacious and determined former U.S. Navy SEAL named Steele who'd escaped confinement in Spence's Georgetown headquarters. The plan's failure damaged the structure of his empire and gave rise to some minor exposure in the press that had been long forgotten. The people who'd fronted for the organization had been conducting legitimate work. It was the back half of the Georgetown headquarters where the core of Double Eagle worked on sensitive projects, known to only a handful of people. Spence rebuilt his empire from his home country of Albania. While still a shadow of its former size and breadth with the surviving part of the US organization still being monitored, he was placing his bets in the States in a few select areas. Most of his inside intelligence apparatus survived, and he was still reading classified reports, including those from the United States, at the highest level.

He often dreamed of a strong and vibrant Albania that had finally turned away from the paranoia of its spotty national past. No more dictators, no more pyramid schemes. Instead, a resurgence as if the legendary Skanderbeg was leading the country once again. Spence looked across the office to the old portrait of Albania's hero on the wall. Larger than life, the man was dressed for the fight: His horned headdress, leather boots and massive broadsword flashing through the air severing limbs or crushing skulls. Nothing could stop him. Spence had his own Skanderbeg outfit but had not worn it in years.

Maybe this year would be the time to fan the flames of pure nationalism once again. Spence mused about leading the country, not from a position as head of one of the largest privately held conglomerates in all of Europe but by officially taking the seat of power and moving onto a different course of prosperity and power, unifying a people that had been downtrodden by their politicians for years, cowed by the threats of their neighbors and still attached to the thousands of post war pillboxes that dotted the countryside. Talk about infrastructure stimulus. What would happen if he called for removal of all those relics of internal war and made a fresh start by breaking the ties with the past? He had tested the waters and had thrown his hat in the ring for the Presidency and intended to win. No half measures but a full-on campaign. Spence's reverie was interrupted by his male secretary for their morning session.

"Good morning, Spence."

"Yes, it is. Thank you, Adam. Shall we get right to it?"

CHAPTER 5

Durres, Albania
August 2023

Two articles in the country's leading daily newspaper, TemA, drew in a well-dressed man drinking coffee at a cafe in Durres, Albania, a coastal town just outside the masthead's headquarters in the nation's capital of Tirana. His polished shoes and neatly combed white hair set him apart from the cafe's other patrons. At first glance, he looked like a retired university professor, reading the day's newspaper. His first language was German, but after nearly seventy-five years living in the country, he could easily pass for a local. Though trained as a naval engineer, the man had a natural affinity for language.

The first article concerned the World Wildlife Fund hiring a diving firm to remove abandoned fishing nets from the Bay of Gelting in the Baltic Sea. The tangled nets were a growing menace to the habitat, threatening the movement of fish in the area and presenting a hazard to boat traffic. While removing a mountain of trawls made of rope, nylon and wire snagged on an underwater shelf, the divers discovered an abandoned typewriter in one of the early nets caught on the rock projection. One diver was curious enough to bring the machine to the surface. Once ashore, the keyboard and rotors placed onto a spindle identified it as an Enigma encryption device which used rotor position, ring settings and a looping internal wiring arrangement to encode and decode messages using letter and number substitutions. The Nazis had used the device to encrypt messages from ships reporting the horrible metrics of war as well as routine requests for replacement parts, fuel and food. According to a local expert, the Enigma machine was a remarkably well-preserved three-rotor model used by German

Navy surface vessels. U-Boats used a four-rotor version of the same machine.

TemA's cover story announced a commercial fish-farm proposed for the offshore waters south of Durres. Hundreds of jobs would be created for the local economy, and the fish trade was expected to spawn hundreds more. Sited in the deep water off the coast, the farm would take advantage of the circular regional currents that washed its shores before heading north into the Adriatic Sea toward Trieste and then back along the coast of Italy before circulating back into the Ionian. The natural flow was perfect to support a large-scale fish farm where the temperature and depth of the water would keep the fish's flesh firm and lean.

The investment in the local economy was heralded from a rostrum set up on the outside patio of a seafood restaurant. A tall avuncular man known as Spence had made the proposal and was its primary investor. A photo showed him at the restaurant providing an overview of the project to a large crowd. He spoke confidently that the project would bring great economic benefits to the country.

"Double Eagle Industries is pleased to partner with the government on this environmentally friendly use of our country's natural resources which will benefit its citizens, especially the people here in Durres. Fish-farming on the scale we propose will prove to be an important element in our future economy. Furthermore, it will be managed by Albanians from top to bottom."

The remarks came months after the same man had announced his intention of seeking the Presidency in the next general election.

What interested the coffee-drinker was the enlarged map outlining the farming area. The offshore lease granted to Double Eagle Industries by the Albanian government was centered on a location known well to the man. While not to scale and without the latitude increments to make a precise comparison with a nautical chart, the area defined amounted to several thousand offshore acres. The man was certain it included a location of particular interest to him. Permits for the venture had already been approved and issued so the matter took on some urgency.

After reading the articles, the man broke his routine and ordered a second cup of coffee, sipping the bitterness and pondering what to do next. Only the well-groomed senior citizen connected the dots between the two news accounts. They brought back a string of memories that watered his eyes and left him a bit dazed. He thought back to the time that he'd fumbled with the four-rotor model of the Enigma coding machine used in the U-boats of the Reich.

In early 1945, the war was winding down, and the dispatches from headquarters carried a bleak tone. Planning for Operation Regenbogen, the "Rainbow Order," had seeped out of Berlin. Scuttling of the entire German U-boat fleet to avoid surrender added a heavy psychological burden to the tough conditions that these undersea fighters endured. Just the fact that the operation was being whispered about throughout the force signaled the nearness of the endgame. The tide had turned. Instead of the submarine force's crisp directives urging its uniformed men into action against the allies, the messages read between the lines that it was now every man for himself. Two weeks before, the well-dressed coffee drinker's submarine had offloaded four of its T-5 acoustic torpedoes at the fortified U-boat base in Saint-Nazaire, France and loaded nearly 15,000 pounds of gold ingots desperately needed by Berlin to sustain the flagging war effort.

Not interested in becoming a martyr for a lost cause, the twenty-one-year-old captain of U-472, assigned to patrol the Mediterranean Sea, decided that he would offer his crew an opportunity to survive. Despite being one of the youngest commanders assigned, he maneuvered his submarine with great skill, surfacing as close to the coast of Italy as he safely could in two locations to release the bulk of the forty-four crew members to swim ashore. Shaking their hands on the deck of the submarine, he bid them a safe swim and a long life before submerging and continuing with a skeletal crew. Crewmembers remembered years later the tears that filled his eyes as his crew filed past him on the deck.

Proceeding eastward, he planned the final maneuver of his underwater hunter. Closing the coast of Albania, he selected an area close to shore where his officers would have a short swim, and the submarine would sink into deep water. Surfacing on a moonless night, the group of five officers stood in the dark cramped conning tower in a quiet sea, watching the lights from the shore. The captain bade farewell to each of them and then gave the order to open the vents. Because of the boat's proximity to shore, scuttling charges were not used. There was no urgency to this final task, and using the explosives might leave something behind that would add to the paranoia ashore. The men stood silently in their shorts as the submarine filled with sea water and gently sank underneath their feet. Left behind on the boat were tons of Hitler's gold and a waterproof box carrying the results of one of the Reich's most ambitious human experiments, known only as Experiment 55. Though tempting to several officers, the idea of swimming ashore with an ingot weighing twenty-seven pounds was a deadly choice. For fear of being discovered, no vests or flotation bladders were permitted to make the swim easier.

The waitress noted his distant stare.

"Karl," she said in a stern voice, "what's gotten into you? Too much caffeine?"

"It's nothing," he replied. "I was just reminiscing about some old times. The coffee was exceptionally good today. I'll be going along now. Goodbye."

CHAPTER 6

Dubai, United Arab Emirates

August 2023

At 6:00 a.m., the drapes on the 140th floor retracted soundlessly as the hot orange sun flooded into the apartment. Dubai was just waking up, and the man looking out the floor-to-ceiling windows of Burj Khalifa, his address for the past three months, lived in what was designed as a large corporate suite. He was the sole occupant of the 6,000 square foot living space with expansive views of the Persian Gulf and the Dubai shoreline. Magnificent.

Little was known about the giant of a man who owned the suite. He bought the residence with a single cashier's check written from a Swiss bank in the name of Smythe. Though purchased in 2020, the unfinished floor was vacant until 2021 when the owner walked in and demanded the key. He presented a passport identifying him as a British subject with a permanent visa for the United Arab Emirates issued at the direction of the Crown Prince.

Soon after arrival, he hired an interior designer catering to Westerners who sought the anonymity of the UAE and its protective statutes that eliminated their exposure to court-ordered restitution and staggering taxes. With her expert help, he divided the unfinished floor into five parts: a master suite, bath with a sauna; a modest office with a voice-commanded, walk-in safe welded to the structural beams of the building; a living room; a guest suite with private bath; a fully-equipped kitchen, with walk-in boxes for frozen and chilled provisions; and a weight room that featured over 2,000 pounds of free weights and stationary machines addressing all the muscle groups.

She selected custom draperies, floor coverings and furnishings for the suite. He ordered all the equipment for the gym. The decorator tried to order artwork and tabletop decorations for each of the rooms and was shocked when the man decided that nothing was to be hung on the walls. They were painted in a neutral palette to complement the floor covering and furnishings. She did ask about the safe, and the man replied that he collected butterflies and that his priceless specimens would be shipped directly to the hotel.

He was rarely seen in public but always made an impression. Some said he was a friend of the Crown Prince of Dubai. Most people believed he was a very wealthy and eccentric investor who enjoyed the unique cachet of the property which was one of the world's most prestigious addresses. A single housekeeper came to the suite three times a week. Groceries were delivered to the floor where the man apparently lived alone.

It was clear that he was security conscious. Only one of the building's elevators served the 140th floor, and it only stopped when a system lockout key was inserted into a control panel located inside the suite. A small vestibule, arranged like a lock-out chamber with separate glass walls built of bullet-proof glass, separated the elevator from the apartment. The doors were interlocked so that one could not be opened without the other door being fully closed and locked. Wall-mounted cameras kept a constant vigil for unexpected or uninvited guests.

A former Alpha Group special forces leader from the Russian Army, General Nikolai Zlodeyev, his real name, needed a private, very secure place to live. He was a fugitive from justice in Russia. There was a standing bounty on his head issued by the Russian president, to be repatriated to face a long list of charges spanning several years. Among the charges were murder, theft of government property, misappropriation, and desertion. He had been tried once for those crimes by a military tribunal, stripped of his rank and sentenced to sixty year's imprisonment without the possibility of parole. He'd made a daring escape on his way to jail, stealing a government airplane and escaping Russia with thirty of his hand-picked special forces soldiers as well as several metal pallets of nuclear artillery rounds and drums of chemical warfare agents.

Landing in Yemen, the General and his crew of fighters lived in a luxurious beach-side compound, surrounded by thick walls, high tech surveillance and a killing zone dotted with land mines and other fortifications to handle aerial assaults. For three months, he had successfully exacted a toll on every vessel transiting the Suez Canal in either direction, holding the rest of the civilized world at bay with his stolen arsenal. Now in Dubai, he lived a solitary, predictable life with financial assets accessible with the touch of a few keys on his computer. Today was a carbon copy of yesterday and the day before, just the way he liked it.

After a brief review of the world markets from a wall covered with curved monitors, the General drank a pitcher of fruit juice with several raw eggs before his morning workout, concluding with a sauna and shower. He began his business day at noontime sitting behind a carved antique Russian desk with a bank of phones and the usual office accoutrements of an international businessman. A circuitous journey had preceded the general's taking up residence at the tallest building in the world.

In December of 2020, after avoiding a US-led Tomahawk attack on the seaside compound in the town of Mocha, Yemen, using a short-range Chinese missile adapted as his personal escape capsule, the former Russian general descended through the cold, dark night. He stared at the UAE coastline and the lights of the inland towns that lay along its border with Oman. He had plugged specific coordinates into his GPS receiver and memorized the map of the area. Relaxing under the full canopy of his parachute, he estimated that his reunion with terrestrial earth would occur sixty miles south of Al Ain, a city built with incentives from the UAE government to lure new residents to the country's interior. With about 800,000 inhabitants, it would provide ample cover for Zlodeyev until he was ready to face civilization again.

After an easy night-time landing in flat, soft sand, the big man took stock. The flesh wound on his side was seeping blood but otherwise, everything seemed to be intact, and he suffered no injuries from his brief space flight and re-entry. He powered up the GPS receiver and read the luminous numbers of his current location as fifty miles south of Al Ain in Saudi Arabia's empty quarter. It was 02:00

a.m. local time. Zlodeyev wrapped himself in the nylon parachute, crawled under the protective lip of a wind-blown sand dune and fell asleep.

After a short night full of dreams, the general awoke to a bright blue sky hosting a hot sun already above the horizon. He freed himself from the nylon bedroll and felt hunger pangs drumming in his empty stomach. Less than twenty feet away in a semi-circle around him was a group of bedouin in a desert squat, drinking tea and smoking cigarettes and eying the large man with suspicion. They were armed with a variety of rifles that were all pointing in his direction. Zlodeyev stood and showed the men that his hands were empty. Standing up, one of the men approached him with a cup of tea, creamed with camel milk and smelling of cardamom. He felt the hot liquid clear the sandy grit from his mouth as it washed into his growling stomach.

"God is great," said Zlodeyev in Arabic. The men all answered the traditional greeting back to him. "Good morning and thank you for the tea. It is good. I'm sorry I cannot offer you some food and refreshments, but I am not prepared to host you properly."

One man carried a battered brass pot over to refill Zlodeyev's cup, filtering the hot liquid though a horsehair strainer, stuffed in its curved spout. Zlodeyev drank the tea and kept his eyes on the group surrounding him. A wizened man with a wrinkled dark face who looked like the oldest of the group broke the silence.

"Do you have any money for us? We are poor men of the desert, but from time to time we must buy provisions, tobacco, and some food for our camels."

Zlodeyev thought that the gathering was no more than a friendly shakedown and wondered if he could save at least half of his gold coins. He looked for the ballistic nylon bag that served as his pillow and found it gone.

"My friends," said Zlodeyev, "I had a bag here with my money, and it seems to have disappeared."

"Is this it?" asked one of the men. He threw the empty zippered sack toward the large man.

"Yes, this is it. All my things are missing, including the money I was carrying."

Zlodeyev continued the small talk while calculating the odds of an unexpected assault. There were six of them carrying old rifles that looked like manhood relics. He doubted that fifty percent of them could be fired. But the odds also predicted that three of them could fire. And then there were the variables of aiming and reaction time. Zlodeyev calculated that he had a twenty-five percent chance of overwhelming the lot without getting himself killed or severely wounded. He'd faced steeper odds in the past and won. Why not now? Each of the men wore the traditional curved dagger in the front of their robes. Knowing he was of no further use to them, like the carcass of a goat picked clean of its stringy meat, ready to be discarded, Zlodeyev needed to get closer. He weighed his options before stretching his limbs. Several of the rifles followed his body.

"So, will you willingly return my possessions, including the money, or do I have to take them back?" He walked toward the leader of the group, waiting for an answer.

"A fight is not necessary. Perhaps you would be willing to share some of your gold coins with us?"

Zlodeyev couldn't help himself. He laughed loudly at the suggestion. It was just days ago that he was collecting millions of dollars daily from the maritime scam he had been running on the Red Sea, charging each transiting ship a toll for using a waterway that he didn't own.

The bedouin didn't recognize that the giant was a fighting machine. Fighting was his alcohol, sex and drugs. As he was laughing, Zlodeyev could see that the group was somewhat distracted, confused by his actions. He had an opening. Bending at the waist, he propelled himself forward like a linebacker taking a bead on a runner for an open field tackle. Scooping up two handfuls of the fine red sand, he flung it at the men in a semi-circle, before reaching the nearest beard. He twisted his neck feeling the muscles tear before hearing the dull crackle of the neck bone of the spine move off its adjacent neighbor. He killed the next man with the rifle butt to the bridge of his nose, bringing the rifle down to firing level before shooting the third man in the chest. Surprise!

He grabbed the man's dagger as he flashed by, feigning left and then right as he faced the aimed barrel held by number four. The gun fired. Zlodeyev felt the round pass by his body as he buried the dagger in the man's throat and kept moving. Number five had a thousand-mile stare on his toothless face and seemed a bit slow on the uptake as the Russian kicked his chin upward and heard his neck snap back as he fell face first into the embers of the campfire. The last of the bedouin was younger, probably still a virgin in terms of killing. The general grabbed his gun barrel and wrenched it from the young man's grip. Looking into his eyes, he saw confusion and fear. The look changed to surprise as he pushed the dagger into his adolescent abdomen.

Zlodeyev sat down heavily in the sand alongside the young man to catch his breath and recover from the adrenaline surge that gave him the strength to turn the tables on his welcoming party without spilling a drop of his own blood. He noticed that the dagger used on two of the bedouin was well-crafted with interlaced gold and silver wires and a rhino horn as the handle. Hammered and folded like Damascus steel, it was an artful weapon and a deadly one in the General's hands.

"Where are the things you took from me?" asked Zlodeyev. The young man was holding his belly with both hands trying to stem the flow of blood. He responded in broken English.

"There in the brown leather bag," motioning with his head. Zlodeyev saw that everything was stained the same earthy brown color and smelled like camels. He picked up several brown pieces of leather before finding his survival stash intact. The GPS receiver signaled the same location. He stripped off his space suit and pulled on the one size fits all balloon pants, likely passed down through several generations, and found a top to match. The smell made him gag.

How do I leave this place? First, he looked at all the rifles. Then the bodies. There was nothing to tie Zlodeyev to the bedouin. He found the young boy in shock and still hanging onto life, his eyes streaming tears and clothes wet with his own blood.

"You will die very soon, my friend," said the general. "If you are in pain, I will put you out of your misery." The boy managed a weak whisper to the offer. Dropping to his knees, facing the boy, and leaning in to hear him, the boy feebly thrust his own dagger at the huge torso. Its point ended inches from the brown cloth of the man's new shirt.

"A valiant attempt my friend." Zlodeyev twisted the dagger out of the boy's hands, pressed the tip to his hairless throat and looked into his eyes as he pushed it to the hilt with his other hand, watching the fear replaced by the vacant look of death. He retrieved his space suit to bury along the way. After another cup of the excellent tea, he bid the men a cheery good morning, unhobbled the camels to wander the desert and set off in the direction of Al-Ain.

Zlodeyev knew that a Russian team of hunters would be searching for him, using satellite sensors, drones, electronic surveillance across the spectrum, and human trackers. They would engage the locals with pamphlets and his picture, offering a lucrative reward for anyone who could narrow the search so they could close in for the kill. Zlodeyev harbored no illusions about his fate but vowed to keep them at bay, even though he was far outnumbered. Though his survival kit was complete, what he needed most was a good hiding place from which he could plan his next move.

Traveling in a westerly direction, and using his GPS receiver, there were sparse signs of life during his first day of travel. He carried food and water for four days, truly a "stranger in a strange land." Trekking in the soft desert sand was exhausting. He headed in the direction of Zarrara, a border site and trading post which supplied the local oil drilling industry with pipe, couplings, and gasoline for the drilling rigs' engines, and a range of field services including oil analysis. There he would find expatriate roughnecks attracted to the desolation of the desert by the high wages and getting as far away from their own pasts as they could.

He pushed himself forward with confidence and determination. His odds for survival and eventually reinventing himself were rising, but he still had a problem. No amount of plastic surgery could disguise his massive frame. At 6' 9" and over 300 pounds, it would take more than a few delicate cuts with a scalpel to disguise him. So, he would be very careful and prepare for the assassins that would certainly track him down. Zlodeyev had faced death before and was not afraid of facing it again but knew that the Federation would send their very best. He'd embarrassed the Russian president, who would not be satisfied until he had Zlodeyev's head on a pike for all to see. There would be no forgiveness or reconciliation.

CHAPTER 7

The Pentagon

Arlington, Virginia
September 2023

Steele's phone began to vibrate as he finished an early morning run around Capitol Hill. He looked at the phone as he opened his front door, recognizing the number.

"Dan, this is Owens. A 07:30 briefing in the five-sided building. I'll meet you at the top of the Metro entrance."

"I'll be there."

After identifying themselves and locking their cell phones in a metal cabinet in the outer room, the two entered a drab, windowless room, taking chairs along the wall. All the seats at the conference table were already taken. They were late. The lights were dimmed as the slide show began.

"This briefing is considered sensitive. The classification has not yet been determined but assume that the information is Special Compartmented Information or higher. Your clearances and need to know have already been established. Let's get right to it. Overnight, a commercial Greek dive boat located here was reported missing." The man at the podium used a laser pointer to identify an area on a chart of the westernmost part of Peloponnesian peninsula.

"This photo was taken three days ago." An overhead shot showed a modern aluminum dive boat anchored close to the rocky shore. A flat-decked barge with heavily rusted sides fitted with a mobile crane lay a hundred yards away. Its deck was tarped, though a section of a carved obelisk and a large black granite sarcophagus were visible on deck.

"Here's the same view this morning. As you can see, the dive boat is missing. The exploration is a joint Greek-US effort to recover Egyptian antiquities carried by the English barque, *Epsilon*, and return them to their origin."

The Navy briefer's voice had an annoying nasal tone that matched the sour look on his face, most likely caused by a last-minute order to prepare a briefing with sketchy details gathered in the recent hours. It was clearly a work in progress. After setting the stage, the briefer then introduced the other half of this tag-team duo from the Department of State.

"Thank you, Stan. As you've already heard and looking around the room, you'll no doubt recognize stakeholders from the relevant agencies. The United States is not interested in a ship load of treasure from Egypt." The briefer paused to see if anyone else caught his humorless turn of phrase. He continued, "or the political intrigue that goes with it. Our British colleagues know about the effort and have been monitoring it. A little history may help put you in the picture. *Epsilon* was enroute to the UK when it sank in a storm in 1802, so we expect some sort of minimal assertion of ownership from them. State's interest is to resolve this crisis without straining diplomatic ties or cashing in any bargaining chips we need to use in the future. Remember the Elgin marbles? That's still an open wound between the Brits and the Greeks all these many years later. Why is it a situation, you ask? The dive team included five Americans that are now missing along with the boat, a chest full of gems and a potentially valuable piece of papyrus outlining the path into the middle of the largest of the three pyramids in Giza. I apologize for all the background. Why is this important or relevant to any of you? Well, one of the missing American divers happens to be the president's son——."

"Lincoln Brewster."

Several people seated at the conference table turned toward the speaker, an old hand in Washington. Everybody knew him as the Blue Man, a regular fixture at these types of meetings. Always dressed in a dark blue suit and blue tie. It was rumored that he helped lay the cornerstone when the Pentagon construction began in 1941. He should have known better. Filling in the blanks for a Washington briefer was a clumsy faux pas.

"Yes, that's right."

The briefer merely acknowledged Blue Man's outburst. "Let's hope the press doesn't connect the dots as easily as you have. Involving them at this stage would be counterproductive."

The State Department briefer continued, advancing the slides to a headshot of the president's son. "As you might imagine, the fact that the president's son is now missing has upped the ante considerably from a diplomatic point of view. The Navy has been monitoring the ship's position using overhead sensors and confirming verbal radio check-ins twice daily. That's been the extent of our surveillance. The White House made it clear that the president wishes to minimize any official involvement because of the ongoing backlash from his other son's business dealings abroad. I'm sure that all of you have been following the stories."

The briefer paused and took a drink of water from a plastic bottle.

"Lincoln Brewster is the son who resigned from the U.S. Navy and became an accomplished commercial diver. Our current plan is a low-key response: to send in a new dive team to see if there is any evidence left behind. We believe Lincoln may have been abducted by unidentified terrorists, who commandeered the vessel and crew and are headed to parts unknown. We don't want to overtly employ the operational or surveillance assets of the Sixth Fleet in this case, and likewise, the Greeks are equally nervous about using their military in a way that will predictably invite inquiries and press involvement which could further complicate the situation. In sum, we plan to send a team to Greece today to look for any clues suggesting what may have happened to the people and the boat."

Steele looked at Owens, who appeared to be sporting his best poker face and knew immediately why he had been invited to the briefing. He would be a member of the US side of the team that would be diving the following morning. Steele mentally packed for the trip as the briefer began again. His planned rendezvous with Garrison would be postponed yet again. Returning to the briefing, he started retrieving files from the library in his brain.

Steele had met Lincoln Brewster briefly two years ago before the president's son washed out of BUDS training, the tough six-month prep school that had to be completed before anyone started to understand what SEAL teams did and how they survived.

Like nearly two thirds of candidates, Brewster rang the bell during Hell Week, where a SEAL trainee's body and mind are stressed to the breaking point. Though there were several calls from the White House seeking to give Brewster another chance, the Navy refused to bend. Lincoln Brewster had all the physical attributes to become a SEAL and certainly possessed the discipline and mental toughness. Attitude caused him to fail. His had been a life of privilege, and he liked to remind the instructors who he was. This was a kiss of death among the tight-knit teams where officer and enlisted team members were like brothers. The rank you wear on your uniform, your name or personal history made little difference when the going got tough.

"So, we've got a delicate situation here with dangerous political risks: the president's son is missing from a Greek dive boat, and there are no tracks leading anywhere. Could it be an inside job? Possibly. Nothing has been ruled out. That's why we need to move quickly and quietly. Are there any questions?"

"What about our overhead sensors? Don't we have coverage of the area that would show what happened? How about the Greeks? Do they have any surveillance of the surface traffic in the area over the last week?" asked a Marine colonel.

"We have scheduled a joint data call with the Sixth Fleet, the Greek government and the Intelligence Community this afternoon. I'll be better prepared to respond to your question once all the information is available. As you know, our overhead sensors have been operating over the Eastern Med monitoring the Syrian situation, but I am reasonably confident that we'll be able to reconstruct the maritime traffic. Are there any other questions? Please sign the meeting log and provide your best contact information. We'll set up daily briefings, and an interagency working group will be stood up starting tomorrow. Invitations to all agencies will be issued later this morning. That's where we are today. Please limit further discussion of this matter. Thanks, everybody."

Steele and Owens returned to the Navy section of the Pentagon's E-ring without speaking. The two filled paper cups with coffee from the Secretary's mess and walked around the corner to Owens' cubby-hole sized office, at one time a janitor's closet. Owens spent at least half his time at the Pentagon as one of the National Security Advisor's military aides.

"What do you think, Dan?" asked Owens from behind his desk.

"Admiral, it's clear to me that the Navy will take point on this crisis. You've been cooking up a response behind the scenes which includes me. Looking at the number of coffee cups in your trash can, I believe this situation hit the fan about 02:00 this morning, and you've been here at the office working since then. You are sporting a five o'clock shadow."

Owens burst out laughing, dribbling hot black coffee down the front of his uniform. He blotted the stain with a napkin and then engaged Steele's dark eyes directly. The time for speculation had ended.

"Accurate enough, Dan. A Gulfstream is scheduled to depart Andrews at 1600 this afternoon. You'll be teaming up with one of your old buds from Team Six, Mac Andrews. And there's more to this story that the briefer didn't cover."

CHAPTER 8

Andravide Airbase

Western Greece
September 2023

After the usual inter-agency tussle, the team heading to Greece swelled to six. Steele and Andrews were joined by representatives from the State Department, the FBI, a well-known Egyptologist from the Smithsonian and Mr. Smith representing the CIA. A sensitive mission involving the president's son attracted attention. Some viewed it as a smart investment in bargaining chips, the bitcoin of Washington, which could be used later to preserve budget initiatives, avoid manpower cuts and polish reputations.

After catching up with all the Special Operations news with his buddy from Team Six, Steele turned into an actual bed made by rotating the adjacent aircrafts seats inward and reclining the chair backs. But it was still like sleeping on a couch. After a restless night, he woke up with a cup of strong black coffee. He pulled a folder from his briefcase and started to read using the built-in lamp above his seat. Everyone else was still sleeping.

A Brief Contextual History of the English barque *Epsilon*

Prepared by the Department of State

In 1798, the Battle of the Nile solidified England's dominance of the maritime domain as Lord Nelson defeated a larger French force in the Mediterranean Sea a few miles from the mouth of the north-flowing river. More important, the defeat bottled up the expansionist

Napoleon for three years, as he had no means of returning to France or communicating with Paris except by courier. He was stranded in Egypt.

The British were quick to pillage Egypt's antiquities, including an odd stone discovered by one of Napoleon's engineers. Years later, linguists found that the stone provided a comparative translation of three languages of the day and enabled researchers to understand hieroglyphics. Dubbed the Rosetta Stone, it became part of the division of property formally directed by the Treaty of the Nile in 1801. Delivered to England in 1802, the Rosetta Stone became the British Museum's crown jewel.

Suddenly, the British became fascinated with everything Egyptian, which prompted a flurry of style-setting among the avant-garde. The interest in authentic Egyptian goods rose sharply. Entrepreneurs reacted to the strong demand signal by funding explorations to gather whatever they could find in Egypt. Particularly sought were stone tablets, sections of columns, jewelry looted from the tombs and the massive death trinkets: carved, lidded sarcophagus boxes. The race was on.

At nearly 200 feet in length, *Epsilon* was built in Liverpool as a coastal trader in 1770. After running aground and losing her main mast, the hulk lay abandoned for years. Seeing an opportunity to cash in on the latest fad, three young businessmen pooled their limited financial assets and purchased the derelict. They aimed to fund a dockyard refit in Portsmouth before sending the three-masted barque to Egypt.

Roland Haberstam, the superintendent at the yard, was a well-known dealmaker, with a reputation in the maritime community of a modern day used car salesman. He knew every trick in the book to make the yard's work look like skilled shipwrights had completed it. To avoid the cost of putting the ship in a drydock, the investors relied on Haberstam's self-serving advice. The yard repaired *Epsilon's* beaten hull from the inside while the ship was waterborne. Her cracked ribs were sistered and mended with thick iron plates covering both the damaged ribs and the adjacent strength members, hewn of a local member of the ash family. The iron plates looked sturdy enough, compensating for the adjacent timber not long enough to be considered a strength member and of a different fresh cut wood that in time would bend and twist on its own. It was an early example of what U.S. Navy ships called a budget yard. Haberstam filled his pockets and sent patched-up relics to sea without a second thought. A deal was struck with the three naive investors to replace the main mast and steering masts for a cut rate price. The term you get what you pay for had never been more applicable.

Finally ready to sail, *Epsilon* moved sluggishly under its square sails. A local ship surveyor declared the ship sea-worthy in exchange for an evening of drink and his choice of ladies offering themselves for service. They recruited a captain in a similar manner. A twelve-man crew was scooped up like a seine net pulled along the bottom in over-fished grounds.

As any sailor knows, a coat of fresh paint can hide underlying defects. What the captain did not know was the condition of the new masts added during the refit. Round beetle holes had been plugged and hidden by a coat of tar. The beetles turned sections of the center mast into a honeycombed structure. What was once strong wood that could accept the stress and strains of holding its square-rigged sails in a spanking wind had been hollowed out in the lower part of the mast that penetrated the main deck and was fastened to the hull just above the keel. Unseen, the beetles had left fungal infestations as they fed on tasty cellulose fibers.

Once in Egypt after an uneventful voyage, the crew proved to be remarkably creative in finding and recovering goods that would bring top dollar back home. Promised a share of the value of the goods plundered motivated the hard-drinking lot to collect everything and anything that bore the design or had an Egyptian provenance. In a few weeks, *Epsilon's* holds had been filled with obelisks, carved statuary, sarcophaguses. The ship wallowed at anchor, long before the standards for loading a ship became commonplace. Cargo was a matter for the captain to decide. This captain's focus was not on ship stability but rather the volume of artifacts that he could haul back to England. More discriminating, the captain filled sea chests with gold artifacts and gemstones and an ancient set of plans which disclosed the route into the interior of the pyramids where a chamber had been prepared for the afterlife of one of Egypt's rulers. The pillaging of architectural treasures was nothing new. It began during the reign of Tutankhamen. The pyramids at Giza had already been stripped of their marble veneer.

Departing Cairo in 1802 for the return voyage to England, where the demand for the goods *Epsilon* carried had reached an all-time high, the ship sailed steadily for the first few days despite the light winds in the Eastern Mediterranean. A storm brewing offshore, fed by the parched desert wind crossing Northern Africa pushed past the high-pressure system. In hours, the barque's captain knew the overloaded ship was in grave danger. He fortified himself with frequent nips of rum from a long, curved silver flask. Square rigged sails were reefed-in with only the traditional aft mast sheet left to steer the ship. Wind-driven seas built from the burning sands of Libya. The period of the storm-driven seas kept *Epsilon* in the trough while the captain set a northwesterly course, hoping to find protection in one of the quiet harbors near the island of Crete.

There were risks there as well. Rocks above the sea could protect. The unseen spires and outcroppings underwater could gut the barque like a sharp knife opening the belly of a codfish. Plowing into swells and sometimes being carried by a following sea, *Epsilon* was getting pounded by a mountainous ocean, tossed around by an angry, frothing salt water and strong winds that showed no evidence of diminishing.

The sheering force of the wind first fractured the thick main mast as its inner core provided no real strength. Loud cracks could be heard over the howling gale. The captain prayed that the little barque could reach the sheltering lee of an island and enjoined the frightened crew to do the same. If he lived, he would become a very rich man. When the mast broke, it took the upper third of its weakened height and rigging into the sea, leaving the stub of a greenstick fracture looking skyward. Lashings and lines were cut away. The small sail on the aft mast was shredded in the wind and looked like a load of fresh laundry flapping on a clothesline. All control had been lost, and the barque became just another piece of flotsam. It seemed their last-minute prayers had not been heard. The barque pushed on a course set by mother nature herself.

Through the mist of the seas cresting in the strong wind, tall volcanic mountains came into view on the port side, and it seemed that the ship might get some shelter on the other side of a rocky promontory off to starboard. A protected waterway loomed ahead, and the crew felt some relief. So did the captain, puffing up his chest as if he planned to do just that. Waves pounded the little craft unmercifully. Each swell caused the boat to heel over, lingering in that position as seawater flooded the decks and found its way below.

The fierce winds rolled the barque on its side, burying the starboard deck edge. With a final sustained blow, and within sight of the solace of calmer water just ahead, the wind increased to hurricane force and beyond as the ship balanced on its rail before the swells lifted the hull and held the barque and its cargo on ship's side. Lashings tore from the attachment points and gravity repositioned the heavy stone artifacts in the cargo holds. Thick iron plates popped off the sistered ribs, as if they were affixed with headless brads.

The barque's rudder was torn off on a rock outcropping protecting the point of land so close that several sailors were inclined to take their chances in the water itself. Those poor souls were flung against massive rocks with hard faces worn down over the centuries. Their skulls burst like ripe melons when flung against the rocks. Sailors hung from the ship's port rail, suspended in their sodden clothing until their arms could no longer hold their bodies. *Epsilon* had no righting arm left to bring the ship back from its starboard side. The wind died down for a few minutes while the ship rolled amid the foamy seas and began to take on tons of seawater. The barque's starboard side became its hull, and the shifting interior cargo served as a weighted keel. With no buoyancy left, *Epsilon* sank in deep water on the edge of a desolate island with a hold full of museum quality treasure, sea chests filled with gemstones and a rolled papyrus thought to provide the interior architectural details of a passage into a Pharaoh's tomb within the largest pyramid at Giza. There were no survivors.

★ ★ ★

Steele wondered if the State Department's author fancied himself as an historical novelist as he tucked the briefing back into his briefcase.

On final approach, with the noontime sun penetrating the water column, the plane flew over the dive site where the sparking blue water separated the Peloponnese peninsula from the mainland. Landing on the generous 10,000-foot runway which was home to a squadron of the Hellenic Air Force's tactical fighters, a military bus met the plane on the apron and transported the passengers to the base operations center. A buffet table held a feast with a mezza of cheeses, olives, several breads, marinated lamb and pureed eggplant, juices, coffee, retsina wine and beer. After shaking hands with another group of officials and the designated liaison, a portly Navy captain from the embassy in Athens, the stand-up lunch set the stage for an amicable yet delicate meeting. Thirty minutes later, a solicitous officer asked the group to take seats in the room next door.

The briefing had the look and feel of dog and pony show that had been polished over the course of the expedition and was meant to convey the importance of the find and to highlight the cooperation between the host government and the United States. After a few organizational charts, a chart was displayed to orient people in time and place. The airbase lay on the far western side of the peninsula less than four miles from the Ionian Sea and the port of Kyllini, located less than a mile from the dive site.

The group viewed a video simulation re-creating *Epsilon's* final moment. A detailed blow-up of selected artifacts and precise location of their discovery followed. Where *Epsilon's* cargo spilled from its holds on the bottom had been gridded and carefully surveyed. The next series of slides captured the artifacts in crystal clear water in situ. Steele was amazed at the size of some of the stones. He had made a trip from Alexandria to Cairo during a port visit there and saw similar things at the Egyptian National Museum in Cairo, though stones this size, barged down the Nile from Aswan were generally displayed outside. How these fragments got loaded on the ship and transported was another feat. Several of the column sections measured six feet in diameter and must have weighed tens of tons.

There was nothing new reported on the intelligence front. Presumably, any video collected from the port authorities, and the data from any overhead sensors had been reviewed. Several photos captured the missing dive boat, a purpose-built craft manufactured in the United States, fabricated of marine grade aluminum plate with welded joints. It was donated to the Hellenic Ephorate of Underwater Antiquities, the group sponsoring the expedition and funding it. The specifications were included on a marketing fact sheet. Steele was familiar with the manufacturer, Munson Boats, located in Washington State, and wondered if he'd ever seen the missing craft. A very capable, flexible craft powered by two 350 HP Mercury engines, trailerable, and weighing in at a substantial 15,000 pounds.

Weather certainly had not been a factor in the boat's disappearance. There was no reason why the divers would depart the dive site. A mechanical failure of the anchor or chain seemed remote. So how does a working dive boat just disappear?

CHAPTER 9

Department of State

Washington, DC
September 2023

Four State Department interns were drinking coffee and openly grousing about their assignments at a table in the cafeteria.

"How in the hell did you two get on the Norway team while Gus and I got banished to the Balkans. What did you score on the foreign service exam?"

"Look, it has nothing to do with any test score or undergrad record," said one of the table mates who looked like his forebears carried Scandinavian lineage in their DNA. Klaas continued,

"The junior officers usually make the choices, and they liked what they saw with us. You know, blonde hair, blue eyes. I think you'll be working with swarthy, suspicious males who wear cheap black suits. Have you met the woman who leads that section? I'm told they call her Brunhilda."

"You guys are so full of it. Heh, Gus, we've got to go listen to that candidate for president of Albania. He starts in five minutes, and Basford wants a summary before the end of the day. Let's go." He pushed his chair under the table and left his remaining table mates with a resigned conclusion, "Yep, we are living the dream!"

A large screen television bridged the gap in time and language for the interns.

Spence spoke the language of Albania, an ancient dialect spoken only by its citizens and those who had migrated to neighboring countries. A hand talker signed, and an AI-generated, broken English translation scrolled across the bottom of the screen. The local Tirana television station broadcast the event live to an audience of an estimated 8,000 people, some of whom were drawn to the venue by the promise of free food. Spence energetically addressed the crowd and made the usual pledges about the economy, health care, and transparent governance before surprising everyone listening.

"My team will work for the people of this country and chart a new course for the future. For too long, we have lived with leaders satisfied with an underdeveloped economy, inadequate public transportation, and an industrial sector that has seen little growth in the last fifty years. We have not kept up with technology which is changing the world around us. We will catch up during my term as your next president."

What shocked many Western listeners were his statements about Albania's relationships with NATO, the European Union and World Trade Organization.

"I pledge to re-examine Albania's membership in several specific organizations to ensure that our country is being served in the most advantageous way. How will the European Union serve Albania? Please offer me a concrete example. NATO has been slow to acknowledge the central issues affecting our independence and our freedom to act, not to mention failing to deal with the ongoing crisis in Ukraine. Let me ask. Can anyone point to a single accomplishment by the World Trade Organization? I believe a thorough, honest assessment of these external institutions needs to be accomplished as a matter of priority. I do not believe in kicking the can down the road, and I know many of you agree with me. We are in the twenty-first century, my friends, but many of our glorious roots are hanging on to traditions which stunt our growth.

Looking inward, there is much to be done on the military front. The brave men and women wearing the country's uniform and serving under the Double-Headed Eagle must be equipped with weapons for modern conflict, wireless and satellite communications systems and an intelligence organization which maintains a constant surveillance of our friends and potential adversaries. We need the ability to anticipate instead of merely react. Isn't it ironic that our American allies left so much equipment during their hasty withdrawal from Afghanistan? We desperately need those weapons systems to modernize our military. I intend to tackle this capability gap as a top priority of my administration."

After pausing for a drink of bottled water at the podium, Spence walked to the front center of the stage and, raising his voice, continued, "Modernizing our military will be the focus of my new Minister of Defense who I am pleased to present to you now."

A mountain of a man stood and joined Spence. His suit was fitted and cut to reveal his massive physique. The two joined hands and raised their arms high above their heads while the crowd cheered. Spence returned to the podium while his man mountain remained at the front of the crowd.

"Ladies and Gentlemen, my choice for Albania's next Minister of Defense is General Nikolai Zlodeyev, a former Alpha Group commander from Russia with a distinguished military career. He is not only a highly trained warfighter and capable leader, but also a skillful planner who will craft the future military blueprint for our country. This brave man can deliver what we need to modernize our forces within a reasonable and affordable budget. We will no longer haggle over guns versus butter. We can and should have both. Albania is now General Zlodeyev's home, and he has pledged his allegiance to all its citizens."

The bold claim excited the crowd. They began waving the Albania flag and well as campaign posters of Spence, some featuring full-color photos of Spence and Zlodeyev under the words, "Albania's Future."

Spence ended his speech on a high, reach for the sky vision recalling the proud history of the country's national hero, Skanderbeg, who had rallied the population and led the people to shake-off Ottoman rule. He ended on a thunderous note.

"Albania will rise again and move toward Skanderbeg's vision for a free country. We will be capable of asserting our independence and military power on the world stage."

"Wow, that speech sounded like it was written by one of Trump's speechwriters," said Gus.

"Sure does. We've got an hour to put together the summary and get the background info to Basford. How about if I start typing and you see what you can find out about Zlodeyev. I already have a background paper on Spence. It's very thin. Frankly, he looks like a vanilla candidate to me. I'll use the info on Skanderbeg that we used last time. The guy's been dead over 550 years, so I don't think there are any updates on the internet," said Tom.

"Sounds like a plan, let's meet up in the conference room in thirty minutes. I'll send a note to the Embassy, and we'll touch base with Hilda. Who knows, a good job on this might get us promoted to another division."

Three hours later, Deputy Assistant Secretary for European and Eurasian Affairs, James Benjamin Basford, charged out of his office, the point paper on Spence's speech and the announcement on Zlodeyev in his hand.

"Mary, please find these two guys from the Balkans" flipping the pages on the report, "Stone and Michaels... and have them come and see me ASAP. Thanks." Standing just short of six feet, and weighing in at 140 pounds, "BB" Basford was a slight, bookish man that most people assumed was a career civil servant who made it to his current position because of longevity. Though his unimpressive features and build didn't show it, he'd been a young, highly decorated fighter pilot in Vietnam who spent four long years as a caged guest of the North Vietnamese in Hoa Lo prison, better known as the Hanoi Hilton.

Five minutes later, Gus Stone and Tom Michaels were standing in front of Basford's desk, breathless from their quick walk from a remote corner in the basement of the Department of State.

"Wow, that was fast, I'm impressed gentlemen. I've read your report and wanted the two of you to fill in some squares for me. I believe your boss is on travel this week, right?" Basford came over and looked at both of their badges.

"Yes, sir, that's correct," said Gus.

"I'm curious about two specific things. First, the dossier on Spence has a major gap. It fails to mention the problem we had with him years ago when he was implicated in a plot to kill the president. Frankly, State kept the story under wraps, and we released very few details on the attempt, but it still scares the hell out of me whenever I am reminded of it. How far back did you guys go?"

Stone answered, "the protocol is for five years, but we went back ten."

"That's impossible," said Basford. "This all happened 2018 or 2019 over in Georgetown. I recall it well because I was lucky enough to be the Duty Officer that night. The FBI raided a K street office building, the Headquarters for Double Eagle Industries, trying to apprehend Spence. I know it's hard to believe, but he escaped the Bureau's raid. It proved to be a very long day for me. Do you guys have the clearance to get into our foreign personnel files as well as the country briefs?"

"Yes, sir," the two answered in unison. Stone continued, "I accessed both databases for the dossier. No new information in either data base so I used the last one and just cut and pasted it."

"No, no, no, that's impossible. Let's go over to the conference table. One of you guys log in and project it on the screen."

After spending thirty seconds getting into the system, Stone pulled up the chronology on Spence.

"Good, now scroll down to 2019, and let's see what we've got." said Basford drumming his pen on the table next to his planner.

One of the first accounts on Spence was a 2019 article from *The Boston Globe* recounting Spence's trip to Boston to receive an

International Rotary award for his philanthropic support of exchange student programs. A black and white photo of Spence accepting the award was attributed to a well-known photographer from the newspaper.

"Keep scrolling," ordered Basford. The next entry covered Double Eagle Industry's presentation of a check to the United Way Campaign in 2018. Staring at the screen, Basford's face flushed with annoyance. Both interns expected to see hives next. Basford rolled into the chair at the head of the table and his fingers flew over the keyboard as he accessed a CIA database on Spence. The same articles appeared. He punched a familiar extension into the table phone and pushed the speaker button.

"Lewis," said the person answering the call.

"Jim, this is BB. Remember that case several years ago Double Eagle Industries over in Georgetown was raided and the primary target, a guy named Spence, somehow slipped through the dragnet?"

"Sure. I also remember the sap who was almost sliced in two by a big broadsword. I couldn't believe the blood. There were a few others taken out of the building horizontally if memory serves. They raided the operation in the back of building."

"All that stuff was entered into the database before we converted to electronic files, right?"

"It sure was. I loaded a ton of it myself. Why, is there something new on the case?"

"Yeah, what's new is that material seems to have disappeared from our database as well as the CIA's. I haven't checked the FBI or Treasury, but I thought you might start with ours and see what you think. Looks like we've been hacked by someone wanting to write some revisionist history. I plan to see the Director at 7:00 p.m. tonight. If you find anything else of interest, please give me a buzz back. Looks like two of our interns have discovered something that could set us back for years. Thanks, Jim."

"You've got it."

Basford leaned back in his chair, momentarily closed his eyes and then returned upright with his palms flat on the table.

"Now. The second thing that sparked my curiosity was the dossier on Zlodeyev. Why do I keep remembering these moments which should have been sent to the TV show 'That's Incredible.' This is the guy who tried to impose a tax on ships transiting the Red Sea and Suez Canal less than a year ago. Unbelievable. He built a luxury condo for his crew of Russian special forces deserters and seeded a mine field all around it. Pulled in an American to set up a maritime ambush. They sank a modern British container ship that refused to pay up with some mines which were stolen from some pre-positioned stocks we kept in Djibouti. What a mess! Containers bobbing all over the place. The channel had to be re-defined. It was in all the papers and ended when the president ordered a Tomahawk strike on the compound in Yemen. Does that ring any bells?" asked Basford.

"Yes, sir" said Stone, "but we thought it may have been a different person. The protocol directs that we use the Department of State's database as the primary source of information and the story you just related is not there."

Basford repeated himself, "That's not possible. Let's pull it up on the screen."

A photo of the general projected on the screen.

Basford said, "I wouldn't want to meet that guy in a dark alley. He's huge. At the time, there was a story going around that he set up a small amphitheater in Yemen where his band of thugs would fight each other and also animals. Unbelievable! Scroll down."

Zlodeyev's biodata looked much like Spence's, ending with his retirement from the Russian military and transition to security consulting for commercial firms headquartered in Moscow. He was living quietly in a modest dacha on the Black Sea. A magazine article showed the general riding a horse along the beach accompanied by a top-heavy Russian model reputed to be one of Putin's favorite consorts.

"Impossible," exclaimed Basford. He pushed his chair back from the table.

"Guys," he said, "I want you both to keep this apparent hack quiet. This is very serious stuff and obviously none of our IT safeguards protected this sensitive information. I'm starting to have a very bad day. You guys did a great job on the report, and you've uncovered a serious breakdown in our IT system. I'll make sure your boss knows about this. Thanks for your time."

The Secretary of State, Rachel Sullivan, walked past Basford's secretary's desk, giving her a broad smile. She knocked on Basford's office door and opened it at the same time. Stone and Michaels were moving toward the door as she entered.

"Good afternoon, gentlemen," she said to the interns, "I'm Rachel Sullivan. Let's see, Gus Stone and Tom Michaels, assigned to the Balkans Division if I recall correctly. Tell me, how is your internship here at State going?"

"Fine, Madame Secretary. We met with Mr. Basford regarding the speech just given earlier today by one of the contenders for Albania's presidential election."

"Well, coincidentally, that's exactly why I came to see BB. Spence's speech set off a firestorm among our allies in NATO and the European Union." She looked at Basford, raising her perfectly sculpted eyebrows. Dressed in a subtle plaid suit, she inherited her lithe frame from her father, a well-known marathoner from Kenya. Her mother, a cherubic Cuban, donated the flawless skin and an ever-present smile. Tall and elegant. Educated as a lawyer, Sullivan found the life of a practicing attorney boring. She enjoyed the constant human interaction of politics.

"BB, my private line has been blowing up. People are fearful of what Spence and his Russian friend might do. As you might expect, they have offered all their support to the US in cleaning up the mess. Last week, the president's son went missing and this week it's a direct threat to NATO and the EU. What's your take on this situation?"

"Well, Madame Secretary, it's far worse than it seems. Not only has Spence set off a firestorm in Europe, but also, I suspect he's behind the hack that these two interns found in our database, where he is portrayed as an angelic philanthropist."

CHAPTER 10

The Pentagon

Arlington, Virginia
October 2023

For the older people working at the Pentagon, uniformed and civilian, Robert Graham was a legendary researcher who dedicated his life to thwart what young Adolf Hitler had created in Germany in the late 1930s. Originally from Poland, he changed his name twice: once when he came under the spell of the Third Reich, and later when he emigrated to the United States. He was the Pentagon's Simon Wiesenthal, a Nazi hunter forged in the ethnic fury of wartime Germany. Graduating from secondary school at fifteen, he entered medical school in 1936, graduating a year before the Germans overran Poland. His field of expertise was the human mind, and his medical degree in psychology gave him a rare privilege. With the ink not even dry on his new diploma, Robert Garbaciok was an apolitical child of rare intelligence and insight. He was recruited by the Germans and sent to Berlin to be considered for a post on the Fuhrer's personal staff.

Garbaciok was among twenty physicians from the major medical disciplines who organized and conducted experiments on human subjects. The framework for the studies were peer-reviewed and were based on the classical scientific method with control groups, use of placebos, and population sizes recognized by the scientific community. Of course, Hitler often had an outcome in mind when he approved the experiments, and the science was a means of giving such inquiries legitimacy.

Once young Dr. Garbaciok was vetted and assessed as posing no security threat to Hitler's inner circle, he became involved with experiments in control and power. Hitler's mesmerizing and impassioned speeches enthralled the nation and then the world. His approach was largely supported by Dr. Garbaciok's work on the speeches that reflected Hitler's position of power and how ordinary people were cowed into animated compliance. Many of those early studies of people's reactions led to several theories which the doctor brought to the Fuhrer's personal attention. His influence grew and soon he was made the Director of Experiments at the tender age of twenty-four.

His age belied encyclopedic knowledge of medicine and his own specialized discipline of behavior. Though early experiments were conducted without using drugs, Dr. Garbaciok soon began experimenting with compounds designed to increase the intensity and recall of the messages. Could he use a drug to make authoritarian suggestions even more pervasive?

Observations regarding the power of zombie organisms to create behavioral change in animals higher on the food chain was a widely quoted article from *National Geographic* some eighty years later. Those who knew the man regarded him as a man before his time, studying behavior in a way copied years later in Western countries.

He consulted widely with physicians, scientists, scholars and even clergymen. It was during this period of inquiry that he became exposed to Western theories of behavior and realized that his intellect was being used for evil. The death camps and round-up of Jews proved to be the last straw. Dr. Robert Graham finally landed in the United States where he first hid within academia then later joined the ranks of the intelligence service, the only one of Hitler's inner circle to successfully flee. Through the war years, his contributions to the allies were valuable in understanding the hypnotic hold of blind loyalty to the madman. Under Hitler, even the educated people became passively complicit in the spread of his brand of control.

After all the years of dedicated service, Dr. Graham's retirement and final departure from the Pentagon were marked by a yellow sheet cake purchased and lettered at a local grocery store and a series of testimonials from longtime friends. His final remarks were brief, thanking his colleagues and again giving the stern warning that

Experiment 55, if ever found, should be considered sensitive intelligence and reviewed by trusted psychologists. He claimed that the study remained relevant and should be mined for methods of mass mind control that could be used defensively by the intelligence and national security teams.

Graham walked out of the Pentagon that morning into a hot blinding sun and elevated humidity. The air was thick and close. He placed a cardboard banker's box in the trunk and started his car, pushing the climate control to MAX AC. Even with the cold air coming through the vents, Robert had difficulty taking in a full breath. He lowered the seat back trying to relax before driving home. When the car ran out of gas the following morning, Robert was in the same position but not having any problem breathing…he was dead.

CHAPTER 11

Kyllini, Greece
October 2023

Kyllini served as the terminus for several ferry lines providing passenger and cargo service to nearby islands. A steady stream of boats used the port. Well-marked and clear of the channel, the nearby *Epsilon* dive site was delineated by a series of large orange buoys and an anchored barge fitted with an over cabled crane for winching up the heaviest artifacts. Part of its flat deck was covered with newly raised ancient stonework of varied sizes and descriptions.

After the briefing, Steele and the senior diver from the Hellenic side agreed to the initial plan in short order. Within the group of Americans who had traveled to Greece, everyone seemed to have diving qualifications and volunteered to be on the team making the first dive. Particularly annoying was the man representing the Agency who felt that his duty was to uncover clues that others might miss. He somehow thought of himself as the only person capable of picking up the trail to the president's son.

What remained of the wreck, a few odd timbers with some exposed copper nails, lay at ninety feet on a narrow shelf that dropped to several hundred feet on the seaward side and to the sandy bottom on the harbor side at 150 feet. The current was negligible, and the dive would begin an hour before high tide. Most of the artifacts had been found strewn along the rocky walls with some of the larger, heavier stonework falling to the seabed. No one knew whether the dive boat was sunk on site or had been commandeered and driven away in the thirty-seven hours since it went missing.

The US and Greek teams each had two divers assigned the morning and afternoon dives with a divemaster and equipment tech for each shift. Because the dive boat was not built with sleeping quarters or a kitchen, the teams were billeted ashore, and the boat left anchored at night, showing only one 360-degree white light on top of the wheelhouse.

Steele took charge: "This afternoon's dive will be a survey of the site, looking for the dive boat and its six-person crew. There will be four divers on this dive, Nick and Christos from the Hellenic side and Mac Andrews and me from the US. The divemaster is Constantine and the equipment tech is Adras. Any questions?"

The State Department representative knew that trouble was brewing on the American side and tried to nip it in the bud.

"State agrees with this plan for the first dive." There were looks of disappointment and flashes of anger but that settled it. The man from the Agency drifted away from the group.

The four divers suited up with scuba gear from the mobile locker parked near at the head of a finger pier and motored out in a flat-bottomed workboat fitted with bench seats and powered by a 25 horsepower outboard, reaching the dive site several minutes later. Steele and Andrews would search the water on the east side, and Nick and Christos would take the deeper western side. Maximum depth was agreed not to exceed 100 feet to permit a no decompression dive of at least thirty minutes.

Gin-clear, the warm azure water defined perfect diving conditions. Visibility seemed unlimited. It reminded Steele of a dive he made in Guam's Apra Harbor on a World War II bulk carrier sunk near the base of the breakwater protecting the harbor. He and his dive buddy took up positions in the pilot house and on the bow of the ship and could see each other clearly at a distance of 300 feet.

Within seconds of submerging, Steele spotted the stern of the dive boat perched at a steep angle on a long furrow eroded in the rocky face of the steep underwater cliff. As Steele and Andrews approached the boat, they saw that the twin outboards mounted on the transom were caught on a rock projection. It appeared that the boat's weight was being held by the engines' lower shafts and propellers. The aluminum transom was bending with the stress, and the engines' housings were cracked. Suspended at seventy feet, the boat could continue to slide down the furrow at any moment. They carefully surveyed the hull, finding the bow free and clear. Swimming along the deck, scuba bottles were upright and strapped into place. At first, the wheelhouse, a square aluminum box with all the steering and controls, looked like its windows were blocked with papers and clothing. On closer examination, the two divers saw a jumbled mass of bodies with their hands bound.

At the rear of the wheelhouse, the entry door was locked. A blinking light attracted Steele. A canvas bag hung on a life ring fixture mounted on the narrow wheelhouse bulkhead. Steele gently parted the lips of the bag and spotted a row of dull green underwater explosives the size of hand-held radios. They were wired to a depth control detonator set for 100 feet, less than twenty feet away. Any underwater explosion would kill Steele and his buddy and turn the dead divers into chum. The boat's precarious perch and the explosives led to some quick deductive thinking. First, the metal housing of the engines could fail at any moment and the boat would be headed into the depths; second, no one could be saved; third, the explosion would eliminate any forensics and likely kill all the four divers in the water.

Steele and Andrews looked at each other through their face masks. The plan evolved naturally, communicated and agreed to via sign language on their way to the surface. Mac Andrews would start the crane on the barge, slowly pay out cable while Steele would swim the lift cable down to the boat and secure it to an aft-mounted towing fixture fitted forward of the engines. It was a long shot, particularly because of the lateral distance between the crane and the boat. Steele would be trying to pull the cable to the boat using the strength of his finned legs. He estimated that the 1 1/8-inch cable weighed about 3 pounds per foot. Pulling it laterally and then descending to the stern of the boat seemed like a workable approach. Steele grabbed the cable by its large, heavy shackle and swam toward the boat, adjusting his approach to a position well above the stern. But he was fighting a losing battle. Swimming as hard as he could, Steele could not pull the length of the heavy cable laterally through the water.

Breathing heavily because of the exertion, Steele was formulating a different plan when he spotted another diver. He rapped the steel cable against his aluminum dive tank to get the diver's attention, but the diver did not respond. Clutching the shackle in his hand, Steele tapped an SOS on the tank. It was the man from the Agency. He swam up to Steele and immediately saw the problem. The two men swam on either side of the cable and just made it to the boat, passing the cable through the closed aluminum chock on the stern. Steele swam as hard as he could to hold the cable in place, his legs burning from the effort while the Agency man opened the shackle, passed it over the wire and replaced the threaded pin.

At the same time, the cable whipped violently as both lower ends of the engines failed, yanking the boat to starboard as it angled toward the barge. The crane's rear support legs lifted off the metal deck with the heavy load. Rolling over the jagged rocks twice, tearing off the boat's railing, its bow door and spilling its loose cargo into the depths, the boat stopped only when its square cabin wedged in a wide rock furrow. As its woven metal threads strained against the weight, the cable emitted a low thrum which reverberated in the water. Both divers swam to the boat, and Steele paused to glance at his depth gage which read ninety-six feet. The anguished cry of the aluminum wheelhouse moving against the rocks signaled the situation was far from settled. It was time to surface and re-group.

With the boat momentarily secure, Steele and the Agency man surfaced near the barge. Andrews set the brake on the cable drum. Still breathing as if he'd just run a fast mile in soft sand, Steele began describing the urgency of the situation on the boat. There was no EOD diver assigned to the airbase. But the base did have a blast containment vessel. So, all that was required was to swim down, retrieve the explosives, surface and deposit the package into a wire-wrapped container that resembled a tall snake basket.

Before anyone could protest, Steele kicked away from the bobbing divers and headed straight for the wreck. Andrews followed. As the faces of the dead came into view, they wondered if one of them might be the president's son.

Steele inspected the canvas bag, looking for other connections not readily apparent. He had an undistinguished history with explosives that nearly cost him his life in Boston harbor a few years before. Every munitions expert seemed to install some sort of fail-safe mechanism that would produce the explosion if someone tampered with the circuitry. The bag's straps were laced around the aluminum bracket. Steele unwound the straps and removed the connectors from the detonator as he took a short breath from his now empty scuba tank. He gave Andrews the universal divers' sign for out of air — a hand slice across the throat.

With just seventy feet to the surface, Steele kicked upward. His breathing had been so fast from the exertion that he needed another breath of air almost immediately. A momentary panic gripped him as his legs spasmed in a sharp pain. He tried to stretch his calf muscles but even that proved difficult. Andrews offered him the spare regulator, and Steele quickly regained control of his breathing and rate of ascent. He pressed the inflator button to fill his buoyancy compensator, but his tank was void of pressurized air. Steele dropped his weight belt to speed his ascent. Finally, the two divers reached the surface.

Andrews pried open Steele's hand and took the canvas bag, swimming it over to the blast containment vessel suspended off the side of the barge. The two Hellenic divers and the divemaster pulled Steele into the boat where he regurgitated the earlier mezza blended with a generous amount of salt water. Mac Andrews' face was the first thing he saw. Steele began to babble incoherently, "the boat, the bomb, the cable's breaking."

"Dan," said Andrews firmly, "It's OK. The boat is secure, and the explosives safed. You almost killed yourself today. You are not superman, remember? That was a bonehead move to go after the bomb without taking the time to engage your brain first."

Steele tried to process the situation. He thought he was still in the water.

"Mac, what about the Greek divers— are they OK?"

"Yep, they are both fine. They are strapping some heavy-duty lift bags to the boat to neutralize its buoyancy so it can be winched onto the barge. We should know if the president's son is one of the people in the cabin before nightfall," said Andrews.

Steele nodded his head. "What a terrible way to go. Those people were murdered."

CHAPTER 12

The Kremlin

Moscow, Russia
October 2023

The planning phase was over...it was time for execution. Six months of endless discussions, studying the Burg Khalifa structure itself and having a thousand experts answer technical questions about the quality of the bulletproof glass, the ventilation system, the water and even the plumbing. Everything had been considered, and now a plan emerged which survived the scrutiny of multiple reviews by the chain of command where its architects were peppered with questions and what-ifs.

In the same large room, General Nikolai Zlodeyev had been tried by a military tribunal for a long list of crimes while wearing the insignia of the Alpha Group, the Federation's elite special warriors. There he'd been put on display, found guilty of serious crimes, stripped of his rank and shackled before being led away to spend the remainder of his life in prison. The drumming out backfired before Zlodeyev left the building. A daring rescue triggered a series of preplanned actions which enabled the general and a cadre of his fighters to escape Russia in a military aircraft loaded with nuclear-tipped projectiles and drums of biological warfare agents.

A hush fell over the men when the president himself entered the guarded room, shaking hands with the impossible mission force assembled at his direction. He took his time getting to the podium.

"Good morning, men. Are you ready to make history?"

Arms shot skyward accompanied by a battle cry signaling the team's readiness and mindless willingness to die.

"When your important mission is complete, I look forward to welcoming all of you back to Moscow and rewarding you handsomely for your victory. You will live well for the rest of your lives, perhaps in anonymity, but nonetheless well, very well." The president paused for the solemn conclusion and call to action.

"Your valiant exploits may be hidden from the world, but you will be known and recognized by your Federation countrymen." He paused and locked eyes with many of the soldiers standing before him.

"Good luck," he boomed, "And bring me Zlodeyev's head in a jar."

Bottles of chilled vodka appeared. Drinking the most expensive brand from crystal glasses engraved with the presidential shield was a brilliant way to kick off Operation Cossack.

CHAPTER 13

Andravide Airbase

Western Greece
October 2023

Steele knocked on the door and found Mr. Smith in his room in the temporary quarters the U.S. investigative team had been assigned on base. He hadn't seen the man since yesterday's dive. Smith took the precaution of looking out the door's peephole before opening it.

Steele stood in the doorway and said, "I understand they are sending in reinforcements. I've been told to work with you."

"Come in, Dan."

Both his room and Mr. Smith's had used the same interior designer. Budget drove the selection of furnishings. A nondescript tile floor supported a single bed, dresser and desk, the same lamps and nightstands with a couch and armchair covered in an institutional mocha colored Naugahyde.

"Before we get started," said Steele, "Thank you for the help with the cable yesterday. If it wasn't for your timely arrival on scene, we'd be in deep weeds. And you have established your diving credentials in spades."

"Glad I could help. I'm hopeful we can find Lincoln. The fact he wasn't found with the others is a positive development, I think. Do you agree?"

"I'm not sure. When we get communications from the people who are holding him, I'll feel more positive."

"What bothers me is that we've gotten nothing from our overhead sensors."

"What do you mean?" asked Steele.

"I'm going to tell you some compartmented information, but I think you have a need-to-know. I got an up-check on you from a guy you worked with in Yemen, so I know I can trust you, but this is something which only a handful of people know about. And I'm not talking about a DC handful."

"I've got lots of tickets but don't know anything about what the president's son has to do with overhead sensors," said Steele.

"You're not cleared for this. Anyway, the first family all have a small device implanted within an upper sinus in their heads which transmits a broad omni-directional locating signal twice a day, at noon and midnight local time. The transmission is two seconds long to avoid detection if they are being held. They insert this tiny gadget through the nose under their skulls. It's so small that it's virtually undetectable, even by an X-RAY. If one of the family is under duress or being held, the device can be activated by blowing the nose in a specific sequence.

We've got several of our national security satellites that have been looking for the signal since he went missing and activated the pinger. We are concentrating in theater but haven't heard a peep."

"That's an incredible capability."

"Clinton resisted the insertion…that's also classified."

"Do you guys expect a ransom note?" asked Steele.

"Yes, but we want to get a fix on Lincoln long before we must deal with some crazy request. Money is easy, but releasing prisoners or giving up in-country sources are difficult and usually put another agency out front," said Smith.

"I can see how that might complicate things."

Smith said, "OK, Dan, let's get back to the reality we're dealing with here. I have an initial plan but would be curious what you were thinking. Go ahead."

"Well, we know the attack occurred mid-morning because the morning team had completed their first dive of the day and radioed an all clear to the base duty officer. They never returned to swap out with the afternoon team. Pretty bold move to make in daylight. I think they probably came in underwater so the only evidence we might find is either on the boat or on the bottom. My suggestion is to take a close look at what's parked on the barge and then start a search of the bottom from the point where it was anchored. We have the exact coordinates from the search grid," said Steele.

"Good. My supposition is the attack was carried out by probably two divers who approached via underwater scooters, corralled the divers at gunpoint, plastic cuffed them and shoved them into the wheelhouse and extracted the president's son. They made it look like a robbery, so the divers played along thinking they'd be fine. It's a good idea to start with the boat. Then we can follow-up under the water. I'll talk to the Greeks. Are you ready to go?"

"Yes, anytime."

"Let's plan to meet down on the finger pier in thirty minutes." said Mr. Smith.

CHAPTER 14

Andravide Airbase

Western Greece
October 2023

As the utility boat neared the barge, the divers stared at the tortured remains of the dive boat on its deck. A Hellenic navy team treated the entire boat as a crime scene after the bodies were removed by base medical personnel. Though some additional minor damage occurred during the recovery and hoisting to its current resting place, the violent movement while tethered to the crane cable battered the hull. Upright, the wreck was supported on its catamaran-style hull.

The Agency man divided the task into four parts:

"Nick and Christos will take the hull and sides. Among other things, I'd like to understand how the boat sank in the first place. The hull is supposed to be watertight. Dan, you take the main deck and the top of the wheelhouse. I'll take the wheelhouse. Watch yourselves on the sharp edges. Let's get together in one hour to assess progress and identify any next steps. OK? Any questions?"

Pulling on latex gloves, the Agency man and Dan Steele climbed aboard. Steele searched the main deck of the boat forward and aft of the wheelhouse. It looked like it had gone through the maritime equivalent of a demolition derby. Once straight lines were gone. The bow door hung open, dangling from one of its cables. A portable davit was missing, its useless socket bent over ninety degrees. Aft, where the engines' lower ends had been torn off, the transom curled upwards before the metal ripped. Steele suspected those parts were still on the bottom.

The wheelhouse exterior windows were shattered, and the structural framing pancaked. On top of the structure, Steele examined the penetrations where the missing radar, antenna and air-conditioner were scraped off and now lay somewhere on the rocky slope. Down on hands and knees, he peered over the cabin roof through the window frame at Mr. Smith.

"No clues topside. Anything in the wheelhouse?" asked Steele.

"Same, drawers with soggy paper. A camera, wallet, roll of electrical tape, pliers. Just what you'd expect to see on a working boat."

Steele spotted a thin white diver's slate jammed between the steering console and the starboard bulkhead and leaned down to retrieve it.

"Look at this." Steele handed it to the Agency man and lowered himself to the main deck.

Written like the undisciplined scrawl of a grade-schooler, the message was written by someone with hands bound behind them:

3 Ninjas skis

APC9

Took Linc

"So, it looks like the abductors came by boat and were dressed to hide any identifying features. What's APC9?" asked the Agency man.

"It's a new submachine gun built by a Swiss company. Believe it or not, the US Army just selected that gun for its Personal Security Details."

"So, they carried some heavy firepower, did little talking, and planned to kidnap Lincoln and destroy any evidence with the charges you found in the bag."

"Yeah, that's the way I see it." said Steele. "Let's see if the Greeks turned up anything useful."

Both men climbed down the ladder to the barge's deck.

"What did you guys find?" asked the Agency man.

Christos replied, "The aluminum hull plates have been embrittled. Look at this plate. That is quarter-inch marine grade aluminum that I broke off with my fingers. It's got no strength. It's either some super-charged galvanic action or other degenerative chemical process. I've never seen anything like it."

Steele examined the chunk of aluminum and asked, "Where did this piece come from?"

"Between the twin catamaran vees"

"The rest of the hull is intact?"

"Correct. Only the narrow strip between the two vees. We were not able to access everything."

"So, we've got some unexplained embrittlement and a diver's last words as clues. Seems thin so far. Let's hope the dive proves more fruitful. We'll head back to the pier to suit up and make our final dive before the forensic experts arrive later this afternoon, OK?" asked the Agency man.

The bottom was littered with chunks of the dive boat that had been ripped from the hull during its recovery. The divers proceeded slowly in a rough line abreast, searching the rocks and sand on the bottom. The Agency man had just signaled the end of the dive when something caught Steele's eye. It looked like a discarded candy wrapper. He saw it was a short ribbon of blue adhesive tape with some block lettering on one side used to wrap the valve on a full scuba tank to keep the O-ring in place where a regulator would be attached: Durres Dive Center. Steele tucked the tape in his vest and surfaced, hoping the others would find something to identify the attackers.

After removing their tanks and weight belts, the four divers faced each other in the utility boat with an open expanse of deck between them. The afternoon sun boiled in the Western sky. Time for show and tell.

Steele withdrew the piece of tape from his vest pocket and smoothed it on his palm.

"That's what I found."

The Agency man look dejected and shook his head. "I found nothing new, but my colleagues are going to find this crime scene difficult. It's spread out all over the place."

Christos was next, holding a battery-powered saw where everyone could see it.

"I don't know where this came from, but we did see some saw marks on the hull. Perhaps the plan was to saw through the hull and the guy just dropped this when he was able to break off chunks with his hand." There were no marks on the saw and the manufacturer's nameplate had been removed.

Nick said, "I found this switchblade knife with skeletal handle." He released a safety catch and pressed a button. The blade flew into position and locked with an audible click. The base of the blade was marked 'Made in Germany,' and it looked like a military piece of equipment.

"Well, thanks to all of you, we know more about the attack and maybe the team arriving this afternoon can get a fix on this material. But clearly, we don't have a smoking gun to point us in any specific direction."

CHAPTER 15

Double Eagle Headquarters

Tirana, Albania
October 2023

Karl was ushered into Spence's office and greeted warmly by the tall man. Impeccably dressed, the man carried himself with confidence and dignity. Spence's internal team had put together a dossier on Karl for the meeting. Little was known about the spry man sitting in an armchair opposite Spence.

"Welcome to Double Eagle Industries! My mother asked me to see you and, as a good son, I was pleased to arrange this. Can I offer you some coffee or something else?"

"No, thank you. I am grateful your mother interceded on my behalf. We've been friends for many years. We met at the local library and still attend the reading group together. She's a wonderful woman. I know you're a busy man, and I sincerely appreciate your time."

The man sat in the armchair, relaxed and gathering his thoughts.

"I've come to tell you a story and offer something of substantial value if you will agree to not make it public."

"Wouldn't you agree that I need to know a bit more about your proposition before accepting your terms?" replied Spence, leaning forward on his arms, smiling and obviously interested in hearing more.

"Yes, I certainly agree. That's fair."

Spence studied the man on the other side of the desk. Spence guessed he was at least ninety-five. He looked fit. His eyes sparkled in his lined but clean-shaven face as he was prepared to tell a story that no one had heard for three quarters of a century. Spence thought it might be connected to the war years since Karl Shehu seemed to appear out of nowhere. No known relatives or family but a common Albanian surname.

Karl worked at a Durres machine shop where he quickly earned a reputation as a mechanical genius, able to fabricate precision parts and repair almost anything with connected, internal components. His work area was always well-organized and spotless. He was also an accomplished millwright who tuned up every machine and showed his co-workers methods of work that went far beyond the knowledge they had gained through on-the-job training. The only formally trained machinist in the shop was fighting a losing battle against the bottle and wanted to protect his job rather than teach the apprentices. Karl took the opposite view and was happy to demonstrate and to mentor the recruits that came in anxious to learn a skill. Post-war Albania lay in ruins because of the actions of the Italians, then the Germans. Thousands of its citizens left for greener pastures in neighboring countries, tired of having to choose sides or engaging the occupiers as armed, rebellious partisans.

"In 1945, I was a young U-Boat captain on patrol in the Mediterranean. Our crew numbered forty-four, and I had four other officers on board. U-537 entered the service in 1943. I became its second commanding officer after the first was transferred because he got too familiar with some of the young recruits, if you understand what I mean. Imagine a commanding officer walking around the boat naked. A pederast of the worst kind."

"Yes, please continue," said Spence.

"It was no secret that Hitler and his inner circle, including the head of the navy, Admiral Doenitz, were becoming desperate. The tide had turned, and clearly the Allies were on the offensive - the writing was on the wall. I made several stops along southern Italy to drop my crew as close to shore as I could get without the coast watchers seeing us surface."

Spence interrupted, "This is all very interesting, Karl, but a U-boat sunk off the coast is of little interest to me, although I understand that wrecks often attract fish which would be good for my project."

"Do you have a nautical chart of your proposed venture?"

"Yes, of course," said Spence as he came around the desk to help Karl over to a conference table covered with a fitted leather top. Underneath was a chart of the coastline with the leased offshore rectangles outlined with a black marker.

"Yes, yes. This is much better than the graphic artist's rendition I saw in TemA." The man scanned the chart put his finger on a point. "The U-537 was scuttled here, just south of Vlore."

"Karl, again, why would I be interested in a submarine that's been on the bottom for all these years? I have a busy schedule today and appreciate your visit but need to move on to other things."

"Spence, I agree completely. I don't want to waste your time. Believe me, having lived a full 100 years on this earth, mostly here in Albania, it's not the rusting hulk that I wanted to trade. It's what my boat was carrying as cargo."

Karl raised his head and clutched his chest with an expression of surprise. As he fell backwards, he gasped for a full breath and stared at Spence, a look of fear and desperation on his face. Karl Shehu died before his head hit the floor.

CHAPTER 16

Andravide Airbase

Western Greece
November 2023

The base infirmary cleared the waiting room where five gurneys were placed side by side. Covered with white cotton sheets, the bodies removed from the dive boat's wheelhouse were set out for identification. Even though they had less than forty-eight hours underwater, changes had already occurred in the hair, eyes, and faces. The divers' teammates filed by and identified the dead to enable the process of notifying the next of kin. A dive buddy is someone to whom you entrust your life. They are a second pair of eyes, spotting hazards, and keeping track of each other. Enduring emotional bonds grew between the men, and the pain of the viewing showed on their faces. The scene had a somber vibe.

The remaining Greek and U.S. divers identified their dead teammates. The bodies had not been subjected to the ravages of the salt water over time. Steele remembered vividly when he had to identify his wife and two young sons after they drowned in the Chesapeake Bay Bridge and Tunnel explosion. Their faces showed the early signs of water exposure, and the evidence of animals large and small finding their next source of sustenance.

The president's son was not among the dead.

Steele's cell phone trembled in his pocket. He looked at the screen and answered the call.

"Dan Steele."

"Afternoon, Dan, it's Owens. I was hoping we could connect. The White House is pinging on me for information. The press secretary is worried about her own credibility and is arguing for a release to the media that Brucie is missing. Is there anything new where you are?"

"Brucie was not with the others pulled off the dive boat. He's still missing, and I'd assume still alive. Maybe kidnapped. I would expect that a ransom note might be the next thing we see. This story will break soon because the next of kin are being notified now. There must be some ambulance chasers here in Greece. Someone will be in front of the camera soon. I think an initial press release would be a good idea. That's one man's opinion."

"Both of us are on the same page. The Agency's gaggle of investigators should be there on site by this time, and you must stay connected with Mr. Smith. I know that's a tall order, but those are your instructions. Mr. Smith will take the lead on this. OK?"

"Sure admiral. From what I've seen so far, the group taking Brucie were professionals who left no trace. I'll track down Mr. Smith and see if we can put our heads together on this again."

"Anything else?"

"As a matter of fact, there is. I'd like to stop in Italy for a few days on my return trip. It sounds as if my assignment will end when the Agency comes in."

"That's OK with me but talk to Admiral Wright about it."

"Great, thanks," said Steele. Sydney Garrison was several thousand miles away in Washington, DC, but their overdue rendezvous might work this time.

CHAPTER 17

Double Eagle Headquarters

Tirana, Albania
November 2023

A professional team of cleaners came into the mansion after Karl's visit and transported his body to a local funeral home. The medical examiner did not order an autopsy given Karl's age and the circumstances of his collapse. He suggested that the man died of a massive cerebral aneurism.

Spence summoned his personal secretary, Adam, into his office.

"Adam, please sit," said Spence, "Can I offer a mild palliative to help you recover from that awful experience earlier today?"

"What are you having, Spence?"

"This is an old cream sherry from Spain that relaxes the nerves and prepares the palate for dinner. I recommend it." Spence poured a small glass and handed it to Adam.

"Exquisite, Spence. Much smoother than their cocktail sherries. Perfect!"

"Two items for today, Adam. Please see that Karl's death is not connected to me or Double Eagle Industries in any way and arrange for a nice ceremony and a fulsome obituary. My mother will be very upset that he died, but she'll get over it. For political reasons, I want it to have occurred at some distance from here. The medical examiner should align the death certificate appropriately."

Spence cleared his throat and shifted gears, anxious to move past the thought of Karl expiring so violently in his office.

"Second, I'd like you to research some records from the last war. Our visitor today was certain about the location of a German submarine he scuttled toward the end of the war. He parked his sub south of Vlore and died suddenly as you know, before revealing the cargo they were carrying. The war logs combined daily reports from each U-Boat captain to the regional commander. Because his boat was operating in the Mediterranean Sea, he reported to Führer der Unterseeboote Italien/Mittelmeer, the commander of U-Boats, Italy/Mediterranean."

"Did the operational records survive the war?" asked Adam.

"Yes, they did. I recall reading that the reports were found by the Allies late in the war at a castle in Germany. The British Admiralty grabbed them, and the Americans have a complete copy. I'd like you to take a couple of weeks to poke around in the archives and see what you can find. There are several archives that have the records. You choose the destination for the research and take your family with you if you can. Before we spend a fortune on a salvage operation, I want to make sure that it's worth it."

"That's very generous of you, Spence. I will talk to Diane and see what a little research vacation might look like. She would be thrilled to see something else this fall other than the smog of the city," said Adam. "Will there be anything else, this morning?"

"No, thank you, Adam."

CHAPTER 18

Durres, Albania
November 2023

The twenty-foot steel doors large enough to accommodate a fully loaded eighteen-wheeler opened on an overhead track as Spence's car drove into one of Double Eagle Industries' high security warehouses. As the reinforced metal panels closed behind the car, two security men holding stubby machine guns exited the car and took stock of the perimeter, questioning the single coveralled man waiting for their arrival. Spence's door was opened. The tall man with thinning gray hair exited the car with a look of excitement, following the coveralls past banks of metal warehouse racks filled with high value merchandise of every description.

After unlocking a separate metal cage shielded from outside view and flipping on bright sodium lights over a series of metal assembly tables, the man welcomed Spence to examine the booty. Three tables were covered with both cut and raw gemstones and four other tables held gold artifacts looted from tombs. A curious papyrus rolled and stored in a watertight case lay on another table awaiting an expert to determine its authenticity. The treasures from *Epsilon* were on display, retrieved from a locked metal storage container on the barge servicing the Kyllini dive site.

Spence paused to marvel at the gems and gold artifacts, putting on a pair of latex gloves to protect his hands from the barnacles and other growth as the stones had hosted saltwater plants and animals for over two hundred years. A tiny crab fell out of a handful of encrusted raw stones, still alive. Some of the sea growth had been scraped off, probably by the divers, but none of the artifacts had been properly cleaned. He directed that the gems be separated, thoroughly cleaned, and inventoried. A trusted local jeweler who had previously transitioned gems into the market or fenced some of the jewels stolen from a trove buried in Kerch, Ukraine would assess the stones as well as the gold and determine the best way to maximize their value.

"Where is our guest?" asked Spence.

"He's inside a sound-proof reefer box we've converted to accommodate visitors."

"Excellent. I'd like to see him."

"This way," said the man.

Spence walked into a small booth where the building's operations were monitored. A series of screens showed the sides of the building, and there was a bank of alarms for intrusion and fire. The superintendent unlocked an interior door into a smaller room that looked like an audio booth used for hearing tests. Foam cones covered the walls and ceiling of the room to absorb any sound. A shower stall, washbasin, and thin mattress on a metal angle iron frame. No telephone, television, computer, reading or writing material were present. The room's sparse furnishings resembled what a novitiate Tibetan monk might find spartan. Toiletries and fresh towels were delivered when used items were passed through the slot for the food tray.

A blank screen came alive, and Spence saw a tanned, blond-haired beach boy slouched in a chair and chained to a stout metal ring welded to the floor.

"How do I communicate with him?" asked Spence.

The man pulled a weighted microphone from the side of the desk.

"Your voice will be altered by this digital voice disguiser."

"Good. Set it for a woman." The man nodded when Spence's order was carried out. Spence listened for several seconds and could hear nothing outside the room.

"Very impressive work, Altin. Well done to you and your team."

"Thank you, Spence." He keyed the microphone and a red transmit light illuminated.

"Good morning. I hope you had a pleasant night. What would you like for breakfast?"

"Listen bitch. Do you know who I am?" he asked. Spence turned off the microphone and shared a laugh with the warehouse superintendent, a man he'd known in Durres as a child.

"I'm told you are an American. Is that true?" Spence asked, trying hard not to laugh at the sound of his own voice transformed into a silky, soothing feminine delivery.

"Yes. My name is Lincoln Brewster. My father happens to the president of the United States. I'd like these chains removed, and I demand to be released immediately."

Finally, the blond received the attention he sought. Spence spoke to him in very clear English,

"President? president of what? I don't understand."

"The United States of America, bitch. If you know what's good for you, release me now."

"I don't believe that you are in any position to make such demands, Mr. Lincoln Brewster. But I would be pleased to take your breakfast order. What would you like?"

CHAPTER 19

Double Eagle Headquarters

Tirana, Albania
November 2023

Spence's personal secretary, Adam, entered the office after the man had completed his daily immersion in world news. The large man waved him in.

"Good morning," Adam said, walking to the chair in front of the large desk. "Well, I've got good news and bad. Which would you like first?"

"Give me the awful news first," said Spence looking across the deck and giving his assistant an expectant look.

"As you suspected, the ancient papyrus retrieved from the dive site was fake. The expert we hired concluded it had been made with the tools and techniques available at the time, so while it is an antique made over 200 years ago, it does not reveal a path to an inner tomb. Our local Egyptologist has seen similar maps of the same vintage and recognized a peculiar hieroglyph in one corner which is the man's signature. He is a well-known forger who extended his creativity to maps."

Laughing loudly, Spence responded, "Thank you Adam. The Egyptians have a long history of separating the unsuspecting from their money. I think this is just a recent example of a scam that's been going on for centuries. Please send the papyrus to the National Museum of Fakes and Forgeries in Cairo. Now, what's the good news?"

"The good news comes from our local jeweler. Though there were many poor-quality stones in the chests, there are some first-class stones which will bring seventeen to twenty million dollars net, after the cost of cutting and faceting."

"Wonderful!" said Spence.

Adam continued, "In addition, the gold artifacts are worth nearly ten million dollars based on weight alone. Most of the gold is twenty-two carat, and our jeweler thinks museums might be interested in some of the undamaged artifacts at a much higher price than the precious metals market."

"That is indeed good news. Ask him to make some inquires, and we'll see what materializes."

"Will do. Anything significant in this morning's message traffic?"

"Not yet, I'm wading through the last stack."

"Fine," replied Adam. "Is there anything else you need now?"

"Yes, please ask Marie to put through a call to General Zlodeyev in Dubai. That's all, Adam. Thank you."

CHAPTER 20

Burj Khalifa

United Arab Emirates
December 2023

Zlodeyev sought out the senior facilities manager of the famous residence the day following his arrival. Introducing himself as a resident interested in the jaw-dropping architecture and construction of the building and the vast facilities infrastructure needed to support Burj Khalifa. The white-haired facilities manager, Reginald Packer, misjudged the level of detail Zlodeyev was seeking when he offered a glossy, single page fact sheet that was included in the information packet in every guest's room.

Once Packer fully understood the request, he gave Zlodeyev an unrestricted access badge, and the big man roamed through the buildings wearing coveralls and a hard hat, often accompanied by one of the imported labor force. He became a regular, joining the maintenance crew after morning prayer at the change of the shift and would share a simple breakfast of soupy cooked beans, long green hot peppers and fresh round bread. Known to be a curious, generous man who got along with the building's workers and got to know them on a personal level, the big man got to know Reginald Packer well too.

A British expatriate, Packer had been recruited from the Abu Dhabi shipyard where he was a consultant at first and then a full-time employee charged with modernization and preparation of the yard to construct its own combatants for the United Arab Emirates navy. He had a stellar reputation from the shipyard community and was a personal friend of the Crown Prince. Well-educated, with a degree in naval architecture from MIT, Packer had worked in the nuclear ships division at Newport News shipyard as a ship's superintendent for ten years. After returning to England, he found himself party to a messy litigation involving his parents' separation and divorce. It was clear that Reginald might be left holding the bag when the dust settled. He had no appetite to pay for his parents' self-destructive behavior.

Responding to a job offer with Aramco in Saudi Arabia, he maintained a very low profile. From there, he was hired by the shipyard and worked for twenty years in anonymity. Things fell into place when an old expatriate friend decided to leave UAE and return to England. The facilities manager's job was a position he had accepted just as the construction closeout inspections were underway.

Zlodeyev's interest in studying the building surprised Packer. So did the occasional gift of a bottle of his favorite highly-peated scotch whiskey, Lagavulin 16, which was a challenge to obtain in the Emirates. Within two weeks, Zlodeyev knew of places within the structure its own engineers had never visited. Most important, he had identified an escape route which he could count on in the future.

Now friends sharing a bottle of scotch, the two men talked about the reality of Zlodeyev's world.

"And there's no doubt in your mind they will come after you?" The facilities manager was incredulous. He continued without a response. "Look at the hotel's security, the steps you've taken related to the elevator lockout. Good God, man, you spent a fortune on the glass we installed on all sides. It would be foolhardy to mount an attack on this place to get to you."

"Ah, Reginald, you don't know the Russians, particularly if the president himself has been embarrassed. It's naive to think that I'm secure here, my friend. They will stop at nothing to bring me down, alive if possible. If they die, too bad. There are no rules or protocols for the operation against me. A determined force enticed with the promise of great future wealth, probably by the president himself. No, my friend, they will most certainly come. It's just a matter of time."

Packer lifted his glass. "To a long life," he said.

Zlodeyev smiled and enjoyed the burn of the liquor down his throat. He would surely die at the hands of Russian operatives that he himself had trained. But it would not be in the Burj Khalifa.

CHAPTER 21

Burj Khalifa

United Arab Emirates
December 2023

Eighteen men gathered in a nondescript metal warehouse just outside the Dubai International Airport. Some had arrived via commercial flights into all the individual states in the Emirates, some via ferry boats from the other Gulf states, and some overland. Nothing obvious linked the men together. Their passports were issued by several different countries. The garb of the men varied greatly. Some looked like tourists, others like local drivers, tradesmen, and utility repairmen. But they were all part of the same mission.

Bright halogen lamps illuminated several pallets stacked with white woven polypropylene bags, each of which carried fifty kilos of rice originating in Vietnam. The top bags were removed revealing a wire cage where the mission equipment had been secreted. Each of the men was now armed with his personal choice of weapon and the tools for their part of the mission: climbing ropes, shaped charges, night vision devices, vials of nerve agent. A series of taxis, ten-passenger vans, and motorcycles arrived over the course of an hour to begin the synchronized operation. Operators supporting the raid deployed on ships in the Persian Gulf while others took positions in the Dubai Mall and other locations in the sprawling city. The operation had many moving parts synchronized by time.

The operation formally began at 5:55 p.m. when two containers on the top of a stack of seven containers high on a Russian container ship just off the coast opened their tops using hydraulic rams. Two ultralight drones flew out of the containers and skimmed the water flying at 120 knots toward the world's tallest building. At

6:00 p.m. the world's largest aquarium, holding some 2.5 million gallons of salt water behind thirty-inch-thick glass, shattered and began to flood the congested Dubai Mall. Thousands were swept away as the water filled the hallways and shops in seconds. Nearly 33,000 sea creatures, including a large collection of sharks, were freed. Simultaneously, the blare of the city's fire brigades responding to a dozen fires halted traffic in the congested city including the major highway leading to the international airport. One fire sprang up near the airport's fuel farm, where thousands of gallons of high-octane jet fuel were stored under the sandy desert floor in massive tanks.

At 6:02 p.m. General Nikolai Zlodeyev stopped his afternoon workout with an uneasy feeling. He looked out his window and spotted two specks in the cloudless sky flying low over the water heading directly for the lobed structure where his suite was located. He smiled to himself. The Federation's finest were coming for him. How many operators were sent, he wondered. He'd planned countless missions against his fortified redoubt and thought he had examined every possible contingency. He expected a direct attack from the sky and a team trying to breach his apartment via the elevator. But he hadn't planned on drones carrying hardened missiles, pickled off by an operator thousands of miles away, designed to penetrate the bulletproof glass that surrounded his enclave.

"Very ingenious," he muttered aloud.

The armor-piercing rounds would penetrate the glass at high velocity and fill the suite with choking smoke. Zlodeyev anticipated an assault from high above his 140th floor would begin within a few short seconds. However, the general knew hope had never been a winning strategy. Just as the rounds struck the bullet-proof glass, he dived headlong into the room serving as his gym, built with thick interior walls and a gas-tight fire door. From there he pushed a button on the wall which opened a hidden floor hatch that ended in the uppermost of two mechanical rooms dedicated to the upper floors. Known as MECH 5, the room also served as Zlodeyev's departure point. The floor hatch was programmed to open once for twenty seconds, re-close automatically and disable the sliding mechanism.

He knew the Federation special operators would not stop their search at his gutted apartment. They would continue until they found their quarry or died trying. None would go quietly into the night. Zlodeyev had a choice. To wait and hope the assault would be halted by UAE's special forces before the searchers found him or to continue his escape. In the corner of Mech 5, he slid open an access panel covering a return air duct which ended in a plenum which collected the air and fed the chillers. The panel lay just behind the building's sharp edge, a two-foot square open shaft that fed stale, warm air down to the subfloor air handlers five floors below the lobby level.

Wedging his body into the shaft, Zlodeyev strapped himself into a harness attached to a narrow wooden board of laminated birch plywood clipped to the continuous lip of the building's outside wall supports where it narrowed to a sharp angle for the knife-edge exterior. The board was fitted with six skateboard wheels on either side. The polyurethane wheels were high-performance optimized for long board riding and speed. His feet rested on a narrow plywood projection a foot square. It was a body length custom skateboard that the general had fabricated in Burj Kalifa's machine shop. Zlodeyev calculated that his 320-pound frame would reach a maximum velocity of about 150 miles per hour because of the foot plate and the friction generated by the wheels flexing against the metal frame. This was his sixth model, incorporating all the improvements made to the original prototype.

He strapped on a full helmet with integrated windscreen. Brake cables were hydraulically assisted and foot operated. After securing the access panel, Zlodeyev pulled the lanyard over his head releasing the pin which held the device in place. His 550-meter trip would take a total of eleven seconds assuming an average descent rate of 100 miles per hour or 150 feet per second. Brakes would be applied 300 feet before touchdown.

Zlodeyev had practiced using this escape route each month since he took up residence. When his feet hit the twelve-foot-thick concrete raft that supported the building, he unstrapped himself from the board, replaced his helmet with an LED headlamp held on the side of the vent with rare earth magnets and began threading his way out of the maze of pipes, wiring trunks and piles that supported the structure above. The ride down was exhilarating. When time permitted, he planned to propose the design for commercial use by amusement parks and ski resorts for use in the summer.

On his initial exploration, he found himself in complete darkness, feeling his way to the access. He remembered the unsettling feeling of seeing luminous eyes and hearing the creatures that inhabited the subfloor. The raft had three feet of headroom, so Zlodeyev crawled around and over the interferences on his belly, writhing through the sand and pieces of welding slag and ribbons of concrete dressing before finding the steel rungs that led to a trap door, a stainless-steel hatch where the structural systems were remotely monitored for any movement. He smiled at the thought of the masked team frantically looking for him amidst the smoke and shriek of the fire alarms on the floors high above him.

Zlodeyev checked his stopwatch and found that he recorded his best time to date: 10.7 seconds. He changed into dark grey coveralls, darkened his face and wrapped a turban around his head. Driving a common maintenance van out the service tunnel, he passed by an anxious armed operator, posted to ensure that the Federation dragnet closed any of the general's escape routes from the Burj Khalifa. The operator was unconcerned about an imported maintenance man leaving the building and let him pass onto the chaotic streets of Dubai.

CHAPTER 22

Burj Khalifa

United Arab Emirates
December 2023

Initial stories from Dubai startled people, making them wonder if the news was a sick cyber-joke. But it just kept coming. The fractured Dubai aquarium flooded the lower floor of the mall with hundreds drowning. An attack high up on the Burj Khalifa, fires raging, traffic snarled so badly that motorists were abandoning their cars to flee the hot flames licking the underside of the major artery in and out of the city.

The morning anchors returned to their desks and reinforcements were called. Cable networks scrambled to find people in Dubai or close by. Camera crews were assembled and deployed. Americans seemed fascinated with any disaster that wasn't happening in their own country. Desperate black-clad men roamed the floors of the world's highest structure, toting ugly machine pistols searching for something. Terrorists? High-tech smash and grab artists? UAE secret police? Dubai was paralyzed and burning.

The grim statistics rolled in throughout the day. What didn't receive much attention was the attack on one of the building's upper floors where rockets blew through the windows and incinerated the flammable furnishings before the flames were extinguished by the building's sprinkler system. TV cameras zoomed in, showing that the exterior of the building had been torched on two sides.

Stories of drones flying into the building seemed to be the most frequent account from eyewitnesses. The countries' recent warming relationship with Moscow seemed to be forgotten in the rush to report the breaking news needed to satiate a public with a need for chaos.

The Federation forces not captured or killed disappeared into the throngs of people gathered in the streets to see what evil had been brought to their country.

By the following afternoon, Dubai had regained a sense of normalcy. There were no fires. The first level in the mall had been drained of saltwater. Living and dead inhabitants of the aquarium were being gathered in trucks and dumped into their natural habitat, the Persian Gulf. The pandemonium was over, but the incident needed an explanation.

In a modest office building near the Dubai Mall with no unusual architectural appeal, the chief of the Emirates' Internal Intelligence Agency addressed a group of undercover police whose job was to keep their fingers on the pulse of the city and to find trouble before it became a reality. They included bankers, cab drivers, tour guides, street sweepers, shop owners, dishwashers and bartenders, all sharing pride in finding problems before they boiled over onto the streets. The group had failed to pick up the signs of the attack on Burj Khalifa and were being verbally taken to task by a thin wiry man with a shaved head.

"So, nothing was telegraphed about this attack, or you have been sleeping at the switch. The Crown Prince wants answers, and we need a plausible story to feed the press. How could we have missed this? How many men did we pick up from the area?"

"Six," answered a man standing to the side. They are in isolation cells and quiet for the time being."

"Not a single whiff of anything? You are supposed to cover this city like a blanket. We are in the business of prevention. Your networks are designed to give us warning about this sort of attack. What happened?"

No crisp responses to his rhetorical question were offered by the group.

The chief spoke again "Find out who put this operation together and plug the holes in our network that caused us to miss this operation. We will meet here again in twelve hours. I expect a much clearer picture then." The chief turned to his Deputy and said, "Al Josep, get the first prisoner to the interrogation room and ask Dr. Ibrahim to join me. Our guests will find their voices soon."

CHAPTER 23

The White House
Washington, DC
December 2023

A single telephone intercept prompted a series of meetings which produced a growing list of possible actions for the Administration to take regarding repatriation of the president's son. It was late fall in Washington, and the maples had peaked, their leaves blowing to the ground and showing splashes of color as the National Security Advisor joined the president in the Oval office. The city had survived another dreadfully hot summer with few domestic problems. But the time of year, unsettled weather, and any police action had the potential to throw a match on the city's flammable chemistry. Even at Christmastime, tension in Washington put its residents under great strain.

Barbara Ryan got straight to the point.

"Mr. President, we've compared the audio from this call with voice prints of both participants and have high confidence that the call is genuine. We believe that Lincoln is being held in Tirana, Albania, and Spence will attempt to secure his release for his own political interests. One of our overhead sensors detected a transmission from his chip, but the angles of the sensor and the chip did not give us any actionable locating data."

"And that son-of-a-bitch, Spence, is about to be elected president? Unbelievable. Sorry, Barbara, this situation has gotten to me. What do you propose?" asked the president.

"Thank you, Mr. President," said his National Security Advisor. "Our options at this stage are limited, but I do recommend several specific actions to get a better fix on the situation and not imperil Lincoln. First, position one of our submarines in the Ionian

Sea where they can help with the monitoring and, if we are lucky, pinpoint the abductors. Second, direct the CIA to activate our regional assets to see if we can get any intelligence on the ground."

"Is that it?" the president asked.

"At this stage, sir, we believe Lincoln is still alive, and we do not want to respond overtly or in a way that might delay or screw-up what might happen on its own," said Ryan. "I expect something to happen in the next seventy-two hours."

"I appreciate your advice on this and agree. Please stay on top of this, Barbara. Send me the decision packages. Let's get moving."

"Yes, Mr. President."

CHAPTER 24

United Arab Emirates
December 2023

Twenty hours after the attack on the Burj Khalifa, the chief of the Emirates' Internal Intelligence Agency had a clearer picture of the attack. The grim tally: Eighty-three Emiratis killed across the city by drowning, fire, or from stray bullets from the terrorists. An additional 120 expatriots and third country nationals died. Nine of the attackers were dead, six men had been captured, some badly wounded, and the internal police were rounding up dozens of potential suspects for questioning.

Interrogations for the first six took place in a very quiet room with sound deadening sheathing on its walls and ceiling. The floor was gleaming stainless steel when the first of the Russian perpetrators was strapped into a dental chair covered with a clean white sheet.

Dr. Ibrahim removed a starched white doctor's coat and faced his first patient in light green scrubs. The Intelligence chief began with the basics: name, nationality and place of residence in Dubai. There was no response, exactly what he had anticipated.

The naked man had the look of a military man who was no stranger to violence. There were deep furrowed scars on his scalp, puckered skin where a bullet entered his body and a tissue excavation in his torso that was not performed in a hospital setting. Here was a hardened veteran who had experienced excruciating pain. The pain he suffered on the battlefield had been instant and delivered from a distance. Looking into the eyes of a skilled tormenter caused the body to act differently. The pain was more intense.

"We know that you are part of a Federation attack on the Burj Khalifa which occurred yesterday at six p.m. We who live in Dubai are proud of our city and are pleased to welcome visitors from around the world. You have upset the tranquility we seek to maintain. It's very important that we learn the objective and details of your attack. Now, you can choose to answer my questions directly, which I assure you is the easy way, or my colleague Dr. Ibrahim will try to motivate you by performing some very painful procedures."

"I know nothing about any attack on your city."

"Dr. Ibrahim, please assist me."

The doctor who held a medical degree by virtue of working with the Syrian resistance had broken many Russian soldiers in his life. This one would lose his arrogant exterior and be whining like a colicky baby in short order.

The Chief took the doctor aside and said, "Ibrahim, I promised to give the crown prince a report before Maghrib prayer so forget about the psychological build-up. Just get him to talk quickly."

Nodding his head in understanding, the doctor reached into a black leather medical bag and withdrew what appeared to be poultry shears. He approached the Russian and lifted his arm. The shears pierced the skin at his elbow joint then the doctor twisted the joint and clipped the skin holding the lower arm from the upper. The arm was removed as easily as a well-cooked chicken wing. Ibrahim shifted to the other arm and positioned the shears as the man found his voice in between his anguished screams. The man began talking, anxious to avoid removal of his other arm. Ibrahim nodded. It was a good start.

By the time the fourth suspect lay on the chair in the examining room, the floor was covered with bodily fluids, chiefly blood, and a stainless bucket was brimming with body parts. Dr. Ibrahim's scrubs were no longer light green but stained like a butcher's apron.

Between the talkative Russians and the efforts of the internal police, the details of the plan emerged. More evidence was found at the warehouse where the team collected their weapons. They had the timeline, the attackers' names, and corroborating statements about the sendoff. Found in the breast pocket of one of the attackers' outfits was a photo of the champagne glass bearing the presidential seal of the Russian Federation.

The crown prince met with his chief just before ablutions for the Maghreb prayer. He listened to the report, asking no questions. He would discuss the matter with his council of ministers the following day.

CHAPTER 25

Double Eagle Headquarters

Tirana, Albania
December 2023

In Albania, the president is elected for a term of five years by a secret ballot among the 140 Parliamentarians and must be supported by three-fifths of its members. Since the election cycle began with a national election voting for a representative parliament months before, Spence had met with every member and actively sought their support. Without doubt he was the best-known candidate for the presidency since it became a capitalist, democratic country in the early 1990s.

The country's campaigns were short and sweet compared to the marathons of primaries, debates, and barnstorming in the United States. Spence made every effort to ensure his victory. He was counting on several other events to enhance his standing in the polls. Having the advantage of momentum, Spence was postered on every street corner in the city standing with his nominated Minister of Defense.

Spence was on a roll. His campaign point man reviewed the polls, which confirmed that the Chief Executive of Double Eagle Industries was leading three contenders as the voting for president was now only weeks away. Both men knew polling was neither supported by a rigorous scientific methodology nor was it random.

"Yes, I am pleased with the results. And with the initiatives we'll be announcing between now and election day, I'm confident of being Albania's next president," the pleasant-looking man exclaimed as he scooted his leather desk chair up to the kneehole of the polished antique desk and stared at his campaign chief.

"Are there any surprises we are not prepared for now, Arvin?" Spence asked.

"I can't think of any. We are holding dirty politics in reserve. You've already reviewed the disinformation initiative, but I don't believe we'll even need it." said Arvin confidently. "Your BBC interview will take place at their studio downtown, and the only hard questions you can expect are related to what you think Albania's position will be vis a vis the EU and NATO. She will also ask about the impact of the tougher immigration standards which you announced. You are well-prepared for those questions. If she asks you about the ongoing conflict in Gaza, just use the 'unhelpful for me to comment' excuse.

Ms. Besjana Spahiu is known to distract the men she interviews by exposing herself with an "accidental" slip of a blouse or hiking up her dress. As you know, she is blessed with exotic skin coloration, very glitzy jewelry and a body that can produce surprising reactions. I'm not worried about that side of things with you so I think your approach should be serious but perhaps a little playful if she tries anything. People know her tactics, and you'll get points for staying on message by recognizing what she'll stoop to for a scoop. No pun intended," Arvin concluded.

Both men enjoyed a good laugh. Spence would prepare by re-reading his position statements and reinforcing his messages in front of a full-length mirror. A car would be waiting for him in one short hour.

CHAPTER 26

Andravide Airbase

Western Greece
December 2023

The longer he stayed in Greece, frustration and confusion became Steele's constant companions. Feeling like he suffered from a permanent brain fog, he began pacing the longest dimension of the spartan room and said out loud "it's time to review the bidding." That was the code for venting to Jill, his wife, mother of his twin boys, counselor, confessor and still today, even though she was dead, his best friend. He often spoke to her aloud and believed that the one-way conversation helped him concentrate. Talking as he walked, intertwining the professional, personal, and political threads, he felt Jill listening patiently. When alive, she would only interrupt to ask clarifying questions or get a better grip on the relationships of the people involved. An active listener, she would dismiss all extraneous thoughts to give Dan her full attention. It didn't happen often, but it gave her insight into the state of his busy psyche.

"Hi, Jill. My head is about ready to explode. Things are not going well. I wanted to bring you up to speed." Steele paused before setting off on a new unexplored diagonal of the square room.

"The president's son is missing, and we've uncovered no clues to suggest where to take this search next. Zero progress. Looks like the divers and support people died a horrible death, after being bound by their hands and locked in the cabin, drowning on the way to the ledge where we found the boat. For those professional divers, it must have been a terrifying end."

Steele stopped his pacing, first seeing the pallid, stone faces of the men laid out on the gurneys at the base medical clinic, then the contorted faces of the grieving families after the awful realization of losing a husband, father or brother. He began to pace again.

"The man responsible for killing you, dear Jill, and our two young sons is running for president of Albania. It's unbelievable. Less than 250 miles away. Knowing that I'm breathing the same air makes me sick. The deep, open wound of losing you and the boys won't heal, with constant pain, throbbing every minute of every day. In the past, I vowed to bring Spence to justice rather than exacting revenge, but it might be a bridge too far. The right thing to do, certainly, but I'm not now thinking about the right thing to do. If I got the chance to put my own bare hands around Spence's neck, it would bring me some sick comfort." Steele raised his arms toward the ceiling.

"I know you would not like me taking on the role of judge, jury and then executioner, and I promise you that I'll do it the right way if I can." Steele wiped away the tears that filled his eyes and choked down the throbbing reality of losing his family.

"As I've told you before, Albania's likely new Minister of Defense is none other than the man who murdered one of my team in Yemen and escaped in a rocket after thrashing me in a fight. He's big and strong. I didn't find any weaknesses last time we met. What can I do if we meet again mano-a-mano? True, I've learned a few tricks when dealing with a big guy from my martial arts friend at the naval hospital in Portsmouth but wonder if they could be used against him. I have doubts. The man seems invincible. What he might do in the middle of Europe gives me a bad feeling. NATO could lose its remaining relevance being tested in the never-ending conflict between Russia and Ukraine if Zlodeyev controlled Albania's military forces. I just want a chance to face him before the Federation sends in their team. I know I can't take on the world's problems, but this is very personal. The world would be a better place without both Spence and Zlodeyev.

Personally, and financially, I'm worried about the future of Pisces. It's shaky at best. Admiral Wright is still recovering. I don't know what his personal long-term prospects may be. I'll have a better handle on that once I get back to DC. I am nervous about Pisces' existence longer term. It's important, but I don't have a vote in what might happen. It keeps me plugged-in to the Intelligence world so I can keep tabs on Spence. Now that he's running for president, maybe there will be enough info in the public domain. Anyway, I may be out on the street looking for employment soon. It reminds me of when we closed on that first house in Virginia Beach. I had to look through all my pants' pockets and in the car console to afford to buy a pizza for dinner. We had less than $18.00 in the bank. You were confident we'd be OK. I'm so happy I listened to you." Steele shifted to the shorter axis in the room.

"There's one more thing, Jill, that's been weighing on my mind. You know about the woman commanding the sub, Sydney Garrison. Months and months have passed since we've seen each other. Now she is in DC, and I'm in Greece. We might as well be on different planets. Both of us are anxious to see if our relationship, if you can even call it that, could blossom into something real. If things work out timewise, I plan to travel home via a stopover in Italy. I'm deeply conflicted. Need you to know that I will always love you, dream about you and hold you deep in my heart. You'd tell me to pursue another partner. I will. But there will never be another Jill. You'll be there until I take my last earthly breath. I love you, Jill." Tears flowed freely down his face dropping on the tiled floor.

Taking several controlled deep breaths and forced exhalations, Steele tried to regain his composure. There was plenty to ponder as he pulled on a pair of nylon shorts, a tee shirt and his running shoes. He was booked on a flight in the morning headed for Italy. The mission to Greece had ended with mixed reviews. Steele was happy to turn over his role in the investigation to the larger team and move on. He just hoped that the move he was planning would have a better, happier outcome.

Troubled, Steele sought the silver lining in the situation. He found none.

CHAPTER 27

Double Eagle Headquarters
Tirana, Albania

Haim Harpazi had worked in Israeli intelligence and on Benjamin Netanyahu's personal security detail during his most recent stint as Prime Minister. His first love was the computer, and he became addicted to hacking. To him, it was a game that pitted him against someone who'd designed the access systems so they couldn't be penetrated by outsiders. Not interested in ruining anyone's reputation, credit rating, or finances, his sole interest in hacking was to prove to the developers their security system could be penetrated. After gaining access to a company's servers, he'd always leave a series of smiling emojis claiming he was able to successfully access their system, always signing the string of happy faces with David, using the biblical image of the single man with a sling taking on the giant.

No one had been able to dig up the dirt on Double Eagle that used to reside on the servers of multiple agencies. It made investigative reporters crazy. The run-up to the election had been transparent, not marred by any claims of election tampering or salacious stories of personal transgressions. Spence had dirt on each of his competitors but held it close in case something dire threatened to derail his flawless campaign.

A local company manufactured the voting machines and was a wholly owned subsidiary of Double Eagle, but the relationship was masked by a trust and a highly respected charitable organization unwittingly headed by the country's first lady.

The big man ran a hand over the thinning gray hair on his pate, steepled his hands in front of his face and spoke.

108

"Haim, you and the team have done a splendid job re-writing our company's history as well as mine and the general's biodata. People don't use their minds anymore. If it can't be found on the computer, it never existed."

"Thank you, Spence."

"Were you able to get in all the databases we discussed?" Spence asked.

"Yes, the government servers were extremely easy to access. The artifacts related to the company's Georgetown operation were all stripped out and replaced with press releases about your philanthropic efforts and good works around the world. Your files back as far as 2012 were cleaned using the updated biography and a variety of stories that you previously approved. And don't worry, I did not leave my calling card anywhere in the western dailies. I expect people will search and then abandon the effort when they can't find anything. In the west, the bar is so low. People have forgotten common sense and determination. They will briefly question their minds and then move on to something easier than trying to find the previous versions of you and the general."

"Very good. I hope you'll stay with us here through the election."

"Yes, Mr. Spence, that is the plan. I am at your disposal. I want to return some of the money you paid for my services. The ease of the task didn't equal your generous payment."

"No, Haim, keep every penny. You have made my election here in Albania possible. Without you, I could never have won. There is another matter I want you to handle personally. I don't want to leave anything to chance, and believe I am still exposed because of that SEAL, Dan Steele, who caused me to lose some of the deep operatives I had in the United States government and abandon our Georgetown operations. A liability." Spence slid a thick folder across the desk toward the other man.

"He's a wily little bastard, Haim. Seems to have nine lives too. Please eliminate him as quickly as possible. I'll leave the details to you. The folder has all the information on the Top-Secret facility where he works in DC, his residence, and daily routine and some recent photos."

"Consider it done."

"Thank you, Haim. Can I take you to lunch today? Kosher Sushi served on a block of ice?"

PART II

PART 4

CHAPTER 28

December 2023
Dubai, United Arab Emirates

The chief of Dubai's Internal Intelligence Agency gave an unusual briefing to the Council of Ministers about how the attack on Burg Khalifa was executed. He was dismissed while the ministers discussed the next steps.

They all agreed that the Russian president should be named as the mastermind of the attack, and he should be publicly shamed for ordering its execution. The details were left to the crown prince and his staff.

A 767-jet liner modified for the royal family and frequently used by the Crown Prince of Dubai for official trips outside the country departed the international airport enroute Moscow with six passengers, the men who'd been captured and started to piece together the event with their confessions. None of the men was looking forward to the return home where they'd jubilantly gathered with the president months before. Today, they were being delivered along with transcriptions of their confessions. The tactic was designed to embarrass the Federation president by pointing to the origin of the attack. How the government-controlled press would handle the story was another question, but the crown prince had made certain that the event could not possibly be covered up.

The plane landed and taxied up to a private terminal used to handle official visits to the Federation, where the full red-carpet treatment would be in full view. The president himself would meet the plane, believing it carried the crown prince. Instead, six bedraggled men, their heads and arms swathed in crisp white bandages, deplaned to a million flashbulbs, recording the event for eternity. Three of the men were in wheelchairs.

Momentarily stunned by the sight, the president greeted each of the men as if they were repatriated war heroes. Each was embraced and greeted warmly, before the president realized that these were the fighters he sent to Dubai. Out of the cargo bay came three open wire containers filled with the fragments of the drones, rifles, handguns, unexploded rounds and weapons used in the attack. The last part of the delivery was a large, sparkling white cooler which bore the crown prince's seal. The president stepped forward rigidly, thinking that a roasted sheep and lamb dinner may have been prepared. He felt the top of the cooler, wondering if the meal had been kept warm during the flight. An aide opened the cooler. Inside was a collection of ears, eyes, fingers, and noses sloshing around in a frothy red liquid. The sight and familiar smell of the decaying body parts revolted the Federation's president. He quickly covered his mouth with a white handkerchief retrieved from one of his jacket pockets.

He had taken the bait, as well as the hook, line, and sinker. He wondered how his staff could put a different spin on the event and his reaction.

Zlodeyev had proved elusive. Two costly raids to kill or capture him had gone sideways, failures that lay at the president's feet. The score was not yet settled, and this most recent embarrassment added to the urgency to the task. The Federation would mount another operation to permanently rid themselves of this annoyance. The president walked quickly past the podium that had been staged for welcoming remarks from both the crown prince and him. The speech prepared for the president by a team of speechwriters and then pencil-whipped by his personal staff would never be given. Instead, the internal press team would issue a statement of praise for the returning fighters who had been treated in specialty hospitals in Dubai for serious injuries sustained in the conflict with Ukraine.

CHAPTER 29

Tirana, Albania
January 2024

Lincoln Brewster was miserable. He'd been held in a soundproof box for almost two months by his calculation. There was no indication of night or day where he'd been held, and he was increasingly nervous that his captivity would not end well. It had been too long. Meals were delivered through a sheet metal letter slot that revealed nothing when it was opened. He assumed that his food was delivered on a regular schedule but could not define what the frequency was. All the food was removed from packaging that might reveal his whereabouts and covered with a sheet of plastic wrap. Hot and cold food was delivered as if he had been assigned his own executive chef.

A ceiling lamp burned all day and all night. Lincoln Brewster thought of himself as a prisoner, though the shackles had been removed a few days after he was captured on the diving boat. He wore a lightweight cotton jumpsuit. The air in the room was fed through a filter and the temperature was maintained with no variation. He guessed it was kept about seventy degrees with the humidity just under fifty per cent. It was a kind of hell on earth, not having a clue where he was or what his captors might be demanding of his family. Savvy enough to know that international kidnappings often ended badly, he had no means of escape and no conversation with anyone he could bribe to become an ally.

His physical health was very good and, after a few days in captivity, he had started some conditioning exercises to keep him ready to escape if the occasion presented itself. Mental health seemed to be a bigger challenge, as he was not permitted any reading material or media to keep up with what might be happening in the world outside his narrow box.

A meal came through the slot, and Lincoln picked up the tray and sat on his bunk to eat. It was a plate with a small fried steak with mushroom gravy accompanied by sliced potatoes and a dish of hot spaetzle with two bottles of water and a thin brownie. The executive chef had set a new standard. So good and filling that Lincoln returned his tray to the slot and lay down on the mattress for a nap. Twenty minutes later, several men wearing blue coveralls entered the room and removed him from the bed to a wheeled gurney.

He was loaded inside a white transit van inside the warehouse and driven to a private airport where he was carried aboard a plane, strapped to a rigid frame stretcher and attended by a nurse anesthetist who'd been ordered to keep him sedated for the entire trip. The flight plan reflected a routine business trip from Tirana to Zurich. But there was no intention of following it. Instead, the plane flew a great circle route to Dubai. The five-hour flight was uneventful.

The plane landed at the private aviation terminal where there was a brief change of crew, including the nurse anesthetist and re-fueling before General Zlodeyev boarded the plane, flying on to Zurich where it was hangered in an isolated terminal. The nurse and two guards stayed with the aircraft overnight. Local cameras caught Zlodeyev entering the five-star Baur au Lac hotel in the center of town accompanied by a four-man security detail, one of whom had a large aluminum transport case chained to his wrist.

With a mid-morning take-off from Zurich, the aircraft arrived at the main terminal in Tirana shortly after 1:00 o'clock p.m. and taxied to an area staged for its arrival. A large crowd of government officials and local dignitaries had been invited to the arrival ceremony. Local and European news outlets as well as the major US networks were represented, easily lured to what Spence had termed a major announcement with important diplomatic and international implications.

Spence stepped to the podium and thanked everyone for joining him for this momentous occasion. People edged forward for the reveal, and Spence built the excitement by making them wait. On cue, the plane's doorway dropped to the tarmac, and people were stunned to see Lincoln Brewster walking down the steps to the podium. Applause broke out as he waved to the crowd. General Zlodeyev followed. Dressed casually in a thin windbreaker over a long-sleeved collared shirt and khaki pants, Lincoln Brewster smiled broadly. Spence met the blonde beach boy and bear-hugged the man as if they'd been friends for eons.

Brewster read a prepared statement slowly and methodically, his emotional state on full display. His tear ducts were working hard with an obvious outpouring of joy and gratitude. He looked at Spence and offered his sincere thanks and certainly those of his father, claiming his successful release from captivity had been brokered by the Chief Executive of Double Eagle Industries. He stopped mid-sentence to personally clap for Spence and wrap him in another bearhug. He'd been accompanied from Switzerland by none other than Spence's designated Minister of Defense, a man of great integrity and patience and someone accustomed to achieving his objectives. Written by Spence himself, the script being followed would make for very positive press.

General Zlodeyev then stepped up, dwarfing the podium with his massive frame. Praising the behind-the-scenes negotiation of the presidential candidate to gain young Brewster's freedom, he recounted the challenge of first identifying the kidnappers, gaining their trust and then convincing them that their actions could lead to terrible consequences. Nothing good could come to anyone involved in such a scheme.

He limited speculation and the range of questions by announcing the terms of the release made it impossible for him to provide any details regarding the kidnappers, but assured the reporters that the release was tied to diplomatic suasion of the presidential candidate along with weeks of negotiation with an entity that could not be publicly identified. No financial exchanges had been part of the release. Not a single lek had passed from Spence to the other side to free Brewster.

The general's charm offensive had worked as intended and tear sheets printed in advance for the press gave them all a good start on the world's biggest story of the year, very timely since the results of the presidential election in Albania could be announced at any time following the audit and certification required by the country's election laws.

Lincoln agreed to have his first conversation with his father made public for the interest of the press. He was delighted to be released and thanked both his God as well as his savior on earth, Spence. It was a joyous occasion. The former captive described his treatment by the abductors as humane but could not give any details about the place of his captivity or any clues as to the nationalities of his captors. He was just very happy to be free.

CHAPTER 30

The White House

Washington, DC
January 2024

The White House exuded goodwill. High-fives were the greeting of the day. Ready to drop everything, jump on Air Force One and repatriate Lincoln himself, an ecstatic president careened around the West Wing with nervous, joyful energy. Holiday decorations had been removed the week before, marking the end of a somber Christmas that had extended into the New Year.

No one could remember the president being in a better mood. The White House Press Secretary was caught up in a fast-moving torrent of emotions, preparing and releasing a statement without the normal vetting process which included a final review by the president. Some cable news channels proclaimed the Spence-Zlodeyev team heroes. It seemed like everyone had swallowed a happy pill washed down with multiple cans of caffeine-spiked energy drinks.

Both Defense and State weighed in with the White House to dampen the enthusiasm. Defense had recreated the flight based on the tail numbers of the aircraft and the Identification Friend or Foe transmissions. The IFF transponder was modified when the aircraft landed in Dubai. They had strong evidence that the same plane departed Tirana, flew to Dubai and then made the return trip to Albania via a stopover in Zurich. Likewise, Basford at the State Department prepared a package for the president's Eyes Only detailing the sordid history of Double Eagle Industries and Spence. General Zlodeyev was also revealed in his true colors. The fact that the Defense, CIA, and State Department computer systems were hacked to change at least these two classified records was made abundantly clear. The president was urged to control his praise and endorsement for those that had won his son's release as they may have been party to the original abduction.

The White House Chief of Staff was busy with the impromptu celebration and left the Defense and State packages unread in his locked office. The press secretary had already announced that the president was flying to Albania to be reunited with his son. His itinerary included a grand dinner hosted by the Albanian president which would include the two men sharing Lincoln Brewster's spotlight: Spence and Nikolai Zlodeyev.

CHAPTER 31

Gaeta, Italy
January 2024

Steele landed in Rome early in the morning, opening his phone while the plane was still taxiing to the gate. The flight from the Greek airbase required a domestic flight to Athens and a connection to Rome. Admiral Wright approved his stopover in Italy after the CIA's forensics team took over the operations at Kyllini. Steele was excited and a bit apprehensive about seeing Sydney Garrison after all these months, but he had to know if the relationship had any wind left in its sails or whether they were luffing. As this date had been put off, doubts began to creep into his mind and his self-talk took on a distinctively negative tone. But he was almost there and looked forward to seeing the woman who had become a part of his life throughout 2023.

His phone automatically picked up the local cellular service, and he had missed several calls from Sydney. He also had a string of text messages that confirmed his worst fears. *USS Newport* had been ordered underway for an operation of unknown duration to a place she couldn't disclose. The boat would leave that afternoon. Steele could not interfere with her duties as commanding officer, but hoped he could spend some time with her before she got underway.

It was 08:30 a.m. by the time Steele cleared customs and immigration and hailed a cab. The trip to Gaeta, located two hours south of Rome, had finally begun. With luck, he could get there before *USS Newport* left port. To be so close and yet so far away.

"Commander Garrison," she answered.

"Hi Sydney, it's Dan. I'm just leaving the airport in Rome and hope to see you before you leave. Is there a chance?" asked Steele.

"Dan, it's great to hear from you. We won't have time for the leisurely lunch by the sea that I'd planned on. Our underway time is 1400, but we've got a classified mission briefing at 1300 with the Commander Sixth Fleet Operations Staff coming down from Naples, so I'll have to send you off before then. But at least we can see each other. It's been too long. I miss you."

"I should be there by 11:00 a.m. We've got a couple of hours anyway. I'd race up there if it were just two minutes before handling the lines to cast you off."

"Wonderful. I've gained sixty pounds and grown a beard since I saw you last."

"I'm glad you've kept your sense of humor. See you soon."

Steele fell back in the car seat elated. "Where there's a will," he said under his breath. He sat back and his thoughts drifted to their last moments together before he was launched into Mocha, Yemen in a man-carrying torpedo. She'd come to wish him good luck and kissed him in a way he still remembered, soft through parted lips that made him feel like a guy ready to take on the world.

Walking down the pier, Steele noted the frenzied preparations for getting underway on short notice. The crew had to prepare for what might be an extended operation at sea. That meant loading frozen provisions, fresh fruits and vegetables, consumables for the ship's store, lubricants, paint, rags, solvents, greases, and cleaning supplies, laundry detergent, medical supplies, weapons, ammunition, money orders, lightbulbs and toilet paper. Everything the boat might need, assuming no port visits and not surfacing for months at a time. The only thing that *Newport* did not need was fuel for its nuclear-powered propulsion and electrical plants.

Steele felt very conspicuous when he stopped at the end of *USS Newport's* brow with his carry-on bag. The commanding officer attended to myriad details before getting underway, and he knew that Garrison would be overseeing completion of the underway check-off list, where the sequenced steps were summarized on several sheets of paper and monitored by the Officer of the Deck. Steele heard the sound of two bells in succession followed by a pause and then another two rings over the ship's announcing system, signaling the arrival of a full captain, a senior officer in anyone's navy.

Standing at a distance from the gangway, he watched the three officers wearing dress blues and topcoats continue up the long steel ramp and spotted Garrison wearing a dark blue sweater over her khakis greeting them on the quarterdeck, the formal deck to receive visitors. She gave Steele an exasperated look before disappearing into the boat via the sail. Thirty minutes later, he heard the shrill sound of a bosun's pipe over the general announcing system.

"Single up all lines."

Next were bells announcing the departure of the visiting captain and movement all over the sub's hull as lines slithered into the water and were retrieved on deck by sailors wearing blue coveralls. Two tugs took positions on *Newport's* seaward side ready to gently breast the boat away from the pier until her bow was headed to the open Tyrrhenian Sea. The working brow positioned aft was lifted off by a crane. Only single lines kept *Newport* in place. Cables were shackled to the lifting eyes and the crane operator awaited the signal to remove the single brow connecting *Newport's* quarterdeck to the pier.

Steele saw Garrison in the sail. She studied the position of the submarine and two tugs. Satisfied, she said something to the Officer of the Deck and topside watch team and then disappeared. A minute later, she climbed out of the hatch in the deck and walked directly to the brow. She saluted the flag still flying on the boat's stern and deliberately walked down the long steel ramp stepping onto the pier and throwing her arms around Steele in an unmistakable embrace. Whispering in his ear, her warm breath on his cheek, she said, "I hope you know how serious I am about us," Then she kissed him, slowly and passionately. His knees turned to jelly. Then she held his face in her hands.

Looking into his dark brown eyes, she said, "Soon, Dan, I'll hope to see you soon."

She turned and walked up the gangplank past open-mouthed sailors wondering what they had just witnessed and disappeared into the bowels of the ship. Steele walked over to the cylindrical pier fixture that held a breast line and waited for the order.

"Take in number two and three lines," ordered the Officer of the Deck.

He stood behind a shoreside line handler who slipped the eye of the line over the flared end of the bollard, catching a glimpse of Garrison in the conning station in the sail. The bosun pipe shrilled over the topside speakers, "Underway" announced the formal separation from the pier. She waved at Dan from the conning tower and then was gone. Steele watched the lines cast off from the tugs as a churning wake could be seen behind the submarine. Steele felt a knot in his stomach as *Newport* headed out to sea.

CHAPTER 32

Washington, DC
January 2024

Steele returned to the United States in a daze. He'd been in Greece long enough to adjust his internal clock to European time but knew he needed to transition fast. A little roadwork with the temperature just above freezing might help. He took a painful run around Capitol Hill, then showered and arrived at the office at 0600. Paul Blanchard alerted him to the fact that the entry security system had been upgraded and promised to meet Steele in the lobby. The new system was based on facial recognition.

"I know what losing a hand is like, but it must be less painful than having your face ripped off. Thank God we were not using facial recognition last July," quipped Blanchard as the elevator descended to Pisces. After the Quantico team finished their investigation, the interior rooms had been repainted. The space had a clean linen smell, a great improvement over the condition of the spaces when Steele left them.

Steele found his desk covered with piles of correspondence, data printouts, non-urgent call slips, letters and other paperwork that would take him the day to wade through. He'd been gone for months, and the bureaucracy never takes a day off. Sorting through the pile, he found an envelope the thickness of a rural phone book near the bottom of the first stack, a package promised to him by Robert Graham when Steele was forced to regret attendance at his retirement ceremony after first accepting.

There was a sticky note from Graham on top of a manila folder:

Dan,

Sorry you can't make it to the retirement ceremony, but I know you've been to lots of them. I expect someone will make some comments, there'll be a grocery store cake and some dixie cups for soda and that will be it.

I wanted you to have this file. First, because I know you'll be interested in the science of it all and to warn you that these findings could be very dangerous in the wrong hands. I would estimate that in 1940, Germany was a good thirty years ahead of the U.S. in the study of human behavior and how to influence it. The study of tiny animals which can change the behavior of other animals as their hosts is particularly alarming. Second, I know you to be a good man and a good friend. If anyone can use this information for the better good, I know you can.

All the best. I hope to see you upon your return from God knows where.

Bob

The folder contained his file marked Experiment 55. The yellowed pages recounted interviews and preliminary findings from several experiments carried out by the Nazis. The subject of Experiment 55 was simply mind control, not of an individual or small group but the masses. Psychologists had distilled a preliminary vocabulary which set the framework for control. The footage from World War II Hitler rallies proved their effectiveness. Follow-on experiments introduced a broad range of chemicals that would amplify both the effects and the persistence of the vocabulary.

In one study, the subjects, all elderly patients at a rest home were invited to a talk by a well-known doctor on the health benefits of sexual contact. The suggestions were so powerful that several subjects began aggressive advances toward other patients and began to copulate on the floor in front of others. By the time the doctor had completed his talk, nearly all the subjects were engaged in some sort of sexual activity except for two women with severe hearing loss. All without drugs or introduction of external photos or other stimuli. A vocabulary of the keywords used in the experiments was attached. Steele understood the consequences of such information falling into the wrong hands and appreciated Graham's insistence that the experiment be safeguarded or destroyed.

In the postscript, Graham wrote that the last known location of Experiment 55 was on a U-boat operating in the Mediterranean Sea. It would be flown from the boat's first port visit directly to the Fuehrer's Staff. Steele's concentration shifted with a knock on the door followed by Cass Thomas' beaming face. Steele bolted from his chair and met Cass with a spontaneous carefree hug in the middle of the floor.

"Cass, I heard you were coming back to work but assumed that was still weeks away."

"Yes, and here I am with a 'returned to full duty' chit from my doctor." Cass kissed Steele's cheek and broke the long embrace.

Steele asked, "How do you feel, Cass, really?"

"It's good to be alive. I've had a few rough moments since your old friends from Albania visited a few months ago. My digestive system is still detoured, and I can't wait until that's connected the way it should be. Other than that, I'm starting to exercise and get back into some sort of shape. I've also discovered that it now takes longer for me to heal than it did in the past." She sat down in a chair on the other side of Steele's desk and looked at him.

"And how was your vacation in Greece?" she asked with a smile.

"Vacation, right. It's a beautiful place, but I suffered through the airbase revolving menu at least three times while I was there. Other than that, there was a lot of work with all my Agency friends who finally took over the effort. It's nice to be home and to see for myself that you are recovering."

"Speaking of miraculous recoveries, have you seen the boss yet? He's been back for about six weeks and seems to be his usual self, although he or more likely Carole have set some new guidelines as far as his work schedule and so far, he's complying."

"Sounds like a positive change."

CHAPTER 33

Tirana, Albania
February 12, 2024

Pollsters began to take a renewed interest in the Albanian election with its controversial candidate, who at this early stage appeared to be the odds-on favorite. The election, held annually in November, required the Parliament, elected by a national vote, to vote for the president. Because Spence dominated the news cycle in Albania and throughout Europe, there was little anyone could do other than watch. There was so much breaking news on the channels in the United States that little domestic interest was paid to an election in a country most people had never heard about and almost no one knew its location.

During his fiery vision speech, Spence had captured the interest of his countrymen as well as the Pentagon, NATO, and the EU. There had been many inquiries made about Spence's past, his current associations and to find out if his bold initiatives were real or just political bluster. Attempts to dig up dirt on the candidate proved fruitless. Spence was a rich, well-mannered, confirmed bachelor whose sole female companion was his mother when she accompanied him to church.

European talk show hosts characterized him as an eccentric, self-made millionaire who wanted to break the historical shackles which held Albania to the past and invest in its future. His company was always very generous and had a well-documented history of charitable works. Politically, he questioned the value of alliances, treaties, partnerships and resisted the traditional polarizing dialog of taking sides.

The votes had been cast, and a hand count was underway. Several polling places were late in returning their ballots because a winter storm had closed much of the country's interior, and the election process still relied on an actual hand count of paper ballots. Voting by mail or electronically had not been made available because of widespread infrastructure challenges. The last step before his inauguration was the final vote of the Parliament to reaffirm his victory. Finally, on February 12, 2024, Spence had his ratified victory in hand. Spence would be Albania's new president, scheduled to be sworn in on April 15, 2024.

CHAPTER 34

Tirana, Albania
April 16, 2024

A talented, self-taught thespian, Spence stepped up to the rostrum. Behind him stood the majestic statue of Albania's liberator and national hero, Skanderbeg. He'd been sworn in the day before as the duly elected president of Albania on April 15, 2024. The park was filled with people believing that Spence would carry out the promises he'd made as a candidate. Better days were ahead. His address was being carried live into the major squares of Tirana on large screen monitors erected by his order weeks before. His first public address would officially outline his vision for the future of the country.

"Good afternoon my fellow citizens," he began, repeating the greeting in the major languages used in the country, then continuing in English. Translation screens streamed his words and a woman signed for the deaf. Spence took a drink of water as the crowd stirred, watching and waiting for his speech. Spence took his time and began.

"When I traveled throughout the country campaigning to become your head of state, I was impressed with the vitality of our citizens, and the eagerness they showed for changing Albania's direction. By any measure, our country has fallen behind our neighbors and friends here in Europe. Why? There are many reasons but foremost among them is what I'd call the albatross of history that we continue to drag along. Our thinking is mired in the past. We concentrated on the rear-view mirror instead of looking out through the windshield. It has held us back as a nation. I am looking at our country's future, not its past."

A pool of photographers and print reporters recorded the event for the world to see.

The tall man ran a hand through his thinning hair and continued, gripping the rostrum on either side, strong, confident and reassuring. He addressed the economy, education, infrastructure, and health care as would any politician, blaming the failures on his multiple predecessors and promising better for everyone. Albania had lost its way in the world, and Spence promised to fix that deficiency right away.

Every new leader is expected to offer his plans for the country's security posture and vision for the military. Spence's vision for Albania 2030 was a striking departure from the passive status quo of the past and got the attention of everyone, including the team at the Department of State.

"As I have said before, I intend to re-evaluate our position within the NATO alliance and assess whether this organization provides the right level of assured security for Albania. Other nations are clamoring for membership, at the same time we are witnessing the troubling and costly conflict between the Russian Federation and a free Ukraine. NATO continues to stand on the sidelines, providing weapons and financial aid, but does nothing to end the fighting. Does Albania wish to continue membership in a seemingly feckless organization to which we subordinate our independence? I think not.

Further, I have invited a Chinese shipbuilding consortium to visit Albania and to determine the feasibility of developing an industry to serve our Navy's needs as well as our broad commercial interests in the future. This will be a multi-year project funded in part by China's Belt and Road economic outreach program that has been so successful in other parts of the world. As you know, many of you firsthand, hundreds of thousands of concrete and steel bunkers were built by Mr. Hoxha during a twenty-year period which ended with his death. They are a constant reminder of his communist regime and the terror which accompanied it. Because these bunkers weigh several hundred tons each, I intend to use them to upgrade the breakwaters that protect our ports so that expansion which I predict can be realized.

Defense Minister Zlodeyev will oversee a re-organization of our land forces and will create a special operations team to deal with delicate military operations here and elsewhere which require a small highly trained force rather than the commitment of a larger army.

I also have had initial discussions within my team regarding Albania's suitability as a Spaceport. Why should we in this country watch the future from the sidelines? As you have likely heard me say before, do we want our beloved country to be a wave maker or a wave rider? My view is that we need to speak up and let our voices be heard here in Europe and beyond. It is high time we broke out of our paranoid shell and stood tall among the free countries of the world.

Let me be clear. Our country must be an active, independent participant on the world stage. My election is a mandate to move out smartly, and that's what I intend to do. I will do everything I can to honor the example set by our beloved Skanderbeg. Thank you and may our God bless the people of Albania today and for evermore."

As reporters took positions around the park with the cheering crowd as a backdrop, Spence waded through the crowd until he reached the statue of Skanderbeg and dropped down on one knee to revere the national hero and to reinforce his pledge to be guided by the historic leader's example. Spence's announcement would be the leading story in Europe for the remainder of the day, and the story that most Americans would wake to later that morning.

CHAPTER 35

Washington, DC
April 17, 2024

At the Department of State, the Balkans team drank fresh coffee and sleepily watched the address from a small conference room in the basement of the building. There was no danger of having the conference room pre-empted by another more important country. At 04:00 a.m., they had the entire building to themselves.

Within minutes, Gus Stone and Tom Michaels were talking to the US Embassy in Tirana to get a reading on local reaction to Spence's speech for a briefing paper for their boss, currently away at an EU meeting in Brussels. The two might have another opportunity to meet with James Benjamin Basford, Deputy Assistant Secretary for European and Eurasian Affairs.

"Good morning, Hilda" said the pair in unison.

"Good morning, are you awake? Did you hear that speech?"

"Yes, we are awake, and we heard Spence's speech," said Stone. "Did he just blow the doors off central Europe or what? Looks like a bold move to me, Hilda."

"Yeah, the Ambassador already has a call in to the secretary, and every news outlet is replaying the address. I've already got a stack of phone messages on my desk. Talk about a wake-up call!"

"Heh Gus," said Michaels, "This is big stuff. Questioning the value of NATO and inviting China into the heart of Europe to build a port city? Are you kidding me? Let's see if we can finish this paper and get it up to BB's office before he comes to work. I want to get some breakfast before we get called to his office."

The two returned to the warren of the State Department basement which was quiet. Most of the State Department rabbits who worked in the building's lower floor were still sleeping and oblivious to the impact and consequences Spence's rant would have on their own countries. Stone and Michaels had just jumped on a fast-moving train, destination unknown.

CHAPTER 36

Durres, Albania
April 2024

Spence's speech captured headlines all over the world. Social media posted and reposted direct quotes from the speech as well as reactions. Something was decidedly different about this meltdown. Everyone seemed to react to the news regardless of age group or social standing.

The speech struck a resonant nationalist chord among the youth of the country who believed they had been used by the world, held back from their rightful place on the international stage and treated like third country nationals in their own country. Those who had gone to war wearing Albania's colors were inspired by the new president's words. The vast majority of those in the middle were fatalists willing to give the new political slate a chance to prove that things would get better.

Chapter 37

Tirana, Albania
April 2024

General Zlodeyev shouldered his responsibilities as the new Defense Chief. He had worked several military and intelligence initiatives into Spence's platform and only needed time and money to carry them out.

Zlodeyev also used his power and position for his other interests. He'd always dreamed of inviting the world's best fighters to a single forum and hosting them akin to the World's Strongest Man competition. His competition would be the World's Best Fighter. There were still myriad details to address, but he'd made some exploratory calls to potential sponsors, and there seemed to be strong interest.

All nations would be invited to participate, and regional competitions would be held to reduce the number of fighters to about thirty who would compete against each other before a fight against Zlodeyev himself. Would ESPN be interested in covering such an event he wondered? What would be different about this series is that it would be a fight to the death. Outrageous. Or perhaps a select group of people could give the contest a thumbs up or down exactly how they had in the Colosseum. The possibilities were endless, and the general found himself thinking about the concept all the time. He also knew that Spence would have to approve the idea before he could hire the people to put on the event. The opportunity presented itself sooner than he thought when Spence came to visit him in his personal gym, constructed after he moved to the presidential palace as a full-time resident.

"Good morning, Nikolai. How is everything this morning?"

"Just great. This is a surprise. I just finished the last repetition in my upper body routine and need a brief rest. What can I do for you today, my friend?"

"I needed to stretch my legs and to ask you to join me for lunch. We'll discuss the week's plans and make sure we are in synch."

"Thanks. That sounds great. I have got a couple of topics I'd like to discuss with you. 1:00 p.m.?"

"Perfect. See you then." Spence looked at all the weight-lifting equipment that filled the basement room and shook his head in amazement as he left the room, making a note to talk to the building's architect to see if the gym might be expanded for his Minister.

Zlodeyev's second surprise came when Spence endorsed his concept for the World's Greatest Fighter competition to be held in Tirana the following summer. Zlodeyev called together his small staff and outlined his preliminary concept for the World's Greatest Fighter and solicited their initial thoughts. Several winced at the idea of a contest ending with someone's death, but all agreed that the concept was outrageous and therefore attractive to the international press. They talked about coordinating and publicizing the event. He already knew who he wanted to run with the concept and turn it into reality.

Beach and Hamilton, LLC was a New York-based PR firm specializing in major international events which could be expected to generate worldwide interest.

CHAPTER 38

Durres, Albania
May 2024

Agron suddenly felt tired, as he was just ending his shift as an X-ray technician at a small urgent care clinic outside Durres. He slid his dosimeter into a reader and proceeded to the locker room to change from his scrubs into a pair of jeans and a t-shirt that emphasized his muscular physique. He swung by to record his radiation exposure and jumped back from the desk when he saw his exposure was off the charts.

"Must be a problem with the reader," he mumbled aloud, plugging the dosimeter into an adjacent machine and watching the needle and the flashing red light. He had absorbed over a thousand times his normal working day exposure. How? The day case load was very light: four views this morning for the on call orthopedic surgeon to help set a young boy's broken arm, a runner's badly sprained ankle, a woman with suspected pneumonia. And then a simple abdominal plate of two hikers who'd been brought into the clinic by a herder who found them wandering in the mountains, vomiting, delirious, and one bleeding from the nose. Severe dehydration was the preliminary diagnosis.

Agron reflected for a moment and then called his supervisor about the reading.

"Any problems with the machine today?"

"No," answered Agron. "And all the cases seemed routine."

The two hikers lay in adjacent beds in the clinic's urgent care wing, both being administered fluids through intravenous bags hanging on a metal stand between the beds.

Earlier that day, the hikers had set out from Durres in the early morning for the Cape of Skanderbeg. The two were brother and sister, twins from Munich, Hansel and Greta. The guidebook reviews were glowing, and they looked forward to seeing the ruins of the castle Skanderbeg built for his wife on the shoreline of the rocky projection which jutted out into the Adriatic.

The sun was still high in the Spring sky when they crossed over a rail line and headed beyond the city to look for a campsite in the Ceraunian Mountains. Several hundred yards into the scrub, Greta tripped and fell flat on her face. When she rose, she looked like a frosted cake, her sweaty t-shirt covered with limestone dust. After brushing off, she looked for what caused the fall and found a buried, apparently abandoned train rail. Her brother, Hansel, kicked away the sandy surface to reveal another track parallel to the first. They looked at the trekkers' guide and did not see the railroad spur on the map.

"Wonder where this goes?" Greta asked. The line seemed to head into the limestone mountains with no apparent destination.

"Let's find out."

The rails ended at the edge of the mountains, which dominate the region's landscape.

A massive limestone face sheared off and buried the tracks with a pile of rubble.

"Well, there goes the excitement for the day. I was thinking that it might be a cave full of Hitler's gold," said Greta.

"Well, we were headed into the mountains anyway," said her brother, "We might as well continue this way up through the valley."

Both looked at the map. "You ready?" he asked.

Two hundred feet ahead, Greta stopped abruptly and followed a stream toward the mountain. It flowed under a rock and had eroded the limestone. She scooped up a handful of the water and then spit it out.

"It's a karst spring, the water is slightly acidic. Which means we've found a limestone cavern. Up for some spelunking?" Greta dropped her pack and stripped naked, pulling on a pair of quick-dry nylon shorts and a t-shirt from her backpack. She lay on her back in the cold water and wriggled her boyish body against the water flow and disappeared.

Hanzel quickly followed suit and joined his sister.

"Wow isn't this awesome," said Greta, admiring the cavern. A crevice in the roof of the cavern filled the void below with bright light and guaranteed some level of oxygen.

Stalagmites filled the cavern looking like a Dali-inspired pipe organ. And a small stream had eroded the bedrock which crossed the floor and exited where the pair had entered.

The railroad tracks spurred inside the cavern and split on both sides of a wide concrete platform fitted with a crane and a rusty steel lifting fixture. Beyond the platform, long rows of metal shipping containers stacked three high disappeared into arched tunnels carved into the mountain.

Greta shivered with the cold, damp interior of the cavern. The twins picked their way across the floor which was covered with shallow fissures carrying water toward the larger stream.

Hanzel pointed to the side of one of the boxes.

"That's the symbol of the Soviet Union, and these steel boxes hold a weapons system of some sort," said Hanzel. Also emblazoned several places on the exterior were the international radiation symbol.

"I wonder if these are still active?" Greta asked.

Hanzel looked down at a row of boxes until he saw one that had been breached by a massive stalactite which had opened its steel side. What he saw inside was a fully assembled missile that barely fit into the twenty-foot container. Three motors were wired to drive a simple elevation system where the missile could be launched through a frangible cover. Several stickers identified the missile payload as containing nuclear material. The missile body had been fractured over time, exposing the guts of the weapon.

Opposite the loading platform, they found a long-abandoned barracks with twelve bunks, a kitchen with two tables and chairs, and a separate room with six toilets, sinks and stall showers. The single wooden desk covered with a thick layer of mold and a rifle rack holding a dozen rusty rifles. A metal staircase zigged back and forth along the shear walls of the cavern to an enclosure cut into the side of the cavern with a view of the platform and the tracks leading to a massive steel door permitting access to the facility.

The pair carefully climbed the stairs and found an operations center with a radio and panel to control the track switches, locomotives, and rail cars entering or leaving the facility. A short-wave radio full of glass tubes covered a table in front of a detailed vertically mounted map of the route between the facility and the individual piers at the port. A logbook lay open on the desk. The last entry was January 1960:

All weapons secure. Radio inoperative. Our crew is divided into two teams for the excavation of the rocks from the landslide. The Lieutenant ordered the remaining tinned food to be rationed. Twelve men assigned. Four dead, locked in the maintenance annex at the end of tunnel one, three are working, four in rest period and one missing.

"I know you're fascinated with the geological magnificence of this cavern, but the condition of these containers tells me that we are being exposed to radiation. Let's get out of here," said Hanzel in a stern voice. Though somewhat decontaminated by submerging in the karst stream, even a brief exposure to radioactive material would lead to several ill effects. Beyond that his knowledge of radiation was limited. Both adventurers were already suffering from nausea, vomiting, and diarrhea by the time they'd gotten dressed outside the cavern.

"What should we do?" asked Greta.

"I think we need to head back into town and let the local police know what we found and ask someone in a medical clinic what to do about our exposure," said Hanzel.

It was late afternoon when a herdsman found the pair along the trail back into town. Neither could travel on their own power, so he loaded them into the bed of an ancient pickup truck and drove to the nearest town with a medical facility.

CHAPTER 39

Shijak, Albania
May 2024

After a cursory examination, the doctor decided that he should punt the case of the unidentified hikers to the hospital in Durres. They were transferred by ambulance and arrived weak and incoherent. Upon seeing them, the ER physician ordered that they be isolated and called the HAZMAT team from Tirana.

"Good afternoon, this is Dr. Kurti from Durres. I've got two hikers with radiation exposure that were found on the road near Shijak. I'll try to get a better fix on the circumstances, but in the meantime, they are isolated and in very serious condition. Neither is communicating, and they are falling in and out of consciousness. Both have flash burns, nausea, diarrhea and are bleeding from the nose and rectum."

"OK, got it. I'll contact the team and get them on the road to Durres. We'll start piecing together the story from there. I'll also send our staff radiologist to your location to assist."

The herder who transported the hikers to the clinic was located, and he led the team to the place he picked up the two. From there, the team fanned out to find the source of the radiation. Hanzel and Greta only walked about a hundred yards before collapsing. The team found their packs lying next to the small stream and began to take some readings. A small amount of radiation was detected on their shorts still wet from the excursion. The stream flowing from the mountainside indicated a high level of radiation.

Bunker 43 had been discovered.

CHAPTER 40

Moscow, USSR
1959

In 1959, Khrushchev began an extensive deployment of weapons to the countries under the umbrella of the Warsaw Pact as well as to distant locations such as Cuba. One of those places was in a mountain cavern near Shijak, Albania. Its proximity to the port of Durres would allow the Soviets to quickly load cargo ships and deploy them without raising any intelligence alarms. The surveillance assets of the United States were limited, and there was not any major interest in a poor country like Albania. More important was the fact that the munitions were assembled to be self-contained in the new form of shipping container invented a few years before. It was a strategic initiative to give the Soviets the ability to rail the weapons into the port of Durres and position armed cargo ships to strike European cities with nuclear weapons. Bunker 43 gave the USSR a strategic advantage in Europe. Its existence was not known outside the secretive planning cell that Chairman Khrushchev had created outside the military chain of command.

The targets would be the major Mediterranean cities within 300 miles of the coast, struck in a coordinated attack that the Europeans would never see coming. The immediate devastation would cause widespread panic and breakdown within NATO military units. Fear would grip the entire landmass — all to the Soviet's advantage. In the attack's aftermath, the Soviets would initiate a ground offensive that would crush any resistance...the Europeans would drive the price of white muslin higher as the white flag of surrender would appear on every village rooftop. Khrushchev may have portrayed himself as kinder and gentler than his predecessor, Joseph Stalin, but he was a visionary in terms of extending the country's borders and its ramparts by expanding his domain.

When Albania pushed back against the Communists a few years later, the weapons, like the Soviet submarines moored at the Pashaliman naval base, were expected to be withdrawn and returned for deployment elsewhere. Clearly, they belonged to the USSR and were loaned to those countries that accepted the iron fist in a velvet glove approach of the Soviets. But surprisingly, they were abandoned and left behind.

When the Russian team came to retrieve the weapons, they found the perimeter barbed wire fence intact as well as the rail spur leading into the mountain. However, the spur ended at least 150 meters short of the mountainside entrance. A massive rockslide triggered by a deep earthquake along the Shijak fault blocked the entrance with thousands of tons of rock, entombing the weapons as well as the guard force tasked with safeguarding the facility and reporting to Moscow. The dozen men assigned to the facility had found it sweet duty. They bought food in a nearby town, and, outside of a rotating watch standing schedule, time was their own. Several had girlfriends and enjoyed the local Albanian beer. They formed their own soccer team which played area teams and were known for their generous after-match parties.

The rocks had splayed the rails and ripped the spikes and hold-downs out of the wooden sleepers supporting the track and leveling the rail bed. Retrieving the weapons would take a massive effort and require local cooperation, which would be difficult given the political situation at the time. The bureaucrat responsible for redeploying the weapons decided that the rockslide provided sufficient security for the weapons and ordered his team to remove the perimeter fence and any signage left to identify the facility. One man reported hearing scraping sounds near the hidden entrance. Dismissing those concerns, the bureaucrat led a hurried prayer and officially concluded the visit.

It was unlikely that anyone would go poking around the rocks looking for treasure. The cavern became a tomb for the Soviet team guarding the weapons cache and began a long experiment on how ferrous metal reacts to the slightly alkaline nature of a limestone cave.

CHAPTER 41

Presidential Palace

Tirana, Albania
September 2024

Spence stood in front of the IAEA team, thanking them for their work in dealing with Albania's first nuclear incident. The team was enjoying cocktails prior to a dinner hosted by the president at the Palace in Tirana. Sealed after months of dedicated work involving multiple nations, Bunker 43 was closed. The weapons had been disassembled and destroyed, and the nuclear material safeguarded and then stored. The logs recounting the last days of the facility's operations, and the skeletons of the crew responsible for the security of the site were sealed by tons of concrete and a thick lead shield that would have to be in place for at least twenty years until the radiation levels decayed to a safe level. The site had been capped to prevent any further surface water from entering and carrying any more radiation into the ground around the facility.

The 500 pounds of nuclear material, found in the missile warheads in spherical containers of small pellets that looked like spinach rigatoni, had been removed from the missiles and loaded into purpose-built casks made of layers of steel and lead used to transport spent nuclear fuel back to facilities for re-processing. Looking like giant dumbbells, the casks with shock limiters on either side of a storage tube were constructed of steel fifteen inches thick. A special armor was manufactured to withstand impact shock, high-intensity fire and water intrusion per IAEA standards.

Spence was the consummate host and generous in his praise for the team. He invited them to stay for a week and to see the country's historic sites as well as its coasts and mountains. Though the team demurred with talk of other pressing projects, they were very appreciative of the attention and praise from the nation's leader.

During a multiple course dinner impeccably prepared and served, the team leader asked President Spence a leading question.

"Do you need our assistance to arrange returning the casks to one of the facilities authorized to process it?"

Spence's response was just a flat no, surprising everyone within earshot with his brusqueness. Over dessert, the team leader was emboldened by the sumptuous feast and several glasses of a very full-bodied, locally produced Cabernet Sauvignon to ask Spence the same question in a different way.

"What, if I may ask, Mr. President, do you intend to do with the casks?"

"Well, the short answer is to put them on the market and sell them to the highest bidder."

The entire table laughed at President Spence's obvious sarcasm. He joined in the frivolity. "Perhaps we'll have a yard sale on Saturday and see if we can attract some buyers," said Spence, setting off another round of boisterous laughter around the table. Tears poured down the team leader's face like the Spring melt coursing over granite in New Hampshire. After what seemed to be an exceptionally long pause, the laughter died. Spence paused patiently to take a sip of wine and asked, "What do you think the market value is for the casks?"

Ashen faced, the team leader replied, "I've never heard that question asked. Given the cost to produce the amount of material we have safely stored, I would think that the price would be in the billions of dollars."

"That was my thinking exactly. To afford the modernization programs that I planned for this country, I need to raise a huge amount of capital and would prefer not to devalue our currency by just printing money."

After the fete, Spence returned to his office. He knew the phone would be ringing off the hook in hours, and he needed to concentrate. After listing the likely buyers of the casks on a sheet of paper and sketching out the terms of an auction as well as the financial process, Spence padded to his suite and had a quiet, uninterrupted night.

CHAPTER 42

Presidential Palace

Tirana, Albania
September 2024

Over a cup of black coffee in the morning quiet of his study, Spence did a quick internet search revealing that thirty-two countries around the world operated nuclear power plants and only nine countries were thought to have nuclear weapons. Israel was assumed to have the special weapons but never admitted their existence. Albania did not appear on either list. Spence felt ambivalence about developing either capability. The country simply could not afford it. The buyers that might bid on processed, weapons grade material would likely be a handful of countries with established programs, no intentions of phasing out their reactors, and with the money to pay for the material. The list narrowed significantly after Spence applied the logical filters.

Spence reasoned that the 2015 nuclear deal with Iran to halt production of enriched uranium cost $150 billion. Part of the money came from a former military purchase from the United States for ships built but never delivered and another part from frozen Iranian assets that were allowed to thaw and be reclaimed by the regime. He recalled the story of a cargo plane full of pallets of various currencies being delivered to the country. Many critics claimed there was no change in Iran's behavior or intentions, but they kept the money anyway, probably fattening accounts which funded terrorism around the world.

The current Middle East conflict provided ample evidence that Iran had funded and even trained the Hamas terrorists that struck Israel in October 2023. While it was difficult to understand the closed loop economics of nuclear energy production, Spence thought that a value of $500 billion might be an appropriate starting place.

He crafted a short sales sheet using the IAEA-prepared summary and identified the material as being ready to ship. The sale would be FOB from Durres, and a thorough safety and security plan would be part of the bargain. Spence smiled when he looked over the draft sales sheet. It would be broadcast by every news agency worldwide and probably activate the situation rooms in the countries that had them.

The terms would be the full payment in US dollars, the shipment could be made via truck, rail or sea with the buyer responsible for all pick-up and delivery arrangements. Spence would require that the bidders and their offers be made public during the sixty-day bidding process. He would assign the bidding process to an independent auditing firm. His Attorney General would be able to translate Spence's scribblings into a legal framework supporting the sale. Formal bids would be due not later than November 30, 2024.

Spence finished his work and placed the draft in his outbox. His secretary would dress up his draft and he'd have a chance to review it with Zlodeyev later in the day. If people were not aware of the small country of Albania by now, they would soon learn of it.

CHAPTER 43

Presidential Palace

Tirana, Albania
October 2024

The NATO protocol was on full display as a band of six ambassadors arrived in Tirana in an official motorcade of armored vehicles that were flown in for the occasion. Each of the Ambassadors represented his own country as well as the alliance itself. The men were attired formally to signal the solemnity of the occasion.

Spence greeted the group at the Palace entrance as they each presented their credentials in front of an eager press corps. The Europeans still wore very ornate uniforms, many with elaborately plumed hats, some of which appeared motheaten, having not been worn for years. As Spence expected, NATO had sent these second-string ambassadors to Albania to persuade him that auctioning off nuclear material for transfer was dangerous and foolhardy. It clearly violated some obscure paragraphs in the Alliance's policies and could serve no purpose in Spence's vision to rebuild the country and make it count on the world stage. The colony of penguins looked silly. Some countries had the audacity to send their third stringers to negotiate with Spence. That made him more determined than ever to set a course where Albania would not be the laughingstock of Western Europe.

Once inside, they were escorted into a sitting room and select photographers captured their smiling faces. The group's leader, a German, spoke first after they'd gathered around a conference table prepared according to NATO specifications, including seniority. The press had been dismissed.

"President Spence, my colleagues and I are here to implore you not to continue on your present course to sell the nuclear material that the IAEA has secured in two casks. We represent the entire Alliance in urging you to stop this reckless action," said the man.

"Thank you, gentlemen, for coming all the way to Albania. I am honored to have you here." Spence rose and walked around the conference room as if pondering what he might say next. Stopping, he resumed his response.

"Last time I checked, I'm part of the same Alliance, yet no one asked me for an input on this matter, so how can you say you represent NATO?" Spence took his seat to a series of harrumphs echoing around the table.

"An oversight for certain, Mr. President. As you know this is a matter of the upmost import…"

"What is the important matter?" Spence thundered, "NATO is an alliance of European partners for mutual defense. Simply put, my economy needs shoring up, and that's what the sale is all about. As I recall, I haven't received a bid from the Alliance for the material, have I?"

The German diplomat nervously shifted in his chair as if he'd sat on a mound of fire ants.

"President Spence, we've come to plead with you to cease and desist this illegal auction and the transfer of the material. Everything can be how do you say, restored, or status quo ante. That's the carrot side of the bargain we carry to present to you. Let me be clear that we are also carrying a stick. Albania will be considered in violation of the accord and subject to penalties up to and including dismissal from the Alliance, if you choose to not accept what I consider to be a grand bargain. It's up to you, President Spence. Are you prepared to be isolated and turn your back on the many benefits of the Alliance that's stood for so many years? NATO has become a rock in the civilized world."

"What Alliance benefits? I don't recall any benefits coming to Albania, my friends. Please explain."

CHAPTER 44

Presidential Palace

Tirana, Albania
October 2024

The phone calls began the following afternoon, preceded by a stack of cables from the allied side of the world, the ones who already had nuclear power as well as weapons.

"Spence, the president of the United States is coming on line one". The call came in at 4:00 p.m. Tirana time. Spence and Zlodeyev sat on either side of Spence's desk enjoying coffee with the speaker phone between them.

"Good morning, Mr. President," said Spence.

"Good afternoon, President Spence," responded the president, sitting in the situation room at the White House, surrounding by his National Security team, the Secretaries of State, Defense, Treasury, the vice president and his military commanders. The only outliers in the room were retired Admiral James Wright and Dan Steele.

"Your announcement about the sale of the old Soviet material surprised me. The goods might attract some buyers that the United States might not approve of, and I am hopeful we might be able to head off any future unpleasantries. You are an honorable man, and you showed me your generosity and good nature when brokering the release of my son. I'll never forget that. Perhaps we could discuss an alternative arrangement with Albania which would provide you a safe and secure means of disposing of this material and at the same time support some of your country's projects through some aid or technical assistance. What do you think?"

"Thank you for calling me. Mr. President," responded Spence. "I must say that this auction has stirred up quite a spirited exchange with many others interested in changing the terms of an open market sale to a quiet exchange between friends. I've had several proposals. My interests are safety and security but also generating cash for our economy. As I'm certain you know, Albania's GDP is less than $20 billion U.S. dollars. I think the price for the material with a floor bid of $500 billion dollars is an appropriate starting place for the sale. Wouldn't you agree, Mr. President?"

"To tell you the truth, President Spence, I can't say that I've run the numbers on what you have, but at first blush, I think the figure is very steep."

"Well, Mr. President, we shall soon see. We are very early in the process, but do you expect that the United States might place a bid?"

"What I had in mind, Mr. Spence, was an agreement which would partially satisfy your economic needs and permit us to restrain the enthusiasm of a country with vast resources but not the temperament to buy this type of material, whether for energy or weapons production. We can simply not afford to deal with countries which have an enhanced opportunity to make weapons of mass destruction."

Spence responded, "Well, I completely understand and hope your bid will reflect your determination. I'm sorry to end this call so abruptly, but I have several nations holding, I believe on the same subject. Before I go, I did want to inquire about the health of your son."

"Lincoln is fine. I appreciate your asking."

"Very good. Hope to talk with you soon, Mr. President. Goodbye."

The president cradled the phone and looked expectantly at a group shell-shocked by the call. The outcome of the call was not as predicted. The pleasant rebuff of the president would not make for good press.

CHAPTER 45

The White House

Washington, DC
October 2024

"Now that this Albanian deal with Iran is moving, I want a plan to stop it," said the president. The Secretary of State, Secretary of Defense and National Security Advisor glanced at each other. They all knew that the question would be asked.

"Well, Mr. President, I have a team working on alternatives but are far short of a plan. With the security arrangements for the transfer and transit, we can't do anything overt, and a covert operation will be tough. I've got my best planners working on it," said the Defense Secretary, leaning back on the couch and concluding that the problem wouldn't go away regardless of how much bourbon he consumed.

The Secretary of State said, "I think we should continue approaching Spence with other incentives to have him reconsider any offers that he gets, specifically from the ayatollah. That may mean more cash, or something else, but my view is that a military action to seize this material could be a diplomatic disaster with lots of unintended consequences. It certainly has the potential to kill our alliances and encourage aggression to solve problems. There are plenty of bullies out there now. We don't need any more."

The president looked at his lined tablet, picked up his pen and then replaced it between two lines on the paper and shook his head. He stared at each of his advisers for several seconds before ending the meeting.

"Look, we have a real problem here, and we must solve it. I know it sounds like a kid who loses the game and gets so mad he threatens to take his ball and go home. The bottom line is that by hook or by crook, we must not let the ayatollah get his hands on what he's bidding for. If we don't come up with something, I'm sure the Israelis will do whatever it takes to stop that shipment. We may be headed to the brink of war with the Chinese and Russians. We are in an untenable situation, and we need a brilliant solution, likely without our fingerprints on it. I know it's a tall order, but we've got to come up with something."

CHAPTER 46

Presidential Palace

Tirana, Albania
October 2024

Big and burley with a white swatch of hair over his left ear where it met his full thick beard, the man standing in the doorway to Spence's office filled the rectangular opening. He looked like a Jersey barrier stood on end. Adam had completed a due diligence process on the man and assessed him as very capable but also risky. Spence decided to interview the man himself.

"So, tell me a little about yourself and your diving experience," asked Spence, wearing a tailored suit and bold red tie.

"Larry is the name. Larry Jackson. I've been diving for my whole life. Mostly working out of dive shops and marinas, doing marine repairs like changing propellers, installing new zincs, hull patches, adding diving platforms and the like. I've scavenged the bottom or looked for lost articles on occasion. Recovered fouled anchors, and freed nets. I dive by myself and don't like to dive with others because they complicate things. No, I'd rather dive by myself."

"Any depth limits?"

"No. I'll dive to where the work is. If it's deep, I usually will stop for a few minutes and hang on the anchor line, so I don't get bent."

"I see. Where are you from?"

"Well, I was born in Louisiana. Been kicking around Europe for over twenty years. Left the States after high school. I've been living and working in Durres for the last eight years. I'm shacked-up with a real nice woman who's lived here all her life. We've got a son and daughter together. Life is good."

"Yes, it is. The job that I would like you to do for me is to find a submarine sunk right off the coast."

"A real submarine? Never dove on a sub before. What kind?" asked Jackson.

"It was a German submarine sunk near the end of the second World War. It's within the area I'm proposing for my fish farm."

"What do you want to do, salvage some nautical artifacts?"

"That may come later. I just want you to confirm it's there." Spence studied the man sitting in the chair in front of him. His bulging, bloodshot eyes, and the spidered red veins on his face confirmed that the man wasn't just sustaining himself by breathing compressed air. He was slugging down whatever he could afford at a local watering hole. Spence decided that he would use the man for a single dive to locate the hull and then bring in some professionals to harvest whatever the sub was carrying. He didn't quite trust the drunk but understood he owned some high-tech equipment which might prove useful.

"I can sure handle a job like that. How accurate is the position of the sub?" asked the big man.

"The location was given to me by the former commander of the vessel, so I assume it's very accurate but want you to verify and confirm its position and depth."

"When do you want it done?"

"Sometime in the next two weeks would be fine," said Spence.

Jackson's eyes darted around the office.

"OK, no problem. If I can't find it, nobody can. $2,000 for the dive plus an extra $500.00 if I find the sub. How does that sound?"

"I'll let my secretary address the financial arrangements. Please give him your contact information, and we'll be in touch before the end of the week." Spence rose and found himself looking up into the bloodshot eyes.

"Thank you, Mr. Jackson," Spence concluded the meeting and shook a beefy, calloused hand. "Good hunting."

CHAPTER 47

The White House

Washington, DC
November 15, 2024

The president marched into the conference room and sat at the head of the table, surrounded by his vice president, the cabinet secretaries, the senior NSC Staff, the head of the National Nuclear Security Administration and a component branch, the Office of Secure Transportation. A single topic was on the agenda — Albania's recent find that they intended to sell to the highest bidder. The president opened the meeting without an accolade or comment about the polls, a signal to all this was a serious meeting.

"As most of you already know, the government of Albania has just begun the process to sell 500 pounds of weapons grade nuclear material removed those Soviet missiles from the late fifties. They intend that the sale will be completely transparent and have brought in a consulting firm to ensure everything is done by the book. While we were focused on the installation in Cuba, our shoe-banging colleague from the Soviet Union was deploying weapons systems to all the countries behind the Iron Curtain. We knew about most of them, where they were, and what type of weapons they contained, but to my knowledge, we never even considered that Albania would host weapons designed for a Soviet takeover of southern Europe. We are not here to perform a collective post-mortem on our failure to know about this stockpile or the plan it supported. I have asked for this meeting because it is vitally important that this nuclear material not be purchased by Iran, China, Russia or North Korea.

The Operations Analysis branch in the Pentagon has put together a top-level briefing that will be presented to you this morning, and I have a few thoughts to discuss about how we might react to what's about to unfold before our eyes."

The Pentagon briefer distilled the issue down to a handful of slides he presented to the group. The first slide listed the likely bidders for the material with an estimate of the use of the material whether for energy or weapons. The second slide provided an estimate of the bidding strategies and how various countries might approach the auction, the third slide provided an overview of the potential threats during the transportation of the casks and the final page recommended actions by the United States. His slides had obviously been pre-briefed to the White House and modified accordingly.

"As you can see, we have several courses of action to ensure that this material is protected and ends up in the hands of the United States or EU, but nothing is certain. The president of Albania has announced that the bidding floor is $500 billion. Bids below that number will be discarded. A final opportunity to bid will be offered before the bidding concludes on November 30. All bids will be posted with the identity of the bidder assigned a code to be revealed only when the bidding ends. By now you may be asking yourself why am I here?

My idea is this. We will divide ourselves into three teams. There will be a USG team led by the vice president that will carry out the routine business of government and any role we might play in the protection of the cargo to its final destination. I don't expect any country will ask for our help. A second team, a Red Team if you will, headed by the Department of Defense, assisted by the Agency will play the Iranians and Soviet Bloc as well as China and perhaps North Korea, and the third group will be headed by me, aided by the NSC, the Chief of Naval Operations, Admiral Wright and a small contractor team."

The president looked around the table silently soliciting comments or proposed changes to the plan. There were none. He resumed talking, "As you know, I am opposed to any opportunity presented to the Iranians that will accelerate their advancement to nuclear weapons. This sale, if consummated, will do just that. China may bid and that would be something that we should prevent, but they already have a stockpile, and it's unlikely in my view that they would be a public bidder. China may help the Iranians financially. Ditto Russia. North Korea is a wild card, but I don't believe they have the means of raising the cash. Could they be a proxy? Sure. I wouldn't rule out anything at this stage. We can try to outbid the competition, but I suspect that Iran will win the bid, which means that our opportunities to stop this sale would be on the covert side. Plausible deniability is important here, and we cannot afford a tactical blunder of someone talking outside of school.

Simply put, we cannot tolerate a nuclear weapons capable Iran and will seek to outbid them in the auction. With our current economic situation and the aid just pledged to Ukraine and Israel, I don't see a way to outbid Iran without triggering a deeper depression and runaway inflation. Both Russia and China could support the Iranian bid from behind the scenes. We need our best minds applied to this problem. Please think about my idea of three teams. I don't want any group think about this but would like a call or email from each of you on what you think. Please make your responses clear and concise. And no comments to the press or your staffs on this. Thank you."

Dan Steele listened intently to the president and immediately knew that the small contractor team he referred to was Pisces. As people were rising from the table, he noticed what appeared to be a Beltway message from the vice president to the CIA director. The vice president had put his index and middle fingers together, and the CIA director had made a slight head nod in response. What did that mean Steele wondered? Then it hit him like a ton of bricks. The vice president had made no secret in his interest for running for president after the incumbent's second term. The VP was communicating that he and the CIA director needed to stay close on the issue and ensure that both their futures were not tainted with actions that were not "approved." The vice president had a history of using approval when it aligned with his interests. This might be one of those occasions.

CHAPTER 48

Durres, Albania
November 2024

Larry Jackson drove a pickup truck covered with rusty dents and bruises towing a white-hulled fiberglass motorboat that he bought from a man in Slovenia who made a living harvesting salt. Piled in the truck's bed were four dive tanks, several rugged composite cases, and a large gear bag. The drive from Durres was about fifty miles. Loud country music blared from the radio. Larry wasn't thinking about the dive. He was concentrating on the generous fee he would collect the next day.

He'd been working hard since he was a kid, trying to eke out a living for his single mother and twin sisters. To survive in southern Louisiana required a physical toughness developed from farming, hunting gators and bullfrogs, running weed and shine, sometimes finding guns when asked. Jackson's physique helped his family survive when others just stopped trying. He protected his mother and sisters and developed a mean, angry personality as a young man. Cold as ice and fearful of nothing.

He remembered his first diving job, the recovery of a large diamond ring that a woman on a pontoon boat had thrown in the water after an alcohol-fueled spat with her boyfriend. Jackson didn't know anything about scuba but figured that he had an air tank on his back and a mask to protect his eyes when he pushed off the dock and started to search the bottom, moving his bare fingers over the mud. Visibility was zero. Jackson was patient. He found the ring in five minutes, feeling its size and shape, wondering what he could get for it at a pawn shop. He just relaxed underwater as the people on the surface were getting nervous and his bill started to increase like the meter at a gas pump.

If the ring was worth $20,000, the fee for finding it would be just as pricey. He really didn't know the man who owned it, but knew he owned a twenty-five-foot pontoon boat named *Easy Money* with a fully stocked bar and a pair of 350 horsepower engines that would push the hull close to forty knots. He'd seen a line of some white powder up at the bar and knew it wasn't from some lost jigger of salt. The man wore a gold Rolex and drove a BMW, so it wasn't hard for Jackson to assume the guy had money. It really didn't matter to Jackson whether he earned or inherited it. Jackson didn't have enough money in his pocket for a six-pack of drinkable beer. He sucked that tank dry before surfacing with the ring in his hand. The man with several friends were standing on the small dock drinking long necks when he dog-paddled over and stood up in the muddy water.

"Did you find it?" the man asked.

"I found two rings on the bottom but need to look at it to make sure it's the one you're after." Jackson bellied up to the dock and looked at the rings, hiding them in his large hands. One was a plain gold band, the other a silver-colored band with a polished diamond that looked like an almond.

"What did your lost ring look like?"

"It's got a platinum band and a tear-shaped diamond on top. It's worth $45,000 and that bitch threw it in the water."

"Well, one of the rings seems to measure up to that description. What kind of reward should a poor man like me expect from recovering it for you?"

"Listen you son-of-a-bitch. You know the damn ring is mine, and I showed you where it was. I would've suited up and found it myself if I had time. I got a couple hundred here for you."

"That's sounds a little light to me. I think my time and effort should be worth more than that."

"OK," he said, "Here are five Benjamins for you. Now, hand it over."

"I'd love to have me a nice watch like the one you're wearing. Can you throw that in too?"

"Are you crazy? This watch is worth almost as much as the ring."

"Well then, why don't you throw in this diving rig, and we'll call it even."

Five women had worn that ring one time or another. It had served him well, and he wasn't about to part with it. The man sputtered his agreement. Jackson had been diving ever since.

He launched the boat and motored out of Vlore harbor and headed south. Twenty minutes later, he maneuvered the craft using his GPS. According to the chart, the submarine wreck was located in over 1,000 feet of water. The paper that he was given by Spence's office just had a location revealed by single tap of some old guy's finger. How accurate could that be? The days leading up to the date the officers stepped off the submarine were cloudy and overcast, so their last celestial fix was old.

He assumed they were using dead reckoning for navigation with maybe a line of bearing from the Vlore light. Jackson was not about to waste time at any depth looking for what might be miles from his current location. He studied the chart and opened a hard-sided plastic case protecting a battery powered side scanning sonar. Programming the yard stick-sized sensor via his phone, he called up a standard two mile east-west square search grid just inside the 100-meter curve at 150' and started mowing the lawn, making passes at five-hundred-yard intervals.

A green light illuminated his phone once the sonar body reached search depth. Jackson moved into the boat's darkened forward cabin and began watching a color monitor of the progress, periodically grabbing a beer from a cooler beside him. Just as the two-hour session was scheduled to conclude, the sonar painted what appeared to be a long metal pipe with a dense projection midships. Jackson noted the GPS coordinates and retrieved the sensor fifteen minutes later. He unscrewed the battery compartment and loaded a fresh battery and reprogrammed the fish to search a smaller area at a higher frequency at the same depth.

Bingo! Jackson exclaimed to himself as the higher resolution provides a picture which reveals the submarine upright, perched on a rocky ledge on the edge of steep cliff that mimics the terrain that rises behind Vlore.

It's mid-afternoon when Jackson sets the hook on the bottom at 120 feet, suits up, sits on the edge of the gunwale and falls into the water. The water is clear and calm. He heads down the anchor line slowly. Visibility is good as he passes 100 feet. A pipe-shaped hull fills his view. His anchor found the large deck gun forward of the sail. The submarine is upright.

The sail has been laced with a tangle of old fishing lines and nets covering a slimy hole ringed with coral and sea grass. Jackson makes short work of clearing the lines blocking the hatch, turns on a bright underwater lamp and slithers inside the boat, being careful not to disturb the silt that covers every surface. Once inside, the equipment seems intact as he sets his buoyancy compensator and gently pulls himself along. OK, he's found it and wonders what Spence's interest was all about.

His curiosity is answered when peering at the deck. The control room's grated deck had been covered with hundreds of landscape bricks that raised the deck at least ten inches. A quick scrape of one edge revealed a bright yellow surface underneath the layer of organisms that had made the brick a home. The blocks have been cemented together so that they didn't move. Jackson's knife point tests the mastic which finally yields.

He does a bit more scraping and sees a Swastika stamped into the ingot's surface along with the weight from the foundry. This is my lucky day he says aloud as he exits the boat and repositions the anchor line so it can be retrieved without fouling. Surfacing, he hangs his gear on a hook bolted to the hull amidships and pulls himself up and over the gunwale. A wire brush removes the growth on the ingot. Larry Jackson is suddenly a very rich man.

As he's re-stowing the diving equipment Jackson ponders his next steps. His clear thinking is jumbled by what he'd just found. Spence knew about the gold on the boat and just wanted to locate the treasure so he could harvest it later. Jackson mulled over his plan forward on the trip back to Durres, the gold ingot cradled between his thighs.

The following day he drove to Tirana to see Spence.

"Well, I used up four tanks of air looking for that submarine with no success. The last location is in water over 1,000 feet deep. It may be somewhere down there. I can organize a deeper search if you want."

"No, not now," said Spence gently. "You've done a thorough search and who knows how far off that location might be. I'm satisfied. Thank you, Mr. Jackson. See Adam and collect your fee. And tell him that I want to give you the bonus you asked for just to recognize your professional effort."

"Thank you, Mr. Spence. Please call me again if you have any diving work in the future."

"Yes, I will," said Spence as he walked the burly diver out of his office.

Spence returned to his desk and picked up a single page report of the surveillance of Mr. Jackson's day on the water. Attached to the report were several photos taken with a telephoto lens. One showed an ecstatic Mr. Jackson holding a dull yellow rectangular object in his hands and kissing it.

CHAPTER 49

NSA Headquarters

Fort Meade, Maryland
November 2024

Everything involving the would-be hero who rescued the president's son was being monitored by an NSA team after Lincoln Brewster had been found. A signals analyst listening to the conversation almost dismissed it until he verified the source of the local call from Durres. It was an invitation to meet at a local watering hole the following evening for drinks and dinner. The party accepted and indicated he would contact another diver named Kustrim to complete the trio. The call details were forwarded up the chain.

The Embassy in Tirana used a local source to surveil the meeting and take pictures of the trio.

Jackson was the last to arrive and joined the other two men who had taken a table in the corner of the dining area and were already enjoying a flagon of beer. He was wearing a large leather man-purse that provoked a few comments from his dinner partners. After drinking half the beer in a long, slow gulp, Jackson opened the bag and showed his future accomplices what he'd brought along. After a closer inspection somehow tested its authenticity, they got down to business.

"I don't know how many are down there but at least several hundred. The recovery plan was hatched over the course of the meal and several rounds of beer. It would begin the following morning. The trio left the restaurant full of expectation and ready to haul in a treasure.

CHAPTER 50

The White House

Washington, DC
November 20, 2024

"Look, my son is back safely. Getting our guys involved in additional operations in Albania seems like we are basing things off the fruits of a poisonous tree if my legal memory is still working," said the president. He didn't make a habit of cutting people off at the knees, but he was firm in his refusal.

Rachel Sullivan and BB Basford exchanged glances, and Sullivan decided to press her point again. She knew that she was on shaky ground but continued.

"Mr. President, the United States has no interest in provoking Albania and its would-be president who was instrumental in your son's return. Nor are we proposing a treasure hunt for Nazi gold. What we do have a vested interest in is the human experiments conducted under the Third Reich. We would like to recover that package to study it if possible or to make sure it falls in no one else's hands."

"Do you think it's worth the risk, Rachel?"

"Yes, I do, Mr. President. Bearding the lion is not one of my usual methods, but the risk is low. We have a solid plan, and this will be the end of our surveillance operations in Albania. We are yards from the finish line and to stop now would be snatching defeat from the jaws of victory." Rachel Sullivan's pushback was direct and compelling. She'd given this last step her best try, and it took days to convince her to take this final meeting. She had to be convinced first.

"OK, Rachel, you've convinced me. In and out, and we close shop in Albania. Agreed?"

"Understood, Mr. President. Thank you."

"As some of you know, I'm headed overseas later this week. I hope everyone has a wonderful Thanksgiving."

CHAPTER 51

Adriatic Sea
November 23, 2024

The operation was a piece of cake. Steele and his diving buddy, Mac Andrews, would be dropped over the submarine's position via helicopter at first light. The topography of Albania kept the dive site in the shadows until mid-morning. There was a remote possibility that someone would see the helicopter or spot the two men dropping from its cargo bay, but there were too many complications involved with transferring between the destroyer and *Newport,* which would stay submerged and be on station within thirty minutes. In the water, visibility was expected to be good, and the German submarine's position was precisely known. If they could get inside the submarine, find the box containing the results of the experiments and rendezvous with the submarine at periscope depth in a total of fifteen minutes, they would avoid any time dangling in the water to rid their bodies of nitrogen and avoid any possibility of decompression sickness, known as the bends. They would dive on the sub, recover Experiment 55 and then be recovered by the submarine operating in support of the presidentially ordered surveillance activities in Albania.

The helicopter lifted off the deck of a Navy destroyer on a dark, overcast night.

"OK, guys," the pilot said through the interior communications system, "our flight time is twenty-four minutes with a time on top of 05:45 a.m. local. The water surface is calm, the current negligible, and the water temperature a refreshing 75 degrees."

Andrews and Steele smiled at each other as they relaxed in the cabin, already suited up and ready to dive. Because of the warm water, both divers were wearing cotton coveralls to protect themselves from the barnacles and other sharp edges that might be found in the metal after reacting with salt water for seventy years.

"So, Mac, how's your new little guy doing?"

"He and Brianna are just fine, and he's growing like a weed. It was great for me to be there for his delivery. Her sister came out to stay with her and the baby during this operation which interrupts my maternity leave, but the personnel folks say I can just start again when I get home."

"Are you kidding — maternity leave for you?"

"Yep. Twelve weeks! This is the new Navy. Remind me to show you the man bun that I'm growing when we get on the sub…that's OK too."

Steele shook his head. "Incredible."

A red dome light illuminated the cabin, the only light on the aircraft. They were five minutes out from the drop site. Steele and Andrews checked each other's gear one final time and stood up.

"I'm starting to like these twin eighties again," Steele said. "Maybe a bit of overkill for this dive, but it was the only thing the destroyer could put together on short notice. Sorry to ruin your Thanksgiving, Mac. You know it was Jill's favorite holiday. Anyway. Ready, Mac?"

"Yeah. Let me read back the plan for possible correction. The plan is simple. We find the sub, ignore the fortune in gold and get the waterproof box with the findings of an eighty-year-old experiment on behavior. How can that still be of interest? Why doesn't the Navy just hire Dr. Phil?"

"Good question," responded Steele.

A crewmember opened the side door, and they looked out into the black night. The only way they could detect a difference between the sky and the water was an occasional florescent flash on the water's surface from a school of fish.

"OK, guys, thirty seconds. Drop zone clear. Over the site in a hover. Fifteen feet."

Both men stepped out of the helicopter and into the blackness together, linking up on the surface.

"Ready?" asked Steele.

"Water feels good. Let's go," replied Andrews.

Disappearing into the inky water guided by the luminescent dials of a GPS receiver, they switched on dive lights at fifty feet. The steep slope reminded Steele of the rugged underwater terrain they'd encountered in Greece. Within two minutes, a different shape began to take shape in the loom of the lights near the target depth. There it was. Eerily quiet, the sub's curved hull filled the beams of their diving lights.

The two swam around to the other side of the sub to see how it was being held against the slope. They found that the steel tube was perched on a rock outcropping, balanced on a narrow area of contact where the midships hull was wedged against a separate striated rock formation which appeared to have been sheared back over the years.

"That looks shaky to me," said Steele through the point-to-point underwater communications system between them.

"Yeah, I agree. A minor underwater tremor or weight shift could probably cause a real problem," said Andrews.

The two divers swam up the outer hull to the conning tower and hatch surrounded by fishing nets that had been cut away.

"After you, Dan." Even at 150 feet, Andrews never lost his sense of humor.

Steele swam down through the hatch and pulled himself along with his hands to avoid creating a dust storm with his fins. Fine silt covered everything inside the hull, though there were places along the deck where the silt had been scraped off with a fin or gloved hand.

Once in the control room, both divers adjusted their buoyancy to be neutral. The floor was covered with ingots. Part of the top layer of gold had been removed on the land side of the deck, exposing several more layers underneath. A short shiny crowbar lay on top of the gold.

Forward of the control room the two found the tiny galley, the size of a mobile hot dog stand to accommodate the crew of fifty. Utilitarian and serviceable. To the side, bolted to the deck was a wooden crate which had obviously been used as an extension of the stove. It was stained from the grease and hot pans leaving black burn rings. Andrews started on the nuts on the steel bar holding the box in place while Steele twisted the flat metal banding straps with his gloved hand. Oxidized to paper thinness, the straps yielded with no force. He passed his glove over the side of the box, revealing stamped black letters on the side and the symbol of the regime — the swastika. They had found Experiment 55. Steele rocked the box forward to assess its heft and reflected about the importance of the likely sodden contents. The two-foot cube would require both divers to wrestle it through the control room and push it through the conning tower hatch. Steele wondered if any of it could be salvaged.

Just as they hoisted the box, a sharp metal-on-metal clang on the outer hull startled the pair. They immediately recognized an unnatural sound. Extinguishing their lights, they listened and tried to peer through the inky black water for signs of what caused it.

Unmistakably man-made, the source of the sound came from another diver. Wearing a head-mounted lamp, he wasted no time unfolding a heavy canvas bag and connecting it to a cable leading up through the conning tower. Digging through the mastic with ease, he filled the bag carrying two ingots at a time. After the strange diver tugged the wire pendant several times, the bag was slowly retrieved and disappeared when it was hoisted up the conning tower shaft. What would the man do until the bag was returned for more gold?

CHAPTER 52

Adriatic Sea
November 23, 2024

Lying on the deck on either side of the galley, Steele and Andrews watched a large-framed diver stack ingots on the deck at the bottom of the conning tower shaft to accelerate the recovery process. Was there more than one diver? Neither man wanted to alert the unexpected diver to their presence by using the underwater communications system built into their masks, but finally Andrews whispered.

"What's the plan?"

Before Steele could respond, there was grinding of the sub's hull against the rocks. The massive diver felt it and quickly pushed off the deck toward the conning tower.

"Dan, what the hell was that?"

Steele did not respond.

"What's the plan? I'm down to forty percent air, and we still need to lug this box to the sub," said Andrews.

"Right, let's grab it and get the hell out of here before our beefy friend gets back. Move," commanded Steele. Even with the adrenal glands supplying additional energy, the crate was surprisingly heavy and awkward.

The unscheduled meeting of the Experiment 55 crate and three divers happened at the bottom of the conning tower ladder. Larry Jackson, the salvage diver, was swimming down the shaft when he reacted violently to an unknown dive light by ramming Steele backward and trying to rip his mask away. Steele countered, twisting his body and using Jackson's momentum until his shoulder crunched against one of the boat's heavy steel ribs. Jackson came back like a wounded animal, clutching a diving knife in one hand. Years of sediment now lifted off every horizontal surface and visibility dropped to nothing. Steele could barely see Jackson's headlamp that cast a pale light source with the power of a Christmas window candle on a snowy night.

Steele said, "Let's get out of here while we still can. Go first, I've got your six."

Andrews felt his way along the deck until reaching the shaft without seeing anything or encountering the other diver. With zero visibility, there was no ability to determine anything except by feel. Andrews was moving up the shaft when he was knocked into the steel ladder by what felt like a large fish. Except this fish carried a large knife with a serrated blade, slashing ahead of him to clear the way. Andrews felt a sharp pinch on his left side as the slasher moved forward, anxious to get to a place with some visibility where he could see and take control of the situation. Larry Jackson wouldn't let anyone stand in the way of the incredible wealth that was within his reach. How did these poachers find the sub? Did one of his partners topside make a deal with someone else?

Without warning, the awful screech of the sub's hull against the rocky incline grew deafening as the U-537 started to slide down the underwater mountain. The sound stopped abruptly a few seconds later.

Steele commanded himself to "orient." He was running low on air, inside an unstable WW II sub at 180 feet with zero visibility facing a massive fighter ready to kill.

"Mac, you ok?"

"Yeah, I think I'm crumpled on the deck in the tower. The big guy just got out. I think he got me with his pigsticker on my left side. The water is so soupy, I can't tell if I'm bleeding or not."

"Abort. Let's get out of here now."

The words were barely out of Steele's mouth when the submarine's hull vibrated once again, and it started sliding down the mountainside. Steele hugged a sturdy round pipe as the slide continued. It felt like the periscope. Heavy equipment was peeling off the bulkheads as rotted straps and once strong metal fixtures failed under stress. As the eighty-year-old steel was tortured by the rocky underwater mountain, the sound inside the metal pipe became unbearable What seemed like minutes later, the slide stopped as the sub found an outcropping to stop its progress. Steele sensed the sub would continue its descent, and his fears were soon realized when the ingots on the control room floor began to lift and slam into the other bulkhead. At least that's what he saw in his mind's eye.

The metal cylinder rolled over the rocks and all hell broke loose. The rollover tested fittings that were not designed to last in salt water for eighty years. There was still no visibility as the sub continued to roll. When would it stop? At 1200 feet? Using his light was impossible because of the sediment in the water. It was like diving in a bowl of Italian salad dressing adulterated with a red rust slurry. The screeching continued, and Steele thought he was going mad. His communications pack was ripped away after it wrapped around his throat like a garrote. Was Mac still alive? Was there a way out? Finally, the sound stopped as the sub plowed into what felt like a sandy bottom and settled. Steele had lost all sense of direction and had no idea of the submarine's position on the slope or the bottom. Their underwater tomb grew quiet.

He didn't know whether the sub was upright, on its side or upside down. The tumble down the mountainside had caused equipment racks to topple over and to fill the interior with sharp detritus. The interior of the sub was a jumbled mess. Steele again commanded himself to "orient" but exactly what that would look like under these conditions was questionable. Cold, dark and deep with no idea how to escape the steel tomb or even conceive of a way to find *Newport*. We are in deep weeds for sure, Steele said to himself.

He heard no sounds of other life aboard the submarine.

CHAPTER 53

Adriatic Sea
November 23, 2024

The underwater drama played out on the surface as well, as the sturdy 3/8-inch cable shackled to the bow mimicked the sub's plunge. At first, the pair in the boat thought they were winching up a very large load of ingots when the bow of the boat momentarily dipped under the surface because of the sub's initial movement. A question flashed through the minds of both men: whether the steel leash would break under the strain or pull the fitting through the hull. Instead, the bow was suddenly pulled under, and the boat upended, dragging the treasure hunter's helpers with it. It was a modern-day Nantucket sleigh ride which happened so quickly that neither man tried to disentangle himself from the boat itself.

Both managed to get free of the diving boat with a few bumps and bruises and surfaced within twenty feet of each other, elated to see that both might live to recount the day's adventure around the bar. Two people sharing the same story would have more credence.

And where was their buddy, Larry Jackson? Rather than pondering the possibilities or even thinking about rescuing their benefactor, they both turned and began paddling toward the safety of the pebbled beach.

CHAPTER 54

Adriatic Sea
November 23, 2024

Steele relaxed his death grip on the periscope and tried to assess the situation. His legs were still supporting him, and he'd somehow avoided serious damage from the debris unleashed by the sub's roll. He needed to find Mac and get out of the submarine before it decided to move on its own again. Visibility was worse now that the sub had taken the bumpy ride down the mountain. Steele was blind and couldn't even see the pressure gauge on his dive console. He had no idea which way was up or down. The only position marker was the periscope he'd clung to during the unplanned plunge into the depths.

Then he heard a slow metallic scraping which sounded close and tapped twice on the periscope with his scuba tank. A two-tap reply came back. Mac Andrews was still alive. Steele slowly pulled his body along on his fingertips, first finding the heavy plotting table in the control room. He tapped again trying to get a bearing on Mac's position. He heard the two-tap response which seemed to be coming from his right side. He turned as close to ninety degrees as he could and continued in the direction of the sound.

Steele felt the flexible curve of a diver's fin first and followed it up to a body which he shook with excitement. Both were alive. Now all that was left was to find a way out of the sub. Without communications, including hand signals which could not be seen, Steele grabbed Mac's hand and they picked their way through the sub. Steele saw a shaft of light pierce the turbid darkness of the water and swam toward it. Miraculously, U-537 appeared to have stopped in an almost upright position, and the conning tower hatch was the most likely source of the light. Steele closed his fist on some of the loose fabric at the neck of Andrews' coveralls and swam up into the conning tower.

What blocked his escape was the macerated face of someone who had been strapped to the outer hull of the submarine as it rolled and slid down the mountain. Miraculously, his dive light survived the ordeal intact and was shining brightly. That was the source of the light. What was left of the big man's face was a shock of white hair matted to the crushed temple held in place with a piece of nylon line. Steele pushed the body away from the hatch and found it covered with several layers of netting and line, tightly bound to the sub's hull. The nylon had been stretched and cut through the body until it reached the thick bones of the legs and torso. The man's ribcage was scraped clean from the sawing action of the lines.

Still pitch black, the visibility improved to several feet while Steele followed his bubbles and headed toward the surface. The glass face of his pressure gage was broken and unreadable except for the thin black needle in the red. With no idea of his depth or location, Steele swam upwards, hoping that his next breath wouldn't be his last. He knew that Mac was breathing but had no idea of his physical condition. Even though he had the nickname "Gills" when he was an active-duty SEAL, there was a limit to the myth that Steele could stay under water forever.

He felt the grip on his coveralls loosen, as Mac was going the wrong way in the water column. Steele again grabbed him by the collar and kept moving toward the surface. His buoyancy compensator was ripped and useless in speeding the trip up. Maybe Mac's was in better shape. A momentary thought but one quickly dismissed because it might risk the precious time and the next sip of air that he drew into his lungs from the exhausted tanks might be his last. At some point, the tanks themselves would provide some level of additional lift, but at this depth, it didn't matter.

CHAPTER 55

Adriatic Sea
November 23, 2024

On *Newport*, Sydney Garrison stood over the SONAR supervisor. They had arrived at the rendezvous location minutes before and were trying to establish communications with the divers.

"What's going on, petty officer Jensen?" she asked.

"I don't know, captain, but it sounded as if the sub plowed down the cliff all the way to the bottom. I've got no comms with the divers. I can't hear anything now."

"OK, stay on it." Garrison turned to the plotting table where the ship's position appeared as a tiny illumination on an electronic nautical chart. The depth of water at the bottom of the cliff was 1,200 feet. *Newport* was blind. How would she search the area and be able to recover the two men safely?

She turned to the watch officer and barked, "Sound General Quarters." An electronic bell pulsed every second and in three minutes, the submarine was ready to fight. Only this time Garrison had taken the action to get everyone throughout the ship to listen for any sign of life outside the hull.

"Get LEO ready to launch. I want a slow descent, after I speak to the crew. Maintain our current aspect." she said.

"Yes, ma'am," responded the watch officer. Garrison picked up the 1MC to broadcast a message to the battle-ready crew.

"Good morning, *Newport*, this is the captain speaking. As you know, our current surveillance mission was modified to include picking up two SEALs trying to recover some documentation on a World War

II German U-Boat that was found on a steep cliff near our current position. The planned rendezvous has not happened. We have lost comms with the divers. Petty Officer Jensen believes he heard the submarine tumble down the cliff. We don't know in which direction or how deep, but we will make every attempt to find them. We are launching our autonomous searcher, LEO, to help us find the sub and rescue our shipmates. Please help them by listening and reporting anything that could be a man-made sound. And if you are of a mind to do so, pray for these brave men. That is all."

She walked to the plotting table and engaged *Newport's* Operations officer.

"What do you think?"

"I think this is a real long shot. We are restricted to a diving depth of 600 feet and, if that sub is on the bottom, that's 1200 feet. We've got no comms and don't even know if the SEALs are inside or not. Our little friend LEO is our best chance." LEO was the ship's nickname for the cooler-size autonomous underwater drone that the boats carried and relied on for hull inspections when underway or for searching for lost objects such as World War II submarines full of gold. The device could follow a pre-programmed search like a robotic vacuum cleaner or be steered by the operator. Its battery-powered propulsion system had a ninety-minute life and could relay real-time images with an adjustable lens pack.

"Agree. It's a dicey situation and I don't think there are any procedures written for it. I'm not too worried about the valves, but I know the Chief Engineer will protest if we exceed the diving depth that's been ordered." She studied the chart and knitted her brow, rubbing her temples with her palms. The Operations Officer knew she was thinking hard.

"Take us down to 800' slowly and maintain an even keel," she ordered the watch officer.

Within a minute, the Chief Engineer appeared in the control room and joined the captain and operations officer at the plotting table.

"Just a reminder, captain, but we are depth restricted by SUBLANT directive. My recommendation is conservative — do not dive greater than 400 feet to give us some margin. We've got four valves on the watch list, and I urge that we don't test them. The result, as you know, could be catastrophic, and will endanger the crew." He paused and caught his breath. When Garrison did not respond, he nudged her with the word "over" as if it were part of his previous statement.

Though she anticipated the visit from her chief engineer and was prepared for his little reminder, Garrison's default reaction was to respond to him in a sarcastic, dismissive manner. She caught herself. Lieutenant Commander Michael Walsh was a professional nuclear engineer and an extremely competent officer. The problem was that he saw things as either black or white. Gray didn't exist for him. Everything was cut and dried according to science and directive. There was nothing that science couldn't explain. She recalled hearing about another such officer that was the scourge of the surface warfare community for years being characterized as a "humorless turd." That's how she viewed Walsh on a personal level. He was just perfect for the responsibility as *Newport's* chief engineer.

"Mike, I appreciate your bringing the restriction to my attention. Should it be necessary to exceed the depth restriction to save the two SEALs we are to bring home, I'll do it." She said it as simply and evenly as she could though the flash of anger she felt had not subsided.

She turned and walked to the LEO monitor to check its field of view and visible range. The operator estimated that LEO's cameras could see about thirty feet. The monitor was searching as it was descending and had a remaining run-time of sixty-five minutes.

The operator called out to the watch officer that LEO just passed by a steady stream of bubbles. The Watch Officer looked at the monitor and spoke before Garrison could. "Follow the bubbles. Straight down. Max speed." Garrison smiled. That's exactly the order on the tip of her tongue when the watch officer stepped in.

The submarine hovered at 600 feet while LEO continued a straight down descent, passing 900 feet. The bubbles seemed steady, and LEO operated with that dogged determination that we expect from our machines. The controller stopped the robot suddenly as two figures filled the screen. One figure appeared lifeless, and the other was struggling to move vertically.

Garrison ordered "Zoom", and the LEO operator provided a closer look at the face looking up. It was Dan Steele. Match LEO's depth and prepare the recovery hatch. Tell the Engineer…"

"I'm right here, captain. Belay that last order." Garrison turned and saw that the engineer brought reinforcements, accompanied by the Executive Officer and the Chief Master at Arms.

Garrison stood in front of the trio as she repeated her command to the watch officer. Then she turned and said in a commanding voice.

"This is USS Newport, not the USS Caine. I'm Captain Garrison, not Captain Queeg. I'm going to take this boat where it needs to be. I will meet with each of you individually sometime later today. Commander Walsh, I want a watch stander on each of the valves. Now, gentlemen, when I turn around, I don't expect to see any of you here. Understood?" Each of the three nodded their heads in silence.

She stared at each one of the men directly in their eyes.

"Now, stand down!"

The control room was so quiet that a deaf man could have heard a pin drop on the gray vinyl diamond tread deck. The captain stood over the LEO operator's shoulder.

"Maneuver LEO to keep eyes on the two. What's LEO's current depth?"

"1050 feet," said the operator.

Garrison could see that Newport's current depth was 900'. Another 150 feet to reach the divers. She directed the watch officer to continue the descent. She would twist the submarine's hull to put them near the hatch where they could be locked in and have a fresh air supply. There was no time left, the one diver still moving was likely out of air and would soon drown. She picked up the underwater comms hand mike.

"This is *Newport*. Do you copy?"

She heard two clinks on the receiver and relayed the plan. At least one diver heard the transmission and was still alert enough to respond. A glimmer of hope circulated inside her head, and she tried to anticipate what to do next.

As *Newport* reached a depth of 1,000 feet, a report came over the interior communications system that the packing in one of the skin valves had ruptured and was spraying water past the valve body into the propulsion compartment. The crew had shielded the valve so that the water was diverted to the hull where it ran into the bilge. No equipment had been damaged. Garrison did a quick estimate of the pressure on *Newport's* hull, over 400 pounds per square inch. She momentarily questioned whether she was being foolhardy or whether she was blinded by the fact that there were two people still in the water with a slim chance of survival, one of whom she wanted to love. If the operation went sideways, and she damaged equipment or injured personnel on the boat she'd be facing a formal board of inquiry and would have to have the strength of her convictions. She was teetering on the edge of continuing the mission or pulling the plug. Getting the pair aboard would be no easy task, and she wondered if the hatch would even open at this depth.

A second valve failed when the packing gland exploded from the valve body, and the heavy valve wheel struck a young engineer in the face, crushing the bones of his face and fracturing his skull. The ribs of the handwheel were buried in the man's skull. The first casualty of the operation? The water flowed into the boat at full force, enough to cut a sailor in half. The crew fought to re-direct the piercing stream and protect equipment. Tight quarters, fighting a knife-edged sword of water capable of slicing flesh and bone in a flash.

Momentarily paralyzed with the news of the second valve failure and likely death of one of her crew, Sydney Garrison steadied herself on the plotting table, drawing in a deep breath to calm her jangled nerves. She only needed a few seconds to focus on the situation at hand which included imperiling the ship and its crew.

She picked up the communications handset.

"This is *Newport.* Hold on to LEO. He'll bring you both to the boat."

The response was two rapid clanks.

Two figures disappeared as they approached the underwater vehicle, but the two sharp metallic raps confirmed that the SEALs were in position.

"Winch in LEO," ordered the captain. "Let's bring the SEALs home."

"Officer of the Deck. Start a slow ascent to five hundred feet. Have the chief engineer call me on ICS."

"Captain, Walsh here. I'm down in the auxiliary machinery room #2. We've got the flooding under control. Petty Officer Jacobson has been transported down to Medical. The other valves seem to be holding."

"Good," said Garrison, "We've started a slow ascent and will not pressure test them further. How badly was Jacobson injured?"

"Not sure, captain, but when I saw him, it looked pretty grim."

"OK, thanks. Please keep me posted."

"Captain, we are at 600 feet and LEO's ninety feet from the boat. We have a team standing by the escape hatch ready to receive the SEALs."

CHAPTER 56

Adriatic Sea
November 23, 2024

Steele spotted the underwater vehicle and surmised that *Newport* must be positioning to pick them up. Andrews was barely conscious and unable to breathe on his own. Steele felt the cylindrical shape before he saw it. He followed the smooth exterior hull of the sub. He thought he was aft on the sub's hull, because of the few hull penetrations in the ship's stern. He pulled McAndrew along the hull and slammed his nearly empty tank against the hull.

Almost immediately it stopped, and he reached the lockout hatch where he might be rescued after using another of his nine lives. Mac Andrews' eyes were wide-open and looking through his mask with a thousand-yard stare. He showed no signs of recognition. Steele felt the lockout hatch shudder and the whining of hydraulics inside the hull. His mind raced to a variety of unrelated subjects. He recalled the book, *The Last Dive,* which traced the underwater experiences of several deep-water wreck divers. One particularly chilling chapter addressed the bends or decompression sickness and some of its long-term effects, assuming that someone might survive the incident. Steele tried to ignore the little voice in his head citing the worst-case effects of the condition and the permanent injuries that a diver might sustain.

"What do you mean, it can't be opened?" shouted the captain on the interior communications handset.

"The hatch must be jammed because of the pressure. Can you raise the boat a couple hundred feet, and we'll try again."

The watch officer started the ascent by giving a series of commands and everyone watched the depth gage in the control room as it gradually moved upward in the black water.

"OK, we are at 500 feet and still rising. Try to open the hatch again."

Steele heard the hydraulics and felt the hull shudder as the heavy hatch was pushed open. Andrews was dead weight, and Steele took his last breath from the tank. He too was out of air. Grabbing Andrews regulator, he manually pushed air into the man's lungs and then took the regulator from his mouth and took a deep breath, just as the hatch opened forward. He swam into the chamber, dragging his dive buddy with him. The hatch closed behind them, but the water level remained. Steele was still buddy-breathing with Andrews. Did someone forget to activate the pumps? To ride a submarine down to the bottom and then get rescued by a sub at 1,000 feet was a miracle. To drown in the sub's lockout chamber was just impossible. Or was it? Steele peered out the viewing port and saw an animated group of sailors and a Chief Petty Officer talking on the interior communications phone.

"No, captain, the pressure is not equalized, and the pumps just can't pump air against the water at that pressure. It's just too high."

"Chief," said the captain, "Rig a firehose to the air test valve on the left corner of the hatch and run it down below to the bilge. Equalize the pressure and then open the hatch manually."

"What about all the water," asked the Chief.

"Don't worry about a couple hundred gallons of salt water. Just equalize and get those men into some fresh air. Now!"

The sub was still ascending as the water level dropped as it was drained. In less than a minute, the pressure was equalized, and the interior hatch was opened with a rush of cold seawater soaking the crew.

"Let's get them out of there" yelled the Chief. "Move!"

Still ascending, the compartment was blown dry, and the inner hatch was opened. Fresh air flooded the chamber.

The blare of the 1MC startled Steele. "Flooding, flooding. Flooding in the auxiliary compartment. Flooding boundaries are set at…" On the living side of the interior hatch, Steele spotted the ship's doctor and a corpsman who dragged Mac Andrews out of the compartment and began to check his vitals in the pool of seawater covering the deck. Steele sat on the grated floor of the compartment unable to move. Mac Andrews was pulled to one side, but Steele didn't think he could crawl out of the compartment on his own. The doctor stuck his head in the compartment and asked if Steele had the ability to continue on his own.

"Yeah, Doc. Just give me another two minutes to catch my breath." He removed his mask, slid out of the tank harness and unbuckled the weight belt and then crawled on all fours out of the hatch, collapsing on the deck. When he opened his eyes, Steele wasn't sure whether he was alive or dead. The view was hazy as if he were wearing a mask that was completely fogged up. His arms and legs felt like he was strapped down. Finally able to focus, Steele saw the bright light of a pencil-sized beam from a penlight and the blue coveralls holding a thin device which magically shined the light against his heavy eyelids. Behind the doctor was the facial outline of someone he recognized. It was Sydney Garrison. Feeling dizzy, Steele's head began to swirl, and he violently heaved, emptying his stomach onto the grated floor and looked up with a frothy ooze stringing from his mouth. Steele collapsed in his own vomit as he lost consciousness.

After ordering both men to sick bay where they would be administered pure oxygen, the ship's doctor took Garrison aside in the small space filled with men dealing with the flooding and transporting the pair to sick bay.

"Captain, we can provide oxygen as first aid, but both these men need a recompression chamber ASAP. They are super-saturated, and their conditions are off the U.S. Navy charts. The nearest Navy chamber facilities are in Naples. I can't predict the outcome but would assess survival at no more than fifty per cent. The barotrauma they've experienced can lead to all sorts of bad things."

"Thanks, Doc. I'll huddle with OPS and see what we can do. How's Jacobson?"

"He's stable but needs surgery. His skull is fractured, and the pressure inside his skull is causing severe swelling. He needs a scan to guide a team of surgeons able to open his head."

"Got it. Do whatever we can for the patients until we arrange a medical evacuation for all three."

Thirty seconds later, the captain entered the control room and found the operations officer at the plotting table.

"OPS, we've got three men who need an immediate medevac."

"Yes, captain. I recommend a front burner voice report to the Pentagon and an immediate message to the Sixth Fleet watch center. My initial thought is to get near Taranto for a boat and then helicopter transfer to Naples. We are headed that way at flank speed and should be able to surface in less than thirty minutes. The base has a squadron of Italian submarines so our surveillance mission might not be revealed."

"Sounds like a plan. Wake up the Pentagon and get the locals ready to receive our patients."

"On it, captain."

Newport's Control Room took on a somber atmosphere. Everyone knew that the prospects for the young engineer and two SEALs were grim. Glassy eyes all around the seasoned crew. They were tough professionals, but a life-threatening situation involving a shipmate shook them up.

CHAPTER 57

Naples, Italy
November 26, 2024

Once ashore, Steele spent eighteen hours in a hyperbaric chamber. Recovery of any sort was questionable during the first hours. A nurse and doctor took him down to the pressure at depth and then slowly returned to the single atmosphere of pressure that we all comfortably live in. Since their excursion with the submarine put them off the decompression charts, the nurse in charge extrapolated the numbers on the conservative side. The compressed air that Steele and Andrews were breathing at extreme depth caused the nitrogen to enter tissues and the blood stream. Returning to a pressurized depth might allow the nitrogen absorbed to be safely released and prevent the death-causing effects of nitrogen boiling off into the blood stream. In addition to carefully controlled time at depth, a bent diver needs a great deal of luck to escape the long-term effects of decompression sickness or DCS. Loss of life, paralysis, balance and disorientation were common outcomes, some temporary and others permanent. Though Steele understood the science behind the recompression and the dangers of DCS, he was anxious to leave the thick metal tube. No one mentioned his diving partner or the young petty officer with a severe blunt force trauma.

The nurse took more blood samples and had a corpsman take multiple X-rays of Steele's lungs, heart, and joints. Finally, he was released to the intensive care unit for another twenty-four hours of observation. The decision on whether he would need another stint in the chamber would be determined in the following twelve hours. No one could really predict how his body might react to the controlled release of so much nitrogen.

Released to a ward, Steele was restricted to the tiny support activity property and prohibited from flying for seventy-two hours. The other patients were mostly Navy sailors and Marines from various commands operating in the Med, sent for specialized medical care beyond the ship's capacity. Steele found petty officer Jacobson. His head was swathed with white gauze bandages, and his body was connected to a wall-mounted monitoring station. He was sleeping or highly medicated after multiple surgeries by specialists. All his vital signs were normal, but what about his senses — Steele would try to get a fix on his condition and prognosis from the staff. He walked around the ward and found the nurses' station.

"Excuse me. I'm looking for another patient brought in for decompression. Navy guy named, Mac Andrews."

"I'm sorry Mr. ..."

"Steele, Dan Steele."

"Yes, Mr. Steele, let me see what I can find out."

Steele found the patient lounge with a telephone and dialed Admiral Wright. The clock on the wall indicated 2:30 p.m. After being patched through by the Pentagon operator, Wright answered on the first ring.

"Good morning, admiral, it's Dan. I wanted to check in. Our dive to salvage the material turned out to be a nightmare. I just came out of the decompression chamber a few minutes ago and thought I'd let you know."

"Thanks. I've gotten some reports along the way. How are you feeling?"

"Right now, I'm not sure. Time will tell. I probably couldn't pass a field sobriety test right now because all the straight lines in the world look curved. I may have to go back in the tube for another session. Most of my hearing is back, but my joints seem to be begging for additional lubrication. The doctor told me that I had some hallucinations in the chamber. Getting bent is not good for your health. I'm grounded and restricted to the base."

"Understood. You need to follow the doctor's orders. Period. This is very serious stuff, Dan. You are lucky to be alive. How's Andrews doing?"

"I don't know yet. I know he needs surgery, but I don't know whether that was done before or after his session in the chamber. The people I've talked to either don't know or have been told to keep it close. As far as I know, I got rid of all the nitrogen in my system and don't have any lingering or permanent damage. Mac's situation may be different."

"I understand," replied the admiral. "We have a few balls in the air, but nothing I can tell you about. Your orders are to continue your recovery, get discharged and report back in one coherent piece."

"OK, admiral. I've got it. I'll keep you posted."

Steele returned to the nurses' station and surprised the nurse he'd spoken to minutes before. She saw him and quickly gathered an armload of charts and headed the other way. An uneasy feeling crept into Steele's body. Was it the after effect of being returned to depth in the chamber or was it because he thought something serious may have happened to Andrews? He spotted the nurse returning to the station.

"Hi. I was the one asking about my diving friend, Mac Andrews. Can you tell me where I can find him?"

"I'm sorry, Mr. Steele."

"Sorry? What do you mean?"

"I asked the doctor to come out and talk with you," replied the nurse who turned her back on Steele and settled into a chair in front of a computer monitor.

A rail thin physician wearing a white coat over an open button-down collar approached Steele.

"I'm Dr. Jamerson," shaking Steele's hand. "Let's go to the family conference room where we can talk privately."

Dr. Jamerson sat across from Steele, his hands folded in front of him. His face was expressionless. His waxy skin seemed to be stretched over his face revealing the details of its bony structure. Lips compressed into a thin line. The perfect hospital representative to talk to families about their unfortunate loss.

"Mr. Andrews' case was complicated because of the knife wound in his left side. He had some organ damage and a small tear in his left lung. We rendered first aid before he entered the hyperbaric chamber with me and one of our barotrauma nurses. His twenty-hour recompression was uneventful. After an hour at 250 feet, his hearing returned, which was a positive sign. The staples closing the wound in his left side were effective. Vitals normal. Yet the initial blood draw was frothy and full of nitrogen bubbles..."

Steele listened to the doctor's voice that sounded like a pre-recorded description of someone already dead.

"Doctor, excuse me. I appreciate the detailed blow-by-blow, but can you just give me his current condition and prognosis? Can I see him?"

"Yes. I talked to his wife, Mrs. Andrews, a few minutes ago. She seemed such a pleasant woman, very patient. She told me about their new baby who is growing like a weed." The doctor ended with a suppressed laugh as if he'd never heard the expression, his waxen skin stretching over his bony face.

"Excuse me Mr. Steele. I didn't want to be inconsiderate. Mrs. Andrews gave me permission to discuss Mac's situation with you."

"Thanks. So, what is his situation?" asked an impatient Steele.

"His situation is still critical. He's still in the Intensive Care Unit, breathing oxygen while we determine if he should be recompressed again. Paralyzed from the waist down. I don't think he will recover the use of his limbs, but some of my colleagues differ with that opinion. Neurologically, he has had some loss of brain function, particularly in his speech center. We call it aphasia. I am not optimistic about reversal of any of his current problems, but we've seen other patients recover all their functions over time."

"May I see him?"

"Not while he's in the ICU."

The doctor stood and turned. Steele watched the flaps of his starched white coat and the spindly legs moving awkwardly as he opened the door and left.

Shocked by the news, Steele remained at the table trying to corral a million thoughts of his friend and fellow warrior, wondering about the human cost versus the benefits of their failed effort to recover Experiment 55.

Though not a religious man, Steele believed that humans were too complex to have evolved without some intervention, and there had to be a higher being involved from the beginning. He was not much for prayer but folded his hands and pleaded for a full recovery of his dive partner.

After three more days of blood tests, physical and neurological exams, and one additional six-hour recompression, Steele was finally ready to be discharged. On his final day, he saw Mac Andrews in the cafeteria. In a wheelchair, Andrews sat at a table without any chairs. Steele quickly joined his friend.

"Heh, Mac. How are you doing?"

His dive buddy stared at Steele and appeared not to recognize him at first. Then he gave a halting response.

"Dan. Good… to see you. I thought… you'd …be back in DC. Already pushing… papers."

"No, not yet. Today's my discharge day. When do you expect to be released?"

"They won't say. Started therapy...On my legs…can't feel them. Can you…understand me?"

"Sure, you are just talking a little slower than normal. What's the prognosis on your legs?"

"Getting…better. But takes time. Brianna is flying. Here. The doctor told me… I shouldn't …ever, dive. Again."

Tears wetted Steele's eyes as he pushed a plastic tray down the cafeteria's breakfast line. His last breakfast in the facility. When he returned to the table, Andrews was gone. Feeling a sudden queasiness in his stomach, he picked his way through the tables, dumping the untouched food into a trash receptacle. Steele knew that his friend would never be the same.

CHAPTER 58

November 30, 2024

Steele felt numb during his trip back to the States. He wasn't sure whether it was the reaction of his own body being tortured by the depths in ways few live to even talk about or whether it was leaving Mac Andrews, his friend and dive partner in a busy, cold clinic in Naples. Sure, Andrews' wife was flying over and that would be comforting. But the uncertainty of his friend's medical outcome weighed heavily on Steele's mind, and he just couldn't shake it. In a way, he felt like he was abandoning his buddy on the ocean floor and returning to the surface alone for some sweet salt air, out of danger, safe and sound.

He played the likely scenarios in his mind, as he drifted between consciousness and sleep. Andrews would be evaluated by a disability board and would likely be retired from the U.S. Navy for medical reasons. Those events would occur almost immediately. He would soon be lost in the shuffle of men and women who join the ranks of the disabled. Care and caring decay rapidly. Those veterans are soon forgotten and left on their own. Capable but not capable enough. Discarded and kicked to the curb for someone else to pick up. The sad reality hung over Steele like a heavy black drape.

Steele wasn't immersed in guilt, but just felt that he didn't deserve any better than Andrews did. Same mission, same risk, same shared experience but different medical outcomes. Fate? Bad luck? Steele's usual unsinkable attitude changed to a lingering sadness about a man who he called brother. He vowed to find a therapist who could bring Andrews back to a full life with full mobility, even if he was never able to dive again.

Sleeping through the flight, Steele was surprised when the attendant told him the aircraft was on the final approach to Dulles International Airport. He found his bag, mechanically completed customs and immigration in a stupor, and took a cab to Southeast Washington without remembering anything. In addition to severe barotrauma, Steele succumbed to a confused consciousness. He fell onto his living room couch fully clothed, not having any idea of where he was or why he was there.

CHAPTER 59

White House Situation Room

Washington, DC
December 10, 2024

The president monitored the two groups assembled to overwatch the transit of the nuclear material. Neither group had met since his earlier meeting when he outlined the task and expressed his sense of urgency. Even as president, working in Washington felt like he was trying to steer a fully burdened super cargo ship using a rudder the size of a postage stamp. Maddening. He called a short meeting of his team to set things in motion. They joined him in the Oval Office.

In addition to the president, the group included his National Security Adviser, Rachel Sullivan, her assistant for military affairs, a designee from the State Department, "BB" Basford, Admiral Wright from Pisces along with Dan Steele and Cass Thomas, and the team's new Intelligence Command liaison, Trevor Mixon.

The president stated his goal of preventing the Iranians from taking delivery of the nuclear material they'd won in the worldwide auction. The transfer by sea would be visible to the entire world, and IAEA personnel would accompany the material during its transit to Bandar Abbas.

"I don't know how to stop the transfer. We don't want to cause a release of the material or exposure to anyone along the route. Minimize loss of life and collateral damage. I do not want to be remembered as the president who started World War III with the Russians. We've been on the brink long enough in Ukraine. So that's your mission impossible. I propose that we all go to Camp David next weekend to see if we can come up with some ideas, when we are away from the usual distractions here in DC and where I know no one is listening. It still amazes me that so much sensitive information gets released to the press, sometimes before it even gets to me.

I arranged for all of you to stay there. We'll have a secure meeting room. If there are others you want to join us, please let me know. I want to keep the group small. Otherwise, I'm confident that this team can come up with all the potential alternatives. The Israelis are understandably upset, and the Prime Minister is ready to attack the convoy unless we guarantee the shipment will not be completed. I can hold them off if we've got a plan, but they are the country at risk here. And they have their hands full with Hamas."

"What about the Russians and Chinese, Mr. President?" asked Steele.

"Yes, you're right Dan. This is a complex problem with unpredictable actors. Along with any options we come up with, each must have some sort of cost-benefit analysis, especially if I must sell the idea to get support for it. Maybe I'm being disingenuous thinking I might be able to execute the plan just on my Executive authority. If this is just wishful thinking, I'm prepared to swallow the mess and put on my game face. I've got a call into President Spence to discuss any alternatives to the auction that the government of Albania just conducted."

CHAPTER 60

Camp David, Maryland
December 14, 2024

The meeting room was swept by security prior to the meeting's start. The group met in the Rough Riders building, which had been outfitted with white boards, large screen displays, and communications terminals if needed. They had been working for several hours when the president arrived at 0900.

OK, where are we?" the president asked his National Security Advisor, wearing a cable-knit sweater. Overnight, the temperatures had dipped, and Washington might get a dusting of snow according to the forecast.

"Well, Mr. President, given the constraints you outlined previously, we've ruled out any overt military action and are looking at the Red Sea for a possible intercept point. The Iranian ship will be escorted by the Royal Saudi Naval Forces and the Egyptian Navy at that point, and we are familiar with those navies and the area. We'll likely need a covert force but still haven't figured out how to neutralize the ship without our fingerprints all over it. Too many eyes and ears in the area, and we're told that several news agencies have filed flight plans to cover the transit through the Red Sea. Night operations will put everyone at risk but how to grab the goods without anyone knowing is a tough nut to crack. We're still working through options."

The president removed his jacket and grabbed a bottle of water off the table.

"OK, I'm rolling up my sleeves and am prepared to do whatever I can to help the team, including the brainstorming part of this. Let's face it, I've given you an impossible task, so let's try to tackle it together. We are trying to solve a problem, so let's drop the protocol and the hierarchy and see what we can do. I picked this team myself, so I'm certainly 100% invested in the outcome. The Red Sea makes sense to me. Please continue."

"We were talking about diversions or using something to incapacitate the crews for the time it would take to off-load the casks and make a clean get away," said Admiral Wright. "I don't know if we have anything that will give us that luxury. How could it be delivered? How will it affect the crew? How do we put this convoy in a bubble, administer some sort of chemical agent to make the people forget who they are, prevent collisions or other natural catastrophes, to open a window to seize the casks. That's where we're stuck."

"Maybe sink the ship and have a submarine recover the casks?" the president asked.

"The loaded casks will weigh in at about 150 tons each. I'm not sure that a submarine can move that kind of weight," said Admiral Wright.

"How do you sink a ship without loss of life?" added the National Security Advisor.

"We just can't make a ship disappear in broad daylight," said Admiral Wright.

"Do it at night. When no one is watching?"

"I think we need to assume that the package will be under constant surveillance."

The day turned into night, and the president ordered dinner. White boards were covered with alternatives and options that needed more study, but no one in the room thought they were any closer to solving the problem given all the constraints the president had imposed. Mentally exhausted, they needed some rest.

"Thanks, everybody. Can we start in the morning after breakfast at 0830?"

Everyone nodded agreement.

"I've got a box of fresh Cuban cigars and plan to enjoy one on the front porch of my house if anyone wants to join me."

Steele returned to his cabin and changed into his sweats and laced on a pair of running shoes. Warming up with a set of six-count burpees, he began to sweat, ready for a run. The nature trail on the east side of the compound would give him a way to shake off the stress of the day. He started to run north. The December air cutting his lungs was fresh and clean. What a day he thought to himself. It reminded him of similar sessions where a special ops team would work for hours trying to develop a workable plan. There were similar constraints in those planning sessions too. He soon felt the sweat running down his back and legs. It felt good to stretch those large muscles after spending most of the day sitting. Twigs and pinecones crackled underfoot, and Steele's pace quickened as he looked up at the clear winter sky.

The route took him back around the Aspen cabin where the president and Admiral Wright were sitting in Adirondack chairs, warm under beaver throws, overlooking the fairway and enjoying a cigar. He cut through the three-hole golf course and was running through the parking lot when he spotted the smokers behind the cabin. Whether it was just smoke or smoke plus the vapor from the cold air, the great plumes immediately connected to the task.

Steele recalled a time when he was in the Red Sea on a US Navy destroyer. The crew had used the calm transit to restore the battered topside paint after a tense deployment in the Persian Gulf as they began the transit home. A dust storm on the horizon swept across the desert in Egypt and seemed to be heading to the spot where the ship intended to anchor. One minute it was a beautiful, sunny day. The next, when the dust storm enveloped the ship, blotting out the sun, the fine red dust particles found not only the fresh paint but every crevice on the ship. Visibility dropped to just twenty feet, and the ship could do nothing except anchor and wait out the storm. Radar performance was poor. The ship was just able to drop the hook before visibility dropped to zero in a blinding wind that would scour exposed skin like a sandblaster.

CHAPTER 61

Camp David, Maryland
December 15, 2024

Day 2 of the president's strategy off-site at Camp David started long before breakfast for most of the participants. Steele had a potential solution for getting the ships in a bubble and covering the activity with a man-made dust cloud, but removing the casks from an escorted, armed warship carrying a twenty-man squad of Iranian Republican Guard Corps still fell into the impossible column. Fueled with black coffee, Steele was anxious to see the other ideas that had percolated overnight.

Trevor Mixon had printed the ship profiles and mounted them onto foam board just to spawn ideas from the group. He had had a restless night too. Others brought ideas to the table that hadn't been raised the previous day.

The president arrived at 0830 ready to work. His face looked puffy, and the circles under his eyes confirmed that he did not enjoy a peaceful sleep. He sat down at the head of the table with a mug of steaming coffee.

"Again, thank you all for being here and trying to tackle this mission. I hope your creative juices were flowing last night. Let the brainstorming begin!"

Sullivan began.

"After supper, BB and I sampled some of the scotch in your liquor cabinet and came up with the idea of closing canal operations during the ship transit with its escorts to give us some separation between the high value targets and everything else."

"Interesting concept. I'm sure that something like that could be orchestrated." Mixson captured the idea on a white board labeled planning factors.

Dan Steele stood and invited everyone to watch the large screen monitor next to Mixon's white board.

"I found this clip taken of a dust storm here in the Red Sea. Bear in mind that I've speeded up the video, so you are seeing this unfold at a five times normal speed."

"How could we time the transit to coincide with a local dust storm?"

"My thoughts were that we could create the dust storm by either controlling the weather or by positioning large fans in the desert to create it when and where it's needed. I don't know if it's feasible or has ever been tried, but it would give us coverage to grab the casks. A dust storm would enable a team to operate just as if it were night and keep the press from knowing what might be happening at sea level."

"Could the crew be put to sleep with something in the air or food or water?

Sandy Matthews sat at the table. "Last night I dreamed about Moby Dick." The comment brought the table to tears while laughing. Sandy realized his faux pas and didn't miss a beat when the team settled down.

"My dream was focused on size…" Again, laughter rang out in the room and several of the participants pounded the table unable to shake it. Even the president just couldn't stop laughing. When he looked around the table and saw someone laughing hard, it began another spasm.

When the room quieted once again, Sandy said, "Let me try to explain this a different way. We all know the bible story about Jonah and the whale. As you all know, Jonah was swallowed. The man had been saved by God and lived in the fish's belly for three days before being returned to the land where God initially sent him to preach. I know you are asking yourselves where this is headed. Trevor has the scaled profiles of all the ships either transporting or escorting. I also had him produce the profile of a large container ship." He picked up an Iranian frigate silhouette and placed it on the hull of the cargo ship.

"A cargo ship fitted with doors on its bow just like our old Landing Ship, Tanks could swallow a ship the size of a Sahand class frigate which we assume they'll send. If the ship was ingested during a dust storm by a ship transiting the opposite direction in the Red Sea, the ship would just disappear with the casks aboard. No witnesses."

"What about the crew, how do we deal with them?" asked Basford. "I don't think that capturing them follows the president's guidance.

Steele stood, saying "what if...what if we were able to get the crew off the ship under the guise of the casks leaking radiation or the ship sinking?"

"Maybe they could make a port visit in Jeddah, and we could steal the ship!" injected Admiral Owens sarcastically.

"The Iranian Republican Guard Corps wouldn't leave the ship, and no commanding officer would risk his ship that way," countered Steele.

"What would happen if the ship were sinking because of navigation hazard, either natural or caused? What would cause the CO to order the ship to be abandoned immediately in the middle of a dust storm?" posed Cass to the group.

"Cass, I think you are on to something," said the president rising from his seat. "It's in the middle of a dust storm that reduces visibility to zero. Maybe a ship collision or mine or torpedo would cause the ship to sink rapidly but with enough time for the entire crew to get off safely, picked off the ship or out of the water by the escorts, before our cargo ship arrives with its large mouth open, swallowing the ship and the casks and continuing course."

The president leaned back in his chair and exclaimed, "Are there other comments or ideas? This Jonah plan just might work. I cannot wrap my brain around the timing and logistics and don't know where we'd find a ship or how or if it could be modified, but I like the concept. The devil's in the details, folks. Can we try to put another level of detail on this plan and start running the traps on its feasibility?"

Everyone nodded their agreement. The president looked around the table.

"We need a point man on this to at least get us through the feasibility phase. Jim, do you think you can coordinate this?"

Admiral Wright studied the president's face.

"Sure, Mr. President, I'll be your Mr. Phelps."

"Thanks, Jim. Let me know when you want to bring this team back for a meeting. I'm confident we'll have a solution."

CHAPTER 62

The Naval Observatory
Washington, DC
December 19, 2024

Because the Naval Observatory had been the customary living quarters of vice presidents, an engineering project had been taken on in the 1970s to install a bunker on the lowest side of the property connected by a tunnel from what was originally built as the Observatory's superintendent's home in the 1890's. As the crow flies, the vice president's home is two miles from the White House. But in all things Washington, the proximity of the residence is measured more frequently by politics, not distance. The bunker was occasionally used by the vice president for private meetings with other officials, when the visitors were not logged in as they were in the residence. Six hundred yards from the residence, sixty feet underground with a twelve-foot cap of hardened concrete, the bunker was private and secure.

After offering the CIA Director a cigar and a snifter of brandy, and going through the ritual of preparing the hand-rolled tobacco for lighting, the vice president spoke directly,

"Look, Bill, I found the president's meeting the other day very disturbing, and the three teams he wants to create a bit childish. What not let the government do its job? But the president whisked his team off to Camp David for the weekend, and we don't know what the hell is going on. Neither one of us can afford the negative press this effort may generate, and I don't want to spend my first year at the White House collared by an investigation, savvy?" The vice president punctuated his question with tapping the first ash of his cigar into a side table ashtray.

"I agree. We are on the same team, and I agree that we've got to stay close during this escapade," said the CIA director, a large man wearing a designer running suit and high-topped sneakers. He too tapped the ash off his cigar and looked intently at the vice president.

"Well, we can try to recruit an inside source or get someone placed on the team who could report to us. Don't you have a couple of interns around we could use?"

Both men laughed and the vice president re-filled their glasses from a decanter.

"Do we still have the capability to listen to the conversations at Camp David?"

"Yes, the transmitters haven't been activated for years, but they are still in place. Why don't we start there and see if that gives us enough of a picture, so we don't have to go through our worry beads every day?"

"Bill, what a sensible idea! What do we need to do to get them activated?"

"Your interest alone is all I need. There will be no record of this meeting, nor will there be a paperwork trail for anyone to follow. It's clear to me that this is in the national security interests of the country and bears on both our political futures. Consider it done."

Their work over, the two men talked about the recent gossip in the Congress and Senate and how the mid-terms might play out. The empty decanter signaled the end of the meeting. The vice president handed a few cigars over to his friend and thanked him for coming. Then he walked back to the residence and the CIA director walked to a separate entrance where his armored limousine was waiting.

CHAPTER 63

Presidential Palace

Tirana, Albania
December 20, 2024

The bidding ended on a sour note. The Islamic Republic of Iran bested the European Union by a hundred billion dollars. Some speculated that Iran would be using the recently thawed money to fund the final offer. The EU sputtered publicly about the loss as did the United States, which protested the outcome and demanded that the bidding be re-opened, declaring that some lonely provision in the terms had not been properly exercised.

After weeks of open bidding, fully transparent to the world, the lottery closed and was certified by one of the top five international accountancies. The $100 million dollar participation fee had been transferred to Albania by all the bidders, including the United States. It was a public embarrassment. The winning bid of $920 billion equated to nearly fifty times Albania's Gross Domestic Product and would fund many of Spence's projects, both public and private. It seems that Europe's red-headed stepchild had successfully snookered all the big nuclear players.

The transfer would be overseen by the International Atomic Energy Agency. Iran would send a Moudge-class frigate, Iranian Republic of Iran ship *Simurgh 79* escorted by a Russian Krivak-class destroyer to Durres to pick up the cargo and return to Iran. The IAEA would embark a team on the frigate and a 24/7 video feed would be provided of the secure deck areas housing the casks. Additionally, news organizations were making plans to cover the transit of the ship via helicopters and drones. Everyone could watch the transfer on TV.

The frustration grew even more intense after Spence formally proposed that NATO provide escort ships for the transit leg in the Mediterranean Sea, Egyptians through the canal, Egyptian and Saudi navies from Port Suez to the Bab el-Mandeb, and India, Oman and UAE for the transit to Bandar Abbas, Iran. Rubbing salt in a fresh wound, some of the players that bid and lost the nuclear auction would safeguard the material to its destination. The irony of the situation dominated the newscasts.

Spence and Zlodeyev sat for lunch in a private garden patio, enjoying the cloudless sky above.

"I still can't believe that we pulled this off, Spence" said Zlodeyev as he forked a piece of fresh fish and shoved it in his mouth. Eating styles clearly differentiated both men. Spence believed dining to be about good food and conversation about things other than the events swirling around the country, while Zlodeyev saw meals as a time to refuel, much like filling-up a car with gasoline and complaining about the rate of flow. Zlodeyev finished his piece of fish before Spence had the first bite.

"Yes, my friend, I am amazed that bold action has once again ruled the day. There are many unhappy people out there but, because the entire world watched the process, we are clear of the criticism. But there will be attempts. I just found out that the president of the United States has asked for a conference call with me this afternoon. He probably wants to make a counteroffer, now that the bidding is closed. I look forward to giving him a lesson in fair play," said Spence, laughing at his own reality. He raised his wine glass to his defense minister.

"You played a huge part in our success Nikolai. You had the idea of selling our radioactive treasure to the highest bidder. Our Treasury received the $250 billion dollars from the national Bank of Iran yesterday as a down payment. The balance will be due when they take possession of the casks in Durres. Iran has assumed all the risks with the transshipment, so I believe we are clean on the contractual arrangements. At first, I didn't think the idea would work, but you made it happen. Salut."

The men clinked their glasses. Spence assessed the wine's fragrance, carefully tasted the wine and assessed its flavor and finish while the minister downed the glass in a single gulp.

A server replaced Zlodeyev's plate with another one with two large whole fish fillets.

CHAPTER 64

Tehran, Iran
December 28, 2024

"Yes, Rahbar-e-Moazzam, I discussed our urgent need to transport the casks from Albania to Bandar Abbas with the chief of staff, your chief of the navy, Admiral Qarabaghi, and the director of the shipyard. All agree that *IRIS Simurgh* is the best vessel to carry out this critical transfer. However, the ship is currently in an important maintenance period which involves drydocking to replace one of its primary diesel propulsion engines. The shipyard commander has studied options to accelerate this refit, but he and your military planners have concluded the ship will not be ready to carry out the mission until the period just before our holiest month of Ramadan."

As the Supreme Leader of the country and Commander-in-Chief, the ayatollah knew that his personal assistant had tried his best to speed up the transfer of the nuclear material. His assistant was a member of the leader's own tribe, a trusted and loyal member of the inner circle. They had been together before the 1979 revolution when the ayatollah came to power.

The ayatollah grunted and moved his hand in a dismissive wave, indicating that he was not happy with the situation but was convinced that trying to change it would be impossible. The delay meant nothing in the larger scheme of things.

"One other matter, your Holiness, is that it would be impractical to impose such a mission on the crew with the obligations of Ramadan, and the celebrations of Eid al Fitr. I know the dates for our holy month will only be known for certain when the threads cannot be distinguished under the light of sunrise. But the day will surely come near the date I have used for planning. Shall I try again?"

"No, I know you have worked hard on this issue. I am satisfied. Tell everyone to plan the ship's voyage after Ramadan."

The advisor bowed deeply and said, "With your permission, I will attend to my other duties."

"Go in peace with God's blessing," responded the Supreme Leader.

PART III

CHAPTER 65

January 16, 2025

An Office of Secure Transportation (OST) subcontractor was awarded the work to build two new casks, exact replicas of the two which would be loaded on the Iranian frigate. The contract was classified and had been awarded without any formal solicitation or competition. Further, the contract terms required that it not be announced in any company press releases. Employees assigned to build the casks were also required to sign non-disclosure agreements. Plus, the company was financially incented to deliver the containers early.

If the schedule permitted, the new casks would be loaded on a vessel in the shipyard. The logistics of getting the casks onboard was another hurdle. At ten feet in diameter and nearly twenty-three feet long, the overall size made handling difficult, but with each cask tipping the scales at ninety-five tons, the weight itself made transport overseas nearly impossible, given the time and distance constraints. The largest cargo plane in the United States military inventory was limited to a payload of 170 tons, so it would take two C-17 cargo planes to transport the two casks. If the casks were not finished prior to the ship's departure, it meant that the ship would have to make a port call that could add a day or more to the ship's transit.

Transporting and loading the real casks in Durres had been tedious, slowed down by the IAEA looking at every detail to make the movement safe. Tests were performed on every piece of hardware to be used in moving the casks from the rural area to Durres and down to the pier where they were to be loaded. Standards labs provided testing equipment in need of calibration which took days and sometimes weeks.

The fact that Islam's holiest month of Ramadan was anticipated to begin at the end of February. The post Ramadan celebrations helped extend the observance from the end of March through the first week in April. That period in the Muslim calendar set the earliest transfer date into May.

Safety was the foremost consideration for the IAEA. They were unaware of the shadow organization in the United States that was planning to rip those carefully prepared casks off the carrier ship.

CHAPTER 66

Department of Transportation

Washington, DC
February 15, 2025

At Admiral Wright's insistence, the president's team vacated Camp David and took over the top floor of the Department of Transportation. In the works for several weeks, the move put the group closer to the White House and accommodated the people whose day jobs were in Washington. Moving was a simple matter of staging a dozen large white boards and a banker's box of planning folders for secure courier transport. The team's progress and decisions were locked in peoples' brains. Wright orchestrated the move to M street in two hours which included a working lunch. Here, in the southeast sector of the district, they had access to secure communications and to the president.

Today's agenda was daunting, and several key individuals had offered explanations as to why they couldn't attend. Since several of the people invited to the meeting clearly outranked a retired admiral, Wright knew that he had to make the meetings mandatory and likely make them daily. The team was behind the planning eight ball, and Wright knew he needed all those brains concentrated on the problem at hand. He sent a short note to the president, asking him to issue the directive under his own hand. That would clear up any confusion as to the priority of this task and the admiral who would lead it. Everyone would clear their desks and see if their deputies were up to the task of leading their respective organizations. He pressed on with the agenda for the morning's meeting. Three topics were to be discussed:

1. Creation of the dust storm; 2. Ship preparations; and 3. Ship identification.

1. The president's team had looked at possible sites in both Egypt and Saudi Arabia to generate the dust storm that would set the stage for the big gulp. There was no shortage of the fine, reddish-colored sand to produce the storm required on either side of the Red Sea. Navy meteorologists modeled a man-made storm and calculated that at least ten dual-turbined aircraft would be required to sustain a thick cloud. Where would they be able to acquire and set up the aircraft required? A continuous brownout required tons of sand. A fleet of bulldozers would be needed. Every question spawned a dozen more.

The ideal way to birth the storm would be explosives placed under a thirty-five-foot-high berm of desert five miles in length. Prepositioned weapons stocks of explosives designed to breech or cut through enemy fortifications would be used to spawn the initial cloud. Local conditions favored placement on the Saudi Arabian side in the desert north of Yanbu, an industrial city created by the government. An ancient port, Yanbu hosted thousands of pilgrims that visited the second of the holiest cities in Islam, Medina. The international airport would facilitate logistics, and the land sixty miles north of Yanbu had a contour that narrowed the Red Sea slightly but enough to reduce the size of the area that needed to be covered by the dust.

2. The whale was another worry bead. To modify a ship sufficiently to enable it to swallow *Simurgh* was no easy feat. At 308 feet in length and displacing over 2,000 tons, *Simurgh* would be an awfully large mouthful. A possible solution was found in South Korea. Sandy Matthews convinced the president to call his counterpart to make it happen. A large container ship was being outfitted and nearing the delivery date to an owner who had already paid for the vessel. A dual fuel vessel able to ply the seas using methanol as well as diesel fuel, the ship was just over 1,100 feet in length. With a beam of 175 feet, swallowing *Simurgh* was possible but only if some significant changes were made to the forward third of the container ship.

One advantage of the ship's new green design was the placement of the bridge and berthing areas. Traditionally, the accommodation block to house the crew had been placed aft. In the new design, it was all the way forward, enabling the captain to see right in front of the ship. Perhaps the identification of the target to be swallowed would be easier.

The customer for the modified container ship remained confidential. Though the shipbuilding community is competitive, suspicious, and tight-lipped, the likely user had been identified as a rich and eccentric Asian who believed future riches lay on the seabed. How the modifications would support that type of exploration was unknown, but the speculation ran rampant among designers and builders alike. The ship's owner had graciously delayed receiving the ship, so the United States could rent the vessel from the home yard for a million dollars per day plus the cost for the building yard to restore the ship to its original design.

To accomplish the mission-specific changes required, to get a ship to sea and then to travel nearly 8,000 nautical miles to meet a ship at a designated spot in the Red Sea seemed impossible, or nearly so. There was no slack in the schedule. Admiral Wright called on a surface warfare officer who had a change of command scheduled for early May. He was the commanding officer of the newest Arleigh Burke destroyer, USS Iowa. Bill "Willy" Wilson would be returning to Newport to be part of a group of planners who performed high-level studies in support of the fleet commanders. The urgency of that assignment paled when compared to the plan for the big gulp.

Wright asked the CNO what he could do to get Iowa's prospective commanding officer over to the operating theater early and to accelerate Wilson's change of command. Iowa was currently at sea assigned to escort US and allied commercial ships from the Indian ocean and get them safely past the ballistic missile firing range that the Houthis were still using from Yemen. Wilson's designated replacement was still in the pipeline scheduled for a course that the CNO himself had designed and made mandatory. The CNO was able to buy a month by simply cancelling the leave plans of Iowa's next commanding officer. Wilson would now be relieved at sea on April 2, 2025, and would be able to travel to Asia the following day.

Wilson was a known quantity, a steady hand. The scope of the temporary assignment was sketchy. Like all military officers, he served at the pleasure of the president, but an officer concerned more about his career than his country would try to duck such an assignment. Wilson was available, had the shipyard experience required, and never shied away from putting his career in jeopardy for such a challenge. His orders were modified to report to the world's largest and perhaps most efficient shipyard in South Korea. This assignment was classified and would not be released to the normal outlets that post the orders of ranking naval officers.

3. Ship identification was a trouble spot, and Steele believed the current plan was shaky at best. He was concerned about ensuring the cargo ship swallowed the right target in zero-visibility conditions. There were other ships in transit and escort ships to consider in the busy waterway. The assumption was that visibility would be reduced to perhaps 50-60 feet, maybe less. A large container ship did not have the ability to turn on a dime. This was a one-shot deal, and it did no good to swallow the wrong ship.

Steele came up with the idea that a laser-designation would have to be maintained on the vessel via an aircraft. But what type of aircraft would be able to see through the dust cloud and maintain a laser designation on the target? Choking dust was problematic for any aircraft. Another idea was floated suggesting *Simurgh* could be designated by an underwater device. Quickly dismissed, the plan relied on *Simurgh's* crew being ordered to abandon ship.

Timing would be everything. If the ship sank too early, then *Leviathan,* the tentative name of the swallowing ship, would not be able to ingest it. *Leviathan* could not turn around and come back for another bite, and the powerplants creating the dust storm needed enough fuel to sustain it for at least an hour assuming that the creation and movement of the dust cloud could be controlled. What would happen if the prevailing wind did not cooperate?

After briefing the team, the number of possible snags spilled over onto two poster boards labeled hard spots. Each one had to be addressed. It seemed like an impossibly long list of issues to deal with as the planning window was too close to the execution time. It boiled down to an execution window of twenty minutes with a single pass.

There was little flexibility in the plan to slowdown or speedup the transit of the two ships. Hundreds of "known unknowns" were being addressed simultaneously. Difficult enough under normal circumstances, but this operation also had the major constraint of being kept secret from the world. There also had to be a plan "B" that would accomplish the same goal. But that came with the clear risk of having the United States' fingerprints on the operation What was the real probability of success? The variables stayed in the hundreds as the team worked the problem. The team was already exhausted and were still facing three more months of tedious effort.

CHAPTER 67

Bandar Abbas, Iran
April 12, 2025

It was a heady day in the port city. *IRIS Simurgh* glistened under the morning sun. Just painted from stem to stern, brass fittings were shined to the high luster of gold, and the crew manned the rail in their spotless white dress uniforms. A stage on the pier had been erected specifically for this important send-off. Thousands of people jammed the pier where *Simurgh* was moored, hoping to catch a glimpse of the Supreme Leader bidding the ship farewell.

The occasion was marked by a parade of military equipment representing the weapons systems installed on the ship and the pride in the nation's armed forces, charged with carrying out God's vision for the country and its people.

The ayatollah gave a lengthy address to the masses and worked the crowd into a frenzy. He glorified the ship and its mission and told the people that the trip was part of a grand plan to eliminate the evil that had been visited on the region by the infidels and their partners, the Satan of the Middle East, Israel.

He applauded the actions of militias that continued their attacks on United States forces in the region and vowed to keep the assaults alive, until there was no American blood left anywhere to be spilled in the name of Allah. He praised the Yemen-based Houthi militias that were still sending ballistic missiles into ships transiting near the Red Sea. The sailors were about to take the cruise of a lifetime, where they would be part of the nation's future history. Beaming parents with grandparents and brothers and sisters in tow yelled and screamed with excitement. Young men wanted to know where they could sign up to join the Iranian navy.

Throngs of onlookers pushed forward as the ship cast off lines and slowly moved away from the pier. Perhaps fifty people were pushed into the water by the crowd pressing forward to get a closer glimpse.

CHAPTER 68

Ulsan, Korea
April 19, 2025

Wilson arrived in the yard after his hurried change of command and a circuitous trip — a helicopter ride from the ship into the Republic of Djibouti in the horn of Africa to Jeddah, Saudi Arabia where he caught a lift from a U.S. Navy C-12 propeller driven transport to Riyadh, Saudi Arabia. Wison spent the night in the lounge trying to sleep before boarding a non-stop nine-hour flight to Seoul and connecting with a commuter flight to Ulsan, South Korea, a short hop of less than an hour. Wilson felt like he'd be traveling for a week by the time he lay his body down at an Ulsan hotel catering to Westerners and shipyard visitors. His body had been tortured from multiple flights, multiple time zones, and extended layovers. If this operation were so important, why didn't someone send a plane to Riyadh to pick him up, he wondered?

Wilson was meeting Sandy Matthews the following morning for breakfast and a rundown on the part of the operation that he had "volunteered" to execute. That meeting would be followed by a luncheon sponsored by shipyard executives eager to understand the extent of the changes to be made to a new ship and the urgency of the timeline.

Over breakfast in an isolated corner of the restaurant, Sandy Matthews briefed Wilson on the mission. Wilson lost his appetite and emptied two pots of coffee listening to the plan. By the end, despite the injection of caffeine, he looked shell-shocked.

"Any questions for me?" asked Sandy.

"Have you ever heard the military term FUBAR?" asked Wilson in return.

"Yes, and if that's your current assessment I have to agree," quipped Matthews. "And I assure you that all the smart people who put this plan together were not drinking at the time, and I'm certain none of them was using recreational drugs. As some Chinese philosopher observed, it is what it is."

The two were picked up in a shipyard car and whisked away for the initial meeting with the executives.

From the top floor of the shipyard operations building, Wilson surveyed the vast expanse of the yard and couldn't believe his eyes. Here was a shipyard producing first class vessels, commercial and military, at an incredible rate. The yard ran as smoothly as a Swiss chronometer. He bemoaned the fact that there was only a single yard in the United States that was producing commercial ships. The rest relied largely on military contracts to stay alive.

Wilson had great difficulty staying awake during the meeting after jovially accepting a tumbler of soju, a traditional clear Korean liquor distilled from rice or cassava and known to have a paralyzing effect on Westerners. Koreans took great delight in getting their guests inebriated prior to important meetings. Though the duo may not have made a memorable first impression, the shipyard would soon learn that Wilson was a no-nonsense taskmaster who intended to stomp on the shipyard accelerator and keep it floored for as long as it took to get *Leviathan* out of the yard and steaming toward the Red Sea.

Wilson met with the planners every morning and with the production team every afternoon. The major modification required the ship to be brought into a drydock where the water would be pumped down over the course of a day, and the ship would be cradled in custom made blocks to support the keel and the major frames of the superstructure. Blocks were giant wooden stacks of curved timbers built to conform with the external shape of the hull, placed in advance based on the arrangement of the frames and watertight bulkheads. Placement of the blocks had to be exact.

Fortunately, a large Liquified Natural Gas Tanker had just been moved from the drydock to an adjacent pier for outfitting, so

Leviathan's blocks could be set immediately. Getting a thousand-foot ship into a drydock was a complicated effort involving hundreds of people setting blocks and preparing the dock to be flooded to receive the ship.

Once the ship was high and dry, the cutting began by lopping off the ship's nose, a bulbous underwater projection which added a percent or two of fuel efficiency over the ship's life. Then the bow itself was cut away to be replaced with movable doors manufactured, strengthened, stiffened, and attached to the hull with machined hinges made of phosphor bronze, cast to receive twelve individual eight-inch diameter hinge pins on both sides of the hull with the strength necessary to plow through seas of any size. Each of the pins weighed 180 pounds. Where the doors joined each other forward inside a two-section retractable stem, the seam had to be watertight to prevent the ship from taking on water with its own forward progress. The main deck was raised twenty feet, eliminating the first two decks of the accommodation block to handle the height of the vessel to be swallowed and strengthened to rake off the ship's superstructure above the bridge level as well as the mast. The winches and capstans used for line handling and anchoring the ship in the bow were removed and a new fiberglass anchor was cast and wired into the hawsepipe. This was photoshopping on a large scale involved retaining an external appearance but removing tons of weight forward. Wilson also had the waterline repainted to look like the ship was lower in the water and fully burdened.

Though the shipyard employed some 12,000 workers, they were already working three shifts, and there was little surge capacity left. Jobs with committed deadlines were at risk of a schedule overrun, something the yard had avoided in the last six years.

Wilson handpicked a small team of naval officers and chief petty officers to be released from their present assignments and join him for an undefined period of temporary duty. Thirty officers and CPOs joined him in Korea a handful at a time for myriad close-out inspections and to prepare for at-sea testing of all major systems including propulsion, steering, operation of the bow doors, fire and damage control, electrical generation and distribution circuitry.

Leviathan's timeline for modifications was eleven days. When added to a voyage of twenty days from Korea to the Red Sea, the timeline was brutally fixed. The pressure was on, and Wilson tried to accelerate every effort he could, poring over the draftsman's drawings and trying to tweak the production schedule to buy more time. Working twenty-hour days, he was able to oversee the round-the-clock three shift modifications being performed at the yard using computer-generated drawings made hours before by some of the best naval architects in the world. Those architects were also under a tight timeline and were ahead of the production team by no more than twelve hours.

The shipyard normally held the trials over the course of several weeks and worked the punch list to deliver a ship without defects. Wilson crammed the shipyard schedule into a single thirty-six-hour period that tested all the critical gear *Leviathan* needed for the mission. Necessary repairs would be carried out in a single day. There was no time for re-testing for this come-as-you-are operation. The few good men Wilson selected were expert naval mechanics and troubleshooters. He'd trusted them with his life before and would again rely on them. Every minute of every day was precious. Wilson lived with the schedule pushing people, organizations and planners to the limit. The Korean shipyard drove each shift hard day after day but the light at the end of the tunnel seemed no brighter than the day before.

As *Leviathan* moved away from the pier under its own power, thousands of shipyard workers who'd worked on the project cheered from the pier. Empty cargo containers piled six high completed the disguise. Below the main deck, the cargo bays had been removed, and the ship's interior looked like a giant open warehouse. Wilson cranked up the speed as soon as he was certain that the massive wake generated by the ship's propeller would not swamp any smaller boats. The bridge seemed to hang over the bow. It was a major adjustment in thinking, and Wilson had jumped back after looking down at the water hundreds of feet straight down, like riding the first car of a roller coaster.

He removed his sweat-soaked ballcap and hoisted himself into the captain's chair on the starboard side of the bridge and fell asleep.

One of his enterprising colleagues had a custom embroidered cover sewn into the back of his bridge chair that featured a wide-open set of glossy red feminine lips with the words Deep Throat embroidered in white letters just past the sparkling white teeth and above an extended tongue. Just over eight thousand miles away was the planned location of the great swallow.

A countdown clock began to tick in Wilson's head when *Leviathan*'s massive main engine had reached full power, driving the hull at a top speed of twenty-one knots.

CHAPTER 69

Gaeta, Italy
April 22, 2025

Under a shrouded skeleton of steel scaffolding covering *Newport's* sail, the fat dorsal fin built up from the pressure hull was modified with a steel cage and curved twin tusks fabricated of high strength steel, its carbide edges beveled like a knife, and projecting ten feet above the top of the conning tower. The sub looked like a primitive sea animal found in the deepest part of the oceans. And that it would be, during the vessel's transit of the Red Sea. Sydney Garrison, protective of her boat and crew, monitored every phase of the modifications, especially any that might affect the integrity of the hull. She would not take any risks with the safety of her crew. She thought back to the recent rescue operation that took her deep into the Adriatic Sea and shuddered involuntarily.

The design had come together as submarine architects and designers struggled to develop a device which would enable the boat to rip the heart out of a surface vessel by brute force, gutting fuel tanks, lube oil sumps, control and monitoring data cables and seawater cooling. A properly designed warship can continue to operate through most adverse natural disasters, but that capability relies on the integrity of the hull and the ability to isolate damage through compartmentation. When flooding cannot be controlled, and tanks containing thousands of gallons of fuel and water are open to the sea, stability and seakeeping are compromised, and the ship invariably sinks into the depths.

Gutting a ship from the bottom over any length would pose enormous problems for the damage control parties who would be the first responders to deal with flooding. *Simurgh's* engines, generators, and auxiliary equipment were placed in large adjacent compartments, below the waterline, and as close to the keel as they could be mounted to increase buoyancy and stability. Watertight bulkheads separated the compartments to enable the crew to isolate flooding as well as fire. If no longer watertight, bulkheads would offer no means to control progressive flooding.

Once the objectives were understood, the naval architects put together a design in short order. The sail of a submarine can be used to punch through a layer of ice nearly ten feet thick so the application of sharp horns to the superstructure posed no significant challenge. After an engineering review, a detailed plan would be sent to the fabricating facility with all the specifications, including the quality of the steel, high pressure welding standards, and the few attachment points which were already installed on the boat's hull. No cutting of the boat's hull would be permitted. This was a purpose-built fixture to be used for a specific operation and then removed, like someone removing an outer coat when out of the weather.

CHAPTER 70

May 01, 2025

A rendezvous between two military ships at sea is a commonplace evolution. Both ships are party to the plan and remain aware of any delays because of weather, higher priority operations or mission-essential repairs. Speeds can be adjusted, the rendezvous location moved, or the time and date modified to accommodate changes. The level of flexibility varies based on the urgency of the join-up.

The rendezvous between *Simurgh* and *Leviathan* was starkly different. There was no rendezvous plan. Only one was military, and the ships were starting their respective voyages over 10,000 miles apart. *Leviathan* had to travel four times as far as *Simurgh*. No communications were established between the ships, but the timeline was so tight that no delays could be accommodated. Thousands of variables stood in the way. Few could be addressed by *Leviathan's* side to improve the probability of mission success.

Simurgh's transit plan had been announced to the world. Television networks already displayed graphics of the ship's course through the Mediterranean and Red Seas, into the Indian Ocean and back to their home waters in the Persian Gulf. No anticipated stops along the way. Transit speed would be twelve knots. The ships would enter the Red Sea on May 21, escorted by the Royal Saudi Naval Forces and Egyptian Navy. Based on the transit schedule and *Leviathan's* full speed track, with zero time allocated for bad weather or propulsion repairs, the president's team established 11:00 o'clock p.m. on May 22, 2025, as S-hour, the S meaning swallow.

Admiral Wright had also decorated the main conference room with a large countdown clock to keep people focused on the end game. No one could miss the six-inch numerals which displayed the remaining time until S-Hour: 21 Days 06 Hours 49 Minutes.

CHAPTER 71

May 2, 2025

Steele felt the weight of mission stress as soon as he began the day. It dominated everything. Not a waking moment went by that Steele wasn't thinking about how to accomplish the impossible without the US getting entangled in an international controversy with major implications. All the threads of the plan had to be knit together on a seamless schedule with no slack.

Creating the dust storm was a critical element of the plan. He worked with meteorologists on the numbers of aircraft engines required to create the dust storm and demonstrated it in the Arizona desert at Yuma proving ground. A dozen aircraft engines were required to operate at maximum thrust to provide a twenty-minute window of cover for the operation. Mechanical engineers were concerned about overstressing parts being held in place at full throttle. More calculations were performed, and other consultants were called in to verify the plan. Everything had to be accomplished under a blanket of secrecy, but Steele worried that bits and pieces of the plan were being openly discussed. Too many people were getting involved and planning was bumping up against execution, a dangerous reality.

How to track *Simurgh* to make sure *Leviathan* would swallow the right ship caused the most worry. The Russian Krivak posed another complication, especially if it were actively engaged in rescuing survivors at S-hour. Steele's mind kept playing back to the good news-bad news scenario. Yes, Mr. President, the great swallow worked perfectly, just as we planned. The bad news? *Leviathan* swallowed the wrong ship.

Myriad details, many of them still question marks, bogged down the ongoing planning and raised the level of uncertainty regarding execution. The probability of success was going down over time, not up. In most cases, a one- or two-day delay could be made up in another part of the schedule. In this case, there was no latitude to delay any task, preparatory event, or planning milestone, however minor. The consequences were far too severe.

CHAPTER 72

Department of Transportation

Washington, DC
May 6, 2025

The president arrived for the briefing early and found Wright in his office holding a mug of coffee and staring out over the city.

"Morning, Jim. I know I'm here ahead of schedule, but I woke up this morning and couldn't get back to sleep. How are you holding up?"

"I'm doing well. If nothing else, this operation is the most energizing job I've ever had. It's got more moving parts than wartime flight operations off a carrier, and a timeline that's next to impossible. I think we are concentrating on the right things, and I couldn't have a better team than the one I've got."

"Jim, in the last few weeks, I've had some people question whether I've got a screw loose. It's hard to remain convicted to something with all the negative voices out there. What do you think?"

"To tell you the truth, Mr. President, the courage of your conviction is motivating. I'm 100 per cent convinced that we are doing the right thing for the country and frankly, the world. The whole team is committed to this operation, and we are all experiencing that 'Man in the Arena' feeling. If you're ready, we can head down to the conference room."

The clock was ticking. Additional precautions had been taken by U.S. Navy specialists to sweep the conference room and eliminate any potential eavesdropping, by circling the room with a length of clear plastic tubing stuffed with a flexible radio frequency cable which generated white noise. The team had taken their seats, when Wright escorted the president into the meeting. As the president panned the table, the strain of the task was evident on the people's faces.

"Mr. President, we have a plan. As a matter of fact, the plan is underway, pardon the pun. Today, we'll brief you on where we are and identify what's needed to execute the final pieces of it. There may be some variations to this plan, but there is no plan B that can be executed without our involvement being revealed. The best way to visualize the plan is with the sand table." Wright stood and pulled back a thin blue nylon cover to reveal a four foot by eight-foot scaled model of the Red Sea that detailed the land on either side as well as the depth contours of the water.

"This is the big picture. As you can see, this is a small section of the Red Sea where the operation will take place."

Wright then moved to an adjacent table, twice as large as the first where the action would take place. A narrow part of the Red Sea was blown up depicted at a scale of 1:1000. The ships involved were three to five inches long, dwarfed by *Leviathan* at just over a foot. The flag of Liberia was painted on its side. Wright used a laser pointer to show areas in Saudi Arabia designated for the dust-storm producing turbines and the underwater features of the area where the frigate would be, assuming the hull were sufficiently compromised by *Newport* for the captain to order his crew to abandon ship.

Leviathan would appear, its bow doors fully open and ingest the ship. The hull steel exposed to direct contact with the target ship had been strengthened, and *Simurgh's* superstructure would be severely contorted, bent, or broken to fit inside the ship.

The president listened quietly, fully understood the fragility of the plan, and acknowledged the lack of a good backup plan. A tic in his left eye fluttered during the briefing, the muscles contracted involuntarily, making his eye spasm. At the end of the briefing, when Admiral Wright asked if there were any questions, the president slumped in his chair and shook his head.

"I have no doubt that this plan could work. It's high risk. It's a stretch."

238

"Mr. President, we all agree that this plan is an elegant solution to the problem, and it is high risk. The only back-up plan is to sink the *Simurgh* in the Indian Ocean in very deep water. The downside of that plan is that we will probably not be able to recover the nuclear material as neatly, and our fingerprints may be on the sinking of the ship. It's deeper water, in the open ocean, but higher risk for the crew's safety, especially if we conduct the operation at night."

"OK," said the president, "I've got it. What are the plan's hard spots now?"

"We have found some newly installed receivers hidden in this room which suggests that some of your top advisors may not agree with the three-team structure you proposed. Though this room has been previously swept, I'm not sure who might have been on the end of the broom. There is obviously a keen interest in what actions you might consider to thwart this transfer. Everything on the intelligence team, including China, Russian, and North Korea, has been crickets. The vice president's team seems to be focused on the day-to-day issues, and I've not gotten any pushback from anyone. Of course we are still early in this fast-moving game. People accustomed to being on the inside are now outside. I'm not sure to what ends they might go to get a peek at our plans.

The Chief of Naval Operations has volunteered to use some of his internal resources to protect this team's ability to plan independently. Because this town is so connected, I also recommend that the CNO be empowered to develop a misinformation campaign to keep anyone outside this room confused or uncertain about our plan forward. I cannot stress enough the need for secrecy of our plan."

"Agreed."

The president looked at the CNO, Admiral Mike Weathers, directly. "I just ask that you give me a heads-up about any planned leaks in advance. I just don't want to be caught flat-footed and say something that's not in synch with the narrative you concoct. This is going to be fun. What's the next hard spot?"

"Identification of the *Simurgh* in the middle of a dust storm with zero visibility. We've looked at several possibilities but do not have a high confidence plan and need one. Dan, why don't you take it from here?"

"Good morning, Mr. President, the positive identification of the ship is crucial, and we know that it must be sensored in some way so that *Leviathan* can take it in a single pass, bow on. Any sort of radiating device will be discovered on the target ship, so the trick is to add a sensor somewhere topside so *Leviathan* can find the target with zero visibility. The best way to accomplish this is to have someone aboard *Simurgh* to place a beacon of some sort between the time the ship is disabled, and *Leviathan* is in position to swallow the target. We risk compromising the plan if such a device is not placed. It just falls apart. We've looked at all the alternatives, and the one with the highest probability of success is having a rider on the ship who can get the sensor aboard and then place it on the mast."

"And who might be able to place such a beacon."

"That would be my job, sir," said Steele.

"How do we make sure that the crew abandons ship and leaves *Simurgh,* so we have separation to swallow the target?" asked the president.

"That's something else that we are trying to resolve. We think some of the IRGC might think they should stay with the cargo. It's possible that someone has convinced them that it's their duty to stay with the casks. We are prepared to deal with stragglers who are found on the ship. The question we are wrestling with now is my cover on the ship, and how I can get the beacon onboard. I'm certain that everyone's luggage will be thoroughly checked and even X-rayed before they board the ship. I could join the team of IAEA inspectors riding the ship or board as an observer from either Saudi Arabia or Egypt. Any of those roles is possible, but getting the sensor on the ship and in the right position is one of the critical dependencies of our plan. Without the sensor being placed before *Leviathan* opens its jaws, the whole operation is thrown into a cocked hat."

The briefing took three hours. Questions were fired from the president and anyone on the team who could contribute something constructive. Admiral Wright was the perfect choice to lead the team. He had the ability to motivate and keep people focused without shutting people down or discounting ideas which others may have dismissed out of hand. A brilliant taskmaster with a great capacity to assess and to evaluate on the fly, he was always out in front of the team, leading the charge, clearing the interferences and being tone-deaf to his own negative self-talk. There was no doubt in anyone's mind that Wright's brain was like a supercomputer. He made everyone on the team think that they too were operating with a supercomputer in their own heads.

As the president left the conference room, he paused when he spotted Wright's countdown clock with the big red numerals positioned over three other clocks showing Washington time, Durres time and the time in the Red Sea at the position of the big gulp. The countdown clock displayed S-Hour: 15 Days 11 Hours 17 Minutes.

CHAPTER 73

Vice Presidential Bunker

Washington, DC
May 7, 2025

The meeting was set up as before, with the vice president joining the CIA director in the bunker located at the Naval Observatory.

"Would you like to have a brandy with your cigar, Mr. Director?"

"No, thank you, Mr. Vice President. I need to get back to Langley to keep piecing this transfer puzzle together."

"Bill, what's happening with the surveillance capability already in place? Did you forget to activate it?" The vice president added "Just kidding" to his remark before sitting down with a double old fashioned crystal glass full of cask strength brandy.

"Things have not gone well with that capability," said the CIA director. "The president brought in the Navy to sweep the place and has succeeded in blanking out all the conversations with white noise. That pissant CNO is probably responsible. He's a cagey SOB. But I've been activating other sources and have a crazy set of operational queries from the president's team that make little sense to me."

The vice president took a long pull on the crystal glass then said, "Give me an example."

"Well, we know that State has been asked to arrange a top priority meeting between Sandy Matthews, you know that Pisces contractor, and the guy who claims he controls the Somali pirates. They operate off the coast but also in the Bab el Mandeb. State pushed back and is now jumping through hoops to arrange something at the president's personal request."

"Jesus, Bill, why would they try to enlist Somali pirates? Are they looking for a military force outside the US?"

"That's a good question. It makes no sense to me. We are also aware of a request from the team to that Danish shipper, Maersk, to quote the availability of one of their container ships in the Indian Ocean from June 1st for a period of sixty days. To be leased by the US Government. I've tried to connect these dots with another half dozen data points on my desk, and I just can't make hide nor hair out of them."

"OK, Bill. Look, we are late in this game and need answers. I know that the president met with his team yesterday down at Transportation where they've set up shop. If you don't have something concrete in the next seventy-two hours, I want to bring somebody in from the president's team and sweat the answers out of them."

"You mean force them to come here and give us answers."

"That's exactly what I mean. I didn't get the title 'The Persuader' as minority whip for nothing."

"Don't forget, Mr. Vice President, I've seen your service record and know what you are capable of. It was a brilliant move to have your career service record suppressed because of classified operations. Absolutely brilliant! I'm heading back to Langley. If I get any epiphanies tonight, I'll call you."

CHAPTER 74

Durres Albania
May 8, 2025

The sea detail was short and sweet after a routine transit from Iran. A large crowd assembled in the port city to greet *Simurgh* on a sunny warm day with scarcely a breeze. Flags were hung on every available upright, most were the black double-headed eagle of Albania, but many Iranian and Russian flags were visible too. Iranian sailors and the embarked Iranian Republican Guard Corps proudly manned the rail, and salutes were exchanged as *Simurgh* passed by both military and civilian ships in the port. On the pier where the ship would moor, a band played a nonstop medley of military marching music.

A blood red carpet lay on the pier where *Simurgh* landed midships, and brows were hoisted before the braided mooring lines were doubled. Power cables, fresh water, telephone and sewage connections were made. Finally, *Simurgh's* captain stiffly marched down the brow and approached a podium where ruffles and flourishes were played by the band followed by formal honors rendered by Albanian Navy sideboys and a grizzled sailor who announced the arrival with the thrill of a bos'n pipe. The Albanian Minister of Defense greeted the captain with a salute and vigorously shook his hand.

Zlodeyev stepped to the microphone and welcomed the ship to Durres in the name of the president. A thunderous cheer rose from the crowd, excited to observe the formalities. The mayor presented the captain with a key to the city and welcomed its crew who were all made honorary citizens. Stepping to the microphone, the captain made a gracious speech and informed the crowd that he was pleased that his ship and crew were selected by the Supreme

Leader to be part of this historic transfer and the beginning of greater friendship between the two countries.

Zlodeyev walked the captain over to the press and introduced him. The captain expressed his appreciation for the turnout, outlined the critical importance of his visit and then answered numerous questions from the local press, European press, and international correspondents. He thanked the IAEA for their efforts to secure the material and to ensure that people would not be exposed to any stray radiation. The international press tried to rattle the captain with questions about his reactions to some European leaders' remarks condemning the transfer and how the whole world be a more dangerous place with Iran in possession of the material. The captain demurred before being whisked away for a formal luncheon in his honor.

CHAPTER 75

IRIS Simurgh

Durres, Albania
May 12, 2025

Simurgh's commanding officer resented the ship-riders who had joined the ship in Durres and ordered the executive officer to ensure that he reviewed the list with an eye toward its reduction. Those unaccustomed to naval ships even had the gall to ask for a private cabin with its own bathroom. Over forty ship-riders had descended on *Simurgh* without much prior notice, and the captain had little control over the list. However, he vowed to change the numbers during the transit of the Suez where he might have the opportunity to remove some of the straphangers who were riding the ship simply to be part of the arrival ceremony or because they felt very important to the overall success of the mission. The XO took the first cut at the list, interviewed the ship riders and pared down the numbers to those mission-critical individuals that were technicians or special security for the casks, shrinking the list from forty-two to fifteen. It wouldn't be that easy. There would be the inevitable protests and calls or messages of support from the organizations the riders supposedly represented.

With additional berths on the ship able to accommodate eighteen enlisted sailors and two additional officers, a third of the crew of 130 men had been displaced from their bunks. They silently resented the fact that these riders had to be given a berth. Where was the crew supposed to sleep? The captain was furious that some of his crew had been summarily assigned to sleep in their workspaces to free-up space. And, unlike US submariners, *Simurgh* sailors were not accustomed to hot bunking.

Fresh water and provisions were also constraints that no one factored in. Shipboard life was carried out according to plan. Times for eating, cleaning, maintaining and recreation were part of the plan of the day, but ship riders thought there was room service or that the galley was open all day long to accommodate their eating needs. Where was the menu? I need to choose my entrée. On the menu was what was prepared and served, like it or not. And no, the galley did not offer room service to anyone.

There was no smoking in the interior of the ship, and the captain refused to adjust his shipboard standards to accommodate the riders. Those who crossed the captain or questioned his authority were dealt with sternly, and he was prepared to mete out his own brand of punishment when needed. But he was also smart enough to know that while many ship-riders were irrelevant to the mission, they were headquarters types, able to kill a successful career with a casual whisper in the right ear.

The single exception to all the rules was Admiral Ghorbani, a headquarters desk officer who now occupied the captain's in port cabin and arrived with two locking steel file cabinets of projects he was working on. With the cabinets came an expansive office chair, custom built to hold the grotesquely fat man in its soft buttery embrace.

Ghorbani took all routine reports, ate alone in the cabin, and rarely ventured out in the fresh sea air. Rolling his own cigarettes from tobacco preserved in nicotine tar and containing bits of dried fruit, the chain smoker filled the cabin with a thick brown citrus haze. *Simurgh's* captain suffered in silence and just kept count of the transit days he would have to endure with the admiral.

CHAPTER 76

Durres, Albania
May 15, 2025

The sight of the Iranian frigate with a Russian Krivak destroyer pier side in Durres generated enough acid in the president's stomach to give him gastric distress. He'd never complained of indigestion, but the transfer of nuclear material had caused his stomach to become very edgy, and he now kept antacid tablets in his desk drawer instead of chocolate covered peanuts.

Both ships had transited after Ramadan and the Eid al Fitr celebration following the Islamic holy month. Some commentators saw this transfer as a resurgence of Islam as a powerful world-wide force. For some, there was much to celebrate.

Prior to the ships' arrival, the casks had been craned onto two flat rail cars, and a locomotive pulled a strapped load down to the port over an eighteen-hour period. The casks were heavy, and everyone took all the precautions outlined by the IAEA. They asked when the wire straps were last tested. Did they have a certification from an independent lab? Did the crane operator have specialized training in handling such dangerous cargo? Had the tracks themselves been certified for the weight? The IAEA team walked the tracks, and even though the spur line into the mountain had just been re-built, they looked for spongey sleepers, hold-downs or missing spikes. No one had ever imposed such process rigidity in Albania. The attitude of the men who moved the casks was simply let me do my job. It took nearly two days to get the casks staged on the pier...when was that last tested? The IAEA inspectors gaped at areas of the platform suffering from classic chloride ion attack. Large portions of the pier's surface, and the cement piles supporting it were scarred. Rusted re-bar was visible in sheets underneath the rubble of concrete.

Loading the casks on the ship drew a huge crowd of onlookers, evidently with nothing else on their daily schedules. Police lights flickered off the buildings, the people, and the casks themselves as both were loaded on *Simurgh*, placed aft alongside the superstructure where they were secured with heavy chains, all tested and certified. Additional straps were attached to the casks' fittings and led to welded cloverleaf fittings in the deck. And when were the cloverleafs last tested? They were made of crisscrossed steel, cast into a deck fitting, and welded into the deck.

The date set for the ship's departure from Durres was May 15, 2025. *Simurgh* would embark a general from the elite Iranian Revolutionary Guards Corps who outranked the ship's captain. The Iranian navy pushed back on that decision and quickly responded by sending Admiral Ghorbani, senior to the IRGC general, to take charge of the ship's transit. 10:00 a.m. was the scheduled underway time. After topping off with fuel and provisions, the crew was anxious to start the voyage. The sooner they left, the sooner they would be home with their families, though during their time ashore, many of the sailors enjoyed the comfort of women who had journeyed to the port to earn some additional money. Tirana was nearly empty of women who made their living that way.

A five-car official motorcade came through the town of Durres to waving flags and throngs of people lining the designated route. The president himself stood on a raised platform in the middle of the presidential limousine, waving to the energized crowd. When was the last time anyone in Albania had seen such an event? The cars stopped short of the pier, and the president was escorted to a podium set on the pier facing *Simurgh*'s starboard side midships. A band played the Iranian national anthem followed by the anthem of the Russian Federation and then the Albanian anthem to a VIP crowd of dignitaries from around the world, including high level representatives of China and the Navy Chief from Russia. Conspicuously absent were the United States and the members of the European Union. The press had been corralled into two areas to the right of the stage and at the head of the pier. There would be no free-for-all at this ceremony, and the idea of providing the press designated areas for their work was decided by Spence himself.

After a long list of greetings and salutations to the dignitaries, Spence began his remarks.

"Distinguished visitors, Ladies and Gentlemen. What began many months ago as a potential disaster to our country has ended here on the pier in Durres. Before us are ships of the Islamic Republic of Iran Navy and the Russian Federation. Out to sea are several NATO ships that will escort *Simurgh* to the Suez Canal, the first leg of its voyage home to Bandar Abbas, Iran. As you know, our friends in Iran have purchased a supply of nuclear material. That material arrived here in Albania when Albania became a satellite of the former Union of Soviet Socialist Republics during the Cold War. However, the relationship was short-lived. The USSR staged nuclear weapons here in Albania earmarked for a campaign to bring Europe into the regime. Hundreds of thousands would have died in that pre-emptive nuclear attack that was never carried out. I'll be clear to my fellow citizens and those watching our small country from all over our planet. Here in Albania, we have no interest in building a nuclear reactor to produce power and do not intend to explore developing nuclear weapons. But we do have pressing modernization projects that will be supported by this sale. This transaction has given us access to capital that will be invested here for the benefit of the Albanian people. Though the sale has been met with sharp criticism from some quarters, let us celebrate this lucky find and let us walk with our heads held high. This is the new Albania!"

Iranian sailors in full dress uniforms manned the rails when *Simurgh* breasted out from the pier, using its diesel engines. The Krivak was already underway and waiting for the admiral's flagship. NATO ships were visible at sea, ready to take screening positions on either side of *Simurgh*. There was no doubt in anyone's mind that the precious cargo would be protected during its voyage.

Joined on the transit of the Ionian Sea were ships from France, Greece and Italy. NATO agreed to escort *Simurgh* to the Suez Canal. The Krivak kept a respectful distance from the NATO ships but would shine its fire-control radars on the escort ships that would keep them at General Quarters for hours at a time. It was an annoying and potentially dangerous activity that ratcheted up the tension. Not only did the escorts need to watch the seas ahead of the cargo to repel any threat, but also, they had to be aware of the Krivak engaging in a practice that could prompt a deadly response.

Cameras mounted on *Simurgh* operated continuously. A live feed was transmitted via satellite to Islamic Republic of Iran Armed Forces in Tehran, the Joint Staff in the Pentagon, NATO Headquarters in Brussels, and Moscow with a lag time of less than five seconds. The same feed was made available as a free subscription to all the major broadcast news outlets and print newspapers.

The topside area where the casks were secured was illuminated. Cask #1 was located on *Simurgh's* starboard side, while cask #2 occupied the same deck space on the port side. A chain ringed both locations, and two armed guards were stationed inside the chain. No one was permitted inside the area. A roving patrol rounded out the shipboard security measures.

The transit to the Suez Canal, more than 1,200 nautical miles away, would take five days, and *Simurgh* would lead a southbound convoy of ships into the canal just before midnight on the fifth day. The only ships transiting at the same time would be *Simurgh* and the ship's escorts. Planners assumed a full day for *Simurgh* to transit the Suez Canal.

While the world's eyes were on *Simurgh* and its leisurely transit, another ship was steaming at its top speed in the Indian Ocean churning the water at maximum revolutions per minute. Nothing was held back. The large cargo ship coaxed all the horsepower out of the engine that was straining to keep up. The order to max speed had been given days ago and hadn't been changed since. There would be no change in the days ahead. When *Simurgh* breasted off the pier in Durres, *Leviathan* was steaming at full speed, with 4,000 miles to go to arrive at Ra's Abu Madd, a small seaport about sixty miles north of the industrial city of Yanbu, Saudi Arabia, and the location designated for the swallow.

The transfer of nuclear material had taken center stage in the president's administration and placed the entire government in a state of extended gridlock. There were no more interviews, no more stopping to chat with reporters before boarding the presidential helicopter. It was an unsettling paralysis, as if the entire nation was prescribed a large daily dose of ketamine.

None of the planning cells in the Pentagon had developed a workable plan. The War Colleges claimed they couldn't get a wargame up and running before the next academic quarter. The president of the United States and the hundreds of thousands on the government payroll were apparently stymied, not able to move off top dead center. The transfer was proceeding with no known issues.

The entire operation was like a final down in the National Football League where there were seconds left on the clock, no timeouts and virtually no alternatives. Needing a touchdown to win the game, the team with the ball was stopped on their own thirty-yard line. When the snap was called, receivers would fly to the endzone as fast as they could run. An eager defensive line would rush their best three penetrators. The rest of the defense was spread out to ensure the pass would not be caught. The quarterback would throw his longest, highest pass with everything he had and hope one of the receivers on his team seventy yards away would come down with the ball in the end zone. The classic "Hail Mary." It was extremely late in the game, and the president visualized the big gulp as his only viable option.

The conference room on the top floor of the Department of Transportation was ablaze with lights in the middle of the night in Washington, DC. The countdown clock didn't miss a beat as the seconds ticked away. The die was cast. 07 Days 13 Hours 05 Minutes.

CHAPTER 77

Tirana, Albania
May 18, 2025

On the internet, General Zlodeyev found a group of locals who enjoyed blood sport as much as he did. They got together monthly for a series of events featuring bare-knuckled fights, contests with men pitted against animals of every description, and physical competitions of strength and endurance. Here, there was no hotdog eating against a clock, but a group fixated on raw brutality.

Accompanied by several bodyguards, Zlodeyev signed up for a challenge that required the utmost courage or idiocy. As a first-time contestant, he would face a group of a dozen strong wild dogs who enjoyed the taste of raw flesh and warm blood. Zlodeyev offered both in massive proportions. The dogs had been captured by herdsmen who lured them with a chunk of fresh mutton dripping with blood. One herdsman was attacked by the dogs and found half eaten in a nearby village. His body had been savagely gorged, flesh torn from his spare torso and devoured. This pack seemed to enjoy the man's organs, as they were chewed right through his rib cage.

The dogs that Zlodeyev would face had been conditioned to fight each other for their daily raw meat. The meat had been withheld for two days before the event, and the dogs were foaming at their mouths in anticipation of a large meal. The Russian wore thick harness leather shorts and a matching top that looked like industrial strength lederhosen. The outfit would protect his internal organs as well as his junk, an American term that the general found hilarious.

The fighting ring was twenty-five feet across, a circle surrounded by a cyclone chain link wire fence five feet tall and ringed with light poles fitted with bright halogen bulbs. A thick layer of fresh wood chips covered the ground and would absorb some of the blood and other bodily fluids inevitably produced by the contests.

Two matches had been held to warm up the crowd. This fight between the general and the dogs would be the Main Event, and people were throwing money down like it would guarantee more blood. An announcer used a wireless PA system to call the evening's highlight.

"Here, in his leather shorts and combat boots is General Nikolai Zlodeyev, a former Special Forces commander with the Russian Army and now the current Defense Minister of Albania."

He ended the introduction with a local phrase meaning let's give it up for General Zlodeyev. The applause was brief. People were anxious to see if the man's legendary fighting prowess could match the hunger and ravenous mouths of the wild dogs. No one had ever entered the ring with this many canines, so the match promised to be a memorable one. Only if Zlodeyev signaled that he was too injured to continue would the fight be stopped. He'd never done that before, and the crowd eagerly awaited the dogs to be released. There were no clowns in the ring, and bettors wondered who might try to separate the wounded from the voracious dogs. The scene looked eerily similar to Rome's Colosseum where gladiators would fight to the death if ordered by the emperor.

Cool night air with a fresh breeze coming down off the mountains — a perfect night for blood sport.

A gate opened in the ring and wild yelping followed the dogs running at top speed toward their dinner. They were a tawdry lot of canines, all large, scarred and hungry. Zlodeyev might knock down the first two but then he would be overwhelmed with the hounds' first taste of blood. At least that's the way the betting was going.

There was no particular breed evident among the pack, but these beasts were the products of mating survivors. Strong legs for running and pulling down their prey ended with untamed, deadly claws. Muscled chests and thick forepaws were visible on all the dogs. And then the mouths. Large teeth and jaws with a bite designed to kill.

The dogs lived and died in a pack where one fearless animal would lead the others until it was killed or unable to fight.

The pack ran toward the lone man standing in the middle of the ring, bonded by a common goal and eager to fight for their share of the next meal. Ravenous, the lead dog looked like a Doberman with short black hair and fringes of an orangey brown on his paws and belly. At his side was a short-haired German Shepherd mix. His tail had been lost in a previous fight, his mouth in a snarl. The Doberman leaped high, straight for Zlodeyev's head and was met with a crushing blow from his right arm. The next two were killed with single blows to the head. Now attacking their prey from all sides using their claws and mouths, blood spurted as Zlodeyev fought off the remaining nine circling him. One dog leaped to his throat and Zlodeyev parried with a forearm. Then, with the dog clawing his leather chest piece he pulled the lower and upper jaws away, breaking the jaw and throwing the dog over his shoulder.

The general knew he had to beat them one at a time. He pried the animals off his bleeding legs and strangled them or crushed their skulls with his fist. Time was on the dogs' side. There were six left when the dogs sensed that their prey was weakening, and they attacked with greater ferocity. For Zlodeyev, it became a race against time. He continued his strategy of taking on one dog at a time, but the physical costs were mounting. Blood poured from his legs, arms and back. One dog attacked from behind, jumping up on his back and attempting to bite his neck while his paws worked in a frenzy, creating furrows of blood in his back, each sweep of his claws and teeth going deeper into his flesh.

Down to four beasts, the tide changed quickly as Zlodeyev dispatched the next two with two sledgehammer blows to the top of their thick skulls, dropping them to the blood-soaked ground.

The two remaining dogs, a mangy rottweiler and wolf mastiff, circled and growled, baring their teeth and feigning a fresh attack, but they seemed reluctant to take on the man who had quickly decimated their pack. They backed off, to live for another fight, another day.

Zlodeyev had won the battle and the crowd reveled in his victory with shouts and clapping, even though most had placed their wagers on the dogs. It had been a monumental event. The announcer came to the center of the ring and formally announced the winner of the contest. Zlodeyev raised his bloody arms to the crowd, which remained at a frenzied level of excitement with the dead fur lumps on the ground and blood covering his massive frame. Though they might have lost money on their bets, the crowd was satisfied with the bloodletting.

After collecting the winner's purse, Zlodeyev left the arena with his escorts and made a beeline to the hospital. He hoped there was not another pack of Russian dogs waiting for him there.

Zlodeyev was propped up in the back seat of his car with a moving blanket underneath him to absorb the red oozing from his bloodied body. One of his bodyguards rode shotgun, and two others were in the car closely following. Driving through the countryside between two corn fields, Zlodeyev struggled to remain conscious despite the wounds sapping his strength. On the side of the road, he saw no birds feeding on the residue left when a harvester cut a wide swath in the tall rows. Odd, he thought. It was horse corn fed to the cattle. The second thing he noticed was a new watch on his driver's left wrist.

"Yuri, I see you have a new watch. Very handsome. Where did you get it?"

"It's from a friend," he said, tugging at his sleeve to cover its black face.

"Kirill, stop the convoy and turn around. I smell a Federation ambush."

After retracing their route for two miles, they found a hay wagon blocking the road, the tractor at a steep angle heading into the deep swale surrounding the corn field. There was no sign of the farmer.

Zlodeyev said, "Fill up that swale with bales of hay so we can drive across the ditch. We'll take the cornfield to the other road. I know those bastards have blocked the road on the other side of the copse just before the hospital. What a great place for an ambush."

As the men approached the wagon a dull thud rang out and the driver, Yuri, fell to the blacktop. Zlodeyev and his men instinctively hit the ground before one of the men saw a puff of smoke rising from the hay. He fired and heard a scream from the wagon. A second round silenced the shooter. Kirill pulled a man from the hay and dropped him at Zlodeyev's feet.

"Yes, another one of my old charges is still after me. Pile the bales on his body and let's get out of here." The big man used a radio to advise the security detail of the ambush and to have them surround the fighters hiding near the hospital.

Three doctors worked as a team to close the wounds on Zlodeyev's body with eighty stitches and hundreds of butterfly bandages. They wanted to keep him in the hospital overnight as a precaution. He refused. Given two units of blood in a transfusion and a massive dose of toxoid tetanus vaccine along with several tubes of antibiotic ointment and strict instructions about wound care, Zlodeyev looked forward to his morning workout the next day. He felt invigorated. One doctor was instructed to come to the presidential palace in the morning to check the minister's body for any sign of infection.

Between the wild dogs and the surprise attack, Zlodeyev had had his share of fun for the day and wanted nothing more than a full night's rest.

CHAPTER 78

Department of Transportation

Washington, DC
May 19, 2025

"OK," said Admiral Wright, surrounded by the working staff of the president's team, "Let me see if I understand this. I agree that we need some sort of beacon or homing device on *Simurgh* to enable *Leviathan* to take the big gulp. To set the stage, it's about 10:00 p.m. local time in the Red Sea. Two ships are heading on opposite courses, so the additive speed is about twenty knots. They are in the middle of a man-made dust storm that reduces visibility to maybe thirty feet. It's dark, very dark. *Newport* releases Steele a mile away from *Simurgh*. Using his 'X-Ray vision,' Steele paddles up to *Simurgh* that is by now sinking after being holed by *Newport's* narwhal lances. The ship is likely at our equivalent of General Quarters, and the crew is desperately trying to save the ship." Pausing after setting part of the stage, Admiral Wright continued.

"There is a fair amount of confusion as the commanding officer studies the chart. A second generator trips offline and darkens the bridge. Confusion now reigns. Propulsion is lost and along with it, there is a loss of steering control, radar, computer systems, and communications. A messenger reports from damage control that the ship is sinking, fast.

The captain orders the crew to abandon ship. You, Steele, are now 250 yards away from the ship swimming toward it. The Republican Guard is patrolling topside looking for anything that might explain the predicament while keeping their eyes on the lifeboats which are now unstrapped and inflating on both sides of the ship. Somehow, you get aboard at the bow without being shot. I don't suppose they will lower a pilot's ladder for you. How am I doing so far?"

"It's an exciting story, admiral, please continue," responds Steele without a hint of sarcasm in his voice.

"Right. Steele levitates to the main deck in sight of port-side sailors wearing lifejackets not knowing whether to jump or wait to be rescued by one of their closing escort ships. From there, dressed as a dripping corporal in the IRGC, he crosses the main deck and climbs outside the superstructure and surreptitiously makes his way to the mast where he climbs the ladder rungs like Errol Flynn in the old pirate movies. He dances nimbly out on one of the yardarms to place an infra-red and high frequency homing device just to the left of the centerline. The beacon must be placed high enough so that *Leviathan's* captain can get lined up for the big swallow, because he cannot distinguish the ship in the blowing dust. As the guards spot him and start firing, Steele gets brushed off the mast as it breaks on the *Leviathan's* main deck and joins other sailors who thought they'd take their chance swimming to safety in the Red Sea."

The admiral takes a long breath as if he's starting a deep breathing routine in a yoga class and then asks, "Did I miss anything?"

"No, admiral, I think you've captured it well. I hope to get inside the superstructure, so I don't end up in the water. As you point out, there are some additional planning factors that need study but that's where we are today."

"Both *Leviathan* and *Simurgh* are underway, and we come up with a plan that looks like it's the first cut of a sketch from Saturday Night Live?"

Everyone at the table laughs briefly before the room gets quiet again waiting for the next shoe to drop. The admiral gathers his thoughts and addresses the team in the direct, clear, unemotional tone that makes people so loyal to him.

"I like the plan but think the probability of success is probably in the single digits. We are scheduled to meet with the president tomorrow afternoon, so I'd say that we need to spend some time working on the details. Let's review again later this afternoon. And I apologize for my Saturday Night Live comment. It's not fair to any of you. OK, let's get to work. The clock is ticking!"

CHAPTER 79

USS Newport

Red Sea
May 20, 2025

Steele bounced toward *Newport* in a rigid-hulled inflatable boat courtesy of a U.S. Navy destroyer making a routine transit of the Red Sea after spending the previous eight months in the Persian Gulf. Using a hand-held GPS receiver, Steele holds up his hand when the boat arrived at the designated latitude and longitude due west of Jeddah, Saudi Arabia and well outside the shipping lanes and closer to Egypt. The Red Sea was so clear that the submarine outline could probably be spotted from the air.

Because the horned beast wanted to remain hidden beneath the surface, *Newport* would remain at a fixed depth deeper than periscope depth to avoid breaking the surface. Steele would swim eighty feet down to the boat and come in through the recovery hatch. Wearing swim trunks, a mask and fins, and carrying a waterproof bag with a change of clothes and his disguise, he took a few long deep breaths on the surface before slipping under water. Immediately, he saw the deadly steel horns. There were no problems with the lock-out hatch at this depth, and he was inside the sub in just thirty seconds.

Greeted like an old shipmate by the chief petty officer who helped him through the lock-out chamber with Mac Andrews after their ride down the mountain on the German submarine, Steele looked around for Sydney and wondered why she didn't come to greet him.

Later in the afternoon, after changing into khakis and a polo shirt, and checking in with the operations officer, Steele knocked on the captain's door and found Garrison sitting at the small desk.

"Sydney," he said softly, "It's Dan. Are you busy with something?"

She turned and he saw her red-rimmed eyes, devoid of their usual lively sparkle.

"What's wrong, Syd?" Steele asked when she did not move from her chair. Steele knelt next to the chair and held her hands. They felt cold.

"I'm having trouble thinking about the innocent sailors who will likely die, when I slice through *Simurgh*. I'll be OK, but it bothers me. I've been seeing dead sailors' faces when I try to sleep and just can't think about anything else."

"Listen, Syd, you know we are timing this operation to minimize any loss of life from either side. The president was emphatic on that point. Are you having second thoughts?"

Sydney put her arms around Steele and hugged him in a strong embrace.

"I guess I'm looking forward to this operation being over. Inside, I feel like a spring that's been wound very tightly and is reaching the breaking point. It seems like I've been living this way for months. Frankly, I need a long break after my change of command next month." She leaned back and looked into his dark eyes.

"I understand, Syd, I've certainly had the same feeling in the past. But I try to focus on the importance of the mission. We are doing the right thing as a country. That gives me lots of hope about the future. I brought you a small gift."

Steele handed her a t-shirt wrapped around something very heavy.

"Let me guess," said Sydney lifting and feeling the shape of the article. "I know it's not a delicate locket with a picture of you. Maybe a very heavy Swiss chocolate bar?" She unwrapped the gift and dropped it on the deck with a loud thud. Retrieving it, she said, "OK, it's a gold bar with a Swastika. You brought this up from the depths?"

"Yes, it almost killed me, but I thought you'd like a memento from that operation. I tucked it under the lockout chamber in the web of an angle iron frame. It's worth almost a million dollars."

"What am I going to do with this? I can't keep it."

"Maybe you can donate it to charity."

Steele comforted Garrison with several hugs and talk of other things.

"Why don't you take a combat nap, Syd. I'm headed to the radio room to see if I have any messages. I'll be back in twenty minutes. Can I bring you a cup of tea?"

"No, thanks, Dan. I'll see if I can change the picture on the inside of my eyelids. See you shortly." She hugged him again.

"I'm glad you are here with me. I will need your strength to get through this," she said.

Less than twenty-four hours left until the big gulp. Sydney relaxed and prepared for the operation. Steele observed no further emotional strife, and she seemed ready to carry out her critical part of the mission. Without it, there would be no swallow.

The two parted after a long, warm kiss when it was time for Steele to head to the surface and make sure that *Leviathan* could identify the disabled target ship.

"Take good care of yourself, Dan. We'll be together soon."

CHAPTER 80

Vice Presidential Bunker

Washington, DC
May 20, 2025

The vice president welcomed the CIA director and Rear Admiral Owens, accompanied by his aide, to the bunker.

"Can I offer you gentleman a glass of bourbon from the great state of Kentucky?"

"Absolutely," said the CIA director, "It's been another one of those days for me. You know, one step forward and two steps back."

"Admiral, what do you think?"

"Thank you, Mr. Vice President, but my aide, Lieutenant Lewis, and I will pass, we've still got some work to do tonight."

"I hope the work doesn't have anything to do with the president's scheme to derail the transfer of nuclear material to Iran.

"No, it's work that was pushed off because of the transfer. We are catching up with the routine business of our navy special operators."

"I'm not aware of any of our special operators being called in on the transfer, or do I have that confused, admiral?" the vice president asked in a condescending tone.

"I'm not quite sure what you're asking, Mr. Vice President. You know the president's team acts independently from the other teams."

"Look. Let me spell it out for you, admiral. I want to know what the president is planning to stop the transfer."

"I'm not at liberty to say, sir. We have all been sworn to secrecy regarding the plans, if any, that are being implemented. If there were anything that would affect your management of the day-to-day oversight of the government, I'm certain the president would make sure you were dialed in."

"Well, the president hasn't told me squat about his plans, so I thought we could have a quiet, off-the-record chat to put me in the picture. I'm sure you can understand that."

"Crystal clear, sir. But again, I cannot tell you anything."

The vice president reached in the drawer of the chairside table and brought out a 1911 Colt .45 pistol.

"Admiral, do you know what this is?"

"Yes, sir. That looks like a standard issue .45 caliber Colt pistol."

"Correct. My grandfather carried this through the rice paddies of Vietnam. He passed it down to my father who carried it into Desert Storm in 1990, and then he passed it down to me. I call the gun Ol' Pappy after my grandfather. I've often wondered how many gooks or rag heads might have been killed by this pistol." The Vice President saw the Lieutenant wince.

"What's wrong Lieutenant? You find those words offensive? I'm sure with all the sensitivity training you've gotten over there in the Pentagon you do. Makes you want to stand up and walk out of the room or put me on report, right? Look, I find the names offensive too, but sometimes it's helpful to remember that war is hell and you can't refine it. Sherman coined that phrase, maybe after he marched to Atlanta. Truth is, I don't know how many Vietcong or Saddam's Republican guard were killed with this gun, but I'm certain it was more than a handful. It's reality, not fantasy or politics."

The vice president picked up a clip from the drawer and rammed it into the grip, then quickly cycled the slide, putting a round in the chamber.

"Sometimes when I can't seem to persuade someone with logic or maybe a political pledge of some sort of support, I bring out Ol' Pappy to see if I can change their mind. Are you nervous at all, admiral?"

"No, sir, but I'd feel more comfortable if you'd remove the clip from the gun and clear the chamber."

"I'm sure you would."

A sharp report echoed off the stone walls of the room when the gun was pointed and trigger pulled. Bleeding through his white uniform pants, Lieutenant Lewis fell to the ground holding his leg and writhing in pain. From ten feet, the vice president of the United States had just shattered the U.S. Navy officer's leg. Bone splinters stuck out from the exit wound which was pulsing blood onto the carpet. Owens applied direct pressure to the wound and pulled out his cell phone to call for an ambulance.

"Now, admiral, just put that phone away," ordered the vice president waving the gun barrel in his direction. "After you tell me what I want to know you and your horse-holder can move out."

Owens moved toward the vice president, shouting "What in the hell are you thinking, you son-of-a-bitch?"

The gun was leveled at his chest.

"Sit, admiral," he snarled, "I'm listening."

"I won't tell you anything. But what I will do is make sure that you get charged with attempted murder. And I will also find a way to get that service record of yours released to the press. You are finished."

"Really?" The gun spat a second time and hit Owens in his upper arm. Owens grasped his arm and bent over from the shock. He then pulled up, distracting the vice president while he opened and threw a small three-inch bladed pocket knife the short distance to the vice president. The blade severed the man's left carotid artery. Owens wrested the gun from his hand and grabbed the vice president by his mane of white hair, pulled his head back and retrieved his buried knife, wiping the blood on the tailored collar of his starched white shirt.

"Unless the CIA director chooses to save you, you are going to bleed out right here in your bunker, sir. Or you can do all of us a great service and let Ol' Pappy speed things along using your own hand. Your choice."

Owens turned to the CIA director.

"I'm taking my aide to the hospital. I will tell them the assailant is still at large."

The clock mounted on the top floor of Transportation was visible to anyone who entered the conference room where people were working at the same time the drama was playing out in the vice-presidential bunker. 01 Day 20 hours 0 Minutes

CHAPTER 81

Arabian Sea
May 20, 2025

A dozen SEALs from Mac Andrews' west coast team helicoptered to *Leviathan* from Oman as the ship continued its high-speed transit to the rendezvous point. Wilson maintained the ship's high speed so he could have time to test the bow doors and to review the survivors' plan with the SEALs. He planned to continue the sprint toward the rendezvous to permit a dry run the night of May 21st. It would be all hands on deck for the event, though there was not another vessel for the ship to swallow. The rehearsal would fall short of being a realistic representation of the expected operation. Wilson imagined the brutal sound of steel on steel and shuddered.

CHAPTER 82

Ra's Abu Madd

May 22, 2025
10:15 p.m. Arabian Standard Time

The U.S. Army Corps of Engineers was accustomed to large projects, particularly in the Kingdom of Saudi Arabia where they built both Royal Saudi Naval Forces bases, King Khalid Military City, remote air bases, barracks and waterworks. Based on their own internal modeling, the Corps designed and built a continuous sand berm thirty-five feet high along a small section of land north of Yanbu called Ra's Abu Madd, a piece of barren real estate that jutted into the Red Sea.

Detonator cord was connected to explosives buried at the ground level with another along the twenty-foot mark. Explosives were spaced every 120 feet. The top fifteen feet of berm would be detonated simultaneously while the deeper twenty-foot sustainer layer would be ignited in a randomized manner to keep the raw material for the dust cloud in the air and blowing out to sea.

A collection of forty military jet engines had been reworked and shipped over from Davis-Monthan Air Force Base in Tucson, Arizona. The engines were placed on poured reinforced concrete bases. I-Beams with six-inch webs were sunk into the wet concrete to accommodate engine mounting on purpose-built test stands. Twenty tanker trucks had topped off fuel bladders at each engine to provide at least an hour's worth of fuel at max thrust. Those twenty trucks remained on standby to refill bladders if required.

The whine of the aircraft turbines operating in close proximity must have frightened anyone within earshot. Explosive charges would be muffled by the sand, but the aircraft engines would be whining at full power. Steele wondered why the team had never factored in the sound as a possible give away that something out of the ordinary was at play.

At 10:15 local time the explosive sequence began, filling the dark night with tons of fine red sand that would soon blot out the night sky over the Red Sea and reduce visibility to zero.

CHAPTER 83

Red Sea

May 22, 2025
10:25 p.m. Arabian Standard Time

At 10:25, *Simurgh's* radar operator reported a suspected sandstorm to the Officer of the Deck. The officer informed the admiral and the captain of the storm's position seventeen miles east of the ship's position. A large blob on the radar without any return except from its fast-moving edge with nothing behind it, the dust storm was moving westward at forty knots and would envelop the ship by approximately just before 11:00 p.m.

Admiral Ghorbani acknowledged the report, while exhaling nicotine from his hand-rolled cigarette.

Asleep, the ship's captain woke immediately and picked up the phone next to his berth, listened to the report, and ordered the watch officer to maintain course and speed in accordance with the approved navigation track. He asked the officer to contact the Krivak destroyer operating on *Simurgh's* port side to report what they saw of the dust storm and to keep him advised.

Before the watch officer reached for the secure radiotelephone handset, the RSNF ship in company, also stationed on the port side sent a radio message to all ships in company that a dust storm was forming off to the east. There was no proposal related to course and speed.

CHAPTER 84

Red Sea

May 22, 2025
10:30 p.m. Arabian Standard Time

On *Leviathan*, Wilson assembled his team on the darkened bridge.

"Thirty minutes to showtime," he said. "Does anyone have any final thoughts on the operation or is there anything else we need to do."

After head shakes all around, Wilson said, "OK, guys. You know what to do. I expect to see the target ship slowing down in about 15 minutes after *Newport* gets her horns into the hull. We've got *Simurgh* on the scope, but we are also seeing the dust storm blotting out any radar return to the east. We are about to go blind, so I hope we'll get some heading information from that beacon Steele is supposed to mount. It's incredible that this entire operation is now hanging on a single guy, and his job will not be easy. Let's man up. Report to me here on the bridge in ten minutes."

CHAPTER 85

Red Sea

May 22, 2025
10:30 p.m. Arabian Standard Time

Steele left the divers' hatch on *Newport* and swam to the surface of the Red Sea. It was a dark, quiet night. What he didn't see were any lights. The dust storm blacked out everything to the east of his position.

Simurgh's bridge was darkened, the only lights visible were small indicator lights on the communications equipment and the hooded radar repeater that displayed nothing other than the ships in company, but the surface picture was being affected by the dust storm enveloping the ships. Otherwise, it was a routine night on the Red Sea, and it was very quiet on *Simurgh's* bridge. The doors leading to the weather decks were dogged down tight. Even at night, the dust-filled air of the Red Sea was warm and humid, and there were no lights that had to be sighted to assist the navigation team. The door remained dogged down as the watch team had a little over an hour to go on their rotation. Large chillers kept the bridge supplied with fresh air, and several members of the watch team wore jackets to fend off the cold. Everyone was looking forward to a little sleep. With the bow of the ship no longer visible, the watch officer was mesmerized by an electronic chart system which depicted the ship in the sea lanes. The radar was of no use.

On *Newport*, a microphone in the ship's general announcing system clicked on.

"Good evening, this is the captain speaking. As you know, we are on a classified mission which will begin in a few minutes. I will not sound the General Quarters alarm but want everyone to man their battle stations and observe condition Zebra for maximum watertight integrity. We will be using our recently installed hardware to stop the progress of a ship carrying nuclear grade radioactive material to Iran. *Newport* is operating directly under a presidential order. I have reviewed the plans countless times and am confident that none of you will be placed in jeopardy. Our hull, the reactor, and our weapons systems will be fine, but we may scrape some paint in this attack. Be alert and keep focused on your battle stations. That is all."

Her watch officers all gave her the thumbs up and proceeded silently to their battle stations throughout the boat. The submarine had been tracking *Simurgh* for over an hour based on discrete frequencies emitted by the ship's hull and rotating equipment. Though they could not see their prey, there was no doubt that the underwater hunter had the target in its crosshairs.

The engineers had agreed that *Newport* should maintain an underwater speed of fifteen knots for the engagement. The officer of the deck ordered fifteen knots and the reciprocal of *Simurgh's* course of 160 degrees. Once the bow of the sub passed the bow of *Simurgh*, the sub would ascend until the steel horns made contact with the hull. Timing was critical as Garrison did not want to test the sail's strength against *Simurgh's* rudder.

"Helm, steer 340 degrees. Confirm closing course."

"Confirmed 340 degrees, head-on aspect."

"Maintain heading of 340 degrees, make turns for fifteen knots."

Dressed in the uniform of the Iranian Republican Guard Corps, Steele could hear the loud construction-site sounds of demolition as *Newport* rammed its horns into *Simurgh's* hard steel underbelly. Under the lower deckplates, pipes carrying fuel, lube oil and cooling water for heat exchangers for all the rotating equipment were being severed, spewing their pressurized contents in every direction. Angle iron foundations for engines, fire pumps, strainers, purifiers, and condensers were rended away, the twisted metal being raked aft along the hull as if the ship was intentionally driving over an underwater pinnacle, an immovable force ripping out *Simurgh's* heart and its major organs.

In *Newport*, the sound was loud, metallic, and excruciating. No one doubted that *Simurgh* had been mortally wounded, gored to death by horns driven inexorably forward by nuclear-powered propulsion system that drove the prongs deeper and harder with each revolution. The cacophony ended just as quickly as it began and once again, *Newport* sought the silence and the solace of the depths. Shocked by the destructive power of the ship without using its powerful weapons system, the crew looked fatigued, not able to comprehend the catastrophe they had caused. There was no need for a coup de grace. Nothing could save *Simurgh*. Unless some external force was introduced, *Simurgh* would fill with seawater and sink to the bottom of the Red Sea.

The water vibrated with the collision of submarine and surface ship, and the sound of metal on metal carried across the calm water. In his mind's eye, Steele could visualize the frightened reaction of the crew, many of whom had never been taught to swim. The dust storm was doing the job of obscuring everything. From the water, he estimated that he could see perhaps thirty feet ahead on the surface of the water. He checked his compass to the reciprocal *Simurgh's* course and treaded water effortlessly. The homing beacon was carried in a small pack on his back made of the same material as his uniform. It was the size of an old sealed-beam headlight crammed with electronics. An integrated battery pack powered both an LED bulb producing more than 300,000 lumens as well as an IR beam.

Shouts from the ship's weather decks grew louder, panicked men trying to yell over the shrieking sound of the general alarm, as Steele swam slowly to the stricken vessel. He aimed a spring-loaded grappling hook toward the ship's anchor, and a thin, spooled composite line followed the hook to its mark. His gloves were part of the rig, and he pulled himself up on top of the portside anchor and beneath the hawsepipe without any undue effort.

Moving slowly through the water on sluggish momentum, *Simurgh* showed no lights, and Steele noted that the characteristic hum of a ship at sea was missing. The hum was the combined sound of propulsion, electrical and even the galley where electric stainless-steel pots were warming some rations for the crew coming off the last watch period of the day. All that was now silent. As a pre-planned response, a squad of the naval branch of the Iranian Republican Guard Corps fanned out along the deck-edge lifelines, ready for the waterborne assault they believed was coming. The guard at the bow pointed his Kalashnikov at the water as if he expected something to break the surface.

Steele made some scratching sound with the grips of his glove, inviting the guard to investigate further. The guard stuck his head under the lifelines and over the deck edge and Steele pulled him through. He went into the water with a splash. Now on deck, Steele made his way to the superstructure without a challenge. The crew was ready to embark into the inflated lifeboats while simultaneously preparing to receive the Krivak destroyer coming along the port side where the inflated lifeboats would be useless after being squeezed between the two hulls.

Taking advantage of the confusion on deck with crewmembers donning lifejackets and getting to their abandon-ship stations, Steele made his way up external vertical ladders which connected the decks. He made it to the deck behind the ship's mast without encountering anyone. Crew members were looking after themselves and unconcerned about a dripping Corps soldier heading in the opposite direction.

The mast was a hollow composite tube, chocked full of power and data cables feeding antennas, lights and meteorological instruments. Steele started climbing the aft side mast using whatever fittings his hands could quickly find. He couldn't believe that he'd made it this far without being spotted when he heard something plink on the side of the mast. Two excited guards on deck raised the alarm about an intruder on the mast by firing their rifles. Steele quickly mounted the beacon with a Velcro strap as he heard more sharp pings around as the bullets struck rigging, mast supports and antennas. As many as four men were shooting from the main deck. Others were making their way up the ship's external ladders for a closer shot.

Steele moved out on the mast's port arm and slung the empty nylon backpack over the spur of an antenna mounted horizontally. High above the water, he heard Russian commands and realized that the Krivak was coming alongside to take on sailors from the sinking ship. He saw the Krivak a second later, its hull being winched in alongside the *Simurgh,* flipping the inflated rafts and popping their inflation chambers.

With the Republican Guard still firing and Russian shooters now forward on the destroyer's main deck, Steele had no choice. He leaped into space, hoping that he could fit between the two hulls merging to take on passengers. *Simurgh's* bow flair ended further forward, so there would be no space when the ships tied themselves together. Steele did not want to demonstrate that his body could serve as a fender to cushion the two hulls and prevent metal-to-metal contact.

He peered down at the narrowing opening between the two ships' lifelines and the unforgiving deck edge that would open him like a turkey at Thanksgiving dinner. He planned to go feet first but needed to see to navigate the narrow, darkened space so he doubled over like a Mexican cliff diver, turned his body and pointed his toes. As he passed through the closing gap between the two vessels, the deck edge on *Simurgh* tore the boot off his left foot, along with a generous piece of flesh. He entered the water followed by a volley of bullets. He descended along *Simurgh's* hull, heading to the starboard side where the lifeboats were deployed.

Steele got to the surface, where the panicked cries of the crew were deafening. There were others in the water who fell off the ship or avoided the lines from the deck into the water. He had two preplanned options. One was to wait for *Leviathan* to swallow the ship and grab the pilot's ladder on either side of the hull or to find a penetration into *Simurgh's* hull and stay with the ship. Steele liked his chances with the sinking steel under his feet. He dove down and searched the hull by feeling the rush of water filling the hull. What if *Newport* only opened a single hole in the ship?

He needed to surface again for more air when he found the gash in the hull. It reminded him of the twisted re-bar jungle that he navigated through at the bottom of the Chesapeake Bay Bridge and Tunnel years before. Swimming through it, he knew immediately that he was in an engine room. The diesel engines were silent but generating steam as the water climbed higher over the hot engine blocks.

As he treaded the surface of water in the flooded space, the air was heavily laden with the smell of hot diesel oil from the engine immersed in water accompanied by the pungent reek of raw fuel. He hadn't counted on fuel floating on the surface of the water and lapping up against a hot engine. The compartment was already flooded within a foot of the overhead, a vaporous haze above that, and he believed he was the only human in the space. With the engine heat and the thickness of the raw diesel fuel increasing, Steele found himself in a volatile situation.

"Two degrees port." Wilson held a small repeater in his hand that captured the signal from the beacon strapped to *Simurgh's* mast. Just like *Newport,* Wilson couldn't see a thing, and the radar performance was degraded, the radio frequency energy being reflected by the airborne sand which seemed like an impenetrable fog. As modeled, the dust storm delivered an environment where visibility was non-existent or severely fragmented for a few feet. He couldn't see beyond the new deck profile that was bulwarked on each side. Reducing speed to ten knots, he ordered the bow doors open at 10:58 local time, flooding the cargo deck with over two feet of saltwater. High-capacity bilge pumps returned the water to the sea as fast as it entered the ship. A three-inch linchpin holding the two-section stem together was pulled as the curved steel I-beams were retracted into the overhead and a sheath fitted below *Leviathan's* cargo deck. The ship's maw, a gaping hole was ready to ingest a 2,000 ton meal in a single bite.

During the transit from Ulsan, several of Wilson's hand-picked crew discovered some paint in a hazardous storeroom and rendered a gaping shark's mouth on the inside of the doors. The crew also cast some foot-long megalodon teeth from some fiberglass resin and a hand-fashioned mold. With the bow doors wide open and the cargo deck covered by a black gauze cloth, what frightened sailors saw looked like something from a mind-bending horror movie. Add some pumping, amplified sounds from a heavy metal band, with flashing strobe lights illuminating the individual teeth, it was a sight and sound that no one would ever forget — the crew was going straight to hell via a huge prehistoric fish's digestive tract. A hungry mouth surrounded by triangular razor-sharp teeth towered above *Simurgh's* deck.

Wilson was hoping for some separation between *Simurgh* and the Krivak, so he could make a clean capture of *Simurgh*, anticipating that the two ships would be side to side when he arrived. When open, both of the forward doors exposed a razor-sharp knife edge that would take care of any lines between the two ships, and *Leviathan's* hull pressure would naturally push the Krivak away from the target.

CHAPTER 86

IRIS Simurgh

10:59 p.m. Arabian Standard Time
May 22, 2025

Steele swam up through a dog's breakfast of engine room debris illuminated by a single bulkhead-mounted battle lantern, half its lens covered with dirty water: paper cups, log sheets, cigarette butts, rags and bedding from the displaced crew. The engine room was filthy, and much of its detritus was rising to the surface to float in the mixture of fuel and lubricating oils. Steele hoped there would be enough oxygen in the space, so that he could take a deep breath while panning the space for the water-tight door or hatch to escape.

He found a pocket of air near the overhead of the compartment between the beams supporting the main deck, believing that he was likely in the after part of the forward engineering space that was flooded all the way to the overhead. Garrison had certainly used *Newport's* horns effectively. Steele put his lips against the cold steel supporting the deck and superstructure above and found some greasy air. Diving down through the soup, his eyes closed, he felt along the bulkhead for the watertight door that would lead to fresh air. He got a mild shock from one of the cabinets he passed his hand over but finally found the door. Running out of air, he twisted the handle of the heavy door that was connected to a network of steel bars that engaged wedges around the door frame simultaneously to make it watertight by compressing a thick gasket around the door's rim. Steele couldn't budge the handle.

After repeated attempts he concluded that the identical mechanism on the other side of the door had been somehow locked to seal the space, probably to reduce the effect of progressive flooding.

Steele glanced at the luminous dials of his watch. S-time was forty-five seconds away. He put his head between two I-Beams and took a quick breath that was a combination of bad air and greasy seawater. If he couldn't leave the engine room via the watertight door, he would have to assume that any escape hatch was likely dogged down tight and locked from the other side. His only escape route was back the way he came, through a jagged hole opened by *Newport*. Steele took one last soggy breath before submerging and hoping he could make it through the maze of pipes, railings, cooling systems and ripped shell plates to reach the outside of the hull. He badly needed fresh air, and time was short.

Swimming to the lower level of the engine room, he felt a heavy, massive shudder of the ship's hull as if it were rising on a high swell. Except this swell was metal, not seawater. Metal-to-metal screeching as the two weighty waterborne objects collided. All the banshees in the heavens were singing together to mark this trip inside a fish of fantasy size and strength. Surfacing again, Steele found no air. His head was pounding with the excruciating sound of metal against metal, thinking that his teeth would fall out of his jaw with the violent movement. The ship's upright angle changed.

Leviathan's jaws welcomed the smaller ship into its mouth, its mast bending on the main deck edge and then breaking off onto the after superstructure. Water began rushing out through the holes in the hull, spilling out onto *Leviathan's* wide cargo deck. Steele fought the surge of water moving forward and was able to catch a breath as the cacophony continued right under the torn and twisted hull of the engine room. The sound reminded him of the high pitch of a multi-tip dentist's drill exploring a dozen cavities simultaneously. An air pocket opened and got slightly larger as Steele braced himself for further movement. He was thrown against the bulkhead of the engine room as the screeching stopped, and the steady hum of an engine reverberated through the twisted hull. Hydraulic sounds soon dominated as *Leviathan* reduced its forward speed and closed the giant bow doors. Moments later, the ship's speed increased.

Steele then looked at the equipment hanging on every bulkhead. The angles of the power panels and piping told him that

Simurgh was on its starboard side, meaning the escape through the ship's hull would be blocked by the *Leviathan's* deck. It also meant that the seawater filling the compartment would drain out at a slower rate. Steele felt sleepy and suddenly very cold. Losing body heat, hypothermia was lowering his core temperature. He'd been in the water for what felt like hours and expected his body's response. Touching his numb left foot, he felt exposed ligaments and tendons and wondered if he'd be able to walk normally again. The ship felt quiet. He wasn't sure whether there were other survivors aboard but simply waited for the next part of the plan to be executed. For the moment, he was alive but trapped in the *Simurgh's* mangled hull.

CHAPTER 87

Leviathan

11:08 p.m. Arabian Standard Time
May 22, 2025

Steele recalled the admiral asking, "How are you going to handle the survivors that stay on the ship?"

Sandy Matthews had a quick answer.

"There is a non-lethal gas developed by the Naval Research Lab that can be used to anesthetize any remaining crew members. They will have no memory of the incident. Our thinking was to put them in a lifeboat and deploy it as we continue north through the Red Sea. We have acquired an Iranian encapsulated lifeboat that can be used for this purpose. That may also cover our tracks."

Steele didn't know how the gas could find its way to the flooded engine room but knew that the plan was to gas the space and then complete a thorough search of the ship's interior spaces once the ship was de-watered. That would take a very long time.

The water in the engine room had dropped a few inches since the big swallow. Steele was shivering uncontrollably, and the effects of the exposure would leave him unconscious if his core temperature continued to drop. The petrochemical fumes filling the airspace did not help the situation. He had a pounding headache and felt a little sleepy with the lack of oxygen in the air. A piece of line floated into view, and he harnessed himself to the bulkhead hoping that someone would find him before he died of asphyxia or fire. He'd survived much worse than this, but to die in a cold, seawater-filled engine room that could burst into flames any second was not the way he planned to go.

Gunfire inside the hull woke Steele immediately. He ignored his cold, deadened legs, and unstrapped himself from the bulkhead. The water had retreated another six inches. One watertight, battery-powered battle lantern gave off a weak glow across the engine room but not enough to see anything clearly. It would have to be done by feel. In the darkness, Steele tried to visualize the gunfire sound outside *Simurgh's* hull. It sounded like a two-way exchange between friendlies and the Republican Guard — he listened to the sound of the weapons, Kalashnikov rifles for the Guards and MP-5s for the SEALs and recognized the sound of rifles that had a sharper, more metallic report than the MPs. The SEALs' fire followed tactical protocols while the Kalashnikovs were being fired by undisciplined soldiers on full automatic.

How many additional ammunition clips the combatants carried was a matter of conjecture. He was certain that he was in the forward engine room, the first engineering space skewered by *Newport's* lances and the first to flood. In the scenarios studied by the team, everyone had agreed that any surviving crewmembers would immediately withdraw once they saw the flooding.

What Steele hadn't anticipated came next in the form of the engine room hatch opening and Arabic whispers between two men, one of whom had a bright LED headlamp that lit up the area in its swath of light like the sun peeking out of a dark cloud. It was clear that the two insurgents planned to lie in wait for the searchers and cut them down as soon as the watertight door was flung open. Steele saw the men check the rifles carried over their heads and then take defensive positions on the short ladder between decks, protected by a quarter-inch diamond plated stainless steel deck plate. These men would be difficult for the search team to root out, and the men were positioned to make the landing inside the watertight door their kill zone.

Steele lay silently on the engine room upper level, exposed with no weapon should the piercing light move in his direction. Any movement would create a metallic sound inside the cavernous space, and he would be quickly found. His skin was not the only risk, as he anticipated the search team would get there at some point, and they might get ambushed just inside the watertight door. Waiting for the adversary to make a move would shift the tactical advantage, and Steele never favored the passive approach to anything. He carefully slid the uniform shirt up his arm and felt the smooth blade of a throwing knife that he always carried on missions. It was a balanced weapon made of Ipe, a dense South American hardwood crafted by a retired U.S. Army ranger.

Steele slowly moved into a position to throw the knife, aiming at the headlamp still glowing about twenty feet away. The overhead beam left little room for his throwing arm. Steele threw the knife when the lamp was trained on the door. He heard it hit something metallic. The light moved to the left, and Steele could see the knife hilt just under the chin of the target. Knowing that the attack came from within the engine room, the remaining soldier would be determined to find the fighter who took his comrade's life. When the light found Steele, it would be followed by a hail of bullets. At this range, it would be difficult to miss. Steele had to move in the darkness. He dropped beneath the water, crawled on his belly down the catwalk as the light began to pan the bulkheads in a methodical way.

Just as the first rounds struck the steel deck edge of the catwalk, the watertight door opened, and a flash bang was thrown into the space that made a deafening sound and created a paralyzing light which immediately blinded any open eyes. The combination of light and sound pressure overwhelmed the senses. Steele heard men rushing into the space and saw their night vision optics glow a pale green. The combatant was separated from his gun while the team used their headlamps to search the room. Steele yelled the word "blue" before the lights turned on him and raised his hands, hoping that the SEALs would understand there was a friendly swimming in the dirty water.

Given a three-question quiz to verify his identity, Steele was escorted to the passageway, where he was searched and then led to the bow where he saw six to eight Republican Guards on the canted deck with their hands secured behind their backs with plastic tie wraps. He was hustled down the ship's twisted accommodation ladder which led to *Leviathan's* cargo deck where he was greeted with a bear hug by Sandy Matthews.

"I'm glad to see you, Sandy. How are we doing?" asked Steele.

"I think we are on track, Dan."

"Where are we?"

"Heading toward Port Suez. I'll take you up to your cabin to clean up. You smell like you took a bath in diesel fuel. Wilson has put the smoking lamp out throughout the ship. I'll meet you in the War Room where you can get up to speed on the operation."

"Sounds good. I need to drink a gallon of water to get the gunk out of my system. My foot got sliced by the deck edge on my way into the water, and I think I need to see a doctor if we have one aboard." Steele pulled up his pantleg to get a better look at his mangled foot. Sandy took a quick glance at the large chunk missing from Steele's foot and gagged.

"Let's get you to sickbay right now. That looks bad."

CHAPTER 88

Leviathan

11:30 p.m. Arabian Standard Time
May 22, 2025

"Any sign of Steele?" asked Wilson to the bridge watch of *Leviathan.* To a man, the ship's Navy crew and Steele's brother SEALs were anxious to find him alive. When the water pouring out of the swallowed ship's bottom began to slow, Wilson ordered the search of the captured vessel. Armed men were posted on the elevated catwalk above the deck where the battered vessel lay. The SEALs were prepared just as if they were breaching a house in Afghanistan looking for Al-Qaeda. *Simurgh's* drawings had been studied, and the ship broken into zones where four-man teams would clear the spaces as they pushed through the vessel from stem to stern, top to bottom. Every accessible compartment would be searched. They would look for survivors, as well as explosive packages that may have been planted by the Iranians.

IAEA contractors would follow and begin the process of removing the casks containing the radioactive material from *Simurgh's* twisted weather decks. A team of engineers would address the fuel oil tanks, coolers and sumps on the ship to remove any hazardous material and dispose of it in *Leviathan's* massive scavenger tanks where it would be circulated and purified for re-use. The ship steamed north through a tranquil Rea Sea toward the southern terminus of the Suez Canal.

Eight prisoners were gassed and placed in the inflatable lifeboat and dropped into the Red Sea. They would have no memory of the events since they were swallowed by the big ship. Their shipmates' memories would be sketchy at best as they were rescued and taken into ports in Saudi Arabia and Egypt. The description of the giant fish's mouth and their inside look at Hell would signal any medical caregivers to be concerned about their mental health. Sailors losing parts of their bodies to the knife edge behind the doors were committed to the deep in a solemn ceremony, collateral damage from the vantage point of the geopolitical balance.

The press picked up the story after being blinded by the sandstorm, the worst in memory according to the Saudi Arabian press. There was wide speculation about what had happened to the ship and the casks of radioactive material. *Simurgh* had simply disappeared without a trace.

CHAPTER 89

Leviathan

4:00 p.m. Arabian Standard Time
May 23, 2025

Seventeen hours after the big gulp. *Leviathan* loitered near the southern tip of Egypt's Sinai desert, well outside the shipping channel. During the transit, its name had been changed to *Athena,* flagged out of Greece, bound for the Pacific. A re-painted deckhouse, and a different deck configuration completed the makeover. Two large kingposts sprouting from the main deck and soaring to a vertical height of over 100 feet were distinguishing identifiers of *Leviathan.* Fabricated by the shipyard of reinforced heavy gauge plastic, both had been lowered and tucked behind the deck edge. Two painted colored bands had topped the ship's stack. Painted over in black and replaced with a large white letter "A", *Leviathan* had been transformed into *Athena.*

Under a bright blue afternoon sky, *Athena* transited slowly eastward toward the Gulf of Aqaba. Steele reconnected with the West Coast SEALs, many of whom he knew from previous missions. They were part of a larger family of special operators from all services who were bonded by the conflicts they had fought all over the world. A large pilot boat drew alongside, and the special operators departed the ship for an exercise with the Jordanian Special Forces. Steele was among them. On crutches, Steele needed help getting down the ladder and onto the pilot boat. *Athena's* corpsman had patched up his foot and loaded him up with big gun antibiotics. He was wearing a soft cast to protect his foot and calf. The corpsman had not seen anything that would cause Steele any long-term problems but reiterated that rest and time would both be needed to return him to an operational condition. His foot was numb and sported several drains to take away the fluids that would accumulate during the healing process.

Athena reached the location of the great swallow at 03:00 a.m. in the morning of May 24, 2025. The night was black but the visibility unlimited, the canopy above full of stars. All signs of the dust cloud had vanished. Opening its gigantic bow doors and slowing to stop, huge hydraulic rams pushed what was left of *Simurgh* out of the ship where it immediately sank to the bottom of the Red Sea with a few bubbles.

International teams with deep diving capability were getting organized to get to the site of the ship's sinking. *Simurgh* was presumed to have found a previously unreported and unsurveyed seamount that the ship struck with catastrophic results. Because of the depth of water, nearly 1,000 feet, there was speculation that the casks might never be found. Deep submersibles would be required to locate the casks, and specialized waterborne cranes and lifts would be required to recover them. Any such project would take months of planning and a fortune to assemble the necessary equipment in the Red Sea.

The escorts pulling into Saudia Arabia and Egypt had tallied up a total of 145 survivors from *Simurgh* out of a crew and riders of 170, and there were eight crewmembers found floating in a lifeboat, so they were still seventeen souls missing. The press had already labeled the commander of the Krivak destroyer a hero for taking on the bulk of survivors from *Simurgh*, including the IRGC general and the ship's commanding officer. Admiral Ghorbani was not among those in any of the lifeboats or on the escort ships. He was assumed to have gone done with the ship.

Suez Canal logs were examined to determine the identity of ships transiting the Red Sea at the time *Simurgh* disappeared. Canal officials repeatedly asked if anyone had observed anything during the once in a century dust storm that completely obliterated that part of the Red Sea. Even the overhead sensors were blinded by the clouds of dust. The Pentagon was clueless.

Iran alternated blaming the United States and Israel for the disappearance of the ship and its cargo. The Ayatollah promised to empty the cauldrons of Hell on the non-believers. A fatwa was recorded naming the leaders of both countries and any of their citizens encountered abroad.

As *Simurgh* settled on the deep seabed, Steele prepared to board a flight from Aqaba, Jordan to Andrews Air Force Base, Maryland.

CHAPTER 90

USS Newport
June 15, 2025

The boat's steel horns had been removed in the Mediterranean and left on the ocean floor. Soon, they would be covered with corals and appear like something natural on the undersea landscape. Days later, *Newport* berthed in Gaeta, Italy for an upkeep period and a change of command.

A gentle, warm breeze swept over *Newport's* hull where sailors in dress whites manned the rail. An elevated platform had been craned into place on the pier, which served as a backdrop for the time-honored ceremony. Extended in her position as the ship's commanding officer and the first woman to command an attack submarine, Commander Sydney Garrison would formally turn over her command.

The piers were quiet for the ceremony which began promptly at 10:00 a.m. Beginning with a prayer and ending with the newly appointed commander stating simply I relieve you and then reporting for duty to the officer presiding over the ceremony, a change of command was a common event in the maritime services. Rear Admiral Jeremy Quinn had flown over to Italy from Groton, Connecticut. His role was to accept the reporting for duty from the new commanding officer and to present Garrison with an award. Part of the ceremony also included the reading of orders of both officers. Garrison would report to the Pentagon's Joint Staff for her subsequent tour. She looked like a Navy recruiting poster in her dress whites, rows of medals under her gold dolphins, lesser awards on the opposite side of her uniform, and insignia over the front of her starched jacket.

The Legion of Merit citation was read aloud by Admiral Quinn, the Submarine Group commander.

"The President of the United States takes pleasure in presenting the Legion of Merit to

Commander Sydney Garrison for exceptionally meritorious conduct in the performance of outstanding service as Commanding Officer, *USS Newport,* from March 2022 until June 2025."

The detailed citation highlighted Garrison's exemplary accomplishments in command. Among those were *Newport's* winning the Battle Effectiveness award for each of the three years she commanded the ship; the ship's participation in Joint and Combined Operations and her winning of the peer-nominated James Bond Stockdale Award for Inspirational Leadership for two consecutive years. *Newport's* performance in several special operations as well as the recent rescue of two SEALs from a deep diving accident were enumerated.

Gushing with pride, Garrison's parents were seated in the front row with several of her Navy classmates and other submariners. Many of her female colleagues hoped that they could navigate through the gaping hole she'd left in the submarine force's glass ceiling.

During the reception, held under a white tent on the pier, guests wished Garrison fair winds and following seas, and welcomed the new commander. He had big shoes to fill. The wardroom officers eyed the new commander and wondered how life aboard *Newport* would change in the weeks ahead.

CHAPTER 91

Gaeta, Italy
June 25, 2025

After a week touring Rome, the Amalfi coast, and Tuscany with her parents, Garrison dropped them at the airport in Rome and returned to Gaeta to pack up her apartment and check in her car for shipment back to the States. The following day, she was driven to Leonardo da Vinci–Fiumicino Airport in Rome for a midday flight to Washington, DC. Steele promised to meet her at Dulles. Garrison had requested sixty days of leave between *Newport* and her next duty station. She looked forward to decompressing after over three years in command and kept focused on her immediate challenge of knowing if Dan Steele was the right choice for her.

Between leaving Italy and reporting to the Pentagon, there would be time to catch up with stateside friends, to spend time with her parents and Dan Steele. Sydney Garrison was looking forward to a new chapter in her life. Little did she know that the next chapter would include the possibility of an early death.

CHAPTER 92

Dulles International Airport

Virginia
June 27, 2025

Garrison's flight was delayed. A bomb threat brought Leonardo da Vinci's operations to a sudden halt. It was rush hour in the skies and on the highways when Garrison landed. Rolling a modern-day folding bag behind her, she spotted a beaming Dan Steele behind the visitors' barrier. After a brief hug and quick kiss, the two walked to Steele's car and started to thread their way through the airport traffic and onto the artery connecting the airport with northern Virginia. Traffic was crawling.

Garrison pulled up her phone.

"Good. My meeting with Admiral Harding is confirmed for 0700 tomorrow morning. I should be ready to travel north by 10:00 a.m. How does that sound?"

"That will work. With this traffic, it will be a short night."

They arrived at the Pentagon City Mall in Arlington, Virginia at a hotel located in the shadow of the Pentagon.

Steele dutifully pulled Garrison's bag as she checked in. After a beer in the lobby bar, where they caught up on the current events since her change of command, they both went straight to her room. Garrison tapped her key card, opened the door and then wheeled around as the door closed and wrapped Steele in her arms.

"I missed you, Dan."

After a kiss that overloaded his senses, Sydney pulled away.

Steele was already shedding his clothes like they were burning his body. Naked and attentive to what was about to happen, Steele stood in front of Sydney and realized that he had just made a big mistake. Sydney was fully clothed and had her arms crossed in front of her body.

"Dan, first, please put your clothes back on. I know that it will be difficult but try. Second, there's nothing I'd like to do more than to make love to you. But the simple fact is that you and I don't know each other very well. And I am not a dog in heat. Here's the challenge. We will walk, explore and enjoy the sights, and I will tell you about my earliest memories as a child up to my life now. You will listen closely and ask me anything you want about me."

"OK," said Steele, "I understand."

"And you will tell me your story, starting from when you were a little boy, your first memories all the way up to the present. I can ask you questions along the way. We will not gloss over this important period of discovery and understanding nor complicate it with any physical activity. Essentially, we are going to learn about each other and once our stories are told, you will feel closer to me or not, and I will have the same opportunity. We'll either continue our relationship or not, but we'll know for certain if we should be together."

Steele sheepishly replied, "I can tell you my story in about fifteen minutes, so I don't understand this rigid schedule." He was still having trouble putting his shorts back on.

"Trust me, Dan. You'll understand it, and it's the only way we can be sure that there's something here other than a strong physical attraction. You and I both know there's plenty of that, but we must put that aside for now and learn about each other. It will be hard, excuse the pun, but there will be no sexual exploration until these stories are told. I know you may find this severe and controlling, but I know it's necessary before we decide anything about our future lives together."

"OK, I understand. I'll pick you up out front at 10:30 a.m. That should give you time to change and check out."

"Let's make it 11:00, Dan. I'll see you in the morning. Good night."

★ ★ ★

They began the trip north.

On that first day to clear the city, Steele was driving the car and telling his story. He just related an early memory about a third-grade encounter with the neighborhood bully, Tim, who enjoyed pushing Steele down after they got off the bus in the afternoon. His mother was shocked to see grass stains on his new school pants.

"What happened, Dan?" she asked as she joined him at the kitchen table as he was bringing out his homework.

"It's that kid, Tim, who lives with his dad just past the Williams' house. He messes with my book bag and likes to push me around after we get off the bus. In fifth grade. A big kid who brags on the bus that he'll beat me up if I ever get him in trouble with his dad."

"OK, so what did he do today?"

"Well, we got off the bus and he pushed me down in the ditch alongside the road. It's got thick grass on the sides and is always wet in the bottom, and he made me walk in the mud."

"Well, I'll call his mother and have a word with her."

"I don't think he has a mom," said Steele, thinking about the beating he'd get the following day.

"Listen, Dan, if he can't be persuaded to stop this behavior, we'll have to go with the second option which I like better anyway."

"What's that?"

"That's where you treat him in kind but do it in a way that he'll stop pestering you."

"What do you mean? I push him into the ditch?"

"More or less. You need to learn how to get some leverage on a bigger boy. Let me show you."

After a lesson in momentum and balance, a confident Dan Steele got off the bus the following day.

"Why don't you walk home in the mud down in the ditch?" asked Tim.

"I don't think so" replied Steele taking an uphill position from the bully.

"Well, you are going to whether you like it or not," said Tim, grabbing Steele's arm.

Steele lowered his shoulder and gave Tim a quick, unexpected push in his stomach that ended up with Tim sitting on the bottom of the soggy ditch. He started to cry. Steele got down to the edge of the ditch and helped Tim up, after he promised to never bully him again.

Sydney laughed, "That's priceless. I think your mom taught you a good lesson."

Steele's voice was hoarse, and bone dry by the time they stopped that first afternoon on the Eastern shore of Maryland for some fresh crab cakes and local beer. They checked in to a hotel in Baltimore's inner harbor. When the desk clerk suggested a higher floor with a king bed, Steele blurted out "great" with Sydney following up with "Do you have anything on a lower floor with two beds?"

"I've got a room with a harbor view on the eighth floor with two queens."

"We'll take it," Sydney replied, placing her credit card on the ledge separating the guests from the staff. Sydney gave Steele the choice of beds and was certain that he'd never met anyone so single-minded.

Later, after dinner and some more talk of the past, Sydney changed and gave Steele a wonderful warm kiss and said "goodnight." Lights out and Sydney just out of his reach.

This trip was going to be like another Hell week for Steele.

CHAPTER 93

The White House

Washington, DC
June 28, 2025

Frustrated, the president couldn't publicly recognize the members of the big gulp operation or tell the story to the press. A few creative people involved put their lives on hold and developed a solution to a major political, security, and world order problem in a few short months. They had successfully pulled off a major diplomatic coup which had no US fingerprints on it. Investigative reporters were scrambling to understand what happened that night in the Red Sea, and it seemed like every country with a submersible in its inventory was back at it, offering help and assistance to the international community, not just the Iranians. How ironic. It would be difficult for the Pentagon to get a meeting roster approved in that time.

The incident had fallen off the front page in the press. The Iranians were convinced the Americans were behind the debacle but couldn't rule out the Israelis. Also suspects were the Russians, who seemed suspiciously silent on the matter, even though one of their destroyers was there to witness the event.

CHAPTER 94

Pennsylvania
June 28, 2025

On day two of their journey, Steele felt more relaxed as the pair drove to Gettysburg and enjoyed a perfect day. Sydney was anxious to see the place where Colonel Joshua Chamberlain and his regiment, the 20th Maine Infantry, gained notoriety for their desperate bayonet charge down Little Round Top on the second day of the battle against the Confederates. Among other actions that day, Chamberlain's heroic maneuver led to the surrender of Lee's army.

That night, they stayed at an inn near Gettysburg and slept in two twin beds that seemed sized for children.

After a breakfast of eggs, scrapple and toast, the pair continued north to Philadelphia. Sydney had three stops on her wish list. A walk through the Reading market, a cheesesteak at both Geno's and Pat's, and a photo of the Rocky statue outside the Philadelphia Museum of Art. That night, a hotel in the old part of the city gave them a view of the battleship USS New Jersey (BB-62) moored across the Delaware River in Camden, New Jersey.

On day three, they explored the Garden State. During the drive to Cape May, Steele reached the part of his life story when Sydney asked about his first kill during an actual operation with the SEAL team. Steele had hidden that memory away in a deep part of his brain but told her that an operation in the mountains of Afghanistan was the first time he'd killed someone. Not a maybe either. A man had charged Steele's position just as Steele's weapon failed. His sidearm was buried under an Afghan robe so the only weapon he could get to before the man pounced was his knife, the same weapon held by his attacker.

Steele parried the first thrust and ended up on the ground with the bearded fighter on top of him. Strong and wiry, the Afghan clamped his legs around Steele's torso and used his free arm and upper body weight to drive the blade into the infidel's chest while maintaining a death grip on Steele's weapon hand. Reacting quickly when he felt the point of the weapon pierce his skin, Steele kicked out of the hold and flung the man forward over his head. The man rolled and came up in a fighting stance before Steele got up off his hands and knees.

Steele buried his head in the man's solar plexus and fell on top of him. The man had lost his air and was momentarily out of commission. That didn't last long. Revived, the man stabbed Steele in his side and pushed him off his body as he rolled to give the American the coup de grace. Steele gave the man an elbow to his temple, stunning him. Dazed, the combatant reacted to the blow and moved his free hand up to survey the damage to his head while Steele pressed forward and stabbed the man in his chest. Blood gushed from the wound as the man gave Steele a sick smile of defeat. It was the smile that haunted Steele. He would never forget it.

It was a story that he had never told anyone. While somewhat cathartic, Steele felt nauseous after relating the details. There was nothing glamorous or heroic about the tale. Steele was lucky to have bested his opponent. He vowed to minimize the details if he needed to relate any other kills to her.

They slowly walked the boardwalk and enjoyed the warm ocean breeze right off the Delaware. Passing by several food trucks offering everything from cheese steaks to Cuban sandwiches, they settled for a fresh fish taco eaten at a nearby picnic table. Sydney suggested a large cone of sweet soft-serve custard for dessert. It was the best ice cream he'd ever eaten. In his head, Steele banked the equivalent of at least three hours of strenuous activity to offset its effect.

CHAPTER 95

Connecticut
June 30, 2025

Sydney didn't have anything on her sightseeing list in northern New Jersey or in the New York suburbs of Connecticut, so the couple drove through to Niantic, Connecticut where she promised Steele the best seafood platter he'd ever eaten. After leaving the Governor Mario Cuomo bridge spanning the Hudson just south of West Point, Steele took the exit for the Merritt Parkway. The tree-lined Parkway gave anyone traveling north a break from the stress of I-95.

"You know Dan, that dark blue Camry with Illinois plates is following us. I saw it in Gettysburg and again in Philadelphia. Do you have someone tailing us?" asked Sydney.

"Not that I'm aware of. I'm in that comfort zone between crises and don't know that I've gotten anyone angry enough to follow us. Are you sure it's the same car?"

"I'm sure it's the same car. I thought you were all about situational awareness. Are you so smitten with me that you can't keep track of your surroundings?" she laughed. Steele blushed and felt hot under his collar.

"I guess you caught me there. And yes, I'm not doing a good job maintaining situational awareness with you next to me. You are a wonderful distraction. Maybe Rickover's ghost is trying to see how you behave after your command."

"Why didn't I think of that?" Sydney laughed again. "Can you pull into the next rest stop so I can powder my nose, and we can get something cold to drink?"

After studying myriad beverage choices, both chose cold water. They strolled down to the car, and Steele spotted the dark blue Camry backed into a spot at the far end of the rest area.

"Looks like we are still being followed. How far is Niantic?" he asked.

"Not far," she said, "we should be there in an hour or so. The big question mark is whether or not New Haven is backed up." She looked at him and put her arm around his neck. "At the risk of killing your situational awareness entirely," she said as she kissed him softly on the lips.

"Wow, I didn't see that coming. I'll try to make it to our destination without thinking about it."

"I've got another story that will keep us on track, and it took place near today's destination. As a young girl, I'd often go with my dad out to the breakwaters and rocky parts of the shore, exploring for whatever I could find. I'd collect periwinkles and pull mussels off rocks at low tide. Dad taught me to use a mask and snorkel and another world opened for me. I wasn't much of a swimmer but was happy to stay in the shallows and look at all the life on the rocks and bottom. He insisted that I drag an inflatable orange buoy behind me for safety and would check on me whenever he surfaced. Sometimes my dad would bring a speargun and try to shoot some tautog. He'd shoot a couple of the fish and bring them home for fish chowder. Blackfish were a delicious, white-fleshed fish with snaggled teeth and a bony head that you'd have to saw through to separate.

It was just another beautiful day in the water when I swam over to a new spot near a short breakwater and suddenly the bottom seemed to be getting further away. Nothing was in reach, so I surfaced and found that I'd been carried out in the current and way past my dad who was looking towards the shore for me. I tried to dog-paddle against the current and could still see the bottom and knew I wasn't making any progress.

My legs were so tired, and I was breathing so hard I almost spit out my snorkel. My dad finally saw me and was able to reach me in seconds because he was a strong swimmer and always wore fins for spearfishing. It felt like it took a long time for him to catch up with me. I held on to the float and never felt so scared in my life. My dad inflated his vest, and we continued out in the sound while he explained the physics of rip currents. Then, he towed me parallel to the beach, and the water stopped moving. Two things came out of that day. First, I gained an appreciation for the power of the ocean and second, I started taking swimming lessons. If my father hadn't been there and aware of where I was, I might have ended up being eaten by a shark or washed up on Long Island. I'm not sure which would have been worse!"

Just before 4:00 p.m., the two pulled into a beachfront hotel right on the boardwalk with lanes for runners and walkers connecting to a public fishing pier jutting out into the water. After checking in, they walked hand-in-hand along touristy shops and souvenir stands and at least one tattoo parlor. Steele suggested a heart pierced with a dagger and the words Death before Dishonor be inked on his forearm.

"I've already got one of those" Sydney said, "but it's hidden."

"I don't believe it," said Steele.

"Stick around and maybe someday you'll find out," Sydney challenged. "Are you ready to devour some fish? The restaurant is about 20 minutes' walk from here, some on the boardwalk and some on the beach."

"Sounds great. So, we don't need to change, right?"

"Nope. It's very casual."

"Sounds great. I am ready for some good seafood."

"Oh, did I say seafood? I'm taking you to a bargain burger joint topped with yellow arches."

After admitting it was the best mix of fried and broiled seafood Steele had ever had, the two retraced their steps to the hotel. He was thankful for the opportunity to begin walking off the calories of the generous portions of everything, drizzled with butter and washed down with local craft beer.

"Great food, and wonderful company. We should do this more often."

"Agreed. It's one of my favorite places."

At 03:00 a.m., Steele awoke and changed into a swimming suit, tee-shirt, and his running shoes. Sydney was sound asleep on the other queen-sized bed, and he tried to be as quiet as he could when opening the door to the hallway. He figured that the driver of the dark blue Camry might try to plant something in their car. If he were doing it himself, he would use the wee hours of the night. If the man were some sort of special operator, he might think the same thing. A big "if" but Steele was anxious to find the man and to find out why they were being followed. There was no reason to lead danger to Sydney's parents' home either.

Steele carried a small penlight and headed to the valet section of the garage. He paused at the door and opened it without a sound, ducking behind a row of cars in the shadows. The garage was well-illuminated. He stayed in place for ten minutes until his eyes were fully adjusted, and his hearing tracked the ambient noise in the garage before spotting their rental car. The trunk was open, and he could see the back of a person working inside. A small well-worn duffel bag had been placed on the unadorned concrete deck. Steele wished he were carrying a firearm but wanted to avoid the hassle of taking a gun across state lines. Even his fighting skills were no match for someone with a gun. He couldn't see the person's face, but he did retrieve what looked like hand tools from the bag. Bomb?

Steele was hidden but still twenty feet away when the individual stepped back, examined his work and then threw a lamp into the bag and closed the trunk. Steele could not see the man's face but approached him soundlessly from behind, until the man sensed his presence.

"Hi," said Steele. "Are you the guy from Triple A?" he asked.

"No," said a deep voice, continuing to walk away from Steele.

"What were you doing in that car?"

The man quickened his pace and did not answer. After a few long strides, Steele caught up with the man and grabbed his shoulder. He whirled around fluidly like an adagio dancer and pushed a hypodermic needle into Steele's midsection. After a half step, Steele collapsed on the floor of the garage. The man dragged him back to the rental car and pushed Steele onto the back seat. Dead weight the man muttered, or soon to be.

Sitting in the drivers' seat, the assailant looked across the garage with the rear-view and side mirrors. Satisfied that the only two people in the garage were now in the same car, he started the car using an electronic device from the duffel bag and drove out of the garage entrance. The gate was up because the hotel wanted to avoid a nighttime parking attendant on the payroll. Slowly, the driver drove one block and turned right at a sign arrowing the "Fishing Pier" and stopped.

Sydney Garrison was awake, laying in the bed thinking — where in the hell did Steele go? Curious, she pulled off her nightshirt and slipped on a pair of shorts and a tee-shirt and strapped on a pair of leather huaraches before heading to the lobby, half expecting to see Steele on a pay phone, and then out to the boardwalk. She saw nothing. Steele had successfully impersonated others. If he were living a double life now and leading Sydney down the path for some reason or other, she would rather find out the sorry facts sooner rather than later. The keys to the rental car were left on the desk in the room, so she knew that he wasn't taking an early morning drive. What was he up to?

She heard a car with squealing tires splinter the "Pedestrians Only" sawhorse at the beginning of the fishing pier. In the broken light, it looked like their rental car. Running to the pier, she watched the car careen between the pressure-treated wooden railings at high speed. Out of control or being driven by someone with a death wish, the car clipped a small information booth, toppling the structure. Could it be Steele? She reached the wooden deck of the pier as the rental car broke through the strong railing at the end and plunged into the water, splashing loudly. As she sprinted down the pier, Garrison thought about what to do next. Would the car still be floating or already underwater?

She reached the end of the pier in time to see the trunk of the car disappear under the black water. It was definitely their rental car. Without another thought, she dived off the pier into the black water, thinking that Steele must be unconscious and oblivious to the fact that he would soon be drowning in twenty feet of water. The last pier light had gone into the drink along with the car, and the moon didn't illuminate a thing in the inky water. She kept her hands in front of her and felt them drive into the sandy bottom. Where in the hell was the car? Searching with her hands swinging wildly in search of the car, she contacted something hard and metallic. She followed the surface, rough with barnacles, and quickly realized she was on the wrong car. Barnacles do not grow quickly, so this vehicle, whatever it was, had to have been on the bottom for years.

She remembered reading the plaque on the pier recognizing a local company for constructing an artificial reef near the end of the pier to create a habitat for fish. Panicked, she twisted ninety degrees and in a new direction. Another car, but it too was covered with barnacles. Feeling a tingle in her legs, she needed a fresh lungful of air. Surfacing and gulping air, she purged her lungs and then dove again, having no idea of the state of the tide or the current that might run by the end of the pier. She only suspected that the man she'd come to love was in a car, probably unaware that his lungs were filling with seawater. A race against time. What were the chances?

Again, she surfaced and took in several deep breaths of the salty air. In the loom of one of the pier lights still standing, she could see several people looking down at her.

"Someone call 911," she yelled.

Feeling hopeless for half a second, she jackknifed back to the bottom. Within seconds, her hands hit a tire. The side panels were smooth, and the car had flipped over on its roof. Opening the door, she found the passenger side empty. She reached across the front seat and found a body pressed against the seat by an inflated airbag. She tore the airbag away from Steele's head and put her arm around his limp body.

Using the air bag, Garrison kicked to the surface as hard as she could. She'd never lifted anything so heavy. Steele was dead weight, and she could only hope that he wasn't already dead, lungs full of seawater and brain beginning to die without oxygenation. When she reached the surface, she was exhausted, gasping for another breath, and not knowing whether she could keep Steele afloat. The air bag was leaking when she took her first full breath and delivered it to Steele's mouth. An early morning fisherman who was also a volunteer fireman jumped into the water with a life ring and kept the body afloat while Garrison continued mouth to mouth resuscitation. Her legs felt like lead, and her own breathing was labored.

The fishing fireman assessed the situation and swapped places with Garrison. Taking a deep breath, he expelled it forcefully into Steele's mouth and was rewarded with a half-digested seafood platter and a sputter. Again, the fireman pushed air into Steele's lungs and finally heard the right response. Steele was breathing, not normally, but breathing, nonetheless.

"Let's swim him toward the hotel beach. I'll continue the mouth to mouth as best I can," said the fireman. "I expect an ambulance down here any second. In another fifty feet or so, you should be able to touch bottom."

"OK," said Garrison. Even with the adrenaline surge, she was not certain of hanging on for even the next five feet.

A blinking EMS truck parked on the boardwalk, and the EMTs met the rescuers in the shallow water in front of the hotel. A crowd had gathered to watch the rescue unfold. The siren and flashing lights had stirred the hotel occupants from their slumber. It didn't take much encouragement to get travelers out of bed to see any ruckus.

The fireman told the EMT that the victim had been rescued from a car driven off the end of the pier.

"He's lolling a bit but breathing on his own. Better get a tox panel. He may have overdosed."

Garrison looked at the limp body as it was transferred to a gurney and announced that she was going with the ambulance. The EMTs moved around the body at top speed, taking vitals, and administering oxygen. An open mic to the hospital ER prepared the team to receive the half-drowned victim and kept them apprised of their arrival time.

It was all a blur. The hand-off was professional, and she heard the word drugs several times. She followed the gurney down the hallway until an orderly stopped her and ordered no visitors beyond this point. She collapsed silently into a chair and started shivering in the cold air-conditioning of the emergency suite waiting room, clasping her hands together and praying that Steele would make it past the ER.

Garrison found the ladies room and thought she'd use the time to make herself more presentable. She stood in front of the basin and couldn't quite figure out what was wrong with her image. No bra. That explained all the looks she'd gotten since arriving at the hospital. No, she was decidedly not a contestant in a wet t-shirt contest. Her purse and small make-up kit were at the hotel. She crossed her arms to hide her breasts and went in search of something to cover her torso. She found a sweater left on a row of seats that would serve two purposes.

"Are you with the drowning victim?" asked a short stocky man wearing a white coat with a name that she couldn't possibly pronounce.

"Yes, I am," she answered. The doctor paused before asking her what he might have taken before going in the water.

"No, nothing. We've been traveling for the past several days, and he had a couple of beers tonight but no, there are no drugs involved."

"That's good to hear. He's not out of the woods yet, but I'm optimistic that he'll recover on his own. All we needed to do was to clear his lungs and pump him full of oxygen. The EMTs earned their pay tonight in spades. We drew his blood and asked for an analysis of whatever he was on. Nothing immediately showed. During the exam, we did find an injection site on his stomach, but it didn't look like he was trying out any recreational drugs. Looks like he got a jolt of a fast-acting sedative like Propofol by someone who wanted him dead. And in a dose large enough for an elephant. He was still out of it when they wheeled him in. Anyway, it's all good now. We'll need to watch him for a few hours while the sedative works out of his system, but he should be released first thing in the morning if he continues to improve."

"Thank you doctor. Can I see him?"

"He's in the ICU now and should be transported soon to a room somewhere on the fourth floor. It's best to check with the charge nurse there."

"Thanks." Garrison wheeled and found the elevators. She charged into the car almost colliding with a man in scrubs exiting the car. Why did he look familiar?

Steele lay on the hospital bed with his head elevated and eyes closed. Sydney tiptoed across the room and watched him breathing a slow regular breath. The small boxes monitoring his vitals were all showing green lights. An IV bag hung from a pole on wheels and ended in his right arm. She bent over and kissed him on his cheek. His eyes fluttered and opened.

"What happened, Syd? Where am I?"

"You took an early morning swim off the fishing pier in our rental car and swallowed a few gallons of sea water in the process. Fortunately, you are alive and in Niantic Memorial Hospital for observation as a strong sedative works its way out of your system. Today is the day we were planning to arrive at my parents' house, remember?"

"Last thing I remember was being in the parking garage watching some guy working inside the trunk of our car. I approached him, and he hit me hard in the chest. I guess I must have passed out."

"Do you remember what the man looked like?"

"Shorter than me, a little heavy set with a partial Van Dyke beard."

"What do you mean a partial?"

"He had a pointed beard that started at his lip line but no mustache. Kind of a weird beard."

"I just bumped into a doctor with the same facial feature. He must be here in the hospital to finish the job. It's 05:00 a.m. but maybe I can get someone from NIS down here to watch this room until you are discharged."

"Syd, do you really think we need more security here at the hospital?"

"Yes, the guy with the pointy beard tried to arrange a burial-at-sea tonight, and you were the one being committed to the deep. I bet he's prowling around now with another hypodermic rig ready to administer. My phone is still in the hotel. Let me grab the room phone and see what the hospital can do. I'm exhausted."

Garrison picked up the receiver and started looking around the spartan room to see what she could use to fend off the killer, who might enter the room any second. She turned when she heard a short rap on the door as it opened.

The same Emergency Room doctor with the unpronounceable last name walked in, and Sydney expelled an audible sigh of relief. He smiled at her and stood by the bed.

"How are you feeling now, Mr. Doe?"

"I've taken a personal inventory. Everything seems to be in place and working normally. And my name is Steele, Dan Steele."

"When you were brought in a couple of hours ago, you weren't carrying any identification except for the hotel passkey in your pocket." The doctor studied the monitors connected to Steele and then listened to his chest and upper back with a stethoscope.

"Everything looks good. Still a little fluid in your lungs, but all your vitals are solid, and you've got 100% oxygen absorption. I'd like to keep you for a few more hours for observation, but we should be able to get you discharged after lunch. Sound good?"

"Yes, I can live with that."

"Breakfast usually starts early. Just eat whatever you want and make sure that you keep up a steady flow of water or juice. The gash in your forehead looks fine but you may develop a headache from that and coming down off the sedative."

Garrison interjected, "Doctor, I think the man who tried to drown Dan last night is in the hospital. He's stocky, has a pointy beard with no mustache. It might help if Dan is identified as John Doe until he is discharged."

"That's easy. Have you notified Security?"

"Not yet" answered Garrison, "but we will now."

"John Doe it is. I will ask the charge nurse to post one of our burly orderlies at the door until something can be arranged. Are you in trouble, Mr. Steele?"

"Not that I know of. But this man, whoever he is, is certainly no friend."

CHAPTER 96

Niantic, Connecticut
July 1, 2025

Both Steele and Garrison fell asleep just as the sun was illuminating the southern shore towns along the coast. The attempt on Dan's life, and his rescue left them both drained. The sound of the lock on the door being twisted woke them. As the white-coated man turned toward them, they could see the point of the beard protruding from his chin. Steele and Garrison stole a quick glance at each other: 'How in the hell did he get in here' was the question on both their minds.

"Good morning, Mr. Steele, I tried to convince my employer that you were no longer a threat, but I am not one to cut off my nose to spite my face. He is very generous when a mission is successfully completed. If not, he gets testy, and there's no telling how he might react."

"And who is your employer Mr.....?"

"My employer is a man named Spence. I believe you've had dealings with him in the past. And my name is Harpazi, formerly a field operative of Israeli intelligence. I wish I had more time, but the circuitous trip from Washington has exceeded my projection for this mission. Now it's also more complicated because of your attractive girlfriend."

"We are in close quarters here, Mr. Harpazi. How do you think you are going to carry out your job and get away?"

"Well, I have prepared a dose of fentanyl for your IV," withdrawing a hypodermic syringe from his jacket pocket. "I'm told the drug recently came into the United States via your porous southern border. I plan to depart the building with the Staff who will be shifted into an emergency high gear when a fire alarm will be sounded in…"

Harpazi lifted his left arm to see the watch on his wrist. "In about 90 seconds."

Steele eyed the man and said, "What will it cost to have you abandon your mission?"

"I am a loyal employee," Harpazi laughed, "I would not terminate the mission for additional cash of any amount. Did you, Mr. Steele, ever try to negotiate a better deal from your intended victim?"

Pulling a tiny gun from his pocket, Harpazi said, "Don't be fooled Mr. Steele. Though this is not a traditional handgun, it fires a 9 mm slug. You've seen what they can do at close range."

As the pointy beard advanced toward the hospital bed, Steele threw a scalpel he had palmed from the ICU at the man's center mass. The razor-sharp cutting instrument penetrated Harpazi's white coat, but then clattered to the floor.

"Interesting, don't you think Mr. Steele? I was in the room when the Israeli Defense Forces' chief asked an executive of one of our nation's defense contractors if he could make a Kevlar-like material that could be applied to the body directly and remain pliable like a thin body suit. Six months later, the CEO brought a fifty-five-gallon drum of the material back and demonstrated it. Because of budgetary pressures at the time, the project never moved forward. It's great stuff. Pliable, transparent, and it affords more protection than traditional body armor."

Steele picked up the IV stand next to his bed and javelined it as hard as he could at Harpazi's head. The IV tubing from Steele's arm trailed the metal stand as it hit the top of the target's head, its hooks leaving a downward smile on Harpazi's forehead. Blood gushed from the laceration, but Harpazi quickly regained his composure with a wipe of his white coat sleeve.

The blood covered his forehead and flowed down his face. Steele and Garrison looked at each other and Steele nodded. Together, they rushed their attacker and tackled him onto the floor. A bullet grazed Garrison's arm as she came in high on the beard's body, her head ramming the man's head backwards as he fell to the floor. That's when the fire alarm began its ear-splitting symphony in a single pulsing chord. Steele used the telephone cord to truss the assailant up and placed him in a chair against the wall.

Once he was secured and Steele was holding the small revolver, Garrison opened the door into a stampeding hospital staff that reminded her of the running of the bulls in Pamplona.

She screamed, "There is no fire! No fire!"

Her attempt to calm the bulls was fruitless. She walked back inside the room and slammed the door. She walked past Steele and the wired-up assailant and picked up the other handset in the room. A voice answered despite the audible competition with the fire alarm.

"Operator, how may I help you?"

"First, the fire alarm is bogus. There is no fire. Second, please ask Security to send two guards to room 411. We are holding the man who set off the alarm and tried to kill one of your patients."

CHAPTER 97

Mystic, Connecticut
July 1, 2025

Early afternoon on the sixth day, the pair arrived at Sydney's home. Surrounded by stone walls, the white clapboard Cape looked like something from a New England calendar. It was thoughtfully balanced on the property's grade, nestled atop a large granite outcrop, which seemed to support one side of the house. Still exhausted from the stop in Niantic and with fresh stitches in his forehead, Steele thought that Sydney must be equally as spent, though she looked fresh and energized. Her mother greeted them with a tray of sweating glasses of iced tea. A long hug with her daughter followed before Sydney introduced Steele. Her mother took both of Steele's hands in hers.

"Welcome, Dan. It's wonderful to finally meet you. How was the trip?" she asked.

Before Steele could answer, Sydney's father opened the front door, and Sydney rushed to greet him. He lifted her off the ground with a hug, and a beaming father strode over to Steele and shook his hand vigorously.

"Very nice to meet you, Dan. How was your trip?"

"Our leisurely trip north was memorable to say the least. I'd say we got to know each other very well," Dan said, smiling.

Sydney sat next to Dan, drinking iced tea and sitting in armchairs in the modest family room which featured an antique cooking fireplace with a swinging, wrought iron crane that must have been forged two hundred years ago.

The house boasted two guest rooms on the second floor with a bathroom between them.

"I'm not sure what you two are up to, but both of you look like you've been through the wringer, and the new gash on Dan's head doesn't look self-inflicted. And what's that bandage under your sleeve hiding?" Her mother's gentle manner disguised a woman eager to ferret out the truth, whatever it might be. Steele was their house guest, but she didn't like being told a tale.

The pair recounted the highlights of the trip. Sydney's parents felt more comfortable and nervous at the same time after the story was told.

CHAPTER 98

Mystic, Connecticut
July 2, 2025

The call from Owens interrupted an early morning hike with Sydney that began at the back door of her parents' house in Mystic, Connecticut set in the woods overlooking the Mystic River.

"The president wants to meet with me tomorrow afternoon. Owens claims he doesn't know what the meeting is about but said it had to be face-to-face."

"OK. You can fly or take the train down."

"Owens said that they will send a plane to New London to pick me up. Details to follow," said Steele.

"Let's hope it's not one of those missions that starts the following day from DC. I think we are making great progress getting to know one another…"

"Great progress. Are you kidding me? We've been together for a week. You saved my life once or maybe one and a half times? My senses are pegged, and we haven't even had any sex?" Dan said, only sorry that the comment about sex slipped out unintentionally.

"It certainly has been exciting. I just hate things being put on ice while you drop in on a crisis. Who knows what the task will be or where it might take you or for how long? Are you the only ex-SEAL who can do these things? It makes me crazy," said Garrison tears welling in her green eyes.

"Sorry for my outburst, Syd. I understand the frustration. Let's not have this call ruin our day. Let's hike to the ridge you were telling me about. I'd love to see the view."

From the ridge, the Thames River came into view in nearby Groton where it wound its way to the ocean beyond. A narrow glimpse of the submarine piers completed the picture.

"I came up here as a young girl and never tired of this overlook. It hasn't changed in thirty years."

"It's spectacular, Sydney. What a great morning. I am enjoying this short hike much more than the daily grind on the highway. And I'm happy to be with you."

Suddenly, the pair melded together with their lips locked. Sydney broke off the embrace gently, still in Steele's arms.

"Dan, it may sound foolish, and I don't want to cramp your style, but I'd like to travel with you to DC. I just can't bear the thought of your heading off on another mission risking life and limb when we are so close to knowing. I can tell you today that I'm completely in love with you and just can't imagine spending my life with anyone else."

"I feel the same way, Syd, and started loving you a long time ago. Maybe I can ask Owens if he can substitute someone else for whatever the president has in mind."

"I think that's a bridge too far. If the president wants you, there must be a good reason why."

"You're right. Maybe this is for something else. You know, I could enjoy being a shoe salesman right here in Connecticut for the rest of my life."

"Hold that thought. In the meantime, we should head back home for brunch with my parents."

Smiling and laughing, the two retraced their steps, hand-in-hand.

PART IV

PART IV

CHAPTER 99

Mystic, Connecticut
July 3, 2025

"You did what?" asked an incredulous Steele, his eyes opening wide with surprise.

"I sent a text to the president's naval aide and asked if we could meet with the president together. She came right back with a yes, as he had coincidentally asked the staff to set up a separate appointment with me next week," said Sydney smiling like a Cheshire cat.

Steele shook his head. An initial flash of annoyance was replaced by curiosity. Later that day the two were shown into the Oval Office where the president was standing ready to greet them.

"This is a very pleasant surprise when two of my favorite operators come to visit." He gave Sydney a presidential hug and then shook Steele's hand and clapped him on the back. He guided them to the sitting area where he sat on one side facing the two.

"Sydney, congratulations on your long and successful command of *Newport*. This last operation was the highlight of my second term. I'm proud of the entire team. Both of you were at the pointy end of the spear. What you accomplished is important for your country and the free world. The operation has just been classified, and I approved a review not sooner than one-hundred years from now."

"Mr. President, if I may ask, why so long?" asked Steele.

"The fact that we were involved in stopping the transfer might alter our future relationships with allies and others. That the winning bidder did not receive the material he paid for is a big deal. It was a very transparent auction. Hundreds of millions of people viewed the bidding page. We reaffirmed our commitment to Israel and gained wider support for our policy of keeping the Middle East a nuclear weapons free zone. The security balance in the region is restored. These gains could be questioned if our involvement was revealed. A hundred years from now, we will be playing with a fresh deck of cards, and I'm hopeful that any reaction to the declassified report will be modulated."

"Thanks. I understand, Mr. President," said Steele.

"As of today, it appears that the plan worked. None of our fingerprints are on the catastrophic loss of *Simurgh*. Not only did we recover the casks, but we also gained intelligence on Iranian forces and their networks. This may help expose their military support for the Houthis in Yemen and other terrorist groups around the world. It will be months before we know what we got from this operation, but let me be the first one to congratulate both of you on this stunning success."

"Thanks, Mr. President, this was a huge team effort, and without all the details pulled together as they were, none of this could have happened. Let's hope that the depth of the sea will hide what really happened," said Steele.

"I hope so. The other internal US teams are dumbfounded with the news that *Simurgh* went down and how those casks might be recovered. Both of you know how hard it is to keep a lid on anything here in DC. And we got a recent intel tip that the IRGC intended to develop a nuclear version of the rockets they are shooting into Israel. They have hundreds of thousands of conventional ballistic missiles that pack a big punch when they hit. Can you imagine what would happen if they started lobbing nuclear tipped rockets into Tel Aviv?" It was a rhetorical question, and Steele and Garrison watched the president pause and shift in his seat, a different subject on his mind.

"I guess you heard the news about the vice president."

"Yes, we did. What happened?" asked Sydney.

"He was meeting with the CIA director at the Naval Observatory when he fell over and suffered a massive heart attack.

There was nothing in his medical record to suggest he was at risk, but I suppose the stress of operating the government independently got to him. He told me privately that he was wrestling with the idea of running for president next time around. I can tell you that campaigning is far more strenuous than the job itself. Later today, I'll go see him in the Capitol rotunda and pay my respects. The burial will be tomorrow at Arlington. It's very sad news. He was a gifted statesman, a solid citizen, and a strong right arm for me. There is a big hole in the political landscape because of his death."

"Now, shifting gears again," said the president.

"Sydney, you'll have to forget what I'm about to say. Dan, I'm ready to take another risk. I should be addressing you as Mr. Phelps for this one. You lost your wife and sons in a terrorist attack on the Chesapeake Bay Bridge and Tunnel years ago. I can't imagine how tough it's been for you to carry that emotional burden in the years since while fighting other battles behind the scenes for this country. We know that the now-president of Albania was behind the plot to sabotage the tunnel and make it look as if the attack originated somewhere in the Middle East, that perhaps Al-Qaeda was to blame."

The president rose and walked around the Oval Office slowly as if reconsidering the impossible mission he was about to pitch to Steele.

"I just made a presidential finding that Spence is a clear and present danger to this country and others in Europe as well as the world. Our alliances will not unravel, but that guy is pulling at all the loose threads. What he tried to do with the transfer of nuclear material is mind-boggling. He's got the Chinese navy planning projects in the middle of Europe. The Russians are studying a potential space port there. Can you imagine? I personally briefed the intelligence committees in the Congress and sought an exception from the ban on assassinations for political reasons outlined in Executive Order 12333 signed by President Reagan. I could have taken the action unilaterally but thought it would be better to outline the rationale and justification to the committees. That said, I got no push back from anyone. No one tried to impose any restrictions on the manner of Spence's removal.

We are in the early planning phase of launching a Special Operations mission to remove him from his position, with prejudice. But I wanted to offer you, Dan, the opportunity to take him out first. This will be your operation. I cannot put a team under your command and will not send a team in without all the planning necessary. It's a high-risk opportunity for you to balance your personal and emotional ledger. We can get you in and provide distant logistics for the operation, and any intelligence that you need, but you'll be operating solo. If you choose to reject this offer, I only ask that you forget this conversation. I will always hold you in the highest esteem regardless. Should you accept this mission, you'll have only a month to plan and to execute it."

There was a polite knock on the door, and the president's naval aide appeared to escort his guests out of the office. Steele shook the president's hand and saw the emotion in his eyes.

"Thank you, Mr. President. I appreciate it. I'll let you know by this time tomorrow."

The president wrapped Garrison up in a hug and kissed her on the cheek.

"Fine, thank you both coming down. Enjoy Independence Day and give my regards to your dad, Sydney. Safe travels and good luck!"

Steele and Garrison were greeted at the curb by a Navy sedan for the trip to Andrews Air Force Base. Their driver was a second-class petty officer, a U.S. Navy cryptologist interpretive. Steele wondered what language he'd studied. A thousand thoughts were running through Steele's mind as he looked out the window at the decayed landscape of the eastern side of Washington. Sydney reached over and put her hand on his.

"A penny for your thoughts."

"Well, my mind is busy right now, and I'm just trying to get an initial fix on this mission. At the same time, I'm wondering how many lives I might have left. I've got mixed feelings about it. With all our storytelling, you never told me you knew the president."

"Dan, do you think that special operations for this country are reserved for SEALs? Though I can't get into any details, I've gotten several calls to the Oval Office to see the president, just like today's meeting."

"Seems like I've been looking at the world through the wrong end of the telescope. Thanks." Steele gave her hand a little squeeze and then pulled away, his mind swarming with random thoughts of Spence, Jill, Jack, his young sons and Sydney.

"Dan, there you go again. You've off thinking like you are a one-man band. Let me help you turn the telescope around the other way. Tell me about Spence."

Sydney extracted a small legal pad and pen from her briefcase and looked at Dan with her eyebrows raised in expectation.

"Syd, I already told you about Spence and his operation. What more do you need to know?"

"Everything you can remember. Everything."

"Well, he's the sonofabitch who planned the explosion on the Chesapeake Bay Bridge and Tunnel and killed my wife and sons. I promised Jill's dad…"

"Remember that old TV show called *Dragnet*?" Sydney asked gently.

"Sure, I've probably seen a couple of re-runs of it."

"The lead detective was a guy named Joe Friday who famously instructed people he was interviewing to tell him just the facts. That's what I would ask you to do. No emotion, just the facts. Now, tell me about Spence."

"Spence was born in the seaside town of Durres, Albania, about thirty miles from the capital city of Tirana. By all accounts, he had a rough childhood. His father was a drunk who beat him every time he got wasted, which was frequently. Spence was an average student. Maybe the product of large classrooms where the teacher might be teaching four or five grade levels at the same time. Like a one-room schoolhouse.

In his early teens, he was bullied by this ex-Army guy who tried to form a little gang to shake down students, steal their lunch money, that sort of thing. The bully used Spence and made his school life as miserable as his life at home. Spence ran away after tenth grade and spent years living on the streets in Naples and Rome as a petty thief. Details are scant, but he did have a juvenile record that was uncovered by the FBI years later. Self-educated, fluent in multiple languages and extremely erudite, he found his way to Vienna where he worked first as a dishwasher and later a tutor to a wealthy family's children."

Sydney put away her pad as they passed through the gate at Andrews for the return flight north. As soon as they got settled as the only two passengers on the small jet, she retrieved her pad and looked expectantly at Steele. The flight to New London lasted just under an hour, and Steele felt like he'd been on the witness stand for hours, recounting Spence's years in Austria before making his way to the United States and going into the business world.

By the time they deplaned and left the airport, Steele had revealed that he had been kidnapped and held in a cell by Spence located in the back half of a building where legitimate business was conducted by the part facing M street in Georgetown. The back half was dedicated to the other activities of Double Eagle Industries. Steele described it as a Gemini operation. Though the details regarding Spence's escape during the FBI raid were accounts that Steele had only read, they put together a sketchy profile of the secretive man and his habits, including his use of a replica Skanderbeg broadsword to split his protege, Jack's, skull and sever his torso in half.

By the time Steele pulled into the driveway of the Garrison house, he felt exhausted. He turned to Sydney.

"Now you can see why I need to start planning. This guy is very clever and will certainly be surrounded by a formal security team and perhaps some personal bodyguards."

"We are almost done," Garrison said brightly, "What do you know about the hikers who found Bunker 43?"

"Only that they were from Germany, a brother and sister, who found a way into the bunker through a stream that had eroded the limestone over the last seventy years."

"Did Spence ever make any public pronouncements about them? Attend a funeral? Where are they buried?"

"Good questions, Syd. Somewhere down in Durres, I suspect. The IAEA got in there very quickly and handled all the details. I don't think Spence was very involved except from the business end. He was the guy who came up with the brilliant plan to sell the material through an open bidding process. Amazing. I thought that those types of transactions were always completed via the dark web, but he made it very transparent as if he were selling a large lot of scrap metal."

"Ok, very helpful, Dan. Let's go in. My parents may worry if they think we are just out here necking in the driveway." She laughed at her own joke, and Steele shook his head in wonderment. What a woman!

"We heard the news about the VP. It's hard to believe. I briefed him less than a month ago in the Pentagon, and he seemed perfectly fine. Stayed awake for the entire presentation. Other than that shocker, how are things in the center of the universe," asked Stewart Garrison.

Sydney glanced at Dan before responding.

"It turns out that both of us have been on the president's short list for special tasks which we cannot talk about. And he sends his regards to you, dad. Dan just got offered an opportunity to address a national security issue and fulfill a promise he made years ago. I hate to sound so obtuse, but that's the way it must be."

"So, is this an overseas operation, Dan?" asked the nuclear physicist, well known in the submarine engineering community. There was no room for error in the Navy's nuclear power propulsion plants, and Garrison had been committed to the zero defects policy that continued in the nuclear-powered world after Admiral Rickover retired.

"Yes, it is."

"How soon do you leave?"

"Soon. I'm behind the eight ball in terms of planning, and I've only got a small window to prepare," said Steele.

"Is this a decision that you must make or is the die cast?" asked Garrison's father, joined by his wife standing by his favorite chair.

"Let's sit down at the table. Does anyone need a cocktail?" Sydney's mother asked.

"Not me, Mom. Dan? I can answer Dad's question," said Sydney. "Dan has been given a timeframe in advance of an organized team going on the mission. They are planning now, so he does have a choice in the matter. It's not an easy choice when you understand all the variables. It's complicated."

"Yes, it is," said Steele. "And I want both of you to know that your daughter, Sydney, is one of the complications. The mission could be dangerous, and there is always the possibility that I might not come back. A week ago, that prospect didn't move the needle much but now it does. I love your daughter and do not want to lose her for any reason. And no, we are not planning to go to the justice of the peace tomorrow morning before I leave."

"Hold that thought, Dan," said Sydney, "because I'm going with you."

Three heads swiveled at the table to stare at Sydney.

All three recovered about the same time and seemed to speak in unison.

"What are you thinking...why would you...Absolutely not...This is no joking mat...You can't be serious...Are you crazy?"

Sydney finally regained control.

"It's very simple. The residence where a man is being held captive will be guarded just like the White House. We can get in the front door and arrange an audience with the man with the right approach. In this case, we could act as the grieving mother and father of the two young hikers who died because of radiation exposure. Since Dan doesn't speak German, and I do, it seems like a good way to start."

Another chorus of simultaneous reactions followed the first. Vehement reactions.

"Why you, you are no special ops…You are not running off with…I didn't know you were an actress…this sounds like a bad movie…Do this on your vacation??

"OK, can we continue the conversation over dinner," asked Sydney.

"I think I've lost my appetite," said her father.

Steele shook his head and said, "No way."

"Can we please change the subject?" asked Sydney's mother. Not another word was spoken until four bowls of steaming New England clam chowder were placed on the table.

"My appetite has suddenly returned," exclaimed her father.

"Mine, too," added Steele.

"And to put a finer point on what Dan said to you," nodding at her parents, "I love him and look forward to spending my life with him. For the record, we have not been cavorting like a couple of teenagers imagining they are in love, nor has he asked me to marry him. This is the real thing."

Set for four with a simple arrangement of several varieties of lettuce topped with grilled sea scallops, the conversation naturally shifted after everyone tasted the creamy delicacy which was thick with chopped clams and red potatoes. After the visit to Washington and the previous day's activities, Steele was hungry, tired and unsettled at Sydney's proclamation that she hadn't even discussed with him. She was independent and spoke her mind. Even after her declaration of love for him, Steele was determined to talk her out of the foolhardy move.

The conversation shifted to Stewart Garrison, who regaled the table with some of his recent trips at sea and the antics of submariners. This was the light moment that was needed for everyone to process what Sydney appeared committed to do. Terrible idea…or was it? The elephant was still in the room.

After dinner, Garrison announced that she would take Steele on a walk around the property. Hand in hand, they walked the wooded land until they reached a bench which offered peeks of the ocean.

"When I was growing up, I would come out here to see the ocean and relax."

"I love the view. It is very relaxing. What's on tap for tomorrow? It's Independence Day."

"I know, I was thinking we might drive over to Bristol, Rhode Island and watch the fourth of July parade. There was some talk about it being cancelled because of the vice president's death, but I understand his wife insisted that the nation needed to return to normal. She said that's what he would have wanted."

"You know, I've never seen that parade. Sounds like a plan. I'm sure it will be a mob scene. What time do we leave?"

"Not sure. I think the parade starts at 10:30 in the morning. We need to leave right after breakfast. Wonder if my parents would like to go? My dad also mentioned something about fishing."

"I'm ready for anything Syd, if it includes you. However, that doesn't include a quick trip to Albania to meet Spence."

"Well, I've been working on the concept based on both of us going. If you want to tell the president no, that's ok with me, too. I'm not trying to be stubborn or make this harder than it already is, just trying to improve the chances of success. You know that, right?"

CHAPTER 100

Europe
July 7, 2025

Following the Bristol parade with Sydney's parents, a day of fishing off the rocky coast of Connecticut in a neighbor's boat, and extended and tearful goodbyes and hugs, Steele and Garrison flew from Boston to Munich. With the tight timeline given by the president, Steele knew that every minute counted in preparing for the trip. Garrison's insistence on being part of the impossible mission force complicated matters. Or did it? What would happen if she suddenly got cold feet and decided to cancel her self-assigned role at the eleventh hour?

Their German passports identified the holders as Gregor and Paulina Leitner, the parents of the twins who died from the effects of a massive radiation exposure at Bunker 43.

After an overnight train ride from Munich to Trieste, the Leitners boarded a bus which followed the Adriatic along the coast and entered Albania at its northern border with Montenegro. The bus ride itself took two days. Steele was defining their strategy using a previous plan developed by Pisces to enter the presidential palace, using an ancient sewer line built in Roman times that had been left in place when the flow was re-routed to a larger prefabricated line with a steeper slope. The new line paralleled the old underground trough and emptied into the river with an underwater outflow to reduce the smell. A new line carrying the wastewater directly to the ocean had never been funded. Spence had added construction of that line to next year's budget.

With the attempted attack on the defense minister still fresh in everyone's mind, Steele and Garrison agreed that the easiest way into the presidential palace was to use the front door. They had good disguises and a compelling reason to visit the president. A professor of earth sciences with several advanced degrees, including one from UCLA, Steele looked the part. Longish, unruly gray hair, a thick mustache drooping past his upper lip, a heavy tweed coat with elbow patches used to cover the thinning material, and baggy wool trousers. He even wore an alpine hat. Garrison wore a rumpled wool suit expanded to the matronly level by adding rolls of a lightweight foam around her narrow waist that closely resembled natural fat. Her suit was adorned with a silver stick pin of a skier. She wore black support stockings to cover her legs. An older, grieving couple on their first visit to Albania.

In Durres, they visited the graves of their son and daughter and laid a handful of fresh flowers at the simple stone marker where they'd been buried together. Both the mother and father were pleased with the plot at a small cemetery near the sea.

They took a bus to Tirana to prepare for their audience with the president the following day.

Steele remembered all the mindless films from over the years where a man would hunt down his target of revenge and face incredible odds getting to his prey. For him, that's exactly what the essence of this mission was about.

CHAPTER 101

Tirana, Albania
July 2025

Professor and Mrs. Leitner carried a letter of introduction signed by the president of Germany, urging Spence to spend a few minutes with the parents who'd lost their children after they unwittingly uncovered the bunker where nuclear material had been stored untouched for nearly seventy years. The pair walked through a security portal like those at airports and were led into a waiting room where other petitioners sat waiting for a private audience with Spence. Both had damp handkerchiefs drawn and blotted their drawn faces constantly with the memory of their children.

Before traveling to Albania, Steele was invited to Langley by a friend who had left the U.S. Navy after his initial tour as a SEAL and transferred to the Office of Naval Intelligence. He then answered an advertisement for the CIA. With his background, he was an easy hire, holding most of the special access tickets required. Knowing the structure and organization of the seventeen agencies that make up the intelligence community was another big plus.

"Morning, Dave, it's been a long time."

"Yes, it has, brother. Welcome to the center of the universe."

"I thought that was DC?"

"OK, maybe we share the center with DC, but this is the absolute center."

The two walked through the security gate where Dave ran his badge over a turnstile and Steele did the same for his visitor's badge. They paused in the lobby to study the wall of stars.

They walked to a conference room where his host fired up a panel set in the table and then typed his password into a small tablet. The screen filled with a close-up photograph of Spence.

'We've been studying this guy since he got elected as Albania's president. Part of that was triggered by the fact that Spence's history in our data base as well as State's was altered by a very sophisticated hacker who replaced our data with some mealy mouth pap describing Spence as a choir boy. Anyway, we started paying more attention to him, and I got tagged to put together a deep dossier on him. I heard through a reliable source that you may be going after him and wanted to alert you to a couple of things.

"First, since the attempt on Zlodeyev by the Federation, Spence has started using a double for some of his public appearances and talking to petitioners as he does weekly. He's always had them but was too vain to think that anyone could stand in for him in any setting. We are told that Spence monitors their meetings, but the double does a very capable job filling in.

Here's a photo of Spence and the double side by side. They look like old twins, right? I've blown these faces up and studied them a thousand times. Plastic surgery has made them look identical."

"There have to be some marks or something to distinguish one from the other," said Steele.

"That's what we thought too. Turns out that we watched hours of Spence footage before we found it. Spence's right eye has a natural tic that pulls back the eyelid briefly. And so does his double. The only difference between the two is the tic's frequency. Spence's tic occurs every two to three seconds. The double has had a tic created in his right eye, but it fires off every five to seven seconds. It's a very small thing, but we thought you should know it before heading overseas."

"Thanks, Dave. Let's get together for a beer when I get back."

"Deal."

CHAPTER 102

Tirana, Albania
July 13, 2025

Ushered into a smaller room for their private audience with Spence, an aide introduced them as Professor and Mrs. Leitner from Germany. The aide presented the letter they carried, which got the conversation started in the right direction.

Spence stood and shook hands with Professor Leitner and his wife and took a seat across a small desk that separated them. He spoke to them in German.

"I'm sorry you've traveled here for such a sad task. What your children stumbled on was remarkable. We are glad to be rid of that material. It is most unfortunate that they died discovering it."

"Yes, it is," said Mrs. Leitner. "They were both avid hikers and truly enjoyed the diverse environment of your country. I talked to them before they departed Durres for the mountains. The were thrilled to be here in Albania."

"Yes, we are blessed with many beautiful natural features in the country. I've heard some people call our country a hiker's paradise."

"That's why they came here. But I must ask, why didn't your government protect everyone, residents and visitors alike, from these terrible weapons?"

"I know it's difficult to believe, Mrs. Leitner, but we were unaware of the facility's existence. It had been closed by hundreds of tons of limestone during a rockslide and forgotten. As you probably know, we've removed all the radioactive material, encapsulated the bunker and shielded it with lead. The facility is permanently closed, and its access sealed. A buffer zone has been established with a high fence, and we have the site monitored continuously to detect any radiation leakage. I can assure you that no one else will be injured at that site in the future. I'm very sorry that your son and daughter suffered from their exposure."

"Yes, I hope these actions will prevent more deaths," exclaimed the professor in English.

"Yes, they assuredly will," replied Spence leaning back in his chair signaling the discussion was over. The aide came into view, but the professor had another question.

Unannounced, the minister of defense strode into the room, and Spence made introductions.

Zlodeyev studied Professor Leitner's face intently.

"Professor, have we met before?" asked the general.

"No, I don't think so. I've spent my entire life in Germany except for my doctoral studies at UCLA. Infrequently, I go to other places in the world to attend conferences, but I cannot recall ever meeting you. And it would be very hard to forget someone like you. You are a very large man."

"Your eyes look familiar. I understand the sad circumstances which have brought you to Albania and hope that you will both find some comfort in your visit."

Spence interrupted, "Why not join us for lunch, Nikolai?"

"Thank you, Spence, but I just received a dozen giant hen eggs from a friend, and they are chilling in the refrigerator. I will blend them with some bulgar wheat and drink the entire lot from the pitcher. Thank you though. Safe travels to you and your wife, professor. Goodbye."

An hour later the big man appeared just as coffee was being served in Spence's dining room. A dried rivulet of yellow ran from his lips to his chin. He approached the table, staring at the professor.

"Spence, may I join you and your guests for coffee?"

"Certainly. How were those fresh eggs?"

"Excellent, Spence, thank you. The protein in the eggs has helped me home in on where I met the professor in the past. I never forget someone's eyes."

Zlodeyev stared at the professor and asked, "Tell me professor, have you ever traveled in the Middle East?"

"Yes, I once visited Riyadh for a conference. I found it a very strange place."

"What about Yemen? Have you been there."

"Yemen? No, not in Yemen. A colleague of mine visited there and told me it was like traveling 500 years back through time. His observation intrigued me at the time but not enough to travel there."

"I see. Perhaps the eggs were not as good as I thought. I have you confused with someone else. Please accept my apologies for the third degree. Let us enjoy our coffee."

The meal ended, and Spence walked his guests to the entrance of the palace and bade them farewell, watching the two as they walked slowly through the courtyard gate toward the city.

CHAPTER 103

Presidential Palace

Tirana, Albania
July 13, 2025

Spence walked back into the palace grand reception room where he met Zlodeyev, agitated and pacing near one of the ornate interior columns. The yellow drizzle on his mouth and chin were still visible.

"We need to arrest those two impersonators. They are assassins from the United States, coming for one or both of us."

Spence guided the big man to a comfortable brocade settee placed against the wall.

"My friend, you seem anxious and alarmed. Now what makes you believe that the professor and his wife are agents sent here to kill us?"

"As I said before, I never forget the eyes. Behind the professor's beard and shuffling limp is a special operator I met in Yemen just before my compound became ground zero for a simultaneous delivery of cruise missiles, which killed my fighters and turned the seaside villa into rubble. We found that bastard and the rest of his team inside the compound walls that were well protected by a wide killing field that we believed could not be penetrated. I learned of the strike just minutes in advance and was ready to take my rocket to safety when he challenged me to fight."

"Yes, my friend, you told me the story of your daring escape, but I don't recall your fighting someone before you blasted off."

"The fight turned out to be complicated. I was shot accidentally in the side when Professor Leitner asked for a hand-to-hand fight. He tried some sophomoric martial arts tricks which didn't work. I quickly overpowered him and left him for dead, pinned between two pallets of nuclear-tipped projectiles. It was quite a shock to see him here today under his own power."

"And his wife?" asked Spence.

"I don't know her. Probably a CIA killing machine. I'm telling you, Spence, those two pose a threat to us. They may be the eyes and ears for a bigger force already here in Albania or coming soon."

"You know, Nikolai, I am beginning to connect some dots. I have asked our friend Harpazi to take care of a former U.S. Navy SEAL who began putting his nose into some of my business dealings years ago and caused the shut-down of the Washington, DC hub of our operations. Could this guy be the same one who gave you trouble? His name was…"

"Steele," said Zlodeyev.

"That's the man you remember too?"

"One and the same. The disguise and cover story were both believable, but we need to persuade them to tell us the details and the timeline of the operation."

Spence paused and remembered the mess created by Steele. He fought back a sudden churn of gastric reflux.

"Yes, I agree. I will double the perimeter security and put the pair under surveillance. I'd like to think of a way to get them back here quietly rather than arrest them on the street and give the press something else to criticize."

"Spence, why not invite them back here for dinner tonight? They could hardly refuse an invitation from you, even if they knew we were on to them. Surveillance would be simplified, and we could keep the press at bay."

"Brilliant. I will have Adam prepare an invitation and dispatch it to their hotel. Perhaps the chef can add something to their entrée to make them more relaxed."

"Yes, that will make it easier for me to pull off his silly beard. We will both get some satisfaction from seeing Steele squirm. The woman can be a gift to our security force."

CHAPTER 104

Tirana, Albania
July 13, 2025

Professor Leitner and his wife walked back to their hotel chattering openly about the charm of the old city and Spence's comforting hospitality. They arrived at the hotel's formal garden and sat together on a stone bench.

"I think our cover is blown. Zlodeyev knows exactly where we met and was just playing dumb. He will tell Spence and tighten security until he knows we are out of Albania. We may be escorted to the border; the only question is whether we'll be vertical or horizontal. How do you read it, Syd?"

Garrison laid her head on Steele's shoulder and whispered.

"I agree. Our cover worked to get us in, but we are probably busted. It's good to know who we are up against. The man in the gray suit pretending to examine the boxwoods on the parallel garden path followed us from the palace. I think it's likely that Spence and Zlodeyev are discussing our future right now. I can't see them just letting us go. We will be picked up on some trumped-up charge like spying, so we can be grilled to see if we are an advance party for an assault. We will just disappear. Your idea of being escorted out of the country is naïve."

"The hunters are now the hunted," said Steele. "And we need to re-think the mission. Spence will turn the palace into a fortress. We've got a few hours to strategize how we can overcome an alerted force and get to the targets. I'm sure that his team is casing the hotel and will probably install some listening equipment, assuming that the hotel is not already pre-wired."

"Do we realistically have that choice?" asked Garrison. "Our planning assumptions are out the window! Whatever we decide, I will not be held as a prisoner servicing the male members of Spence's staff. We need to make some quick decisions about go or no-go and then get moving in the right quadrant as soon as possible. The timer in my head is starting to give me a headache."

Back in the hotel, they removed their costumes and changed into running clothes. They would hash out the options in the open air where any eavesdroppers would have a hard time hearing. Tirana's landscape offered level running on wide avenues. They jogged for ten minutes without talking, losing anyone trying to tail them.

"Dan, I am anxious to hear about the options that are multiplying in your head."

"I am too," he replied, spotting an open park bench where their conversation could be private.

"Here we are. A great place to have a tactical discussion. No pressure — just kidding. We need to execute before they arrest us. And by execute, I mean either to carry out the mission or to hop on the quickest public transportation out of here. I regret your getting involved, Syd. For me, it's a chance to avenge the loss of Jill and my two sons. If I get killed, so be it. But you didn't need to be part of it."

"You're right, but don't forget, I chose you and this mission of my own free will, regardless of the consequences. It's too late to think we could possibly pull the plug and get out of Tirana. I would rather take a risk and try to accomplish something that's long overdue. I'm all in until the end. Now, how do we get back into the palace?"

"I'm still trying to figure that out, but think we need to jog back to the hotel and come in through the little shopping center on the lower floor. There's an escalator from the shopping area into the hotel, so we might be able to get to the room without being seen."

Just as they started their jog, two police cars, sirens blaring, demonstrated a pincer movement, blocking the couple's path. They were trapped, feeling like a pair of animals flushed out of the wild and now paralyzed with shock. Guns were holstered. The policeman in charge approached Steele directly, asked his name, and handed him an envelope. It was official correspondence bearing the Albanian national seal.

The policeman looked at Steele directly, not paying any attention to Garrison.

"Professor, you have been a difficult man to find, even in our small city. I apologize about the intrusion on your afternoon but would have lost my job if I didn't promptly deliver this letter to you."

Steele opened the letter and found a formal invitation.

> Please join General Zlodeyev and me for a casual dinner tonight at the Palace at seven o'clock.
>
> I will send my car and driver to pick you both up.
>
> Sincerely,
>
> Spence

Steele glanced at Garrison before speaking to the policeman.

"Yes, my wife and I are delighted to accept President Spence's kind invitation. Please inform his secretary. Thank you."

The policeman came to attention and gave Steele a snappy salute. He waved a hand toward the cars, signaling his team to move out.

"I guess we just got our way into the palace front door. We've got plenty of time to go back to the hotel, shower, take a nap, and then get ready for dinner. Things are just falling into place, Syd."

"I get the feeling this may be the last supper," she said.

"No this is a piece of unexpected luck. We are welcomed into the target area, fed a nice dinner and will take care of business between petit fours and coffee. Let's head back to the hotel so we can plan for what will surely be a memorable evening with old friends. Do you think anyone would mind if we arrived early?" asked Steele, smiling.

CHAPTER 105

Tirana, Albania
July 13, 2025

Steele and Garrison left the hotel via the kitchen, taking a circuitous route to their access point, finding the manhole cover after clearing away a thick layer of leaves. They descended into a branch line of the ancient sewer system serving the palace. The floor of the clay pipe was damp. A breeze flowed down the line bringing a constant supply of fresh air that displaced the damp smell of a forest floor after a heavy rain.

"The breeze tells me this pipe is open some other place. I have the uneasy feeling that we may not be the only ones down here."

"You are right. There's no other way to explain the air flow."

The narrow pipe required something between moving on all fours and a belly crawl. Though the terminus was only two hundred yards away, the trip was exhausting.

"Here's our hatch. This ends in an old cold frame just beyond the kitchen."

Steele pushed the round cast iron plate. It didn't budge. Garrison got to her knees, facing Steele, their bodies pressed against each other under a vertical access.

"Need a hand, sailor?" quipped Garrison as she pushed upward with Steele.

Something rolled off the manhole, and Steele was able to maneuver it to the side. The area seemed abandoned, full of old cookware, a discarded sink and stacks of dishes — the leftovers from a kitchen modernized multiple times over the years. Steele noticed a glass greenhouse further from the house and wondered why he'd never seen that structure on the house diagrams.

Garrison leaned against a large copper pot.

"Maybe this is an appropriate place and time for you to reveal the next phase of this brilliant tactical plan, don't you think?"

"It's still evolving, but we should discuss the options. We are ninety minutes in advance of our invitation, so I'd say we are on schedule."

"I found this during the crawl here," said Garrison, holding up a shiny brass cartridge shell. She handed it to Steele, who examined it closely with his headlamp.

"Surprising, it's a .22 caliber long rifle cartridge without any manufacturing marks. This looks like something the teams might use overseas, but I think we would have been told if the mission timeline had been accelerated. Don't know how it got here but please keep your antennae up. We may not be the only dinner guests tonight."

The pair entered the house via the kitchen, passing by a dishwasher who looked like he was trying to sleep and to clean a large stockpot at the same time. They took the main staircase up to the living quarters. Spence's office, sitting room and bedroom occupied the left side of the building's second floor, including the formal balcony where Spence would wave to the daily crowd of Albanians who would travel to get a glimpse of the president and to pay their respects. Spence never missed an opportunity to appear before his people or the cameras.

As they moved quietly along the center hallway, both froze when they heard a muffled conversation and a door close. They were exposed with no place to hide. A man with a suit over his arm and a fabric measuring tape hung around his neck entered an elevator and disappeared.

"Why didn't we just take the elevator?" Garrison asked.

Steele ignored the question as they proceeded down the wide, carpeted floor until they reached the door the tailor had opened.

Steele looked at Garrison and said, "OK, we go in, find Spence, and I put him out of his misery. Then, we stroll back through the main floor and return to the root cellar and leave town."

"Don't you find it odd that we don't see more people? This is the country's equivalent of the White House, and I can't imagine why it's not a beehive of activity in the late afternoon."

"Right. It seems odd to me too. Let's move."

The last room on the left took a full quarter of the building's second floor. The doorknob turned silently, and they found themselves in Spence's private sitting room. Steele motioned to continue to the hallway leading off the main room and connecting to the bedroom. Entering the darkened hallway, they passed a large unoccupied bathroom and entered a bedroom with a hand-carved bed of epic proportions. A rounded lump lay snoring in the middle of the bed. Steele held up a closed fist and continued to creep around the side of the bed, withdrawing one of the Ipe knives taped to his forearm.

He pulled back the cover slightly and saw Spence's face as he plunged the knife down with all the force his body could muster. It was the moment of truth for Steele, for Jill, and for his sons. What he stabbed was the head of a full-sized Spence mannequin which never reacted to the knife that went all the way through his neck and into the mattress.

At the same time, three interior doors opened, and three armed men lowered their submachine guns and wordlessly motioned Steele and Garrison away from snoring mannequin and the windows. They were handcuffed with plastic ties and marched down the hallway into the large meeting room where the president's cabinet often met. The pair ended up sitting on a love seat separating two long sofas covered with the same brocade.

Minutes later, Spence entered the room and greeted the couple warmly. His kindness and generosity would fool most people. He had a charming personality and an engaging manner with the capacity to focus intently on the subject at hand, never giving any hint that he was distracted.

"Ah, welcome Professor and Mrs. Leitner. Or should I address you as Mr. Steele and Ms. Garrison? Didn't you bother reading the invitation? Our dinner is planned for seven o'clock, an hour from now. And casual must mean something different to Americans." He turned to the guards and ordered, "Take them to guest room Alpha and remain posted outside the door. Escort them down to the turret room at seven o'clock."

Spence stood, watching his orders being carried out, amazed that Zlodeyev was able to remember Steele by his eyes alone.

Guest room Alpha featured bars on the windows and multiple surveillance cameras constantly watching its occupants. Metal fasteners were ground down so they couldn't be removed, and several violet beams shown across the polished wooden floor. No escape. Each of the large closets contained clothes for every occasion in both their sizes, so complying with the casual part of Spence's invitation posed no problem. They took turns in the shower removing the grime from the crawl in the sewer line and selected beautifully tailored clothes for dinner. They were now prisoners with no cover and nowhere to run or hide. It reminded Steele of the contrived civility in the early 007 movies.

The door was unlocked just before seven o'clock, and the pair was escorted to a formal dining room where Spence and Zlodeyev greeted them. The dining table was set for four people with a bouquet of fresh flowers and an elaborate silver service, crystal glasses and embroidered linen napkins. A state dinner with two hosts and two assassins.

"Mr. Steele and Ms. Garrison, let me welcome you a second time to Albania." Spence raised his glass and offered the toast from his seat at the head of the table. "It's a delicious cocktail sherry from Jerez, Spain. I hope you'll both like it."

"Have you added anything to it?" asked Steele.

"No, I would not alter a drink of this magnificence for any reason," said Spence evenly. "You are our guests this evening."

"We did notice the bars on the room," offered Garrison. She was wearing a crisp cotton dress with a floral print, a handmade replica of a dress made by a well-known European fashion designer.

"Yes," said Spence, "I'm afraid that some security measures are necessary."

The first course was served and eaten in silence. Spence broke the tension.

"I hope you enjoy this small plate. It is cold blackened tuna caught this morning in some netting that I'm trying out for the fish farm that will be up and operating by year's end."

"It's delicious, Spence," said Garrison.

"Thank you, Sydney. May I call you Sydney?"

"Of course."

"I'm curious, Sydney, why would a woman like you would be interested in the submarine service? Isn't it still dominated by men?" asked Spence delicately.

"Yes, it certainly is. I got interested in submarines because of my father's work. It was a dream that took years of effort. My success will pave the way for others. As Dan will tell you, there are only a few things that are restricted for women in our Navy. Although he's been retired for some years now, I'm still on active duty."

"Isn't it a bit strange that you find yourself in this predicament?" asked the general, not as gently as Spence, but still in a respectful tone of genuine curiosity.

"What predicament?" questioned Garrison, cool under the host's clumsy attempt to rattle her.

"You sound like one of those State Department spokesmen being interrogated by the press corps," said Zlodeyev. His tone sounded as if condescension had replaced curiosity. His lips compressed, tired of the cat and mouse game.

"What do you intend to do with us?" asked Steele.

Spence replied, "Nikolai and I have not really worked on a timeline or an agenda for your stay. One option might be to sell you back to the United States. What do you think the president would pay for your safe return?"

"Not a penny," said Steele. "We are here to settle an old debt, and he has nothing to do with the visit."

"That's not what I understand, Mr. Steele. One of my informants got it wrong. Are you a betting man?"

"No, I always knew that the odds were with the house and never felt comfortable when the odds were stacked against me."

Spence leaned back in his chair and said, "One diversion that the defense minister and I have discussed is an opportunity for you, Mr. Steele, to engage my friend in another fight tomorrow morning. If you win, you and Ms. Garrison will be escorted to the border and allowed to leave Albania under your own power. If you lose, you'll be without any power, if you know what I mean." Spence chortled into his napkin, enjoying his turn of phrase. "We believe the president himself sent you on this mission, and he will pay for your repatriation regardless of your condition. Does that sound reasonable?"

"No, not really. But I would be honored to kick the general's ass back to the Russian prison where he belongs," answered Steele evenly, baiting the general. "Excuse my language, Sydney and Spence. I'm sorry to have lowered myself down to his gutter level."

The general glowered but said nothing.

"Well, it's settled," said Spence trying to regain control of the dinner, "now that those details are set, I'd like you to enjoy our entrée tonight, a fire-roasted wild boar with morel mushrooms in a truffle sauce. It's really a pity that you two can't truly be our houseguests. There is so much about our country which you both would find fascinating."

"Too bad. We'll have to be on our way tomorrow after the match, unless the general just wants to throw in the towel now," offered Steele, still unable to get any response from the big man, except a muted grunt signaling that he heard the comment.

After a sumptuous meal of local meat and vegetables, the dinner finished with a rich chocolate cake topped with a red, black and yellow flag and a hand-carved river castle in honor of the German guests.

"Obviously, our chef prepared this lovely cake before he knew you were not German citizens but American assassins. Do you recognize the castle?"

"Yes, Berg Eltz located on the Moselle River. The chef did a wonderful job. My compliments," said Garrison.

"Now," said Spence, "To complete the evening, perhaps you'd like a short tour of the palace and finish with a glass of port before retiring."

Zlodeyev stood and said, "If you'll excuse me, I need to check on the security arrangements for our guests. Goodnight." He turned and left the room without waiting for Spence's response.

The tour ended in a reception hall where the three were served a chilled glass of port wine. They stood under an illuminated portrait of Gjergj Kastrioti, a hero known to Albanians as Skanderbeg. Spence provided a short history of the man he much admired.

"Imprisoned by the Ottoman Turks and trained by them as a military leader, Skanderbeg renounced Islam years later. He deserted the Sultan's army and led several hundred Albanians out of the territory where they'd been impressed into service. Over time, he built a 15,000-man army best known for its fast movement, guerrilla tactics, and capability to win against larger forces. Quite a leader who Albanians love to this day."

"Yes, we all love Skanderbeg. If it weren't for him, we'd still be living under another country's flag instead of our own," said a man who looked exactly like Spence, joining the others with a glass of port in his hand.

"Good evening, President Spence. I just finished giving our guests a brief tour, and we ended here."

"A good place to finish the evening. Did you tell them the history of Skanderbeg?"

"Only the executive summary, President Spence. As you know, they've had quite a day, and I think they need to rest before tomorrow's activities."

"Yes, I agree, Mr. President. I hope that you'll both be comfortable in the guest room."

"Good night," they proclaimed in unison.

Both men shook hands with Steele and Garrison and turned the couple over to a trio of armed guards. They were escorted directly to the guest room and locked inside.

That night, Garrison nestled close to Steele in the king-sized bed, and the two whispered under the covers.

"How are you going to fight that behemoth and live to talk about it? You know he intends to kill you," she said.

"I can't beat him in a fair fight and know that he doesn't know what a fair fight is. And I can't leave you as the spoils of war which belong to the winner," said Steele.

"You can win the fight, Dan. Just use your brain. I know that Zlodeyev is a smart cookie too, but he's not as smart as you are."

"I think you are overestimating my intellectual skills. Don't forget that this brilliant tactical plan of mine put us behind bars in the target's own house. So close and yet so far. And now it's confirmed that Spence has one or more doubles. Very clever."

"Yes, we are in quite a quagmire, but we'll also find a way out of it. I'm confident of that."

"The other issue on my mind is how to tell the real Spence from his double."

Garrison agreed, "I studied the man we had dinner with tonight and how he reacted to the man that came to join us at the end. They've done a terrific job creating the double. I didn't see anything to distinguish one from the other. I think the only way to sort this out would be to bring up a subject that will make the real Spence squirm and give himself away either by body language or a response that only he would know. What do you know that would push him to that level of stress?" asked Garrison.

"Not sure. Something about Jack, who was more like a son to him than any other member of the Double Eagle inner circle. The guy seems unshakable to me. He's calm, cool and collected as far as I can see."

"Isn't Jack the guy that Spence hacked to death with the famous Skanderbeg sword?" asked Garrison.

"Yes, that's the one. Jack saved my life by helping me escape from captivity in the Double Eagle Headquarters cell and down this escape chute that I had no idea even existed. He gave me some covering fire and allowed me to escape. Jack was beginning to understand who Spence really was."

Garrison surprised Steele by pulling off her nightgown and reaching for him. The irony of it all. Their first time making love as prisoners in a distant palace, guarded, and with the prospect of Steele dying in the fight the following morning, mission incomplete and danger on all sides. Steele blotted it all out and moved with an unabashed passion that had lain dormant for years. He wondered who might be watching, but that reality flash lasted only a second as he wrapped his body into hers. Together, they were both transported to a different place, far away from Albania, Spence, and Zlodeyev.

CHAPTER 106

Presidential Palace

Tirana, Albania
July 14, 2025

The sun poured through the floor-to-ceiling windows, waking Steele at the same time the bedside phone rang.

"Yes," said Steele.

"Good morning, sir. May we set up a small breakfast for you now?"

"Certainly."

Moments later, a linen-covered tea cart was pushed into the room, heavy with fresh fruit, eggs, meats, fish, cheese, and a basket of breads. A steward poured two cups of coffee in oversized café au lait cups and announced that tea service was also available.

Steele wrapped himself in a thick cotton robe and went to the cart.

"Syd, coffee with cream?"

Sydney sat up in the bed and confirmed her choice. He brought two cups to the bed along with a handwritten card from the tray inviting him to meet Zlodeyev at 9:45 a.m. for the match that would begin at 10:00.

The coffee was delicious, strong and freshly brewed. Pillows piled behind her, Garrison leaned on Steele's shoulder and drank her coffee in silence.

"I'm worried about you, Dan. Your safety. I have no interest in accompanying a flag-draped aluminum box back to the States. Right now, I'm thinking about a small peaceful seaside cottage in New England, drinking coffee just like this as the sun rises over the sea, and the smell of the incoming tide washing over you."

"Hold that thought. Right now, we don't have the ocean or the sunrise, but at least we have each other. I wouldn't trade that for anything. Syd, I don't see how we could break out of here before the match. Our only chance is to beat Zlodeyev and to take Spence's offer of a one-way trip to the border."

"And how do you intend to win against that massive brute? He looks like one of those World's Strongest Man competitors. I know you are very strong and tough, but realistically, how do you plan to fight him?"

"I can beat him, Syd, and I must beat him. I must beat him for us! We are leaving here together, upright, not horizontal."

CHAPTER 107

Presidential Palace

Tirana, Albania
July 14, 2025

Steele and Zlodeyev walked into the fighting ring, sited under an old grape arbor, overgrown but still producing dark red grapes used for heavy port wine. Zlodeyev's head was just inches under the bottom of the grape leaves. Fresh white sand, a foot deep, was spread over the ground to the sturdy posts supporting the vines. The hand-hewn uprights were wrapped with canvas. Several chairs lined one side of the rectangle covered with an awning to protect the observers from the hot sun. At 10:00 a.m., Spence and Garrison were the only spectators in view, but the armed security force was close by, and there were faces behind windowpanes on the back side of the palace. No one would miss the opportunity to see Zlodeyev in action.

"I understand this is a return match," said Spence, "let it be fair and conclusive. And again, please remember there are no rules for the fight. He leaned over to Garrison and whispered into the hand covering his mouth. "Seems like a non-sequitur, no?"

"Yes," she replied, nervous at the sight of Steele's slight frame compared to the rippling hulk of Zlodeyev.

Spence again leaned toward Garrison and asked, "Have you ever seen anything like this?"

"Only on television."

Both fighters wore cotton shorts. Zlodeyev's body glistened in the morning sun as he began to sweat in anticipation of the match. Spence's double arrived and stood behind Spence's chair. Or so it seemed. It was impossible to distinguish any difference between the two men.

"Are each of you ready?" asked Spence, getting a head nod from both Steele and Zlodeyev. "OK, let the games begin," announced Spence, "Ready the clock for the first three-minute round."

Zlodeyev and Steele met each other in the middle of the ring for the customary stare-down, a fist bump initiated by Zlodeyev and then walked to their corners, marked by a blue square of cloth for Steele and a red one for the Russian giant, before returning to the center of the ring. The double, or Spence himself, clinked a spoon against an empty wine glass to signal the formal start of the fight.

For the first thirty seconds, the fighters were content to circle, testing the reactions of their opponent to a series of feints and some bobbing and weaving.

Zlodeyev opened with a huge round house punch which would have knocked Steele out, if he didn't nimbly side-step the huge fist. He got in a quick counter to Zlodeyev's ribs, an impenetrable cage which seemed to be made of curved high tensile strength re-bar. After backing away, Zlodeyev closed with vengeance, throwing punches as if his jackhammer arms were powered by an air compressor. He backed Steele into a corner post and offered a brutal uppercut which Steele blocked with his forearm. The force of the blow lifted Steele off his feet and left his arm tingling. Steele dodged the next punch and heard the arbor post crack with the force of Zlodeyev's punch.

Both men moved back to the center of the ring. Steele had no options if he wanted to live. He tried to kick each of the cast-iron posts that were Zlodeyev's legs before sending a twisting punch into his solar plexus. Steele saw a surprised Zlodeyev wince as he took the blow, which set him back on his heels. Steele followed with a series of strong punches to the kidneys before Zlodeyev bear-hugged Steele and threw him to the sand.

Steele got back to his feet, wondering why Zlodeyev hadn't squeezed him to death with the bear hug. It was the same move that he recalled from Yemen, the last time he faced the giant. Where is the chink in his armor, Steele wondered as the two worked toward the middle of the rectangle. Did he have a glass jaw? Weak knees? None of these were apparent. Steele waded back inside Zlodeyev's reach and pummeled his flanks when the buzzer signaled the end of the first round. Neither fighter had landed a knockout blow, and no blood had been drawn.

Steele took a chair next to Garrison, and she handed him a bottle of cold water. Steele inspected the bottle and found the cap intact.

"Nice activity for a sunny morning abroad, wouldn't you say?"

"I think it's awful, and I'm just thankful you are still in one piece."

Steele replied, "It's hard to get my head in the fight after last night."

"You better get your head in the fight pronto, sailor. Better yet, get into his head and knock him out!" Garrison commanded. She clawed his arm in a friendly way as Steele got to his feet.

After a one-minute break, one of the Spences called the second three-minute round using the same wine glass and spoon. Zlodeyev was ready to get down to business. Steele got past his defenses and threw several uppercuts to Russian's chin and neck, surprising the Russian with his quickness and the power of his punches that were just shaken off. Then Zlodeyev charged forward for a takedown, knowing that his size and strength would be more advantageous against Steele on the ground. Steele tried to avoid the takedown but did not escape the giant as he grabbed Steele's legs and pulled him down. Zlodeyev pounded Steele's knees and thighs unmercifully as he tried to move up further on Steele's body. Steele landed blow after blow on Zlodeyev's head and the back of his neck, without any apparent effect. Zlodeyev inched forward steadily, keeping his head down along Steele's thighs.

Zlodeyev lifted his head, and Steele threw an elbow square to the bridge of the colossus' nose, enabling him to twist away and jump to his feet. Clearly frustrated, Zlodeyev grabbed Steele's arms and worked his legs like industrial pistons driving pilings into bedrock. Each ram to Steele's midsection lifted him off the ground. Steele realized the fight was close to over if Zlodeyev continued the barrage to his chest. It was only a matter of time before the pistons would drive his knees into Steele's face and skull.

In desperation, Steele concentrated all his energy into a kick on Zlodeyev's planted ankle. He heard a satisfying snap of tendons as the top of the ankle was violently pushed off the other bones permitting an erect posture. Zlodeyev grunted with the injury but kept up the assault by using his strong leg planted on the sand. Steele paid for his ankle assault as Zlodeyev finally connected a blow to Steele's chin, drawing blood and having Steele see the entire galaxy of stars. So ended the second round.

Steele sat down and threw back his head with a gulp of cold water to calm the fire which raged in his gut. He chided himself for not opening the fight, for not finding his opponent's weak points, for not fighting for his dead wife and boys. The thoughts drew fresh energy into his worn body. After seeing Zlodeyev limp to the other side of the ring, he knew that he'd wounded the giant. He expected Zlodeyev to try to control the fight above the waist, using his arms and head to secure victory. Did victory mean death? There were no rules. Zlodeyev could toss Steele around like a rag doll or, if he were able to put him in a submission hold, just slowly squeeze the life out of him. Steele vowed to capitalize on the injured ankle and see if he could gain some leverage to explore Zlodeyev's flanks. The wine glass sounded for the final round. There would be no draw.

CHAPTER 108

Presidential Palace

Tirana, Albania
July 14, 2025

Demetri Korloff endeared himself to the kitchen staff in a short time. He proved to be a hard-working, friendly member of the team, and his efficiency had come to the attention of the chef. Though his job was to wash dishes, pots and pans, and take care of the trash, he volunteered to help the staff with household chores throughout the palace.

Because the addictions of his mother passed through the umbilical cord directly to the fetus, Demetri had suffered through his childhood schooling with a learning disability, short attention span and a poor memory. At home, his life was a living hell. Spankings for not controlling his bowels. Beaten for his uncontrolled screaming at night when visited by the demons of his life. To avoid punishment, the boy learned control and patience at an early age, something that proved valuable in his present assignment. He claimed a Greek heritage being raised by a distant relative after his parents abandoned him and chose to drive off into the sunset fueled by alcohol and drugs.

Of unremarkable height and weight, Demetri was blessed with a forgettable face and the skills of the close-in, face-to-face killer. He would stalk animals of every kind and prided himself on being able to sneak up on birds and hold them tightly until they no longer tried to escape. A tactical genius, he'd come to the attention of the Federal Security Service of the Russian Federation, the modern-day, reimagined KGB. An older operative took a personal interest in honing the boy's already skillful killing methods with the addition of modern weaponry. He quickly became the go-to resource for critical assassinations, always working alone.

Demetri lived a quiet life in Crimea near the coast, fishing and hunting for his larder, reading books and listening to classical music, which soothed his busy mind. Mute — another condition caused by rough treatment at the hands of his parents, had caused aphasia. A school nurse suggested that Demetri may have suffered physical trauma to Broca's area, the part of the brain involved in speech production, and suggested a neurological exam which the family claimed they could not afford. School records labeled the boy as a slow developer. He learned to sign as a child but was shunned by most other children. His hearing was unaffected, but he seldom acknowledged it, choosing to listen to conversations where he was dismissed as a deaf mute. Gifted with a kind of extra sensory perception, he could also read people's minds as if a conversation were taking place on a different level.

From time to time, he accepted assignments from the Federation's president himself in the form of a dossier found in his mailbox. Further details were not necessary. Demetri would find, stalk and kill the target just the way he stalked animals as a child. Control and patience were the keys to his remarkable record of quiet kills and successfully eluding any authorities. He seemed to just vanish in thin air after a mission.

Zlodeyev had been a different kind of target. Demetri watched his movements, learned his habits, and saw firsthand his interactions with others who worked as part of the presidential staff. Zlodeyev was cautious and suspicious. He would prove a capable prey. Demetri watched the fight from the first floor of the palace where he gathered with the kitchen staff. Leaving the others after the first round, he signed that he had no interest in the match or its outcome.

"I see enough blood on the plates that come into the washroom," he wrote on a tablet as he left the group and took a long path through the thickly wooded area that ringed the palace on all sides. Once he knew about the fight, Demetri had hidden a long gun in the branches of a beech tree that grew between two large pines. It was wrapped in a piece of gray canvas which matched the tree's trunk and branches. Green foliage covered everything else. Two high branches in the crown gave him an unobstructed line of sight under the arbor's canopy at eighty yards. After climbing the tree, Demetri got into position and started his deep breathing before the wine glass signaled the start of the final round. It seemed like a perfect time to complete his assignment and leave Albania. He was tired of washing dishes anyway.

CHAPTER 109

Presidential Palace

Tirana, Albania
July 14, 2025

The big man limped to the center of the ring, tired of the fight and weary of Steele's probing. Determined to finish the contest early in the final round, Zlodeyev showed no other signs of weakness to his opponent. Steele anticipated he would go for an early takedown and then pound Steele's body and his head with fisted hammer blows which could not be fended off. He threw a few punches to distract Steele before using his legs to power a takedown. Steele anticipated the move, but Zlodeyev's speed surprised him. Steele landed a solid kick to Zlodeyev's head as he was taken down. On the ground, his legs were encircled by Zlodeyev's massive arms, applying an increasing pressure on his limbs, which became numb in seconds.

Steele pounded Zlodeyev's head and neck but was also fighting through the pain of his legs being crushed. It felt as if his bare bones were being squeezed together in a vise. Steele clapped Zlodeyev's ears repeatedly without success and then tried to stimulate a deep nerve in his neck. The vise-like grip suddenly relaxed, and Steele could once again feel his limbs and the rush of blood to his feet. Steele stood up and stomped both of Zlodeyev's ankles, waking him up from a momentary pause.

Quickly back in the fight, the giant faced Steele on two damaged ankles. Steele saw him withdraw a thin piece of what looked like a steel wire from the waistband of his shorts, thinking he wants to push that wire into my throat and through the roof of my mouth and then twist it around in my frontal lobe until I have a seizure and die. He'd probably withdraw it as I fall to the ground, and Syd would never know what finally did me in. Maybe a few drops of blood from the nose and a small puncture in the neck under the chin. Fast, effective and almost undetectable. But he'd have to get it there first.

Steele planned his next moves in lightning speed. First, he lowered his head and rammed Zlodeyev to the sand with his head on the man mountain's upper chest, pulling his head up and jamming it under the big man's chin. Then he rolled off, kicked his massive knee and tried to elbow his left temple. Zlodeyev wrapped him in a hydraulic bear hug and slowly began squeezing the air out of his lungs. Steele had limited tricks in his kit bag but kept his knees pounding the man's sides as fast and as hard as he could. He felt the point of the steel on his back and knew that Zlodeyev would try to probe his spinal column when he could get the right angle.

Steele headbutted the face of the man until both of their faces were pouring blood. He repeatedly struck the man's nose until it looked like a shallow bowl of macerated strawberries. Still the probing on his back didn't cease. More pounding left Zlodeyev unable to see, Steele unable to breathe. Steele used his head as a ram on the Russian's jaw, and the blind Zlodeyev was unable to protect his head. Still his grip did not loosen.

Steele had enough oxygen to support another blow or two before he passed out. Their upper bodies were slippery with fresh blood. Steele feigned a move forward and slipped out the vise by bringing his arms up and slithering down his opponent's wet torso. He quickly fell to his knees and gulped in huge breaths of air. He heard a long groan from Zlodeyev who was rubbing the sticky blood out of his eyes. The wire was hanging from his hand with a loop around his middle finger.

Spring steel was drawn though a die at room temperature and had the ability to retain or return to its original form after bending. It was a favored tool of assassins who hadn't managed to learn the mechanics of the garrote. There were limitations, but its stiffness and ability to penetrate skin and organs and retain its shape were legendary in the killing trade. It could puncture quickly and forcibly. A well-aimed thrust was all it took. Steele charged, grabbing the hand with the steel and ramming it into the man's neck, producing a geyser of arterial blood.

Winning that battle was short-lived. The giant roared to life, blood pumping from his neck where Steele had nicked his carotid artery. He pushed a dazed Steele to the sand, jumped on his torso, his 330 pounds pushing the air from Steele's lungs and pinning his arms to his sides with his upper leg muscles. Zlodeyev began hammering his opponent with giant piston arms and fists of iron. Steele was able to move his head and to accept glancing blows, but he knew the end was only a matter of seconds. His head was being pounded into the loose sand. Short of a miracle, Steele would die here in the bloody sand, failing to carry out his pledge to Jill and his sons.

Zlodeyev laced the fingers of both hands together for a death blow to Steele's head. The joined fists looked like the business end of a steel forging hammer. Things happened in slow motion as the doubled fist started its downward trajectory, interrupted as Zlodeyev's head jerked forward, the doubled fist inexplicably losing its momentum on the way to Steele's forehead.

Twisting his torso, Steele sustained a restrained blow that sent tingles through his arm before it went completely numb. Zlodeyev fell heavily on top of him. It took all of Steele's remaining strength to push the giant's body off his chest. Rolling on his right side, he saw a clean entry wound in the back of his opponent's head. Steele hadn't won the fight, someone else had won it for him.

Suddenly, the security forces were dashing pell-mell from the palace to its perimeter. Only a handful of the guards knew that Steele and Garrison were the imprisoned guests of the president. Some ran toward Zlodeyev who was still moving despite an exit hole that removed most of his forehead. Others crouched low and quickly closed off any escape for the shooter, thought to be hidden in the thick foliage of trees that surrounded the interior of the property, protected by a ten-foot ornamental wrought iron and an antiquated system of surveillance cameras that worked irregularly. That too was included in Spence's budget.

Steele dug himself out of the small hole of compacted sand under him. He saw Garrison moving toward him. Both Spences were seen entering the palace across an outdoor patio. Steele wiped the blood out of his eyes and shook off the pain. Parts of his body were still numb, and Steele felt dizzy as they ran after the two Spences. Where would they be going? Was there a hidden safe room? Would it be on the second floor or in the basement?

Steele pressed the elevator panel for the second floor, the lights indicated the car was coming up from the basement. The car was empty when it reached the main floor, but Steele saw some fresh grains of sand on its polished floor. He hit the override button inside the car, and the car headed down. The safe room must be in the basement.

"I wonder if we'll run into any security down here? I've got a steel wire from Zlodeyev but nothing else. Maybe there are weapons in the safe room. We could be heading into an ambush," said Steele, still trying to catch his breath.

"Or Spence and Spence could be planning to wait things out in the wine cellar."

"Right, we can start looking there. I suppose that the cellar is large, and it may serve as the safe room."

The elevator doors opened in the middle of an unfinished basement with a dirt floor. The first door they spotted was labeled Zlodeyev's gymnasia and was set into a wall of recently set cinderblocks that emitted a smell of fresh mortar. The door was guarded by a keypad entry. Past the gym, the stone foundation of the palace was visible past a draped area with furniture used for state dinners, grand balls and other events.

Steele and Garrison panned the room and ran to the opposite wall, following it down the length of the back of the palace, until they reached an intersection wall made of the same foundation stone. A massive door made of timbers and decorated with repoussé copper grape vines. Albania's heads of state were clearly serious about their wine and had been for a long time.

The door handle was a polished brass ring which gleamed against the dark timbers. Steele swung it open.

"Steele, what are you doing here?" asked Spence. Three men who looked like identical triplets asked the question in unison. Steele answered with a statement.

"Now, I can kill all three of you, but that seems unnecessary. Two of you must agree with my thinking. I only want to kill the real Spence, but I really don't know which one of you is the real Spence. Let me say a few words and observe your reactions. Perhaps we'll be able to determine the real villain and the two of you who are along for the ride might live. Are you ready?"

All three nodded at the same time in the same manner.

"Did you abduct Lincoln Brewster from Greece?"

"Yes." All men answered at the same time and directly. Steele shifted to indirect questions.

"Let's see, how did your secretary in Georgetown die?"

"With a bullet to the head," the three responded in unison.

"What caused you to split Jack's skull with Skanderbeg's sword?"

The three men glanced at each other and said nothing. Were the doubles trained to respond only to the questions they knew the answers to? Spence would know what the doubles knew plus more, and he was a gifted actor, even under duress. But what gap might exist in the doubles' knowledge of Spence's life and why?

Spence was too proud a man to reveal the pain he endured as a child at the hands of a man who preyed on children and made him his personal whipping boy. Those hurtful memories had been blotted out long ago, hidden away by success and an overactive ego. Steele held that single card which might evoke a response from the real Spence from the "fight or flight" sympathetic nervous system which reacted autonomously to external triggers. Was it enough? Steele wondered. The three men were clearly bored with the questions that

Steele had fed them and seemed oblivious to the mayhem happening on the grounds. Steele knew that this game needed to end if he and Garrison were to leave the grounds on their own power. It was time to play his best and only card.

"Spence," said Steele looking at each of the three men in turn, "do you ever think back to your childhood tormenter, Gjon?"

None of the Spences spoke, but one of them emoted a nervous system tell that was unmistakable. Spence clearly had a massive amount of self-control but did not control his amygdala, the tiny locus of the brain which sends an alarm to the hypothalamus that begins the body's involuntary reaction to high stress. Only one man's hands gripped the arms of the chair, the back of his hands turning white with tension. His heart rate skyrocketed, and a vein in his head swelled as the man responded to the stress of hearing the name of the man who'd been tortured and died as Spence looked on. Steele said "Gjon" again in Spence's face and got a kick and a weak punch in return. The president tried to regain his composure, but it was too late. The other Spences retained their passive demeanor, wondering what the fuss was all about. They knew nothing of Gjon at all.

"Well, Spence. It's just you and me. Prepare to meet your maker."

"Mr. Steele I really don't understand your intentions," said Spence, nervousness creeping into his face as pandemonium reigned at the palace. Sirens were blaring from every part of the city vectored toward the palace, and the president had been left unguarded in the confusion. The guard force took their eyes off the ball and didn't even connect the dots that Steele and Garrison were prisoners, not guests. The security forces had not learned the importance of pre-planned responses.

Steele knew that the guard force was armed, but also knew that Zlodeyev would not trust them carrying live ammunition in their weapons. The first response to the shooter who killed Zlodeyev would be to empty clips into the foliage hoping to either wound or flush out the killer who was hiding in the trees. The guard force seemed paralyzed and took no such action. Why, Steele wondered. Then it dawned on him that Zlodeyev would not be a victim in his own house. The guards were firing blanks.

"Spence, I will make my intentions as easy as one-two-three. Believe me, you'll understand completely." Steele raised his bloody hand holding the piece of spring steel looped over his middle finger. He gripped Spence's skull and looked directly into his eyes. One of Spence's doubles fell off the chair and remained on the stone floor with his back against an empty wine barrel. Frightened, he lost control of his bladder and lay in a widening pool of urine. The other suffered from paralysis which glued him to the chair.

"You killed my family and part of me in the Chesapeake Bay Bridge and Tunnel explosion. Now, for my son, Alex, number one," Steele announced as pushed the steel into Spence's neck and through the rope of the left carotid artery.

Steele withdrew the slender rod. The rate of the blood pulsing out of Spence's neck confirmed that his blood pressure was sky high.

"Number two, for Alex's twin brother, Andrew." Steele pushed the rod into the right carotid until fresh blood squirted out, wetting his hand anew. Spence gulped as he realized his life was draining out of him onto his shirt and his pants. The beige cushion of the chair was absorbing blood very well. Spence was still very much alive but began to feel the chill that comes to the body with massive blood loss.

"My wife, Jill, was my best friend and a wonderful mother to our twin sons. When she left this world, part of her mother's and father's lives ended as well. They've never been the same."

Spence felt the rod under his throat inches back from the chin and between the bony structure of the jaw. The soft tissue of the throat has no protection other than its location. But precious little protection from a stiff wire pushed north toward the skull.

"Wait," said Spence. "I am the elected president of this country. You can't do this to me. Guards!"

"Yes, I can, and I will," countered Steele his dark eyes aflame with an animal-like determination.

"I have money. What will it take to stop this and get me to the doctor? Please, you don't have to do this."

"Yes, he does." exclaimed Garrison. She covered Steele's bloody hand with hers and pushed the thin wire into Spence's jaw.

"This is for Jill," she yelled.

The rod went through Spence's gaping mouth and at least up into his frontal sinus cavity before stopping. His eyes were fluttering as Steele pulled his finger out of the loop and left the wire in place.

CHAPTER 110

Tirana, Albania
July 14, 2025

Steele and Garrison left the wine cellar and followed the foundation wall to a worn pathway that led to a steel door with barrel bolts securing it from the inside. Steele slid the worn bolts open and found a tunnel leading to a small glass-enclosed greenhouse. It was used by the cooking staff to grow fresh herbs, young lettuce, and to store bags of onions, potatoes and other root vegetables without braving the elements. In the summer, thermostatically controlled louvers controlled the heat inside the structure. Sited where its living contents would receive at least eight hours of sunlight on bright days, even in the winter. After surveilling the outside activity at the palace, Steele and Garrison ran the short distance to the abandoned sewer line they used to gain access to the palace without being confronted by anyone. Steele threw back the cover as Garrison led him on the hands and knees crawl.

Responding to the slaughter of the defense minister, the uniformed police and Spence's security team were out in force, concentrating on the palace's perimeter for the shooter. Oddly, no one was assigned or interested in looking for Spence. It had been less than fifteen minutes since the alarm was sounded. The dragnet would initially be centered around Tirana followed by additional surveillance of the surrounding towns and transportation hubs.

When they neared their initial entry point into the early roman sewage conduit, Steele said,

"Keep going."

After another fifty feet, the dry clay pipe they crawled through joined a branch line of the modern system where they could proceed upright though they had to trudge through the fresh filth. Garrison dressed in a fashionable cotton dress for the fight and verbally complained about the route to freedom that Steele had chosen. Steele was clad only in bloodied shorts. He and Garrison were on the run.

They sloshed for a quarter mile until they reached the main line which was like a fast-moving storm drain after a heavy overnight rain. After several hundred yards and several bouts of vomiting, the two reached an observation platform built into the side of the pipe that could be accessed by a set of re-bar rungs set in the concrete. Garrison and Steele climbed up the ladder. At the end of the catwalk was a steel door leading to a concrete vault like a basement bulkhead. Steele opened the steel door and saw the entryway was ringed with a chain-link fence with a padlocked chain to protect it from the city's hooligans. The pair scaled the chain link fence and dropped in a small stand of evergreens growing near the riverbank.

The main sewage outfall of Tirana opened into the Lana River. The outflow discharged fifteen feet below the normal river level which carried away the effluent quickly. There were several construction projects underway to build new drainage systems and treatment plants to process the volume of the growing city's wastewater and to protect the many wells that provided fresh water for the suburbs, but proper sewage treatment would be years away.

"OK, Syd, you remember swim call, right?"

"After what we just jogged through, I'm ready for anything," she responded.

They entered the water upstream of the sewage discharge near the base of an auto bridge which they hoped would provide a modicum of cover during their swim. Steele removed a section of a fallen tree caught on one of the bridge supports for them to swim alongside.

The pair found the river a sanctuary far from the activity at the presidential palace that was fanning out from the site of the murders. Swimming across the narrow river at midday, even near the bridge, afforded them little cover. Three hundred yards downstream, on the other side of the river, they found the hide where Steele opened a waterproof bag and retrieved two sets of clothes, identity papers, a cell phone and a stack of both euros and the local currency, the Albanian lek. Garrison hated the idea of getting dressed without first washing but that would have to wait. She insisted that Steele look the other way and ducked behind a thicket of cattails to change and to apply a packet of permanent hair color that would turn her reddish locks dark brown.

They still had another twenty miles to cover before they would escape what had to be a widening dragnet. The air was filled with the sound of sirens. Roads leading outside the city would be the first controlled through checkpoints. A small motorbike was stashed in the brush that would carry them to Durres.

"What do you think Syd? Should we hide here and wait for nightfall or press on?"

"I think the search will widen and intensify over time. We may have a small head start but need to keep moving before everything is shut down."

"I agree. Nice outfit."

Steele punched Rami's number into the cell phone and heard the friendly baritone answer immediately at the other end.

"Rami, we are enroute. How are things at your location?"

"Nice to hear from you, my good friend. The port is locked down hard. Nothing in or out by sea. The perimeter is being patrolled by the local police, and I just heard on the radio that the Albanian Armed Forces have been ordered to report to their bases. It's a mess here."

"We hope to see you soon."

A German architectural firm had been selected to design Spence's commercial fish farm processing plant in Durres announced during his campaign. The company put the project on the fast track and construction had begun near the fishing fleet marina on the seaward side of Albania's largest port. The docks would be expanded to accommodate the fishing farm vessels that would discharge their finny cargoes directly into the plant. Most of the current fishing fleet consisted of eighteen-meter steel boats which dragged the bottom or operated purse seines.

Steele and Garrison were now wearing khaki trousers, work boots and polo shirts embroidered with the company's name, *Stellis*, topped with numbered white plastic hard hats. Official, clip-on identity cards hung around their necks on lanyards. The pair were now Friedrich Hoffman, a structural engineer, and Elsa Becker, a commercial design supervisor.

With her arms wrapped tightly around his waist, Steele maneuvered the underpowered motorbike, picking the back roads to the southern side of the port where a series of beachfront hotels accommodated a growing number of tourists. The eurozone was taking a beating, and Europeans were searching for budget destinations. Durres was one of them. It was a circuitous route, less than thirty miles, but both agreed it would provide the surest way to the fishing marina where *Iklim* was berthed. A twin-masted Turkish fishing boat, *Iklim's* propulsion, communications, had been reworked and armaments added by the U.S. Navy to provide a capable ship supporting special operations teams that could venture on the seas or into ports where a visible military presence might be counter-productive.

The motorbike was parked in a self-service bicycle rack. Steele and Garrison hailed a taxi and sat in the back seat as the warm summer air filled the interior. It carried the scent of the hundreds of people queuing for ferry service, waiting for a train, engaged in shipyard work or stevedores unloading cargo ships using overhead cranes. A fresh breeze coming off the water helped to dissipate the working smell of the city.

"Durres amphitheater," said Steele.

The taxi stopped at the pedestrian area near the old roman structure that was bustling with shops and eateries and a stone's throw from the fishing marina. As they walked toward the port, they heard bits and pieces of conversations and breaking news on televisions and radios. The situation was not clear, but the general message was that the president and his defense minister had been murdered at the presidential palace. Security forces from the police and other armed forces were looking for an unknown number of assailants, including a western couple.

Large ferries and container ships could be seen across the water at the long docks. Adjacent to the main train station, the ferry terminal was jammed with passengers and vehicles. Four ferry lines shuttled passengers and cars between Italian ports and Durres. Albania's largest port was in constant motion, especially during the summer months when the beaches were crowded with travelers. Everything had ground to a halt.

The fishing fleet moored at the northern part of the port, protected by a new breakwater nestled close to the city and away from the hubbub of the ferries and train station.

Hoffman and Becker walked up to the gate leading to the fishing pier guarded by an Albanian policeman whose rumpled uniform signaled the port's perimeter might yield more easily than they anticipated. Some of his early lunch stained the blue fabric with an olive oil sheen which matched the liquid still on his chin and the corners of his lips. He was badly in need of a shave.

"Good morning," said Elsa in German. "We are trying to get to our company's construction site over there," pointing with her finger to the facility's foundation taking shape a few hundred yards away.

"I do not speak German, but understand you want to get to work site, yes?"

"Yes, thank you," said Garrison.

"Your papers, ju lutem...please?" asked the rumpled sack in English. A shoulder mounted walkie talkie was being used by hundreds with no discipline. Oversubscribed, the frequency was being clobbered by urgent messages from emergency responders, the traffic police, and the activated armed forces. The policeman noticed the fresh stains on his shirt as he turned down the volume to the constant chatter.

"Of course."

"Everything looks to be in order. Normally, this entrance is always open for fisherman. I hope you can understand the precautions we are taking even here in the port city to find the criminals responsible for the murders in Tirana. However, I cannot open the gate for anyone. Those are my orders."

Steele leaned in asking again if he and the lady might be permitted entry, flashing several fifty euro notes under the flap of his breast pocket. The guard smiled. Bribes at all levels of the Albanian economy were common.

"Well, because the harbor is locked down, I can't see any harm in making a small exception this time. Let me look at my dispatches from this morning."

The man opened his breast pocket and brought out a very poor copy of the two westerners wanted for questioning in the murders. Steele was staring at a picture of Garrison and him taken by the hotel's security camera. Despite the quality, it was clearly them in different attire.

"What happened to you?" the policeman asked Steele, looking at his puffy face, broken nose, blackened eyes and several lacerations open and oozing from his face.

"I walked into a café earlier today near the shipyard, and some of the night shift pipefitters didn't like the way I combed my hair."

"You should go to the doctor and get those cuts properly dressed and sutured. That area near the shipyard should be off-limits to the town's visitors. I've told my superiors many times, and they just don't listen to someone wearing two stripes. It's a dangerous part of the city. I'm sorry it happened to you."

The policeman stuffed the dispatch back into his pocket, folded the euro notes and placed them into his pants pocket. When his hand returned it was holding a pistol. Steele's arms shot from his sides and grabbed the policeman's wrist with both of his, twisting the gun from his grasp. Now disarmed, the policeman began to yell into his walkie talkie's microphone.

"I have the Westerners at the fishing mole. Help."

Steele ripped the communications brick from the man's shoulder and silenced it.

"Open the gate," Steele commanded, pointing the pistol at the man's chest.

The policeman removed a keyring from his belt that looked like it held at least 500 keys. He thumbed through the bulging circle and found a key that opened the rusty lock. Steele was amazed that he found the key so quickly.

The policeman dropped the keyring and held his hands in the air while Steele removed the shackle. Steele grabbed Garrison's hand and swung the gate open and began a fast walk. He heard the policeman from behind him.

"Is that any way to treat an old friend who's been watching out for you these past few days?"

Shocked, Steele turned around and watched Sandy Matthews remove his hat and mustache.

"Sandy!" said Steele as he immediately hugged his friend. Let's get out of here!"

The three walked down the worn pathway to the fishing side of the breakwater where Rami tied *Iklim* stern first to the finger pier just behind the stone breakwater. At eighty feet long, the twin masted former sailing vessel dwarfed the Durres fishing fleet. Its modifications were invisible to the casual observer. They navigated the narrow wooden gangplank, while the crew cast off the lines, and *Iklim* roared from the pier, powered by a single marine gas turbine. Traveling over forty knots in less than thirty seconds, Steele stumbled into the wind and collapsed on the forward deck, exhausted. Rami shook him on the shoulder, and Steele just looked into his dark eyes and said, "mission accomplished."

Always the consummate host, Rami welcomed Garrison aboard and then escorted her through the ship and down to Cabin #1. He opened several built-in drawers holding a variety of women's clothing and then showed her to the head which featured a shower.

"There is plenty of hot water and Turkish towels. I suggest using the antiseptic soap first and then the Spanish flowered soap that looks like a variation of mortadella. We have no set schedule, so take your time. I'll try to get Dan into the other head so he can wash the stink off his body. Please put your clothes in a plastic bag, and we'll dispose of them at sea."

A fresh breeze came off the Adriatic Sea as the boat took a southerly course toward the Strait of Otranto separating Albania from Italy by only thirty-nine miles before widening into the Ionian Sea. *Iklim* gently rolled with the swells, and the ride was smooth even at the high speed.

Below decks, Steele tossed his clothes into a plastic bag and showered, pulling on a pair of shorts and tee shirt. After a cup of expresso in the mess, he headed topside. It was good to be alive. At the helm, Rami asked, "What's our destination?"

Steele replied, still in a daze from the activities of a very long week.

"Let's cruise east toward Antalya."

For the first time since he could remember, Steele did not have any pressing obligations. Both of his arch enemies were dead. Garrison's schedule was more urgent. He needed more rest and decided to ignore the effects of the caffeine and return to his cabin for a combat nap. As he was unlatching the door, Sydney's head appeared from the doorway of cabin #1. She stepped into the hallway and kissed Steele. He felt like he had just kissed an electric eel. She pulled him back into the cabin. She felt strong yet soft at the same time. Steele felt he was being embraced in a cascade of scented flowers.

Later, when Steele fell asleep, he dreamed that he found himself in a large city where Spences seemed everywhere. He saw them going into stores, at stop lights and walking on the sidewalks. There were hundreds of them on the city streets.

Steele awoke in a sweat. Sydney was gone. He'd had a nightmare. But he knew what he'd done at the palace, and Spence could not possibly be alive.

The last thing he remembered from the nightmare was seeing sweet Sydney sitting in a side chair in a long cotton blouse. She had an odd look on her face and a bullet hole in her forehead. On the desk close by was a single sheet of paper with a handwritten message.

Mr. Steele,

Just remember, I have a very long reach.

Spence

Or was it a dream?

Steele knew he was still on *Iklim*, and it was the middle of the night. The sound of the diesel engines hummed below as he pulled on his shorts and raced through the lower deck to an interior ladder going topside. With his long arms, he landed on the main deck in one long pull. He walked past the dull red lights in the pilothouse and followed the deck edge until he saw her sitting near the bow. The moon turned her red hair into gold. He crept forward quietly on his bare feet.

"May I join you?"

"Yes, please do." Sydney had a blanket around her and opened one side for Steele.

"Dan, this could be heaven on earth. The sky is clear as a bell, and I've never seen so many stars. The ocean is fresh and clean. I feel invigorated and at the same time so relaxed, so free."

Steele put his arm around her, and they watched the sea as it gradually turned gray just before sunrise. At daybreak, the sun rose majestically into the clear sky over *Iklim's* bow, and the water started to change colors. The sun's rays signaled the start of a new day with flying fish breaking the surface and pods of dolphins frolicking ahead of the boat.

A magical time, a time to forget about the past and to move together into the future.

ABOUT THE AUTHOR

John P. Morse's novels are set in the near future, drawing heavily on his Navy career as a surface warfare officer serving on six combatant ships, two afloat staffs, and ashore in the Middle East. He deployed in all oceans of the world and commanded two ships. Parts of his military service record remain classified. After retiring from the US Navy, he worked for a large defense contractor for 16 years developing both domestic and international business. His widely acclaimed first novel, *Half Staff 2018*, introduced his principal protagonist, Dan Steele, and took an inside look at domestic terrorism. *Chokepoint* followed, offering the evolution of a modern-day maritime swindle in the Red Sea based on a model from the Ottoman Empire. *The President's Hail Mary* takes a credible 2025 look at the frightening reality of nuclear weapons proliferation and the human elements tied to it: power, greed and justice. An accomplished diver, his world-wide diving experiences are reflected in Steele's underwater adventures. He and his wife, Carole, divide their time between southern New Jersey and southeastern Massachusetts.

www.johnpmorse.com

Made in the USA
Middletown, DE
29 June 2024